A Better World

ALSO BY SARAH LANGAN

Good Neighbors

Audrey's Door

The Missing

The Keeper

A Better World

a novel

Sarah Langan

ATRIA BOOKS
New York London Toronto Sydney New Delhi

An Imprint of Simon & Schuster, LLC
1230 Avenue of the Americas
New York, NY 10020

This book is a work of fiction. Any references to historical events, real people, or real places are used fictitiously. Other names, characters, places, and events are products of the author's imagination, and any resemblance to actual events or places or persons, living or dead, is entirely coincidental.

First Atria Books hardcover edition April 2024

ATRIA BOOKS and colophon are trademarks of Simon & Schuster, LLC

Simon & Schuster: Celebrating 100 Years of Publishing in 2024

For information about special discounts for bulk purchases, please contact Simon & Schuster Special Sales at 1-866-506-1949 or business@simonandschuster.com.

The Simon & Schuster Speakers Bureau can bring authors to your live event. For more information or to book an event, contact the Simon & Schuster Speakers Bureau at 1-866-248-3049 or visit our website at www.simonspeakers.com.

Interior design by Kyoko Watanabe
Illustrations on pages 3, 4, 32, 40, 69, 144, 204, and 333 by Alexis Seabrook

Manufactured in the United States of America

1 3 5 7 9 10 8 6 4 2

Library of Congress Cataloging-in-Publication Data

Names: Langan, Sarah, author.
Title: A better world : a novel / Sarah Langan.
Description: New York : Atria Books, 2024.
Identifiers: LCCN 2023039801 (print) | LCCN 2023039802 (ebook) | ISBN 9781982191061 (hardcover) | ISBN 9781982191078 (paperback) | ISBN 9781982191085 (ebook)
Subjects: LCSH: Elite (Social sciences)—Fiction. | LCGFT: Thrillers (Fiction) | Novels.
Classification: LCC PS3612.A559 B48 2024 (print) | LCC PS3612.A559 (ebook) | DDC 813/.6—dc23/eng/20231020
LC record available at https://lccn.loc.gov/2023039801
LC ebook record available at https://lccn.loc.gov/2023039802

ISBN 978-1-9821-9106-1
ISBN 978-1-9821-9108-5 (ebook)

For Frances Carolina Petty

PART I

The Sinking Ship

Resident Guidebook for Greater Plymouth Valley

Welcome to PLYMOUTH VALLEY

*Designed by Mr. Share's Kinder Class

Plymouth Valley at a Glance:

- PV is **BetterWorld's crown jewel**, named the most beautiful place to live in North America three years in a row!
- Population: **4,501**
- PV's K–12 school system is a **blue-ribbon winner!**
- Town mascot: the **caladrius**, of course. 😊
- Once the main producer and exporter of **Omnium©**, the multipurpose synthetic that launched BetterWorld into the global corporation it is today, PV shuttered its mill and is now a home base for high-level executives. But the Omnium keeps flowing. There are now over 1,000 Omnium production facilities worldwide!
- PV boasts a **self-sustaining farm**.
- The local customs in PV are collectively referred to as **Hollow**. So, holla, Hollow!
- PV's **survivor shelter** boasts the only private nuclear reactor in the country.

Holla, Hollow!

The Sinking Ship

"Some people aren't suited. It's nothing personal," Jack Lust said. "They're simply a wrong fit."

This guy was a clown. The creepy kind. Linda Farmer didn't like him, but she smiled at him because she had to.

"For instance," Jack said. He enunciated every syllable like a disappointed preschool teacher. "Character is paramount. When we hire people who are going to live in our town, mix with our top-level executives, *become* top level, we need to know they'll behave."

Linda nodded as if to say: *We have character! We ooze character!*

"You'll have no cause for concern with us," Linda's husband, Russell, said. They were sitting together on the sunken couch, looking up at Jack Lust in the high wingback chair like a couple of kids who'd been caught doing something bad.

"Our community is small and like minded. We prefer collaborative types. It's counterintuitive: to get to this place that you're at today, an interview for a coveted company job in a jewel like Plymouth Valley, you must outshine all your competition," Jack said. His bespoke black suit hugged his bony body like shrink-wrap. Linda pegged him at a vim and vigorous seventy-five years old. Cosmetic surgery, healthy living, clean air—company town people kept it tight. Nobody in their seventies looked this good on the outside.

Jack was accompanied by a small entourage of likewise elegant men, none of whom he'd introduced. Two appeared to be taking notes and two were security, waiting outside the Farmer-Bowens' apartment door. Linda hadn't checked—this had all moved too fast—but she suspected that the leather straps across their chests held pregnant holsters.

"But once you're in Plymouth Valley, you must be a team player," Jack said. His primness, his perfect posture and absence of expression, vibed to her like contained rage. This was a huge leap in all logic—it *definitely* wasn't true—but he reminded Linda of one of those guys you hear about on the news streamies, who murder people in weird, excessively neat ways. They lure the random unhoused into their lairs, then exsanguinate and store their blood in jars on their freezer doors. They sneak incrementally larger arsenic doses into a friend's tea over months and years, just to watch with secret pleasure as their hair and teeth fall out. But she was thinking this only because she was nervous. This three-piece-suited company shill had a lot of power over her life. Her family needed for Russell to land this job. My God, they needed this job.

"Your record is the strongest I've seen in a decade. You must have worked night and day to get to this place. Am I correct?" Jack asked.

"Yes," Russell agreed. He was nervous, trying too hard. She didn't blame him. "I had days off, but I didn't take them. My inbox was always too full."

"The next step is to bring you to Plymouth Valley to interview with our science department. This is a rare opportunity. We almost never open our doors to outsiders. Even when we outsource, it's typically through other company towns."

"I'm so honored," Russell said.

"It *is* an honor. But it's an honor you've earned," Jack said.

Linda grinned at the compliment despite its smugness. "What's it like inside a company town?" she asked.

"They're all different. Plymouth Valley is the best. Very safe. Very happy," Jack answered. His beady eyes connected with hers. He didn't smile. She pictured the shining, bright kitchen in his perfect company town house, maybe a severed head or two in the subzero freezer. It was a game now. A tension release that made this interview less horribly momentous. "If you're lucky, you might see for yourself. If you're even luckier, you might get to stay. The reason I'm here, that I asked to meet you in particular, Linda, is that these hires can get tricky. Relocating and housing entire families is costly for the company. We avoid it when we can."

"Totally," Linda said. She waited for him to say something like: *But we'd be glad to have you! The more, the merrier!* This didn't come, so she elaborated. "We're a very happy family. The twins are practically grown. They've never been in trouble. None of us have been in trouble."

"We know that from the background check," Jack agreed.

"Thank you . . ." she said, flustered. Had she and Russell agreed to a background check? They must have.

"What I'd like to impress upon you both is that Plymouth Valley is a privilege. We have many customs. To an outsider, they might seem peculiar. But you'll understand them with time. The longer you live in Plymouth Valley, the clearer the picture."

"We're prepared for anything that comes," Russell said.

Linda nodded, suppressing a cough. She'd heard that company people thought outsiders carried disease and didn't want to give anybody the wrong idea, even though this year's super bloom was hell on her allergies. "We're easy people. We get along. We can adapt to any culture," she said. She had no idea whether this was true. They'd only ever lived in Kings.

Jack leaned forward, talked even more slowly. Did he think they were half-wits? Yes, she realized. He did. And it probably wasn't personal. He likely thought everyone he knew was a half-wit, and that went double for outsiders. "The first year is the hardest. But if you make it in our town, if you're accepted, you're set for life."

"Great," Linda said.

"Your children will be set for life."

"We'll be the luckiest people in the world," Linda said, smiling big, eyes wide, voice enthusiastic but not flirty. "I'm so glad you've come, Mr. Lust, so I have the opportunity to tell you in person. We're all in. One hundred percent."

Jack surveyed the apartment for the first time. He'd avoided this before, made a point not to look at all, as if to spare them the shame. Now, he didn't compliment their framed kid-art hung askew, or the rack over the dining room table, from which she'd hung long spoons that, in moments of whimsy, they all played like an instrument. It wasn't a nice place to live. The furniture was threadbare, the big screen cracked. Josie's dirty soccer crap had migrated to the corners of this living room like rats' nests. Still, you had to admit: their apartment on Bedford Avenue had character. The Farmer-Bowens had character.

"Our predictions show that this part of town will be underwater in ten years," Jack said.

"That soon?" Linda asked.

Jack nodded. "We're not worried about that in Plymouth Valley. We've thought of everything. We *have* everything. We think of PV as the last lifeboat."

"I'd like to emphasize how hard I'll work to make this happen. To make myself and my family an asset," Russell said.

"No need to emphasize anything," Jack said as he stood. He didn't grunt like most seventysomethings. He was creepily graceful. *Exsanguinator*, she thought. *Heads in a freezer*.

"Thanks for your time. Someone will be in touch."

His entourage preceding him like they'd choreographed this, he was at the door. He shook both their hands, firm and with eye contact, but still didn't smile.

From their window, Linda and Russell watched the men in tight black suits cross the weed-broken sidewalk and city detritus–sprayed lawn: paper waste, dead tricycles, rusted tires. Jack stepped high and wide like all of it was dogshit.

The black van pulled away.

Linda hacked four wet, pent-up coughs to clear her lungs, then asked, "Does this mean you're getting a second interview or *not* getting a second interview?"

• • •

This happened in a different but nearly indistinguishable world.

It was the Era of the Great Unwinding. The institutions, laws, and even the bridges and roads that people had come to depend upon were falling apart. Everything got automated, but broken-automated.

You called your health insurance to ask why they'd dropped coverage despite cashing your check, and your complaint got fed into a system that took three months to process it. By then you no longer needed the surgery because your appendix had burst. The on-call doc had saved your life, but they'd done so without getting prior approval from said insurance company, which was using that as a reason to deny your claim. You appealed this denial, which took six months. In the meantime the hospital's collection agency repossessed your car. This was a thing. It happened in banking, hotels, libraries, schools, the IRS, and every other bureaucratic system. Some version of it happened to everyone.

The weather stopped making sense. Fires and storms raged. Blackouts rolled through the country like waves at a Kings' Stadium Dodger game. A lot of people stopped making sense, too. They were angry and mad and sad all the time. They were indignant over all they'd lost. They were indignant over what they'd never had. In the absence of knowing how to fix any of what had gone wrong, anger spread like a virus, building from one person to the next. Its expression was a delicious release that felt like action.

This unwinding had been happening for decades, accelerating with every passing year. Then a hydrogen bomb accidentally detonated in the Middle East. For two days all over the globe, smoke blocked the sun. The anger went still. Everything went still.

But humanity is resilient. It recovered from this nearly fatal wound, and it persisted, even as it carried its pain with it. The anger returned. The sound returned. The light returned. People ventured out again, resuming the same arguments they'd been having, only the tone was one octave more panicked.

No one could say whether or how things would get better. They wanted to believe that they would. But the organism, the human condition, was sick. There arose no healer to guide them. No strong, honest Prometheus. Alone, they saw no obvious path to health.

Linda Farmer had been a part-time pediatrician at a free clinic for almost fifteen years. Russell Bowen had been a science adviser with the regulatory department at the EPA. They'd lived in the same Kings apartment all that time, hoping to save up money to move to one of the gated communities over the bridge in Jersey, but never managing it.

Mostly, heads down, they stayed positive. The world was falling apart, but they were okay. They had a home, they loved their kids and one another, and their work had value.

Their marriage was typical, in that it was unlike any other marriage and utterly idiosyncratic. She talked when she was happy, and also sang, and maintained ongoing monologues with herself when alone. He talked when nervous but was otherwise laconic. She felt things deeply and expressed those emotions. He held his feelings so close he often wasn't aware that he had any. For instance, if asked a simple question like "Did you like your father when you were growing up?" Linda would have beamed happily and said she'd loved him very much, then described all the good memories she had about him and a few bad ones, too. There were plenty of bad ones. Russell would have looked at the person who'd asked, thought for a moment, and replied with sincerity: "I don't know. I've never thought about it," and been very happy once the subject was changed.

Opposites attract. Linda and Russell complemented one another, each fulfilling a need. And then the kids came along, and life happened faster. They spent less time together. Their differences became a problem.

The years accumulated small crimes between them—words spoken in anger, dismissive behavior, rolled eyes. Sometimes, Linda picked fights. After long, exhausting days at the office, where he was treated badly, Russell didn't have it in him to fight back, and ignored her. This made her angrier. She teased in a mean way to get his attention. (*You're awkward, nerdy.* And once, during a very hot argument that she still regretted: *You're weak.*) He retreated deeper. Days later, licking their wounds, needing the house to function, the food to be cooked, the bank statements to stay black, and the kids to feel safe in an unsafe world, they came together. They still loved one another, after all. This love was apparent and deep. So, they pretended the fights had never happened. They left resentments behind them, like a dirty river.

Then Black Friday came.

The news streamies were clever for once, likening Congress to a mad King Solomon, who'd made good on a bad promise and cut the baby in half, rendering both parts useless. The federal government slashed more than a million jobs.

Russell showed up to work and found his entire department weeping like mourners at an Irish funeral. At his desk, he found a box, his name misspelled in Sharpie: *Bussel Rowen.* No severance. No unemployment. No nothing.

In the face of such an emergency, they put aside their resentments and got along better than they had in years. They were still a team. They were the Farmer-Bowens.

Six months after Black Friday, they were sitting at the dining room table beneath the hanging spoons, itemizing unpaid bills on a yellow legal pad. It had been weeks since their "pre-interview" with Jack Lust, and despite Russell's many follow-ups, they'd heard nothing.

"We could sell my engagement ring," Linda said.

"I looked it up already," Russell admitted. "Even the good places won't pay more than a few hundred dollars for a half-carat diamond."

"Oh," she said, twisting the diamond around her finger, imagining him calling pawn shops, which should not have felt like a betrayal, but nonetheless did. "I talked to Fielding about more hours. She said next month I can do seven days a week, which'll give me overtime. But it's only temporary. The clinic can't really afford overtime."

"How much is that?" Russell asked. His voice was flat, his movements slow. He'd tried to use his time effectively, sending résumés, making calls, cleaning the house, engaging the kids for the first time since . . . ever? But he'd lost weight since Black Friday, his button-down shirt hanging off scarecrow shoulders. Without work, there was a hole in him.

"Hmm . . . an extra two grand next month, but then back to my regular salary—four grand a month. Plus, we'll all need to be on my health care, so that'll take us back down to . . . twenty-five hundred?"

Dutifully, methodically, Russell wrote this out with his mechanical pencil.

"The Jam?" he asked.

With all the trains down from so much flooding, the Jam was their only way out of the city. More practically, a car is a kind of house, with four walls and a roof. You can live in a car.

"Naw," she said. "It's worth more to us than the cash."

"College fund?"

"We'll get killed on the taxes if we cash that in," Linda said, trying hard to greet this logically. But more than her ring, or her winter coat, or even her hair, she loved that college fund. It represented every ice-cream cone never bought, every vacation never taken. It meant they'd done at least one thing right.

"Forty percent penalty. It'd be a huge waste," Russell agreed. Then again, that money might float them. The Legal Aid lawyer had told them not to waste another dime on rent—just wait for the eviction. Then use this college fund to rent something smaller and deeper into the messy part of town. But what then? That money would run out, too, eventually.

People were dropping out all over this city. One day, they were your coworker or neighbor or that harried parent at drop-off with the crazy hair. The next, they were squatting in abandoned buildings. They were *the disappeared.*

She'd been denying it for a while now, but the inexorable weight of it hit her right then: her family might become the disappeared.

"Russell," she said, her voice cracking. She was trying not to cry, but it was happening. He didn't react right away, and she knew it was because this was too much for him. He felt too bad about how things had turned out.

"Don't mind me. Ignore me," she said.

"It's okay," he said, soft. "Let's just get through this."

That was when his device rang. Instead of an area code, the screen blinked a steady stream of rolling names. A scam, she assumed. Another grifter offering water rights in Siberia or sham iodine pills for radiation. Russell answered it anyway, probably for the distraction.

"Yes, this is Russell Bowen," he said. His spine perked, his voice coming to life. "That's right. I met with Jack Lust . . . Really? That's great. Thank you. Thank you. Thank you. That's great."

As he talked, his eyes watered. He circled *college fund* instead of crossing it out, then made a sunshine of exclamation points all around it, and she felt a great and gruesome sympathy for him, for all of them, for the whole messed-up, unwinding world.

• • •

BetterWorld was one of the smaller multinationals, known mostly for a polymer called Omnium, whose main ingredient was recycled plastic. Hailed as a miracle product, Omnium was used for things like rope, clothing, bags, packaging, fabric, upholstery, machine parts, and even ship sails.

It was biodegradable in the presence of a GRAS-rated (Generally Recognized As Safe) solvent called GREEN. You applied GREEN at home, in your bathtub, and your fabric turned into a thin green slurry that ran right down the drain, or you deposited your Omnium at local collection sites, where it was taken to special waste facilities, and the solvent was applied there. GRAS-rated products were the "natural flavors" you might find in a bag of chips, or the thickening agent in your fake milk. In other words, they were so safe you could eat them.

Quickly after BetterWorld's founding, Omnium replaced plastic as the most popular global synthetic. BetterWorld couldn't make enough of the stuff, opening mills across the globe. All that plastic in the oceans shrank. Dolphins, whales, and sea turtles—the ones that could tolerate the acidity—lived to swim another day. The company prospered, extending its reach into pharmaceuticals, banking, construction, and mining.

Though in recent years sentiment had turned against the big corporations, whom protesters accused of resource hoarding, BetterWorld was spared the worst publicity hits. They paid the highest wages to contract workers, contributed to charity, and had literally cleaned the planet. Or they'd done their part cleaning the planet. The planet needed significantly more tidying to sustain life over the next few generations.

Plymouth Valley was BetterWorld's crown jewel. Located along a distributary of the Missouri River, it was established as the site of the first Omnium mill. Though that mill had closed in favor of larger-capacity factories across the globe, the town was reconceived as the seat of operations, where BW's top executives lived.

Over the course of Russell's interview process, Linda read everything she could find about Plymouth Valley. There wasn't much. High walls protected its residents from crime. A filter called the Bell Jar cleaned its air. Their mascot was something called a caladrius, a bird indigenous to the area whose cartoon likeness BetterWorld used as its emblem. Their local culture was called Hollow. Like most company towns, its architects had built a subterranean survivor shelter.

In his old job, Russell had reviewed the safety and efficacy of polymer-based products. Jack Lust was interested in hiring him as a science adviser in BW's Plymouth Valley office. He would follow Omnium from creation to disposal, read and initiate studies, and testify on his findings.

With unemployment hovering around 25 percent, people all over the world were trying to get into company towns—places with laws and order and guaranteed work. Places where you could go to the grocery store and exchange pleasantries without getting shot by a stray bullet. But like everything else, even company towns were shrinking. Access to outsiders was practically impossible. Unless you were born to the privilege, you had to be exceptional. A genius, even. The residents weren't the 1 percent. They weren't the .01 percent. They were the .000001 percent.

After that phone call, BetterWorld's search committee flew Russell out to Plymouth Valley. He stayed three days. Linda spent the time acting falsely cheerful and sometimes genuinely cheerful: *Dear God, what if he got this thing?*

"Well?" she asked when he called on his flight back home.

• • •

While Russell spent the day at the library, studying for his final interview, she prepped the kids.

"We're flying out in two days," she explained. "They want to meet the family. No cussing. No rudeness. No interrupting. I need you to be on your best behavior."

"What the fuck?" fifteen-year-old Josie asked. To correct for her own childhood, in which the people around her had nourished their secrets like beloved lap dogs, Linda had always encouraged open discussion. Lately, as it pertained to Josie, she was starting to think she'd overcorrected.

"If your dad gets this, we're moving," Linda said.

"I'm not moving," Josie said. "I'm the only sophomore starting center forward in Brilliant Minds' history."

Linda explained the situation in plain terms: there weren't any other jobs.

For Hip, who was neither a good student at Brilliant Minds Prep (a prep school only in name), nor a big man on campus, reality clicked right away. Either the Farmer-Bowens moved up to Plymouth Valley, or they moved down and out, to someplace much worse. He nodded. Behind his glasses, his eyes were wet.

"I don't get it. You hate company towns. You said they're for uptight assholes," Josie said.

"That's because I didn't think we'd ever get invited into one," she answered. "Now, I think they're great."

"What about my team? Our apartment? Why can't *you* get a job, Mom?"

"I tried," Linda explained. "Most of what I do's been automated. The work's either in free clinics, where the pay isn't enough to support our rent, or with really rich people as a private doctor, and I don't have those connections, Josie."

Josie spent the afternoon kicking a soccer ball against the brick-walled back of their building. Feverish—that allergic cough had bloomed into a bronchial infection—Linda cleaned the kitchen, mopped the floor, disregarded the bills piled on the counter. She made a snack for Hip, who had food anxiety bordering on anorexia. He liked lentils and he liked tomatoes and sometimes he picked at brown rice. She left the plate on the table as a hopeful temptation. God bless this kid, he ate every bite, then told her to sit down—*take a load off, Mom*—just to make things easy.

Hours later, Josie returned through the back door, the bib under her armpits and around her neck sweat-drenched. Russ finished his research. Hip came out from his room. Having arrived from separate places, they all four sat at the supper table. In poker terms, this job, this potential move, was a Big Blind. They had no idea what was coming. But they were rational people. They understood that this chance was their best option.

• • •

They caught the BetterWorld private jet at the airfield in Ronkonkoma, then zoomed over the congested tri-state with its patched, sea-broken roads, its kudzu and mold creep. They flew over the Great Lakes, and then the plains of Iowa. The closer they got to Plymouth Valley, the more the country flattened and spread like pulled dough. The land turned brown. Houses were dilapidated. Rusted tractors and combines perched silently along desiccated grain fields.

"Jesus, it's *Ozymandias* out here. I had no idea it was so bad. How are they even growing corn and wheat?" Linda asked.

"Wait," Russell told her.

From a plane's-eye view, they passed Plymouth Valley's border wall. A lush oasis emerged. The Omnium River wasn't the dirty Hudson of her childhood. It was blue. As they descended, she saw solar-powered cars cruising paved roads. Hedges stemmed long driveways that bloomed into outsized houses, all lined in neat rows.

"They've got a pipeline to the big aquifer. The Ogallala," he said. "The corn farms were about ten years from depleting the whole thing, so BetterWorld bought them out. I get the argument against company towns like this, but it's not really resource-hoarding if everybody else is resource-destroying."

Upon landing, Russell kissed her quickly, waved to the kids, and joined the search committee to convene with the BetterWorld board of directors for a daylong gauntlet. Zach Greene, one of Jack Lust's many assistants, introduced himself.

"Color me lucky!" Zach said. Like Jack, he put weight on every syllable, enunciating all his letters. They all talked like this, she would later learn. It was the PV accent. "I'm PV's resident tour guide and I get to spend the day with you fine people. Whatever you do, please do not think of this like an interview. It's just for fun!" Then he did prayer hands at them, his fingers bisecting his curlicued goatee. "Please have fun!"

Fun?

Like the one Jack had worn, Zach's suit was skintight. But instead of black, it was bright yellow and pink, and styled with zippers like a tracksuit. Unlike the Omnium fabric back home, which people tended to toss after a season, his was lined and double stitched.

As they rode in the back of Zach's giant white SUV, past the airfield and south along the self-sustaining farm and the field of wind turbines, everything seemed extra crisp, like kids' drawings that have been outlined in metallic.

They passed a park with a wide swath of green ahead of a playground. Colorful maypoles lined its roadside. Grosgrain ribbons hung down, their edges grazing the ground. These encompassed every color, including black.

"You've heard of Hollow?" Zach asked.

"A little," Linda said. The air was so clean that she could feel the swelling in her bronchi and sinuses go down: a literal loosening in her chest and back, a squeak under each cheekbone. It felt so good. "It's the culture here? There's not much online."

"There wouldn't be anything. You've probably already figured out we keep our business private. This place is the repository for Better-World R&D. Lots of corporate secrets. We're a satellite no-fly zone, and we store everything important in analog," Zach said. "But you have it right. Hollow's a set of customs based on gratitude. Some outsiders think it's a religion, but it's not. We're secular. We just enjoy tradition. We've got four local festivals. You just missed Beltane—that's what those maypoles are about. It's terrific fun. Lots of competitions. Lots of winners and losers. The winner becomes the annual Beltane King. It's been Keith Parson every year for the last fifteen. The man's a legend. So strong! If you move here, you'll get to see his crowning in September."

"I'd love that. We all would, wouldn't we?"

"Yes!" both kids gamely agreed.

The ride was smooth—no potholes, no jerking electric power from chewed-up converters. When they got to the residential section, she noticed dog shelters punctuating the front lawns of the large, free-standing houses. These had low mansard roofs over rectangular bases.

"Do many people here have pets?" she asked.

"Oh, no," Zach said. "With the caladrius, we discourage that. They're lazy guys, but in the spring they tend to hunt in packs. Domesticated animals don't fare well here."

"The caladrius is your mascot, right?"

They stopped at a flat, grid-shaped intersection with freshly painted meridian lines. "There's one!"

Out from one of the shelters, a funny-looking creature appeared. Its plumage fanned like that of a peacock, only its feathers were all white, its neck was stubby, and it had carnivore teeth. It reminded her of a squat vulture.

"They're real?" Josie asked with an amused laugh. "I heard about them, but I wasn't sure. But I also didn't believe in narwhals until someone showed me a picture. I'm still not sure I believe in narwhals."

"You're narwhal agnostic," Hip said.

Linda shot them a *simmer down* look.

"The caladrius is definitely real!" Zach answered. "Genetically engineered, obviously."

The bird waddled but didn't fly. Linda wanted to be charmed, but its dirt-crumbly undercarriage dragged as it waddled. It seemed, somehow, inbred, like those dogs whose eyes spontaneously pop out of their sockets. "Are they friendly?"

"They know we feed them," Zach said. "Friendly would be a stretch. But that hardly matters. What matters is that they reproduce very quickly, making them an excellent food source. Very high in the B vitamins and iron. They were invented to replace chickens, but they turned out to have fragile lungs. They're dependent on our Bell Jar. That's why you've never seen one outside. They can't survive."

"And they live here, in doghouses on people's lawns?"

"Birdhouses," Zach said. "They're heated for winter. Very comfortable."

Linda watched the sad thing. Found herself pitying it as it wobbled like a drunk. "Why?"

"We could pen them all up on the farm, sure, but they're our birds. We made them. Why not honor them? Why not take individual accountability for their survival, because the existence of these creatures might also one day mean our own survival?"

"Huh," she said. "I guess that's smart. More ethical than factory farms, for sure."

"We're smart!" Zach announced.

Their first stop was town. Zach took them to Parson's Market, whose produce was so fresh it seemed about to burst, then to the fabric store, where residents had their clothing and upholstery made bespoke. Last was Lust's Bakery, apparently owned by Jack's cousin, where they settled into a table with donuts and day-fresh goat milk whose cream rose to the top. Linda dunked. Made noises of pleasure. Stopped doing that, as it sounded obscene.

Zach explained the rules. Like most company towns, BetterWorld had done away with salaries. Instead, it offered benefits. There was no cap on dependents. Families could have as many children as they pleased. But more than two was frowned upon. Cars, houses, meals in restaurants, education, health care, and everything else in PV was free. New employees paid a small settlement deposit that was refundable, so long as they lived and worked in PV at least twelve months. This kept the company from losing its investment.

Employees underwent annual reviews every year for twenty-five years. The first review was the toughest. "It's a test, to be honest. The whole year's a test, to make sure you fit, and also to get you to fit," he said. "But isn't it worth the extra effort to live someplace so safe?"

"What are the exam questions?" Linda asked. He looked at her blankly. "How are we tested?" she followed up.

"Nothing formal. It's really just for fun. You'll understand as you go. Most people work out fabulously." Quickly, he moved on, telling her that if they passed those twenty-five reviews, they'd receive what was called a golden ticket: they got tenure and could live in PV for as long as they wanted, and retire there, too. Children had grace periods. They were allowed to stay with their families until they turned twenty-two, at which point, presumably, they'd secured their own employment. "Then, they get jobs in PV and live next door to their parents, like me!"

There wasn't an elected government. The big things were decided by the BetterWorld board of directors. The rest was decided by volunteers who worked together in clubs like the PV Beautification Society and the PV Civic Association. Laws were identical to those on the outside, and when people broke them, which was rare, PV retained a small police force and typically outsourced criminal trials to the justice system in New York. Misdemeanors it handled on its own.

"You seem organized," Linda said, noticing the passersby outside. Like Zach, they dressed in tight, brightly colored clothing suitable for both exercise and work. "But what happens to the people who don't pass their first review?"

Zach made gratitude prayer hands, bisecting that terrible goatee once again. It looked like a gigantically hairy slug had died on his face. "The same thing that happens to the people who don't pass their twenty-fourth reviews. They leave Plymouth Valley without golden tickets, but with excellent résumés. You can't lose. This place opens many doors—"

"How much is the deposit?"

Zach put his hand on Linda's arm. It felt performative. She liked him better than Jack. At least he smiled, even if it was fake. Still, his personality was . . . greasy. "Don't you worry about the money. That's never an obstacle."

When they toured the local K–12, they learned that all the meals were fresh, the teachers had PhDs in their subjects, and university-level courses began in seventh grade. "You'll notice everyone has notebooks. We don't believe in screens. Screens are for consumers. Our children are producers."

"Is this place magic?" Linda asked, because back home, all the exams were online, only sometimes blackouts erased everything, and the kids had to take them two and three times before getting an automated, often erroneous grade. Last year, a clerical error had removed Josie from the honors track in math, so she'd been remediated. It had taken Linda six months and the threat of a lawsuit to get her back in Honors Trigonometry instead of Building Blocks of Mathematics. Hip lost his lead seat in cello when the music department was canceled. His heartbroken orchestra teacher tried to give him the school-issue cello as a parting gift, but the assistant principal confiscated it, so now that cello sat inside a locked room on Clark Street, getting dry rot.

After the school, they drove north. Zach tuned the radio to the only station that got reception: Plymouth Valley Radio, which was also volunteer run. The Brahms violin concerto played. "The hills look like baby cartoon bunnies and kitties and puppies holding hands," Josie said. She was intimating what they were all feeling: this place was too good to be true. And also: *Were the Farmer-Bowens good enough for it?* Everybody but Zach laughed.

"But they kind of do," Hip said.

"Yup," Linda said. "Or cherubs. Baby angels."

"God is dead," Josie said in an unnaturally deep voice. She and Hip laughed. From the passenger seat, Linda shot them another *stuff it* glance.

"I've always thought they looked like caladrius," Zach mused.

"Oh, I definitely see that," Linda said.

"Me too," Josie agreed.

"Yeah," Hip said, adding now to the story. "That ripple in the hill looks like wings."

They pulled up a long, circular driveway. At the center was a giant colonial three stories tall, with a wraparound deck. "Should things work out, this house will be yours," Zach said.

The kids went bananas. They ran from room to room, claiming potential bedrooms, standing over the fireplace like it was magic: *Does it work?* Hip asked. *We could roast marshmallows!* Josie cried. Then she did a hula hip dance, shouting, *S'mores!*

The thing about fifteen-year-olds: they act like they're thirty, and they act like they're three.

The smart house was four hundred square meters and came with a maid. Handprints opened every door. The windows darkened or became transparent by voice command. Food got ordered and delivered that way, too. Though the furnishings tended too much toward red velvet and gold paint, it was sumptuous, with the kinds of small details, like plaster molding and blown-glass door handles, that cost a fortune back home.

When Linda'd seen pictures of places like this—screenies showing trillionaire lifestyles—she'd never really believed they existed. She'd assumed they were fantasies generated by sophisticated AI.

. . . Russell was great at his job. But was he *this* great? Was anyone?

She breathed, practically high off the sweet, clean air (it was so fresh!), and pictured her family in this big house, walking from room to room, laughing. They could host plenty of dinner parties. The kids could invite scores of friends to basement sleepovers. With all that company, she'd keep the fridge permanently stocked and she'd never have to say: *Sorry, no milk this month; no fruit this week; it's all cans until the farm shipments arrive*, because they lived on the farm. It was all here.

Their tour ended with the underground shelter. There were six entrances across town. The access point Zach chose was at the lip of Caladrius Park.

They climbed down a stone staircase, where Zach pressed his palm against a steel door. It opened, leading to a wider, grander set of stairs with bright motion lights that tripped as they walked down, down, down, until her ears popped.

"Cave-in is impossible," he said, as if reading her mind. "This structure is meant to survive a ten-kilometer-wide asteroid. It's stronger than Offutt Air Force Base. Better funded, too."

The landing brought them into the Labyrinth, a five-kilometer network of winding tunnels that ran the perimeter of the actual shelter. To defend against invaders, walls moved and tunnels led to dead ends. You had to know your way to penetrate the belly of the place.

They walked a long stone hall until they came to a crossroad. Looking in any direction, each crossroad led to another crossroad. *Labyrinthine* was accurate. It would be easy to get very lost.

"Watch," Zach said. He pushed his hand against the wall. Like footage of high-speed cell proliferation, a glinting, handle-like protrusion birthed from the stone. Zach pulled on that. A four-by-four strip of wall separated from its base. He let them through, and the wall closed behind them, blending utterly.

"Super cool, right?" Zach asked the twins with put-on excitement. It's hard to get your tone right when talking to a teenager. They smell phony like a gas leak. He didn't get it right.

"Kinda, yeah," Josie said. "Unless we're trapped and die here."

It was cheerier now that they were past the defensive shell and inside the actual shelter. The floors were Spanish tile, the air dry, the soft lights following their movements like flowers in bloom.

"Is this technology using intuitive biometrics?" Hip asked.

Linda had never heard of intuitive biometrics. The world moved fast, and it should not have surprised her that her son knew something she did not. And yet, every time this kind of thing happened with either of her kids, she wondered: Where had they learned this? What was the shape of this future they were about to inherit, and would it be very different from the present she inhabited?

"Exactly!" Zach said. "You'd do well here to study that, by the way. We always need engineers. This shelter is the only place in PV where dayworkers aren't permitted. That means we have our executives and our scientists—the best of BetterWorld—but we also need nuclear engineers, biotech specialists, architects, and even plumbers and sanitation specialists. There's something for everyone. This doesn't just have to be a buy-in for Russell Bowen. It can be a buy-in for your whole family."

They toured the shelter's various amenities: two libraries, several gymnasiums and lecture halls, and a sustainable garden. The bathing areas were communal, and the bathrooms were the European style, using little water, and connected to sewer pipes that funneled into a large tank with a bilge pump that pushed its contents to the surface. They also passed through the barracks: deep round rooms with spacious bunks, and an enormous kitchen, painted light blue and equipped with giant industrial ovens whose vents made a complicated architecture along the ceiling. Entire rooms on either side of it were stocked with canned and frozen goods.

"This is the showstopper," Zach announced as they came to

another set of stairs, going down, down, down, for what looked like a half kilometer. The landing was open, but she could see metal pipework down there, and more tunneling. She was relieved when Zach pointed instead of descending. A day of touring had mashed her leg muscles into cooked spaghetti. It wasn't so much the exercise, which she was used to, as being on someone else's schedule; having to act cheerful and enthused was exhausting.

"There are three nuclear reactors built for the sole purpose of transmuting radioactive particles in North America. These absorb and stabilize radioactive nuclei. In other words, they reverse the harmful effects of nuclear radiation. We have one such reactor. Fat Bird is online and standing by. No matter what happens outside this town, Plymouth Valley will survive."

"You're kidding. That's a nuclear reactor?" Linda asked as she peered over the railing and down.

"A mini one. In the event of ambient radiation, we're safe. In the event of a direct hit, we're still safe. Though we'd have to live down here for a lot longer than any of us would like."

"How long?"

"I can't speak for the rest of the world, but it would take twenty-five years to clean the Bell Jar. We could surface before that, but the snow would be neon green."

Back home, the streams shrieked all the time about nuclear disaster. She'd never allowed herself to worry about it. The whole idea was too scary. Now, she gave it real consideration. In the chaos of the Great Unwinding, no one was watching the nukes. No one was safeguarding the reactors out in Asia or Pennsylvania, and making sure they didn't leak now, or in transport to the bottoms of mountains, upon decommission. Leaks had happened in Nevada. In New Mexico, too. As for Tehran, it was uninhabitable.

"Don't let me scare you. We hope never to use it," Zach said, patting the stone leading down with pride.

"Right," she said. But a survivor shelter industry had emerged over the last few decades. Companies had them and rich people had them and some families even pooled all their money together to reserve single spots, as if these places were Noah's Ark, and they needed at least one of their own to survive . . . Would people really spend trillions on something they'd never use?

"We'll cast shadows for eternity," Hip said in that awed way kids have, when they're too young to know the apocalypse isn't cool. They think they'll survive it, and from the wreckage learn kung fu.

"What shadows?" Linda asked.

"When it hits," Hip said. "Our bodies'll melt against the walls. We'll cast shadows for eternity . . . Or until the octopus robots scrape us off and throw us away."

"You wish," Josie said. "We'll be vaporized. Atomized. Sub-atomized. Silicone life-forms from the fifth dimension'll be breathing us from colonies on the moon."

"Your father and I've kept you safe for more than fifteen years," Linda said. "Inside or outside, there isn't going to be a bomb. Stop saying that."

"Totally will," they said at the same time.

"There might," Zach conceded.

Linda looked down into the darkness. Something looked back with beady eyes. It was lighter than the pitch, its movement slow, its size gargantuan. Fear lit up her hind brain like a pinball hitting jackpot.

"What is that?" she asked as she reared, arms extended to hold Hip and Josie back.

"What is *what*?" Zach asked.

"There's something down there."

Making prayer hands, Zach grinned with fascination as he leaned over the metal railing. "I don't see anything."

"It was moving," Linda said.

"Maybe a bird or two. They wander in sometimes."

Linda peered into the grim. "The caladrius?"

"They sneak down during festivals. It's perfectly safe. We've put up electrical fencing around the reactor to keep them out."

"It was big, though. Huge."

"I don't know what else it could be," Zach answered with a note of impatience.

"My mom has a big imagination," Hip said.

"She really does," Josie agreed.

Linda watched the dark. It was still now. Nothing there.

They lingered, Zach delighted by the grand architecture, Linda wondering whether this shelter's cold, dead walls would one day nourish the last pocket of humanity. Then they were heading out through turns and winding halls. Zach talked. Linda pretended to listen. On her mind was the thing in the dark.

Surely her kids were right. She'd imagined it. Even so, its beady eyes had seemed intelligent. Knowing.

"Hollow's tenets are three-pronged: First, through good works, we recognize the disparity between our little town and the outside world. Omnium is a good work, but we also contribute to charity.

"Our second prong is ceremony. Each residence is equipped with at least one Hollow altar, where residents offer tokens of gratitude. This is optional. The four Hollow-based festivals are mandatory. These take place on Beltane, Samhain, Thanksgiving, and at the Plymouth Valley Winter Festival. We bunch them around the cold months to keep things interesting. You'll especially like the Winter Festival," he said, directing this last comment to the kids. "It's the best party on earth.

"Hollow's final prong is the feeding and caring for our caladrius. When they're sick, we nurse them. When they're cold, we ensure their roost is properly insulated. Circle of life. To cull the population, we sacrifice them regularly, particularly for our town-wide feasts. They're delicious. You can eat the eggs any time, too.

"There's more to Hollow, but it's not worth getting into." When he saw her worried expression (Not worth getting into? Had she done something to hurt their chances?), he added, "People learn through experience. That's the best way."

"Right," she said. "We hope we get to be a part of it!"

Linda watched closely as Zach pressed his hand against the wall. She now saw a faint seam. It looked like a spiderweb crack, only the crack spread in five directions, for the placement of fingers. The handle emerged.

Then they were on the other side, in the wild Labyrinth. "Can you guess which way is out?" he asked. They each pointed in a different direction. None was correct. The stairs were straight past the crossroads and then left. They walked up, up, up. Her ears popped again. As soon as they saw sky, the kids ran ahead, grateful, she suspected, to be out from that covered place and in the open.

"What do you think?" Zach asked.

"Incredible," Linda said.

"Overwhelming?" Zach asked.

Linda considered buttering him: *This is the town of my dreams! It's the best place in the world! I'm not freaked out at all!* But despite the clown outfit and the greasy personality, he seemed smarter than that. Or maybe *smarter* wasn't the word. Cunning. More cunning. "Yes, it's a fantasy. Perfect in every way. But overwhelming for that reason, too."

"You understand that we don't let people tour. Certainly not entire families unless we're already prepared to make an offer."

Linda waited, her breath caught in her throat.

"You're a fine family. The kind we look for, to create a little variety, but not too much variety. Your husband will be offered the position."

The kids were laughing now, each on one end of a seesaw, threatening to make the other go flying. It was heartening to see them acting so free. Back home, she didn't let them out. It was school and home and don't talk to strangers.

"I'm so grateful," she said.

"Is there anything holding you back?" Zach asked.

"No," Linda said. "We're in."

For the first time, Zach cut the bullshit. She saw it happen on his face, in his demeanor. His posture slackened. His voice became less grand and more like that of someone she'd once met on a nearby barstool, during her wild days. "Seriously, Linda. This town doesn't work for everyone. We follow Hollow. We believe in community. Acclimation that whole first year can be grueling. If you don't want to commit to all that, this isn't for you."

She could tell him that they had nothing else. She could tell him that compared to outside, this place was a literal paradise and they both knew it. But she kept it short. "We want this. Very much."

"Wonderful. Interview over. I told you it would be painless!" Zach said, clasping her hand between his lotion-soft fingers. "Welcome to Plymouth Valley!"

• • •

That weekend in Plymouth Valley was the vacation they'd all needed. They swam in the Omnium River near the old mill and ate like horses. As if their bodies were healing from poison—which, given the particulate content of New York's air, seemed likely—they slept like the dead. She and Russell had sex for the first time in weeks, and it wasn't the itch-scratching kind; it was *luscious*.

Because their assigned house wasn't yet ready, they stayed at one of the guesthouses on the farm. After supper, she and Russell went for a walk. The sky went vivid red as the sun set.

"Well?" he asked.

"It's storybook."

"They want us in two weeks. I think that's enough time. Don't you? We'd need to get here before school starts, anyway."

"Are we absolutely sure this is the right thing?" she asked.

"Even if we could have our old life back, my job, would you want it, after seeing all this?"

She looked out at the sun, which in that short time had sunk behind the wall, leaving the farm awash in a sullen afterglow. "No."

For this first time that she could remember, Russell got down on his knees. He was wearing his usual pleated trousers, a button-down shirt. "It's a house with stairs. It's fresh air and the best schools, the best everything."

Of course we'll move, she wanted to say, and she knew that they would. It was logical. Inevitable, even. But she was thinking of the shadow down in the tunnels; it had felt so knowing and real. She was thinking of Jack, who'd avoided looking at their apartment, under the false assumption that his eyes on the detritus of their messy lives ought to cause them shame.

"I know I haven't done the things I was supposed to do, partnerwise," he said. "I've left a lot on your shoulders and maybe I should have asked. I should have asked. I know that now . . . I understand why you wanted that divorce when they were little. I get it, now," he said, like he was forgiving her for something. He was being the bigger person. "But it worked out for the best. You did good with them. The kids. I love you and I want us to survive. I want our family to survive. We need this."

Russell was not a communicator. She'd been hoping for something, *anything*, like this, for a long time.

He wrapped his arms around her waist, his hot breath pressing into her groin. "This can be a fresh start. We'll be different. Better. Like we used to be."

She wanted to believe these words and was glad he'd said them. They were pretty. "Thank you. I appreciate that. I know I should just be happy about this. I'd be crazy not to be overjoyed, and I am overjoyed. But there's something about this town that frightens me," she said, realizing just then that it was true. "I mean, the big house. The free everything? I can live with Hollow. The parties sound like fun and I'm happy to feed some ugly chickens. But doesn't it feel like there's a catch, here? Like it's too good to be true?"

"It *is* too good to be true," he said. "There's always a catch."

"But what is it?"

He looked at the place where the sun had fallen. "I don't know. They say the first year's the hardest, but they've assured me that so long as I do the job, we'll pass the review."

"So long as we're a good fit. It's a little ominous, isn't it?"

"They seem to like us."

"Do we like them?"

"Does it matter?" he asked. "It's like those old game shows: a prize behind a door. Do we take the cash that won't last us six months, or do we trade it for whatever's behind door number two?"

She shrugged, knowing the answer but still uncertain.

"I wanted this my whole life," Russell continued. "A company town. Can you imagine if my dad was still alive? This is probably the one thing that might have made him like me. But now that we've got this brass ring, I can see that we'll lose something, too. In a way, everyone here will be our boss. They'll have experience and connections.

We won't. That'll be tense . . . My whole life is tense. I've always felt uncomfortable around other people. It's probably why I got fired even though they needed me to run that department—"

"No—" Linda started to interrupt, but Russell stopped her.

"—I'm not good with people. I know that. You don't have to protect me from it. I know I wasn't popular over at the EPA . . . Around here, they don't seem to care about whether I go out for drinks or crack the right kinds of jokes. They care about the work. It'll be fine for me. Better than home. You're the one who'll need to adjust. You like your friends. You like mouthing off."

She felt no need to defend herself. She knew it wasn't an insult. She *did* like her friends. She *did* like mouthing off.

". . . But in the end, I don't think any of that will be a problem. We'll get used to it. I know Jack's a cold fish, and from what I saw of Zach, he wasn't great, either. But the guys in my department were okay. I think the people who live and work in this town aren't so different from us. You'll find your friends. I'll . . . I'll work. We'll feel good, physically. We'll eat well. It's unfortunate that this place is so cut off that we'll never be able to have visitors. But very quickly, I think you'll forget what's left behind. We all will. That's the trade-off. For you more than me. We'll become the kinds of people who live behind walls."

She said what she'd known she'd say all along. "Let's bet the college fund on door number two."

• • •

There was hardly time for good-byes. She reassigned her patients and sent out a brief email—not enough, but all she could do. Her mentor, Dr. Fielding, called the day they left.

"You can't move to a company town," Fielding said. She'd just turned seventy-eight and was still practicing despite a hacking cough, which she'd x-rayed in the office, and self-diagnosed: *Stage four. Guess I should have gotten more X-rays!*

"Pretty sure I can," Linda told her.

"I'll up your hours. Overtime for three months," she said, her voice all rasp and exhale. Linda pictured her, vaping in the supply closet. It was illegal to do indoors, but no one in the position to enforce such things was paying attention.

"Not enough," Linda answered.

"Honey, you can't even vote there. Stay in New York. It's a broken democracy, but it's a democracy. You think if a bomb drops, you'll want to survive it? You won't."

"I have to do this," Linda said.

"You've got a career here. What do you have there? They can dress it up as the prettiest pig at the prom, but it's still a pig. Those people can't handle real life. They're not living, they're avoiding death. It's a tomb."

Linda was trying hard not to cry. She'd been thinking about her young patients all day, imagining their parents reading the prosaic note she'd sent: *Dear families—I've loved serving you for the last fourteen years but now it's time to move on. I wish you the best!* Some of those children were very sick and needed her to testify in housing court about the effects of mold in their bedrooms. They needed regular paperwork filed to get their medicine. They needed Dr. Linda Farmer.

"If we don't get out of here, it might be my kids who are patients."

"The mom card." Fielding sighed. "Okay, you win." Then she told Linda to take care and keep in touch, to punch Russell in the nuts for her, which she often said, about everybody. And then the Farmer-Bowens were gone. Their belongings packed and shipped by BetterWorld, they boarded the private plane without encumbrance. She watched the outside world get small beneath her feet. A speck of nothing beneath the great blue sky.

ABOUT THE CALADRIUS

- The caladrius was engineered by top BetterWorld scientists for use as an alternative food source.
- They require little sustenance and no hormones to rapidly gain weight.
- Like lobsters, they never stop growing. They haven't been around for long enough to test the theory, but it's estimated they can live for up to one hundred years!
- They're a perfect creature for husbandry, leaving 10 percent the footprint of chickens.
- The original rugged individuals, caladrius avoid their own kind, only grouping to hunt when food is scarce or during spring mating season.
- They're highly sensitive to pollution. Once outside Plymouth Valley's walls, they fail to thrive.
- Their DNA comes from preserved fossils in Pompeii, which BW scientists revitalized.
- It's believed that our caladrius originate from their namesakes–the ancient Roman creatures once thought to be mythological.

LEGEND OF THE CALADRIUS

- Ancient caladrius were employed by early Roman physicians to eat the sickness of kings. Once full, they flew into the sun to burn that sickness away and purify the land. In practice, the physicians slaughtered them. 😟 The populace ate the cooked remnants of the bird as a kind of communion. 🙂

FUN FACT!

- Emperors Caligula and Claudius kept ancient caladrius at court.

CHAPTER 4 SUMMARY: The Convergence of Magical Thinking with the Great Unwinding of the Modern Nation-State

Points to Remember

- Scarcity hastened institutional corruption.
- Excess deaths quadrupled. Life expectancy plummeted to sixty-two years. It was lower for refugees, who on average lived just fifty-seven years.
- The populace in walled-off company towns remained healthy, with life spans extending into the triple digits.
- The mid-twenty-first century was characterized by a rise in magical thinking, a skepticism for the scientific method, and the emergence of violent religious cults.

Definitions

- **Narrative**—the framing of reality into an emotionally resonant story.
- **Magical Thinking**—the employment of narrative to scaffold a specious belief system in which unrelated events are made causal.

Looking Forward

In chapter five, we'll revisit the Great Unwinding, characterized by climate devastation, mass dislocations, and the rise of magical thinking. We'll continue our case study of Plymouth Valley, in the colony of South Dakota.

—From THE FALL OF THE ANTHROPOCENE, by Jin Hyun, Seoul National University Press, 2093.

PART II

The Last Lifeboat

That summer, there was no trial by fire. No coiled snakes on springs popped out from jars and stunned them; no shopkeepers wore electric buzzers when shaking their hands: *surprise!* They arrived on a pretty June day, their car rolling down a bucolic street to a great house waiting just for them.

In the silence, they unpacked. They learned to work the smart house. They read the many, many pamphlets all newcomers were given. They ran errands and cooked meals from fresh ingredients on a six-burner stove. They even met the caladrius that had declared 9 Sunset Heights its own. A female from the looks of the full egg collector behind her shelter. They filled a bowl with dried worms from the Hollow section of Parson's Market and slid this softly into the recesses of her domed home.

Sometimes, younger kids rode bikes down the street. Nannies and parents strolled their children, too. But these spontaneous acts were mostly limited to communal parks. Passersby stuck to Main Street. The few people they met were very polite, offering big smiles and welcomes and gratitude hands. But there was a division between the PV natives and the Farmer-Bowens. Linda didn't fight it. She enjoyed this lacuna between the loss of one world and the adoption of the next.

Slowly, she stopped worrying so much that the other drivers on the road were going to roll down their windows and scream over imaginary slights. She stopped checking for her purse in the grocery store, worried there wasn't enough money. She stopped panicking every time the kids left the house. The real sea change happened one evening after dinner. In the brightness of summer, Hip and Josie went for a walk without her. They stayed out for two hours. She spent the time wet-eyed and wanting to text them, though, from looking at the location share, she knew they were safe. She needed to release the tethers she'd tied to them. But you get accustomed to certain fears. It takes time to unlearn them.

• • •

Russell worked long hours. He loved his department, where everything was clean and modern and the people were helpful. He was still getting his footing, organizing multitudes of data, but he seemed happy. Linda landed a weekly shift at the local hospital but pushed the start date to September to coincide with the beginning of school.

With so much free time, she and the twins explored. They walked the produce groves, met the livestock on Parson's Farm, and hiked the hillside to the north, which was so steep that no one had bothered to build a wall. They read analog books in the library and researched Plymouth Valley's history. They baked. They swam in the river, then dried themselves in the sun. Despite her fears of lurking things, they ventured down into the Labyrinth, trying and failing to memorize its wild perimeter.

Between time's drumbeats, the family talked in ways they had never talked back home. Josie was sorry about leaving Kings before her playoffs. *I let them down. They were my team,* she explained. *And now, if we stay here, I'll never see them again.* Hip confessed that he wasn't sorry at all to go. More self-aware than Linda had imagined, he told her he'd gotten into a rut back home. He'd been feeling sorry for himself. Here, no one knew him as Josie's uncool brother. He could start fresh.

Feeling she ought to match their honesty with her own, Linda told them she'd been relieved to stop her clinic work. At least for now. She hadn't realized how much the suffering of those other families had weighed on her. She felt light lately. Russell, a man who'd historically been absent even when present, joined the fun. One Sunday night, while playing an actual board game like from the old screenies, he announced, "My dad was a mean piece of work."

This came unprompted and unrelated to the conversation, delivered just before a dice roll. The rest of them looked at one another, bewildered.

"He was," Russell continued, almost talking to himself—amazed, somehow, that he'd found himself in a room with people who wanted him there. "He never played with me. This is honestly the first time I've done a board game. He and my mom fought a lot before she left. It was so much noise. And then she was gone and I was a burden. Just my being alive was hard on him. He hated the idea of having to think about me. I hope I've never made you feel that way," he said, as if just then realizing that what he thought mattered to them, that his role as their father carried real significance, and so did playing Monopoly with them on a Sunday night.

"What the literal hell, Dad?" Josie asked. She was a person who'd always known she had a place in the world. The notion that someone she loved could be so lost was horrifying to her. "You're just avoiding because you know you won't get doubles."

But Hip was more thoughtful. "Your dad wasn't nice?"

"No," Russell said. "He was mean. Or I guess the truth is that he wasn't mean to everyone. Just me. Because he hated me."

"Sorry," Hip said. "You're not mean. You're nice."

Gruff, chagrined by his own surprise confession, he said, "Thank you, Hip."

That was all nice and good. A lovefest that made them closer than they'd ever been. But after two months of this, the Farmer-Bowens were done talking. They'd reconnected, like all the banal parenting screenies told them they were supposed to do. Their bodies were rested. The accumulated stress of their old lives had debrided. The slow pace had grown dull. It was time to open door number two.

PLYMOUTH VALLEY GUIDE TO OFFERINGS

As a sign of respect, please remember to regularly clear your altars, replacing offerings at least once a week.

Offering schedule:

Beltane–Samhain: The warm months have arrived! Suitable offerings for June–September include wildflowers, clover, honey, and dried berries. After the crowning, a chill in the air and red in the leaves brings harvest. Ideal offerings include: pomegranates, squashes, root vegetables, pumpkins, sprouts, seasonal fruits, and seeds.

Samhain–Thanksgiving: Increasing cold means more substantial sacrifices! Offerings include fresh eggs, legumes, and grains.

Thanksgiving–The Winter Festival: It's go time—the meatiest offerings of the year! These include feathers, bones, leather, and meat.

Winter Festival–Beltane: As our days grow in length and lightness, so, too, our offerings. Suitable totems include: valued personal items, children's toys, homemade drawings, and stuffed animals. Anything that's fun and loved. In order to facilitate the process, all children in the PV K–12 craft weekly offerings in their art classes. Interested adults and young children can enroll in crafting during these months, at the PV library.

Offering deliveries take place every Saturday. Please notify your quadrant representative if you prefer not to make offerings.

A gentle reminder from the Plymouth Valley Beautification Society

Door Number Two (Competitive Sports)

It was a crisp morning in mid-September. The sun was bright, the clouds few: a perfect day for a soccer game.

Linda and Russell headed out early to get team snacks for the Rocs' first game. Lust's Bakery had been open all night and the food smelled like caramelized sugar and yeast. After great deliberation, they picked two dozen yeast-raised donuts plus a thermos of hot tea for the spectators and fresh fruit for the kids.

"Is this good enough?" Russell asked.

Linda shrugged. "I mean, they're donuts and they're fresh."

"What more could anybody want?" he gamely finished.

They came home to find Hip studying a scissor kick instructional on one of the PV-issue devices they'd all been assigned while Josie popped headers against the caladrius shelter. Typical Josie, she poked at things to get reactions. The bird was a miserable creature that they'd sarcastically named Sunny. Sunny spent her time in the back corner of her shelter, a twin set of beady eyes in the dark. If you tried to tempt her out with a dried worm treat, she lunged.

Hello, Sunny! You're in SUCH Sunny spirits!

While they'd been out, the PV Beautification Society had delivered a package. These came every Saturday, neatly bundled in brown grocery paper tied with Omnium string. Inside: a bouquet of fresh wildflowers.

"Should we try it this time?" Russell asked. The altar was a three-quarter oval carved into the plaster at the stairway's landing with a Geiger counter mounted inside it, which was supposed to sound in the event of ambient radiation. This seemed to Linda like overkill. If a nuke drops or a reactor melts down, you're probably not going to be caught off guard by the ambient radiation.

The pamphlets had made very clear that altar offerings were optional. They were supposed to be a fun tradition that fostered a common sense of purpose. But who were they for? Sunny? The gods protecting them from nuclear war? Was it for the people of PV? Did they, in a roundabout way, worship themselves?

"No?" Russell asked.

She plopped the flowers into the vase on the mahogany secretary that came with the house. No altar today. "I'll get there. But not yet."

PV could be very confusing. They'd been told that their orientation pamphlets covered every aspect of PV life, but she still wasn't clear on this town's rules. For instance: a Beltane King was being crowned next week, but what did that mean? What happened at a crowning? Was there a bureaucratic aspect to a Beltane King's position?

Last month, they'd had a nuclear drill, the whole town descending designated stairways and entering through the Labyrinth to the inner sanctum. The Civic Association had even gathered the caladrius (Sunny included) and penned them in the underground stockyard. The Farmer-Bowens had played cards for two hours, then gone home with everybody else. But in the event of an actual emergency, were they supposed to pack bags? When did the inner shelter lock? If you were out of town when the alarms sounded, were you shut out for good?

She wasn't complaining. Life in PV was a step up. Linda hardly ever coughed anymore and because of that, her energy had doubled. The food was great. Hip's appetite had turned ravenous in the face of so much fresh food. He'd grown two inches. Josie's acne had healed. Russell, her worrier, hadn't put any weight back on, but he'd stopped losing it. Everything here was wonderful. They had only one problem. She'd come to understand, through many thwarted efforts, and especially since the kids' school and her hospital shift had started, that no one here seemed to like them or want to be their friend.

Plymouth Valley killed with kindness. Lots of handshakes in stores, at school drop-off, and at the ultramodern ER. Lots of cheerful hellos, peace signs, and prayer hands waved by pedestrians and drivers alike. Lots of: *Don't you just love it here? Isn't Plymouth Valley the best thing that's ever happened to you?* But it was a hard, impenetrable kindness that had no tangible outcome. Linda could spend half an hour talking to some nurse or parent or shopkeeper and think: *We're friends! They're so great! We're going to hang out all the time!*

But even when she managed to trade texts with these new acquaintances, their exchanges never led to actionable plans. No one had time to come to the Farmer-Bowen house for dinner. No one could be bothered to answer Linda's more practical questions about how one might build equity in a town that didn't cut paychecks. They certainly didn't offer insights into which employees got approved for golden tickets and could stay for good. *Check the pamphlets!* they'd sometimes say. *Everything you need to know is in the pamphlets!*

This was not true. The pamphlets were cute. They contained bullet points and bird drawings and stock photos of multicultural people. They did not offer sound financial advice.

Hoping to get a better lay of the land, she'd called the PV Beautification Society, the Civic Association, and the PV Parent Association, asking to join. Very politely, they'd told her they weren't entertaining new members until after the Winter Festival in January. Due to lack of interest, there weren't any religious services, so she had no way of making friends at choir practice or at juice and cookie socials, either. At a loss, she asked the admins at the high school and the nurses and docs at her hospital what they did for fun, and could she please join them. Their response was awkward bewilderment, followed by: *I don't do anything! I'm so busy!*

So busy!

Russell hadn't complained about it—complaint wasn't his nature—but she knew he was having a hard time, now that the dust had settled. Sure, they were friendly. But the level of engagement stopped there. From what Hip and Josie had told her, the kids at PV High were just like their parents. They smiled and exchanged niceties but wouldn't share study notes or save seats. “We eat at this empty table behind this big beam,” Josie explained. “That way it’s less humiliating that we’re by ourselves.”

She’d called Zach Greene last week, leaving what she’d thought was an innocuous message: *Hi, Zach!* she’d said. *I’m so sorry to bother you, but you told me to call if anything came up. My family is having a devil of a time making friends! I’m wondering if we could talk about the culture here and what’s expected. I want to make sure we’re not offending anyone.*

Two days later Zach texted: *Hi, Linda! Remember, these things take time. I’ve scheduled you for an appointment at my office in the Quality of Life Building on Main Street. My earliest is October 18 at 2pm. We can discuss your failure to adjust then!*

She’d looked at the device, thinking: *Failure to adjust? Really, Zach? It’s like that?*

This is temporary, she repeatedly told the twins when she found them sitting at the kitchen table, bored. She was determined. They just had to keep trying. Life in this perfect town *had* to work! So, as they headed to this first soccer game of the season, she slapped on a happy face, even as she thought: *If one more of these phony residents flashes a peace sign at me, Imma projectile-vomit directly into their dumb mouth.*

• • •

They left a half hour early for the soccer field. Russell and Linda unpacked on the lowest bleacher. Josie took pity on Hip and helped him right his uniform (he’d fastened his shin guards outside his socks), then worked on scissor kicks with him. “You got it!” she said, though he clearly hadn’t gotten it.

Linda wore old jeans and a sweatshirt. Russell went local in a high-end, bright blue-and-green Omnium tracksuit. “You look hot, hot stuff. It’s all good. We did good,” she said, surveying the donuts, which had retained their interior heat.

“Is this the right place?” he asked.

It was five minutes before the game. But no one except the Farmer-

Bowens had arrived. Linda checked the team schedule, checked the location. Made sure they were a match for the third time. She started to text Coach Farah.

"Don't," Russell said.

"Why not?"

He shrugged. She knew why, even if she couldn't articulate it in words. She got this feeling, when she was talking to people around here, that she would be tolerated for just so long, and as soon as she caused problems by asking a complicated question or needing something, the conversation would be done.

"We'll feel like assholes if it's the wrong field," she said. "She's the coach. It's literally her job to tell us where the game is at."

He sighed, which she understood meant *okay*. She pressed SEND.

Two minutes before start time, the gate opened. Both teams (the Rocs and their opponents, the Gryphons) and all their support spectators pushed through and filled the field in a friendly, coordinated pack.

The Gryphons headed for the opposite side of the field, the Rocs for the Farmer-Bowens' side. Russell squeezed one hand inside the other, shoulders tight. She'd known him long enough to sense his internal monologue: *These snacks aren't good enough.*

"Twice-infused bergamot tea? Donuts?" she offered cheerfully.

Though healthy and strong, the Roc parents looked to be in their fifties through early sixties. It was a town where people lived long lives and had few children. Aside from some second spouses, she and Russell were the youngest of them. She'd expected most families to be nuclear, straight, and pigment deficient. About two-thirds were exactly this. But the rest ran the gamut. Regardless of where on the spectrum of race, gender, and family constellation they fell, most had been in this town for so long that they shared more similarities than differences. Their movements were similarly purposeful and languid. They didn't cuss or raise voices. Unless they were senior board members, they dressed brightly. And they loved to smile.

In response to Linda's chirping, they brandished mugs filled with tea or healthy green parsley and fennel–scented juices. Alternatively, they pantomimed gratitude with prayer hands, then made excuses about having just eaten.

The game began. Because cheering wasn't allowed, the sidelines stayed quiet. Like sad shopkeepers, she and Russell stayed behind the bleacher step where they'd set up, Linda sampling a donut out of boredom, Russell arranging and rearranging them into their comeliest permutation: a pyramid, of course.

At the first substitution, they abandoned their shop and joined the thickest group of sideline parents. Ever the optimist, Russell plied them with small talk: *Where do you live? How long have you been in PV?* These received short, pleasant parries, all in that stilted PV accent.

Linda listened, her patience like a cup drunk dry.

Russell put his arm around her, started babbling. "My wife's a fabulous diagnostician. People all over the city brought their kids to her when their own docs couldn't figure out what was wrong. Her old patients still call for advice—or they try to. It's hard to get through. She misses her old friends." Then he grinned, broad and shit-eating. "I don't miss anybody. I've been working so hard the last twenty years to get into a place like this that I never had time to make friends!"

The Roc parents listened without much reaction. By now, they'd probably already heard about Russell, Linda, and their kids—the first corporate outsiders to arrive in Plymouth Valley in north of a year. But they didn't say: *Welcome! So glad to have you! We'll be your friends!*

"So, what do you all do for fun? I noticed both teams arrived together. Did you pregame at someone's house?" Russell asked, and for his own sake, Linda hoped he'd walk away from this well. There wasn't any water here.

"Can we come next time?" he asked.

Nobody answered. They used the excuse that the break was over and turned their attention to the field for kickoff.

She and Russell headed back to their donuts. He looked queasy, brow knitted, eyes downcast, so she kissed his cheek.

"I was doing all the talking," he said.

"Yes."

"You're the talker. You could have helped," he said.

She looked at the field. The absence of cheering lent an ominous quality to the game. It all seemed more important than it deserved to be. "What could I have said?"

His face stayed stony, though she could tell he was thinking hard. "I don't know," he admitted.

Just then, the Gryphons' left forward kicked the ball so hard that it passed through the back net of the Rocs' goal. The Gryphon touchline erupted in rhythmic, coordinated claps. The Roc touchline stayed hushed. It was weird. In a town this small, they all knew each other. So why not cheer your friends on the other team when they did an amazing job?

"Jesus, they're serious about their soccer," Linda said.

"Poor Hip," Russell answered, his eyes on his son, who had been benched since the beginning of the game.

Linda's heart sank. Hip didn't look bored, like the small, young-looking girl beside him, who also hadn't yet played. He looked embarrassed: all those scissor-kick tutorials for nothing.

Josie wasn't faring much better. Repeatedly, she'd been open and in perfect position to score. Nobody'd passed her the ball.

Linda reminded herself that this was natural. These kids had all been playing together for years. It would take time to incorporate Josie into their rhythm, just as it would take time for these sideline parents to figure out what to do with her and Russell. Still, Josie seemed so eager out there, just bursting for the chance to prove herself.

With such a small population, soccer was the only fall sport in Plymouth Valley. The league was advertised as no-cuts, with everyone aged fourteen to eighteen playing at least a few minutes in every game. The PV brochure advertised that the purpose of these town-wide leagues was to build character and community. *Join!* it exclaimed. *You can't lose!*

Despite Russell's objections (*I'm not trying to be mean here, Linnie, but the kid's got two left feet. I don't think you realize what that's like. You can't just* decide *to be coordinated*), she'd forced Hip to join, thinking it would help him break out of his shell and make some friends. Parents were barred from practices. This was the first time she'd seen the Rocs play. Knowing now what this league was really about, she regretted signing him up. She wasn't even sure she should have signed up Josie.

Once the ref whistled for halftime, Russell was back at it. Reluctantly, wishing this were over already, so she could go home and stress eat some cold donuts, she joined him. "That's your boy? He's got feet like a quarter horse!" Russell joked to one dad, then turned to somebody else and said, "Your daughter's the best goalkeeper since the steel trap!" His voice wheedled, radiating frenetic desperation. *Like me*, it begged. *Accept me and my family!*

They gave short answers. Eventually, Russell stopped trying.

Linda noticed a lone man about ten meters down the touchline. *A parent?* Was he sick of these jerks, too? She headed in his direction, knowing that if she hung around the tracksuit crew much longer, watching them passive-aggressively gnaw her husband's balls for breakfast, she'd lose her temper and say something she regretted, like: *No offense. I'm sure you're all nice people deep down. But right now, I hope the frigging earth opens up and swallows you.*

She was speechifying all this to herself, her lips moving, as she walked toward the lone, brown-skinned man, who appeared Middle Eastern in origin.

"Hi!" she called. He was standing in profile. "I've got two. Josie's the shark, Hip's the minnow. But he's a crafty minnow. Which ones're yours?"

When he faced her, she gasped. He was wearing a child-sized *Plymouth Valley Gryphons* soccer shirt that rode halfway up his adult belly. A full hand width of baggy skin protruded, centered like a belt-eye by a deep and hairy belly button. Over this, he wore an open jacket whose cuffs squeezed his forearms. *Demented* wasn't a common look for residents here, but he wasn't wearing a dayworker badge.

"I just come to watch the games," he said. His brown pupils skittered. Possibly, he was on drugs. Equally possible: his endocrine system had suffered so many insults that he'd become unregulated. She'd seen kids with these kinds of eyes in her pediatric practice back in Kings. The chronic stress forced permanent chemical imbalances.

"Great way to spend a Saturday," she said. And maybe it was. Then again, was he saying that he didn't have a kid playing this game?

He was unusually young for this crowd—definitely under forty, with a full, moplike head of black hair. He eyed her up and down, and maybe he thought the gesture was neutral, but he seethed.

Her imagination ran away with her. *This is what's behind Plymouth Valley's veil of smiles*, she thought. Then came a disconcerting image: a bloody, gristly grin under a curtain made of lace. The red soaked the white.

Suddenly, Russell was beside her, his arm on her shoulder. She jumped, then laughed as he extended his hand. "Hi! I'm Russell! We're new!" He'd been introducing their family in exactly this way since their arrival in PV and until now it had annoyed her. Startled from her mind-set by this unaccountable man, she realized that it was funny: *Hi! We're new! Like us, we're new! Be our friends, we're new!*

Fuck you! We're new!

The man ignored Russell, directed his words at Linda. "You keep an eye out for your own. They lose their way in the tunnels."

"What?" Russell asked. "Who gets lost?"

Dismissing them, the man turned his attention back to the field, upon which no one was playing, because it was halftime.

Linda nudged Russell, who seemed to have no idea what was happening, or whether they were supposed to stand there out of politeness. "I like him," she said as they headed back. "We're best friends now."

"He seemed *wrong*," Russell answered with confusion. "Was he mad at us? What was he talking about?"

"I think he's just mad in general. Like, nuts. Which is an improvement over these jackasses," Linda answered, index finger pointing at the sideline parents. Russell looked to make sure they hadn't heard, then pushed down her hand, the ghostliest of grins flitting across his face.

"You're too much," he said, amused.

"Yes," she agreed. "But they're driving me to it."

By the time they'd returned, the game was back in progress. A couple of the parents had filled their mugs with the bergamot tea while they'd been gone. "This is pretty good! I appreciate you!" one of them said.

"Thank you!" she answered. She was trying, but her voice sounded fake to her own ears. What kind of jerk-off doesn't like warm tea on a brisk day? What kind of neighbors don't eat the snacks you bring, just to be polite? Just pretend, then throw it away when no one's looking, for Christ's sake!

The game continued, strikes and counterstrikes, until a fat caladrius wandered onto the field. *Fweet!* The ref in shining black shorts and a bright orange shirt blew his whistle. Everybody took a knee—Josie a moment later than the rest. The ref rushed to lift the bird, gingerly as balancing an egg in a teaspoon, and carried it off. Another whistle and the game resumed. Two more goals for each team made a tie, then two overtimes, then sudden death.

"They still do sudden death?" Linda asked. Back home, they'd banned it. Even during championships, everybody just lived with a tie game.

To her surprise, the coach's husband, Amir Nassar, answered. He was eating a donut, which he must have just grabbed. Was it possible that the Farmer-Bowens were, ever so slowly, growing on these people? "Yes. It's rough on the goalie, but it's the only way to know who wins," he said without taking his eyes from the field.

"There's only four teams in their age group. Do we need to know that bad?" she asked.

"They're used to competition," Amir answered. And then: "Josie'll get used to it, too. She's good."

"What's sudden death?" Russell asked. Back home, he'd always worked weekends. He'd never been to a game. She explained. Sudden death meant seven penalty kicks each against two very stressed-out goalies. The Gryphons went first, scoring three points. The Rocs went next. After six efforts, they scored two goals. One kick left.

But then, another *fweet!* The ref beckoned the coaches to the field, then pointed at the bench. With a dawning horror, Linda realized that the ref was pointing at Hip. According to PV rules, it wasn't legal to have a kid on your roster and bench them the whole game. There were six other subs and they'd all played. Even the runt of the team had gotten five minutes on the field. The ref was clearly telling everyone that Hip needed to play.

Oh, no, someone moaned.

Linda looked around, couldn't determine who'd said it. But she didn't like it.

The ball was placed. Coach Farah Nassar, who'd never responded to Linda's text, beckoned Hip to kick it. Linda's hands closed into tight fists. He was going to be the last player to kick the ball—to tie or lose the game.

The entire field watched. Because the game had gone on for so long, the nine- to thirteen-year-old division and all their parents were on the sidelines, waiting to take possession of the field. Beside her, Russell got still and tall while Linda's center of gravity went low. She followed it, leaning her hands against her thighs. "You can do it," she whispered.

Hip secured his safety glasses, measured five paces back.

"Kill it, Hip!" Josie hollered from behind the halfway line, forgetting, until the ref flashed his yellow warning card, that even players weren't allowed to cheer.

Hip charged. His foot missed, mostly. The ball dribbled lazily. The game was lost.

Except for the Roc parents, everybody—and there were *a lot* of people—burst into uproarious, syncopated clapping. What an incredibly close game!

"Unacceptable," a parent nearby whispered, and another whispered back, "Why'd the ref wait until now?"

"That kid does NOT belong on the team!" Amir Nassar shout-whispered, kicking the grass hard enough to peel a divot from the dirt.

Linda caught his eye. The guy'd just publicly blasted her fifteen-year-old—a kid!—but he didn't mug shame. He held his ground. For Linda, a bull of a person when it came to her kids, this was the equivalent of waving a red cape. She started toward him. Russell's long hand clamped her shoulder, squeezed a soft warning.

The moment passed.

The Rocs congratulated the Gryphons by lining up from opposite directions and slapping hands. Afterward, they didn't separate but formed a clumpy swarm that headed for the north end of the field, where their spectators joined them. Like stray bees banished from the hive, Josie and Hip stayed behind. The next four teams took possession of the field, moving goals and sidelines to make two smaller fields of play. Linda and Russell approached their twins with cautious smiles. "You guys, what a game!" she cried.

"I suck," Hip answered.

Josie eyed the departing Rocs and their parents. A few, including Amir and even Coach Farah, were looking in the Farmer-Bowens' direction, accusation written on their faces. "They suck," she said.

• • •

Linda tried to console the kids—*Gee, these people really do love their sports!* And *Josie, you were open so many times. I can't believe nobody passed! Still, you're both playing so much better. I was really impressed.* But they weren't having it. Even Russell stayed pensive. He gathered all the uneaten snacks. Halfway between the garbage and the car, he halted. Everything here was free. No point carrying twenty-two donuts back home, where they'd just go stale.

"Trunk?" she asked, unwilling to waste all that food. "I'll eat at least a few of 'em!"

The town was split into four quadrants. They lived just inside the border of the southeast end, with what she'd been told was a respectable address. The northern quadrants were for the top people. The southwest, the least desirable area, was for retired residents and the less skilled essential workers who kept the town and shelter running.

Three kilometers east and south, Linda cut the engine at the center of their circular driveway. Dirt-smeared Josie jumped out. "So long, suckas!" she called, having recovered her good spirits, or at least gaining enough composure to fake them. Glum Hip slid over, went out the same way.

Linda was about to get out, too, when she noticed Russell beside her, his top hand draped diagonally over the one beneath it, spindly fingers splayed. He looked tired. Exhausted, even.

"You okay?" she asked.

He squinted at the giant house. Except for the bird scat on the lawn and shelter, it was unnervingly pristine. Dayworkers constantly cleaned and repaired, but they were quiet about it. You had to look to notice them. "A little of column A, a little of column B."

"The soccer game?"

"A lot of things."

"Like what?"

"I'm glad we're here, but it's hard."

"Yeah."

On plenty of occasions over the years, they'd argued when they should have joined forces. Life is stressful. Eventually, you have to let the pressure out. Sometimes the safest target is the person sleeping in your bed. But maybe they'd matured, or maybe they both understood that the stakes were too high to fuck around, because since the Bussel Rowen incident, they'd been very much on the same team.

"Are you upset about the dirty birds?" she asked, hoping to cheer him by making light. "The meaningless politeness? The competitive soccer? The thing they call *Hollow*, that they claim isn't a religion, but kind of sounds like a religion?"

"Yes."

"Which one?"

He was the kind of person with permanently wet eyes. Even she had a hard time discerning whether he was about to cry or just being thoughtful. "I keep missing everything. I keep getting everything wrong," he said, a reluctant confession.

"How?" she asked.

"Everything I do, every interaction I have, feels like it's a second too early or too late. It's as if I'm just slightly off the same dimensional plane as everyone else."

She nodded, because she understood the feeling, this unrealness, though she wouldn't have described it in terms of dimensional planes.

"Everything here feels *off*, doesn't it?" he asked.

"Yeah," she agreed. The cutesy pamphlets were off. The gratitude prayer hands were off. The pathologically polite people masking what was beginning to feel like real cruelty were off. Then again, the world was falling apart. Living inside high walls with abundant food and energy and water and watching hypercompetitive teen soccer games felt a little like being a circus elephant balancing on a beach ball, trying to run in place while the entire big top burns to the ground.

The vibe, inherently, was wrong.

"I'm having trouble at work," he said.

"How?"

He shook his head, the muscles of his face tugging in contradictory directions: a grin, a grimace, a scowl. He was unmoored, she could see. "At the office. It's all smiles. You know those smiles."

She nodded.

"I can't break through." He sounded frustrated with himself. Ashamed, even.

"You were at the office until almost two in the morning last night," she said. "Are the rest of them clocking those hours?"

He stabbed the radio dial with his finger. Static played through the speakers, and he stabbed it again, quiet. "I don't know *what* they do. They don't tell me. Half of them are supposed to be subordinate, but they don't act it. They're nice about it—they pretend to agree with me. Then they do whatever they want. I told everybody we weren't taking lunch; I wanted the data back on a clinical trial the London office is running on Omnium safety. Then I went to the john and when I got back, they were gone. The papers I'd left on my bench were gone. My computer was off, and my work hadn't been saved. I lost hours. I had to do their work *and* mine. It's still not all done."

"You're kidding me. That's insane."

"I'm not kidding. It happened."

"Can you talk to Heinrich?" Heinrich was his supervisor, who reported to the board of directors.

"There's something Heinrich told me yesterday. He dropped it like a bomb."

This couldn't be good. "Bombs away."

"There's a lawsuit against Omnium. The hearing's in October—it's the reason I'm reviewing this data. Heinrich said that the outcome will define my future here. I'm sorry—our future."

"What does that mean?"

"In the annual review. If I haven't helped them successfully defend their case, we're out."

"Then you have to win the case," Linda said, her voice echoing shrilly inside the car.

"Yes, but how?" Russell fiddled with the radio again. His hand slipped and the volume went high: *It's hard work to stay this fit but it's worth it to be a part of the festivities*, said a squeaky, high-pitched male voice. And then came the disc jockey: *And there you have it, from the mouth of Keith Parson, our very own Beltane King!*

It was jarring and too happy. Russell turned the dial back down.

"The lawsuits don't hold water, but I need the data to back me up before we can get them dismissed. The problem's getting the data."

"And Heinrich won't help you?"

"I think this is the test. I'm supposed to show I can deliver without Mom and Dad cutting my greens for me. If I screw it up with bad testimony, they can always appeal the judgment, hire someone else to do my job—someone inside, that the staff likes. The person under me, Nanny . . . did you meet them? I don't think so. Well, it turns out they thought they were getting my job. Everyone did. I think the entire department is mad about it. I'm just some outsider. What I'm saying is, we might not even make it to the first review. We could lose our deposit."

"Oh," she said.

Russell's fists stayed tight. "I'm doing something wrong. I don't know what it is, but I'm saying the wrong things or I'm not saying enough or . . . I don't know. I'm not good with people. I try. I really do. It's the EPA all over again, Linda."

She scooted over the center console in order to be close to him. In her mind, she committed this act with fluid grace. In reality, she flopped. Russell tried to help and got kneed in the thigh. Then they were sharing the shotgun seat, both smooshed together. It wasn't funny. Not a tension breaker. He looked annoyed, which she had to admit was a reasonable reaction.

"First, fuck the EPA. They were too stupid to know the gem they had in you," she said. "Second, I had this thought at soccer. Since we moved here, I thought people were just standoffish, you know? They're not used to new people. Plus, we're more than new. We're not transfers from Palo Alto or some other company town. We're literal outsiders.

"But always before, I talked to one or two people and that's it. I took it personally, which is funny, because I keep telling Hip and Josie not to take this shunning personally. But that's impossible. It feels terrible to be left out . . . It occurred to me today that they're all acting the same, like they're following instructions. They excluded us from the pregame, even though, for the sake of having a winning team, they should have sucked it up and invited us. For the sake of the lawsuit, they should be helping you. Honestly, it's weird nobody's invited us over yet, just in case we turn out cool, or you get promoted to something crazy important. It's just common sense. Nobody's that cold without a good reason. So, I'm wondering: Do you know what the pamphlets say about golden tickets? Are there a limited number?"

"I read both. I think there's just two pamphlets on that? Neither said," he answered.

She made a raspberry. "Those frickin' pamphlets. What idiot wrote them? I swear to God, it's like they're taunting me . . . Is it possible they don't like new people because it's musical chairs? Helping us might help them out of a job? Only it's not just a job? It's everything they've ever known? We get tenure, and then not just one person, but possibly a whole family who've lived here for generations loses it and has to live outside? They'd have to be terrified of something like that."

His hands loosened and he laid them flat. "That would make a lot of sense."

"I'd haze us if those were the stakes," she said. "I'd do worse."

"No, you wouldn't. You invited every lost duckling you ever met to our house for dinner back home," he said.

"If I'd lived here my whole life and was scared, I might," she said. "Anybody might. They think the outside is Armageddon."

"It is, a little. So, what do we do?" he asked. They were sitting close, and it was dumb, but she felt happy. Most of their marriage, she'd been a kind of interchangeable cog in the Russell Bowen ambition machine. But since Black Friday, they'd plotted together. They felt like a real team. In moments like this, she could forget the bad stuff, and remember the Russell she'd first met at Sluggs Bar, who'd been too nervous to look in her eyes, so instead he'd fascinated on the moonshine bottles behind her. *You're unconventionally attractive, but attractive nonetheless*, he'd said. She'd laughed, then realized he was serious and told him, *Dude, I'm regular attractive!*

"We tried nice. That hasn't worked. I think we push back. You said Heinrich doesn't read your reports. He just passes them to the board of directors?"

Russell nodded.

"Then put it in the report. The work you assigned, and how much of it didn't get done. Name names and see what happens."

Russell looked horrified. "Name names?"

"Why not? If that doesn't work, ask to hire an assistant. They'll hate that. They don't want more people—it's too expensive. Say you need one, though, because your own team's lazy and you intend to meet all the deadlines."

"I won't make friends that way."

Linda shrugged. "Heinrich sounds like middle management. The top people didn't get this far without cracking a few eggs. They'll see what you're saying. I'd do it."

Unburdened, Russell sighed with fondness. "I know you would. I thought you were going to break Amir Nassar's nose."

"He had it coming."

"He did," Russell agreed. "I'm almost sorry I stopped you."

"Ohhh," she said. "I wanted to sucker punch him so much. I mean, get over it, dude. It's a soccer game. Live your own life."

"Yeah," he said. "But then you'd have punched a guy in front of a hundred witnesses."

"I wasn't really going to do it."

They chuckled.

The sun's yellow rays shone down through a hole in the passing clouds like a spotlight over their new house. Even from far away, she could hear the kids screaming as they wrestled. You'd think they'd have outgrown the half nelsons, Irish toothaches, and noogies, but when they were on their own and no one was looking, they played together like puppies.

She considered her family, and where they might go from here. Maybe the Great Lakes, though she'd heard that unless you had roots there, you weren't wanted. You were considered a refugee. Maybe Canada, but they kept a tight border. She could always get a job with Fielding back home. But they would lose so much if that happened. Between the pollution and the guns and the Glamp, the city was literally rotting. How many years would PV add to their life expectancy? Ten? Fifty?

"Whatever happens, we'll be okay."

"How?" He looked at her with those bright green eyes that hadn't changed since their youths. She'd thought, when she met him, that he'd grow into himself. He'd fill out. Learn to feign ease in social settings. But that never happened. Even at forty-two, there was something youthful and gentle about him.

"We'll manage. We did it before."

"But it's worse now. There aren't any jobs. The air's worse. There's nothing."

She didn't want to cry. It would only upset him more. "I don't know."

At last, he took her in his arms. "I'm sorry to burden you," he said.

"Don't be. I need to know these things. It's important you told me. You used to not tell me things and I hated it. This is better."

"No," Russell said. "I mean, I wanted this to be easier for you. For the kids, too."

Years ago, she'd been in the habit of ruining good things—like screwing strangers to prevent them from becoming friends. Recognizing that she liked him that first night they met, that his opinion of her had *mattered*, she'd taken him to Sluggs's bathroom stall and screwed him two whiskeys in. Then she'd cleaned up like it had meant nothing to her—left him alone in the stall and ignored him the rest of the night.

You'd think a guy would be furious after something like that. But he hadn't scared easily. He'd stuck around that night, and many nights thereafter.

"It doesn't work like that," she said. "You're not some kind of money machine."

"I know that logically," he said. "But it is my job. To make the money."

"No. Your job is to be Russell." She kissed him. She'd always liked his lips. They were especially soft. He kissed her back. It lasted, and deepened, until it began to feel unseemly: two middle-aged parents making out in their own driveway.

"To be continued," he said with a raised eyebrow. He could be so nerdy. She found it charming.

Gauntlet

They figured, if they were going to find a way out of this, it would be easier if they plotted together. That Sunday, Russell showed Linda the Omnium studies he'd compiled for use as testimony. These were classified—meant for his department only—but he needed the advice. "Am I right that the sample sizes are too small here?" he asked.

"They're a joke," she agreed. "Jesus, there's no data on ethnicity, gender, or even their state of health at the onset of the study."

"That's why I assumed there was missing data," he said.

"I wouldn't bother with any of this. Just get all the landmark studies that set precedent, and maybe order some new ones. Then you're in direct contact with the labs. You can cut out all the underminers in your office. You'll need the board to push the court case. Tell them even some Podunk expert witness from the panhandle would tear this crap apart. You had no choice but to order new studies. Nanny lives in fantasy land if they thought this made any sense at all. I'm shocked, actually. The only way an opposing science team would go along with this data would involve a bank deposit."

"You think?" he asked.

"Oh, yeah. I think."

"But they don't need to bribe anyone. Omnium really is safe as apples. I don't get these studies they delivered. They must know it's all junk. They're supposed to be the smartest people in the world."

Linda shrugged. "Nepotism. This company—this town—has been

around for eighty years. Maybe they used to be the smartest people. Now they're inbred."

He looked at her for a beat, trying to figure out whether she was joking.

"I might be serious. I'm not sure," she said. "But if this is the kind of work they're dealing with, it makes sense they'd need someone like you, from outside. You've got better cards in your hand than you think."

• • •

That Monday, she went to her morning hospital shift. They'd plotted a plan here, too, deciding she should ask for more work, maybe get on her own golden ticket track.

"Do you have any tips on fitting in around here?" she asked the PA, Greg Hamstead, after they'd cleared the whiteboard of a paltry two patients. Kids here didn't have emergent health troubles. The hospital was clean and modestly sized, had a small-town feel though the technology was high end.

"Tips?" Greg asked. There were a lot of Hamsteads in the directory. She guessed he was third generation. "People come. People go. Try to be the people who stay."

"And how would I do that? I'm seriously looking for guidance, here. I welcome constructive critiques."

"Don't worry so much."

"Why not?"

"Causes wrinkles."

Linda made a sour face, because there's useless advice, and there's the abyss.

Right before her shift ended, a harried man with wild eyes scuttled through the doors. He walked top heavy, his back bent as if carrying a great burden.

"Poop," said Greg.

Poop?

Linda recognized the guy as the same one she'd seen at the soccer game. This time, he wore baggy jeans and a sweater, but his countenance carried that same buzzy anger. Even from a distance she could see that his eyes weren't focused. They may as well have been turned inward. The expression *blind fury* came to mind.

He bypassed admissions, a mandatory stop for all visitors, and headed straight for the elevator. The security guard rushed to intercept him.

"No you don't!" the wild-eyed man shouted. His anger was a palpable thing that filled the hospital floor like poison gas. "I know you keep them here. I KNOW IT!"

From Linda's experiences with violence on the outside, the scene was a punch before it happened. Someone would be hurt. There would be blood.

The guard spoke calmly, his words inaudible to Linda. Like a hand steadying a trilling alarm, he muffled the man's shaking rage. The guard continued, practically hypnotic, as the man's posture slumped even deeper.

"No," the man groaned. He covered his face with his hands and began to weep. It was a disconsolate and finite sound.

The elevator door opened. Limply, the man allowed the guard to lead him inside.

"What's that about?" Linda asked.

Greg appraised his sensible white sneakers, which were laced to the very top eyes. "Guy named Percy Khoury. He lost his kid last January. It happened in the tunnels. He gets confused, comes here looking for him. Thinks we're hiding the kid, that we kidnapped him. He walks the whole town and the tunnels, too. It usually means he's off his meds. You'd think they'd have come up with something better than lithium in the last hundred years. Patients hate lithium. He's our lead nuclear engineer, or, used to be. People have been patient—he's a hard guy to replace. Not everybody likes spending all their time down in the tunnels. And he's stronger than you'd think. He went rogue one time. Took four of us to hold him down."

It occurred to Linda right then that when she met the man, he'd been wearing his dead son's shirt, watching his dead son's former soccer team.

"What happened to the kid? How'd he get lost?"

"Freak accident."

"He must be in so much pain. What do you do for people like that?" she asked.

"Therapy. Meds. Psych on fourth floor. But if that doesn't work, they can't stay. This town isn't equipped for people with severe mental illness. They need more help than we can provide."

The elevator's FOUR light goes dark.

• • •

The building was shaped like an *H*, green space filling the open places. Dr. Chernin's office was at the far northeast end of the second floor, and under his name the brass sign read: MITCH CHERNIN, DIRECTOR OF EMERGENCY MEDICINE.

She knocked a few times, heard scuttling. Though it was midday, the suite of offices all down the hall was sleepy. She had the idea that half of them were vacant. It took a long while before Chernin answered. He was a medium-height, slender man in his late sixties with white hair and eyebrows. No dye, no cosmetic surgery or collagen fillers. He looked his age. Behind, his room was dark, the window to outside inky. She'd clearly just woken him from a nap.

Nervous, she talked fast and extended her hand. "So sorry to disturb you! I'm Linda Farmer, the Monday, eight-to-noon shift. I wanted to thank you in person for the job."

He accepted and shook, his grip limp. It took another few seconds before he seemed present and oriented. "Yes, Dr. Farmer! We meet at last." He scooted out and shut the door behind him. "Have you eaten?"

She shook her head.

"Come! Let's have lunch!"

They got cafeteria sandwiches and sat on a bench in the green space. He was slow-moving and frail, though he also gave off the impression of intelligence. "You need to know that flu season is late fall," he started. "That's busy, but your busiest time is winter. People get downright morose, especially right before the festival. Inpatient psychological tends to reach its height."

"Why?"

"Long nights, short days. Yes, yes. That's the easy answer. But I've long had a theory that it's a kind of cognitive dissonance. The world outside keeps sliding farther away."

"You think people are bothered by what's happening outside?" she asked.

"I do."

"But they never talk about it," she said. "They don't even seem to acknowledge there's anything beyond PV's walls."

Chernin lifted his eyebrows. "They doth protest too much."

Through small talk, she learned that he'd lived in PV for more than thirty years but hailed from Pittsburgh. "You'd be surprised. Plenty of lake and river cities are flourishing. It was a great place to ride out the Great Unwinding. We'd have stayed. But then Louis got ALS. He's my husband. I targeted company towns because I knew he'd get the best treatment. I was lucky. They don't hire outsiders much anymore. It's a wonder you're here."

"ALS thirty years ago?" Linda asked, making a low whistle.

"PV has extended his life significantly. I'd hoped for a cure, but the decline's been steady and accelerating."

Linda offered a sympathetic frown. They were shoulder to shoulder and his white coat was crisp. He reminded her a little of her father, who'd also been quiet and kind. A still, deep water of a person before addiction to Glamp got the better of him. "Caretaking can be hard. Do you get much help?"

"Help? Oh, yes, yes. It's just me at night. We have someone who comes while I'm at work. I had to commit some favors on behalf of the board for the additional benefits. But such is the price of survival. Is it not?"

Around them, staff relaxed on benches. A new mom still in her delivery gown nursed her baby with the help of an eager lactation consultant. "I don't know much about survival here," Linda said. "I'm still learning."

"And what brought you to our town?"

Linda gave the speech. "My husband was in synthetics regulation with the EPA. His position was terminated, so he sent out feelers and got very, very lucky. But also, he's a numbers genius. He can look at any study and know whether it holds water. He's one of the last people working who knows how to run a statistical analysis and find probability outcomes without a computer. They don't teach that anymore. He's an autodidact when it comes to mathematics. They're lucky to have him."

Chernin chewed his sandwich, his mouth politely closed until he was done. She realized what made him so different from everyone else she'd met: he bore no false enthusiasm. "Yes. Most people are very nervous when they first come. They're pleasers. Very eager. Plenty stay that way."

"Am I like that?"

He was looking ahead. "No."

"Is that bad?"

"I was like you. I'd say the adjustment was more difficult, but we do all kinds of things for love," he said. "Yes, you seem to be managing the transition just fine."

She surveyed the green space, trying to find whatever had caught his eye, but the courtyard was quiet. The hospital behind them was quiet, too. A set of caladrius strutted along the bench across the way. They ground their teeth on the soft pinewood of the seat back and she realized why all the outdoor furniture here seemed chewed.

"We're having a hard time."

"That's always the first year. It's trial by fire," he said.

"Is it because there's only a limited number of golden tickets—we're competition?"

"Partly," he said. "It's also the culture. People have behaved this way for so long that they don't know why they're doing it. It's detached from any credible, original reason."

"Thank you," she said. "It's nice to hear a straightforward answer. Jack Lust and Zach Greene both framed the first year as a kind of gauntlet. Is there something specific, a real test of some kind?"

"Just the annual reviews," he said. "People here won't want to accept you. You'll have to find some task to fulfill that makes you impossible to replace. That's the test. Perhaps you've found that task already. It sounds as if your husband is essential."

She noticed that the skin along his lips and under his eyes was flaky and dry. Bad diet, possibly. With a sick spouse, probably no one was reminding him to take care of himself.

"Do people sabotage new employees to keep them out?"

He raised his white brows, making his eyes seem wide. "I've made it clear that kind of thing isn't acceptable in my department, but I suppose it happens."

"Any tips? It's happening to my husband and I'm a little worried."

Chernin shrugged. "Everyone finds their own path. If you stay, that's the right thing and if you leave, that's the right thing, too."

"I'd prefer we stayed. Do you think there might be more shifts available for me? I was thinking that if I had five days, then I'd be tenure track."

His eyes remained distant. "The shift you got was controversial. I took it from one of our senior attendings. It's going to slow his own tenure. He's not happy."

"Thanks for the one I have, then. I'm grateful. Please don't take it back."

He made somber prayer hands at her, and she thought it might have been an unconscious tic, an automatic response to her use of the word *grateful.*

"I heard about a free medical clinic around here. I sent them my résumé but I never heard anything. Do you know anyone involved? Is there any way I could get an introduction?"

"ActHollow? That's not for you. The people involved are very high rollers," Chernin said.

"I can handle high rollers."

"We all think we're in a rush but it's never true. This will reveal itself. People reveal themselves. Then you'll make your decisions in the light."

"So, what can I do? How can I help my family?"

"Wait," he said. "There's nothing else."

• • •

They ran out of plots, tried to invent new ones.

Events that occurred over the rest of the week: that night, Russell brought home the recommended bird jerky treat for Sunny from Parson's Market. "Is that jerky *for* birds or jerky made *out of* birds?" Linda asked.

Russell turned the wrapper over, to the illustration of a happy cartoon caladrius with an unrealistically clean ass. The power of advertising! The print was too small to read without his glasses.

"Both," Hip said. "They can eat anything, including their own kind. The jerky's made of caladrius and it's caladrius food. It's food safe for people, too. I read it in the PV husbandry manual."

Linda made a gag face.

"Cannibal birds!" Josie hooted.

Tuesday, Hip's lunch got smashed. He'd been getting napkins while Josie had been stuck on a long cafeteria line. They came back to find a fist print in his soy salad sandwich. They explained what had happened to the lunch lady but were told that every student received only one lunch, no exceptions. What happened after that was their own problem.

"They said what?" Linda asked.

"The cafeteria people don't like us," Hip said. "I don't think any dayworkers like us."

"It's the small pleasures in life," Josie added. "Like forcing some rich, company-town kid to go hungry."

"Which kids did it?" Linda asked. "Should I call the school and complain?"

They had no idea who'd done it. To their faces, the kids were sugar sweet.

Wednesday, Josie came home crying because Farah and Amir's linebacker-sized kid, Arnie, had tackled her during practice. "We're on the same team!" she cried. "And nobody called foul. They just kept playing!" After that, Linda asked whether the kids wanted to stay on the team or quit. Hip chose to quit. Josie, feeling bad about having left her Kings team prematurely, wasn't ready to let go. To cheer her up, Linda set up cones in the backyard after dinner. She and Hip worked with Josie on her speed, agility, and ways to take Arnie down, if it came to that.

Thursday, Linda stumbled upon a group of people from the Beautification Society sweeping rotting flower petals and breaking down maypoles in Caladrius Park. They'd pulled the black ribbons off and kept them separate from the rest. "Can I help?" she asked.

"We're not taking new members," a dainty blonde in tight, electric blue jeans told her. "You should put yourself on the waitlist."

Linda goggled. "But there's a rake. No one's using it. I could use it, and then I'd help."

"I'm sorry," the little blonde said. "I don't know how things work where you come from, but around here, we follow rules."

Hear Ye, Hear Ye:

Come Celebrate Plymouth Valley's Annual
Crowning of the Beltane King!

Refreshments will be served along South Faerie
Street

Friday, September 21
Caladrius Park
5-7:00 p.m.

Sponsored by the Board of Directors:

John Parson Junior * Lloyd Bennett * Rachel
Johnson * Jack Lust * Addisu Getachew * Paolo
Lopez * Mary Coburn * Lucien Keefe * Allison
Williams * Jonathan Newhouse *

Crowning of the Beltane King

Friday was the big day. Their first Hollow event.

"I'm all nervous about this," Linda whispered to Russell. He'd been let out of work early, and as a family they'd driven to the Beltane Crowning, parking three blocks away and joining the stream of people headed for Caladrius Park.

"Same here," he whispered back so the twins up ahead didn't hear.

They arrived at a crowd twenty people deep, the ceremony already in progress. An elevated outdoor stage had been set up beside the tunnel entrance. The flower arrangements and maypoles were gone, replaced by cornucopias filled with root vegetables and gourds. Since the park was on a slope, it was easy to see everyone in attendance, even from the back.

She'd read that the Beltane Crowning was a new tradition. Residents had agitated for a holiday during the five-month dry spell between Beltane and Samhain, one that would mark the end of summer. It wasn't mandatory but the Farmer-Bowens weren't going to miss the chance to meet more (and hopefully friendlier) residents.

The people onstage were PV's biggest hotshots: the entire board of directors. Dead center in the only chair, a magisterial piece of red velvet and oak furniture, sat the chairman and founder's son, John Parson Junior. He was over one hundred years old, and though his posture was straight—no osteoporosis—he looked desiccated as a cadaver.

Parson stood and slowly walked to the microphone. "And now, the Beltane King!" His voice was soft and strangely childlike.

The Beltane King climbed the stage. His name was Keith and she'd read that he was Parson's grandson. He looked about thirty years old, with a plain, pleasant face and a disproportionately stocky build. He wore black shorts and a black tank. The bare skin coiling out from this uniform appeared like thick lengths of boat rope.

The old man strained to lift the gilded crown and place it on young Keith's head. It was the color of polished ivory.

"Bones?" Josie asked.

"Can't be," Russell answered. "That's some kind of synthetic, painted white."

Then another board member, a very handsome man in his late fifties, handed Keith an aluminum torch composed of three spherical cones welded together like a wrapped bouquet. Keith flicked something along its edge and all three cones ignited with small, smokeless flames. Hydrogen, she guessed. Not propane—that was too rare.

"Our season of planting and new beginnings has arrived," Parson said in that high-pitched voice that Linda suddenly remembered from BetterWorld commercials as a kid. That's right. Before all the bad publicity against them, the big companies had streamed tons of commercials.

"The strongest among us, our champion, shall represent the spirit, knowledge, and life of Plymouth Valley, and via his physical sacrifice, ferry us through our dark winters, and usher us back into light."

Keith started to hold the torch over his head. His arms were too thick to meet there, so he held it out instead.

"Hail Satan," Josie said.

"Shh!" Hip whispered.

Parson looked like he had more to say, but he was too tired. Jack Lust helped him back into his chair. The tall, handsome man resumed on Parson's behalf. He had a winking, thousand-watt smile, as if to say: *This town, these festivals, and Hollow itself—it's all a little funny, isn't it? Aren't we having some silly fun?*

"The King Beltane will now run the tunnels!" he announced.

In perfect syncopation, everyone clapped. The Farmer-Bowens joined two beats late.

The Beltane King descended the podium, then down the steps into the tunnel entrance. His light disappeared.

The crowd erupted in hushed, excited conversation.

"Eighteen minutes!" someone said. "He's been letting himself go."

"Fifteen," said someone else.

"What's happening, again?" Linda asked.

"I think he's supposed to run the Labyrinth," Russell explained, pointing. "In that way, out on the other side of the park. Five kilometers. My guess is they're taking bets on the time."

"When they say everything's in the pamphlets, are they fucking with us? Because all the crowning thing said was that we'd get refreshments," Linda said.

Not much later, Keith emerged from the second tunnel entrance at the north end of the park. Slick with sweat, torch-first, he burst across the field, serious as a bullet.

"Did he teleport?" Linda asked.

The crowd erupted in gleeful, rhythmic clapping. Panting in a way that made Linda want to get the man a saline intravenous drip and maybe an electrocardiogram, Keith returned to the head of the crowd.

"Time is fourteen minutes and forty-one seconds," the handsome board member announced. "That's a personal best!"

More claps. Getting better at this, the Farmer-Bowens joined, matching the beat. "How is fourteen minutes possible?" Linda asked.

"It's possible. Some of the soccer team can run that fast," Hip said. Linda cupped her hand to her ear, so Josie repeated, hollering loud enough that some of the crowd turned.

Keith was up on the podium now, sweat drenched. He was a seriously big dude with a neck like a sea lion, but his skin had a greenish, unhealthy hue.

"That crown's not synthetic," Hip said, softer than Josie's holler.

The bones were slender and twined, like supple sticks.

"It's the birds," Linda realized. Bird bones are hollow. Easy to twist.

All four Farmer-Bowens looked at one another, none clear on whether they ought to be impressed, amused, or disgusted.

The bell rang, announcing the food and libations stalls had opened.

Servers with huge platters waded through teeming crowds of cliques. Linda meant to try the mead but lined up too late. The event soon ended. In large groups, people dispersed. The Farmer-Bowens walked slowly toward their car. By the time they got there, no one was left on the street. Everything was closed, though a scattering of houses were brightly lit. From behind ink-filled windowpanes, they heard muted music and laughter. Inside a colonial on Park Street, a bottle smashed, then raucous shouts of "Opa!"

The Farmer-Bowens passed these exclusive parties without comment.

That night in bed, she said, "I don't think I can take much more of this."

"I don't know that we'll have to," Russell said.

They made love without passion, two scared people offering shy, inadequate comfort.

The Invitation

The hazing got worse. Saturday's soccer game against the Alkonosts from the southwest quadrant was a slaughter. The Rocs lost 5–1.

Linda and Russell tried starting conversations, but they did so with less enthusiasm than last time, and they were met with less enthusiasm, too. With Hip beside them, witnessing their freeze-out, Linda felt worse and more responsible. No one passed to Josie. Halfway through the game, she gave up waving her hands in the air to signal that she was open.

A tide had turned. A judgment cast. Perhaps by now, they'd have been expected to have learned the secret password. The magic handshake. But they hadn't, and now they really were outcasts.

On the drive home, Linda thought about how shitty these people were acting, as if all of Plymouth Valley were a life raft, and no one could be bothered to make room. She mentally composed a collection of questions for Zach in advance of their October meeting: if Russell lost his case, or was unsuccessful in pushing the hearing until he had the necessary data to testify accurately, would the Farmer-Bowens get kicked out immediately, or would the powers that be wait until his June review? Surely, if leaving wasn't their choice, they were entitled to their deposit . . . Right?

As she pulled in, she noticed a large SUV parked at the head of their driveway—the fancy A-class hybrid kind that only the most important people drove. No one else was allotted the gas.

Were they getting kicked out so soon? With dread, the exhausted Farmer-Bowens all got out.

A gorgeous woman in a shearling jacket stepped down and out. "Dr. Farmer? Linda Farmer?"

Though she was in no mood, Linda slapped on a smile. So did Russell. The kids, sensing the prompt, smiled, too. "That's me!"

The woman, who was as tall as Russell, looked to be in her late forties, but fit and rich, with growth factor–injected laugh lines and large, perky breasts. Possibly, she was the most beautiful woman Linda had ever seen. "You're hard to track down. I've been sending texts all morning!" she called as she closed the distance between them.

"Texts to me?" Linda asked. "I'm sorry! I forgot my device."

"Don't you always carry your device?" It wasn't rude. A friendly scold. Her accent wasn't thick, either. She talked almost as fast as an outsider. "How'll you know if your kids need you? Or your husband?" She winked at Russell and the kids.

Linda's charm tank had run out of fuel. She meant this funny, but it came out bitchy: "They'll use their words? I've been with them all day?"

"Oooh. Peppery," the woman purred.

"I'm sorry. That was rude," Linda said.

"But I like pepper. I like outsiders, too. I used to be one." She turned to the kids. "You're Josie and Hip?"

Warily—tired of niceties—the kids agreed that they were.

The woman shook Russell's hand, too. "Russell Bowen, right? So great to meet you."

Then she was back to Linda. "I've got that right, don't I? You're the new pediatrician who's looking for work?"

"Emergency and general—" she started, but the woman cut her off.

"—Faboo! We convene tonight at Sirin's Bar and Grill to talk strategic operations and budget, and after that we have dinner. You'll be arriving for the dinner part, around eight."

"Tonight? Is this about the medical clinic? Will I be interviewing for a position?"

"Maybe! If it works out, great. If not, I'm sure we can still be friends."

Linda nodded like this made perfect sense, though it made no sense. The rest of her family had backed up, all making their best efforts to seem polite and benign. "I'm sorry, but who are you?"

Chuckling like they were in on a joke together, the woman gripped Linda's forearm. It was the first time anyone aside from her family had touched her since moving here, and she realized right then that she was very lonely. "Right! You're new. I'm Daniella Bennett."

"Are you related to Lloyd Bennett?" Lloyd Bennett was Russell's boss's boss; BetterWorld's CEO, to whom Heinrich reported.

"Please extend my salutations!" Russell chimed.

Salutations? What were they, aliens?

"I will absolutely salute him," Daniella said in a teasing way. Then, to Linda: "You can come? It's a great group. I'm a bit of a bitch. We all are because poop it. Someone has to assert themselves among these sheep." Then she laughed. "I mean, Hollow? Get out of here with that nonsense. It's so many rules! How can anyone possibly remember all of them? Don't even get me started on the birds. Can't we just eat chicken?"

Linda didn't dare laugh, but she grinned.

"We're a great group. We work hard to make things better. Then we reward ourselves with too much red wine. We really do need a doctor. Say you'll come?"

• • •

They looked up the charity, ActHollow, and its members in the *Who's Who* directory, a hefty print book updated every year that listed every resident in town and provided folksy page-long biographies. Everyone involved in ActHollow was a hotshot—a board member or related to one.

"This could be big," Russell said.

She spent too long getting ready, practicing answers to imaginary questions in the mirror: *It's true, my grades weren't good, and I tested at the bottom, too. Not everyone comes from the same place or has the same advantages. I'm an excellent doctor now.* In her imagination, they grilled her, their comments adversarial. (*Why did you move to part time after your twins? Don't you have any ambition? Are you sure you're capable of implementing our technology? It's far more advanced than anything you saw in New York.*) In reply, she made an award-worthy speech that brought them all to weeping tears. In the end they hugged her and told her she was both hired and also the coolest person they'd ever met. By the time she left the mirror, she was wet eyed, too.

Sometimes she wondered: Was she crazy or charmingly whimsical? Unclear!

Finally, wearing jeans, boots, and an old wool sweater (the Omnium tracksuit seemed too casual, and the bespoke stuff she'd ordered from PV's clothing store, Fabric Collective, hadn't arrived), she came down to find her family in the kitchen eating pizza. They were physically healthier since the move, but this relentless hazing had chafed. The skin under Russell's eyes was dark. The twins had lost their zest. Everyone seemed soggy, like cereal left in the bowl too long.

"What time do you think you'll be home?" Russell asked.

"No idea. If I'm late, don't wait up. You need the sleep."

He nodded with relief. "You nervous?"

Like Hip, he'd eaten half his pizza slice very neatly, the bites evenly sized, no crumbs. The plate and water glass were equidistant from the computer. *He* was nervous, she could see, which was making her *more* nervous.

"Nope!"

The Night of the Fire

"No more tables tonight," the host said. They wore a neon blue tuxedo dress with ruffles, their glitter-decorated dayworker badge pinned to their breast pocket like a corsage. After glancing at Linda in her outsider sweater and jeans, they looked straight ahead, as if she'd profoundly failed at the general task of existence.

"I'm here for Daniella Bennett," Linda answered.

Like magic, their eyes popped and they snapped to attention. "Oh! Follow me!"

Sirin's Bar and Grill was located in a former stone church, the oldest building in Plymouth Valley and the only edifice that predated the town. The large altar in back had been repurposed as a bar and bandstand. Crowded tables fanned out like spokes on a wheel. Linda stopped when she got to three pushed-together four-tops, where about half the Roc team parents caroused. She'd curled her hair and applied red lipstick. Her jeans fit snug, revealing decent curves and a still-perky ass. She didn't look PV, but she did look good.

Amir did a double take, seeming at first not to recognize her, all dolled up.

"Where are you headed? I didn't know you came here." He was drinking a double shot of something alcoholic and brown. Mead, probably. This was a Roc parent get-together, from which the Farmer-Bowens had been excluded. They showed zero contrition, nor any indication that they ought to at least pretend.

"I'm meeting a group called ActHollow."

At the mention of Daniella Bennett's group, the others stopped chattering and gave the conversation their attention. "ActHollow! How'd you snag that invitation?" Amir asked, his voice sharp, even as he grinned. It was an affectation she'd grown to recognize as classic Plymouth Valley.

"They're interviewing me for a position."

"Well, tell her I say hello. In fact, once you're done, tell them all to come over and have a drink with us," Amir said. He seemed to think about it, then added, "You can come, too!"

"Yes, tell them we say hello!" added the goalie's mom, an administrator in Russell's department who'd never acknowledged Linda before this but was now flashing prayer hands. "Tell them Ruth Epstein says hello!"

Linda scanned these people whose acceptance she so badly wanted. They kind of sucked. "Will do!"

She caught up with the host along a wide service hall. They slid open a stained-glass door, then retreated, leaving Linda peering into a private room.

Three women sat along the far end of a rectangular table, papers messily strewn between them. "Linda, you clean up great, you hot bitch!" Daniella cried as she stood. She hugged Linda hard enough to accordion-out her breath. "If I weren't married, I'd be *on* you!"

"Holy bananas. You're SO strong!" Linda gasped.

Daniella kept holding her with warmth. Her tight blue denim coveralls fit like driving gloves. "Free weights. Lloyd likes a little wrestling between the sheets. We old marrieds have to keep it spicy."

It was so charmingly inappropriate that Linda laughed.

"I say anything. I say everything. I'm radically honest," Daniella said. She held Linda an extra beat before letting go, and Linda had the feeling the gesture was intended to steady: *I invited you, and I have your back.*

Next came Rachel Johnson. She was a bone-thin Black woman in her late thirties. Her smile was etched with premature wrinkles. Either she was a smoker or chemically treated faces were so normalized around here that Linda'd forgotten what natural aging looked like.

Linda'd seen her at the Beltane Crowning—she'd been onstage with the rest of BetterWorld's board. She was BetterWorld's compliance director, whatever that meant.

Rachel shook Linda's hand. "Welcome. You're gonna *hate* this town!" she said in a jokey way.

"I hope not. That deposit wasn't cheap!"

Rachel winked with sly good nature as the third and final member of the group, Anouk Parson, kissed Linda on both cheeks. Her open mouth left saliva. Linda made a conscious effort not to wipe it away.

"Disregard our resident gadfly. You'll love it here. Greetings from the first lady of Plymouth Valley!" Anouk gushed in an incredibly thick PV accent. You could have floated heavy metal on it. She wore a loose, ankle-length dress topped with a patchwork shawl that looked like the back of someone's couch. Linda had read in Anouk's lengthy bio (two pages instead of one) that in addition to being a prizewinning poet and Plymouth Valley royalty, she was the town historian.

The women returned to their seats. Unlike the people in the main room, the clothing here looked tossed together, the makeup undone. They seemed relaxed—comfortable in their skin. Linda didn't get the feeling any of these women clapped in syncopation. Or, if they did, they led the rhythm.

"Come, Linda! Be my favorite!" Daniella called, indicating the empty seat beside her.

Panting from nervousness and trying hard *not* to pant, she sat. Directly across, Rachel gathered the loose papers into a multicornered pile. Linda spotted some of the words in bold black: *MRI; X-ray; Requisition for Surplus Medical Equipment.*

"I hope I didn't interrupt your meeting. Do you need more time?"

"We just finished," Daniella said. "Did you find Sirin's all right?"

"The GPS did most of the work. It's the happening place."

"The *only* place," Daniella said. "We're a peanut of a town. You're coming from New York?"

"The Great Melting Pot!" Anouk said. She lifted the bottle at the center of the table and poured something burgundy and thick into Linda's goblet.

Daniella raised her glass. "To Dr. Linda Farmer! Who was gracious enough to drop everything on a Saturday night!"

"To Linda, our next victim!" Rachel cheered.

"To Linda!" Anouk joined.

They toasted and drank. "Is this wine? I get why people in screenies go crazy for this. It's like candy," Linda said.

"Shipped direct from New Zealand. Those mining executives know how to build a company town," Daniella said.

"Please. This crap is jet fuel. But it's better than mead," Rachel said, making a yuck face.

"Everything with you is a complaint," Anouk said.

Rachel winked at Linda, and Linda decided she liked her. She conveyed a messy realness. She also liked Daniella, who vibed phony, but also funny and competent. Anouk was a maybe. She seemed removed from the real world in a way that was specific to Plymouth Valley.

"My husband and I are having a War of Roses," Rachel explained. "He's the fourth member of this charity—does all the logistics, my general partner in crime—but he hasn't come to a meeting in a while."

"—What's he done now, the fink?" Daniella asked.

"—The divorce thing again. I don't know where he thinks he'll go."

"—You know I love him, but he's an emotional Tehran," Daniella said.

"—Oh, no! The divorce thing again? We'll offer some pomegranates for a satisfactory resolution," Anouk said. Except for Anouk, who talked slowly, the other two chattered rapid fire.

"It'll take more than a bloody pomegranate to get Kai off my back," Rachel said. "I was hoping you'd send Keith over. Have him wear his Beltane Crown; stand outside the house and stare into Kai's bedroom, looking terrifying."

"He'd poop his pants," Daniella whispered, scandalized.

"That's the goal," Rachel said.

Anouk huffed with exasperation. "The last thing Keith needs is to get in trouble for wearing a Hollow costume outside a festival. Daddy already thinks that this Beltane King thing's gone to his head."

Rachel noticed Linda quietly tracking all this and sighed. "Blah, blah, blah. Other peoples' problems are so boring."

"Not at all," Linda said. "I'm sorry you're going through this, but it's a relief to hear people say what they're thinking. I don't get that very often around here."

"They're islands within islands in this town, aren't they?" Rachel asked. "Not even they know what the hell they're thinking."

Linda tried to be diplomatic, made a wide eye.

"Yes, how's your adjustment going, Linda?" Daniella asked.

Linda blushed. "I love it. The people are so nice. I can't believe we got in." Her voice was an octave higher than usual, her head nodding like a bobble doll's. When she lied, she tended to oversell.

"Oh, they're nice to you?" Rachel asked. "You're the one exception in the history of this town?"

"Don't put her in the hot seat. She doesn't know us," Daniella said, her black brows gathering toward the bridge of her long, bulbed nose. Then, putting Linda in the hot seat anyway, she asked, "Are they truly nice? Are they inviting you to things?"

Linda nodded her head, then shook it. Rachel's wine-red, eyetooth-prominent smile spread slow and amused.

"I hate this hazing thing! I'm nice to everyone," Anouk said. "I can't abide people who aren't. They don't belong. Linda, you'll have to give me names. I'll have Daddy investigate. We can't be a thriving community if we reject fresh perspectives. It's a Hollow tenet—we need new genes in the pool."

"They're a wet bag'a'dicks," Rachel said, finishing her glass and pouring more. She topped everyone else off, too.

"I get it," Linda said. "There's a limited number of spots. But the vehemence of our ostracization has taken me by surprise."

"*Vehemence* is one word for it," Rachel said.

"Yes, but what does it mean?" Daniella asked.

"Spiritedness. Sometimes I think you do that on purpose," Anouk said. "You want to soothe everyone's egos and let them think they're smarter than you. But I'm a genius. I literally have a 165 IQ. My ego doesn't need that." Then she turned to Linda. "Daddy says people are scared because there's less spots than there used to be. We used to cap our population at 5,000 but we lowered it to 4,500. Contraction's a normal part of every company's life cycle. Even Plymouth Valley needs to expunge in order to purify."

"Right. Totally," Linda said, trying to hide her shock that she'd just heard a grown woman say *Daddy* for the third time in a single night. Then: "The one thing that surprised me was that soccer here still employs sudden death."

"Ooooh noooo," Rachel moaned. "Your kids don't play soccer, do they?"

Linda's voice got high pitched and squeaky. "The pamphlet said it was just for fun!"

Rachel shook her head. Daniella made a sympathetic frown. Anouk covered her ears, like she'd just heard something savage.

"I should have known. I can't believe I'm so stupid. Poor Hip—that's my son. He's just fine at it, but he's not great, like the rest of them."

"How would you have known?" Rachel asked, then indicated the outside of the room with her hands, to the wider expanse of the restaurant and the town. "These people wouldn't have told you."

"Rachel exaggerates. Most people are lovely," Anouk said. Then, voice lowered, as if admitting something: "But the schemers love to compete. They make soccer . . . traumatic."

"My kids swim," Rachel said. "Lessons five days a week. That way they don't get fat but they also don't have to deal with the bullshit. Sign Hip up for that. But at the pool. Don't let him swim in the river. It's got an undertow."

"Really? We swam all summer and it was calm."

"Don't do it again," Daniella agreed. "It takes you by surprise. Only people who don't know any better swim in the river. But Rachel, is it called an undertow? What makes an undertow?"

Rachel answered, and Anouk shook her head, sure that Daniella was feigning her witlessness. Linda felt a flutter of gratitude. She'd been hungry for helpful direction. By that standard, tonight was already a success.

"Do you all put offerings on your altars?" Linda asked.

"Every week! It's more about ritual than belief, like mistletoe and Christmas trees," Daniella said. She tossed this out like a stock line she'd repeated many times before.

"You should do it," Rachel said. "Everybody does it. I'm an atheist and I do it."

"Absolutely do it. It's what makes us Hollow. All company towns have specific cultures. Ours is more ornate, but it's really not much different than Palo Alto or Buenos Aires," Daniella said.

"You're forgetting the birds. The birds are weird," Rachel said.

"Riiight?" Linda asked, her wine kicking in, her East Coast coming out. She was glad when everyone laughed, even Anouk. Rachel saluted with her wineglass.

"You'd think they could fly, at least," Daniella said. "The birds, I mean. Not the citizenry."

"—New meaning to the word *shitstorm*," Rachel said.

"—It's everywhere," Linda said. "The dayworkers must clean the stuff constantly."

"Stop!" Anouk said, but without much annoyance. "The caladrius is a regal creature."

"—Fine," Rachel said. "But nobody needs to freeze like Jesus Christ is on the cross when one of them wanders in front of a car. The Festivals could use some sprucing, too. Less competitions and weird rituals, more booze."

"I've agreed to that! I told you, this Beltane thing excites Keith too much. I want him to rest. You have my vote!" Anouk said.

"—Rachel's making some changes once Anouk's dad retires. Well, she will if she gets Lloyd's CEO position. Lloyd's set to take over as chairman. But Parson will remain honorary leader, and Anouk will always be first lady around here," Daniella said, this last part clearly for Anouk's benefit.

"*If* being the operative word. Lots of people want to be CEO," Rachel said. "Now that we've bored you with nothing you care about, would you like to hear about the clinic—?"

"—Right!" Daniella interrupted. "We should tell you about that. Jack Lust said you're at the hospital. Do you like it?"

Linda imagined Jack leafing through her résumé, felt a funny crawl down her spine and then around, into her gut: *exsanguinator*. "I do! Dr. Chernin only has openings for one half-shift a week. I'd like more work but there aren't spots."

"Chernin," Rachel mumbled. "A tower of Jell-O."

Linda raised an eyebrow; Daniella redirected: "Forget that job. Kids here don't get sick. You're better off with us. You'll have something to do."

"A few get sick," Anouk corrected, "but it's usually outsider children carrying epigenetic trauma. The rest of us live until our telomeres are gone, usually into the triple digits." She looked to Linda, seeming to expect agreement from the scientist of the house.

"Sure," Linda said, and she knew she should stop there, but the wine had loosened her tongue. "Just because environmental damage is heritable doesn't mean outsiders are an inferior species. I mean, have you ever read *The Time Machine*? It's possible that damage, though undesirable in the short term, promotes resilience over generations."

Anouk clapped her hands together. "A scholar! I knew it! I've been in a wasteland with these two philistines. Linda, you *must* study with me."

"What's a philistine? It sounds like a horse," Daniella said, and Linda silently agreed with Anouk; Daniella was playing dumb. But it was funny.

"It's a person who eats trash," Rachel said.

"What?" Anouk asked, aghast.

"That sounds right," Daniella joked.

"Did you want to interview me now?" Linda asked.

Everybody laughed, even Linda. This was going much better than she'd expected.

"Don't think of this like a job interview. We're desperate for a doctor, and we've only got three candidates. Jack already called in your references. Dr. Fielding of the Kings Children's Clinic says 'hello' and 'come home,' by the way. But don't go home. You're the front-runner. The other two are in their eighties, and they'll be part time if they do it at all. You'd basically have to flip a table to mess up. It's really just a question of whether this is a fit, for you and for us. So I guess we'll just dive in. Linda, why did you become a doctor? What makes you interested in pediatric medicine?"

A question, at last. Linda had prepared something trite. Instead of that safe story, the truth spilled out. "You all know Glamp, don't you?"

Everyone but Anouk nodded, so Linda explained. "It's a drug that was marketed to poor, rural communities when I was growing up. It was made of papaverine and pure THC. Those are the active ingredients in opium and marijuana. They said it wasn't addictive. But it was. Worse than fentanyl. They didn't just sell it at pharmacies; they sold it at supermarkets. They recommended it for babies with colic. They called it a health supplement, which was how they avoided FDA regulation. I don't know who the manufacturers paid off. They obviously paid somebody.

"My parents were academics. They were nervous people, you know? Always worried, freaking out practically, about global warming and equality and stupid crap they saw in the streams. They used to get each other so worked up, and I remember thinking: *Why not just worry about dinner? I'm hungry and I'd like dinner.*

"It made them vulnerable. They took Glamp for anxiety. And then they couldn't stop . . . I was protected in a lot of ways. I had a roof. I had a community where people knew me."

She looked around, worried again. No matter how freely they talked, these were sheltered women. Maybe they couldn't handle this. But she'd been alone for months. With the spotty signal, she didn't get to talk on her device with old friends. She didn't get to decompress Monday mornings with Dr. Fielding, either. Her feelings had built up. They needed a place to go.

"This is heavy, and I don't mean to be heavy," she continued. "But I want you to understand that my decision to be a doctor wasn't arbitrary. Medicine isn't lucrative. I could have gone into pharmacology or data analysis like my husband. I became a doctor because of everything I saw when my town fell apart. Glamp hurt so many people. I wanted to help them. I've only ever worked in clinics. I thought this break from that, since I moved here, would be a relief. Like I said, I've seen a lot, and it was often a burden. But I miss the work. I don't like being idle. I don't like spending a whole day at some rich hospital just to oversee the application of a butterfly bandage—no offense to PV intended. I want my kids here. I want them at the rich-people hospital and the rich-people everything. But it's a big world outside this Bell Jar. Aside from family, medicine is my purpose, and I want to help that world. If you have an opening, I hope you'll try me out."

Everyone was quiet. Linda worried. "I'm not always so serious. I'm not a killjoy."

"I like serious killjoys," Rachel said. "I married one."

"Well, if we're going to bare our souls, me next!" Daniella said. "I'm an outsider, too. You probably guessed because I don't talk like everybody else. I grew up in Vegas. My third-grade teacher was awful. Taught us nothing and never in a good mood. He was too lazy to grade papers, so it was always group projects . . ."

She raised her hands, indicated her own face and body. "I always looked like this. I never had an awkward phase. You'd think it's all advantages, but you'd be wrong. It's too much attention. It makes you a little crazy. And it's not all good attention. It's mostly bad. People used to try to buy me off the street from my mom. Not just foreigners . . . The decent people give you space. They hate you because they assume you have everything they want. They assume you've never had to work. But they give you space. The problem is, space leaves room for the monsters . . .

"Anyway, somebody'd followed me to school in third grade. I think he worked at one of the casinos? Or was he a parking attendant? I don't know. I purposely forgot. He broke into my classroom. My crappy teacher came right out in front of me. I don't know how he knew I was the target, but he did. He took the bullet for me. I played dead underneath him. It's a blur, what happened after that. I think one of the guards finally took him down, or he shot himself? There's a definitive answer, but I really don't remember.

"I was lying there, nose to nose with this poopy teacher—Mr. Angle, like isosceles or scalene. We called him *Mr. Scaley*. Only eight-year-olds would come up with something like that . . . I remember it being wet and warm underneath him. Who knows if it was blood or urine. Is that awful? I shouldn't have said that! Linda, you broke me open like a coconut! Anyway, I promised myself, when it was happening, that I'd get out of Vegas. Out of places where I could be followed around, or if I did get followed, at least I'd be in charge . . . Rachel had some really bad things happen to her, too."

"Uh, yeah," Rachel said, in a way that indicated *really bad things* was an understatement, and also that she wasn't inclined to share.

Tears welled in Linda's eyes. The pressure of this move and now this interview had made her too sensitive. Still, it seemed to her that the three of them represented an ocean of people, and they were the only ones who'd come out, and survived. What was happening with her patients right now? What about all those people she and Russell had known over the years, who'd disappeared through cracks, as if the world weren't solid, but a sieve?

"I'm sorry that happened to you," Linda said.

"Me too. But it's over."

"Yes," Linda said, looking around the pretty glass room.

"I've seen lots of things, too," Anouk said. "I've been through bad things. It can be hard, even in the Bell Jar. I know that's difficult to believe."

"It's not," Linda said.

Anouk lowered her voice. "Daddy says other people haven't had my advantages and it's not right for me to complain. I put my feelings in my writing."

"I'll have to read it," Linda said, her judgment against Anouk lifting just a little. Big Daddy, chairman of BetterWorld, son of its founder, sounded like a pill.

"And we do help!" Daniella jumped in. "We have everything we need for our pediatric clinic. The space, the equipment, the legal. The office even has airlock filtration, so it's practically as clean as the Bell Jar. The only problem has been staff. We can't hire from the outside because BetterWorld isn't contracting any new people. We have to cull from our existing pool. Ideally, you'll see patients a few days a week. As we grow, you'll hire staff and manage the place, or hire a manager if you'd prefer to spend your time with patients. Once the position goes full time, you'll be tenure track for a golden ticket. Of course, all that's contingent on results and success, so that we can plead our case to BetterWorld's board of directors and Anouk's dad. They're the ones with the wallet."

"This all sounds great. What does success look like?" Linda asked.

"Healthy kids!" Daniella said.

"Can I get a look at the clinic?" Linda asked.

"I'll send the entire prospectus Monday," Rachel said. "We were just getting the details together before you came."

"You don't have to worry about safety, even though the facility is located beyond the walls. We'll make sure you're protected," Daniella said.

"That's not a problem," Linda said. "I'm used to being outside."

"You'd be surprised how fast you get un-used to it," Daniella said. "The rest of us will discuss your application and get back to you. But this is all very auspicious. Propitious? Whatever it is, you can go ahead and get your hopes up. In the meantime, hazing's for suckers. Yours is over. Once people know you're with me, the invitations will rain down."

"And me," Anouk chimed. "People care what I think, too. It's not just because of my dad. It's because of all my literary awards."

Rachel looked up, realizing she was expected to say something. "I have no time to hold your hand. But good luck."

Linda laughed. "Thanks! I'd appreciate any help you can offer," she said. There was no way that acceptance in this crazy town would come so easily. There had to be more to the test than this. But if these women could help just a little, she was grateful.

• • •

Linda would look back on that evening and identify it as a watershed. If it had continued uninterrupted, her family's success in Plymouth Valley would have been assured. Reviews would have been passed, assimilation achieved. But that's not what happened, because a young brunette rolled open the stained-glass doors, disrupting everything.

"Daniella!" the brunette cried, her voice so jarringly high pitched that Linda winced. "I *thought* that was you!"

Very, very slowly, Daniella's full lips spread into a smileless grimace, like a macaque before it attacks. "Gal Parker," she pronounced.

Gal issued prayer hands, shined a sheepish grin. She was a heavyset, light-brown-skinned woman. Overweight wasn't a common look in PV, making her the unicorn of body types.

"ActHollow's Saturday meeting! What a crazy coincidence! I was just getting some takeout," Gal cried, breathless and excited and vibrating with youth. "I was afraid I was gonna have to leave here without saying good-bye!"

Nobody answered. The pause was too long. Linda scanned faces, saw that Anouk appeared openly annoyed, her eyes narrowed, her chin receding like a turtle's into her ugly shawl.

"Can I join?" Gal didn't wait, just pulled the free chair to the space opposite Daniella, like a second head of table. "Can I have a glass, too?"

"Gal, this is private," Daniella said. "You're too busy, I'm sure."

"Busy with what?" Gal asked. That high-pitched voice seemed put-on and babyish.

"Packing?" Rachel asked.

Gal shot Rachel a wounded look. "I don't leave 'til Monday, and the only thing that belongs to me is my kids."

Daniella looked about to chastise Gal. But then, as if Gal were a ball of infinite energy that would bounce and smash against everything in the room unless carefully handled, she stopped.

Gal turned to Linda. "You're the new doctor. My wife worked at the clinic, but she moved away. Daniella must be interviewing replacements. Did they tell you it's informal? They love saying that. But nothing's informal here. It's all on the permanent record."

"Gal, I don't want you scaring her," Daniella said. "Come back another time."

"Am I scaring you, Linda?" Gal asked. Her cheerful voice turned scratchy with bravado. Though she was acting casual, she'd clearly summoned her last shreds of courage to walk into this room. She was shaking, her forehead damp with sweat.

"I don't know?" Linda answered.

"Really, Gal," Daniella started. "It's not the time—"

"See? She doesn't mind." Gal grabbed Anouk's half-filled water glass, topped it with wine, then sat back down and sipped the diluted pink result.

"Delicious!" Gal pronounced. She looked past glaring Anouk to Daniella. "To the chosen ones!"

"Gal," Daniella warned, in a way that seemed to mean: *Shut up and go away.* But Linda had the feeling that unless physically forced, this woman wasn't going anywhere.

Quietly, with glances and nods, Daniella, Rachel, and Anouk seemed to decide something. They chose not to make a scene. Instead, like this was a middle school cafeteria, they moved their chairs closer to Daniella, leaving Gal with extra space.

"What does everyone think about Principal Jackson?" Daniella asked, once they'd all settled. Her voice was intentionally soft, so that it would be hard to hear on Gal's end.

Meanwhile, having gotten a seat at a table where she wasn't wanted, Gal lost steam. She shot pleading looks at the rest of them, which went unrequited.

The waiter came with bruschetta and more wine. Linda slowly sipped, reminding herself to pace it out. Two glasses of mead was a lot for her, and this stuff definitely had more than the 2 percent alcohol of mead.

Just as Daniella was announcing that while she liked Principal Jackson, she was worried the woman lacked connections to the honors track at BetterWorld University, Anouk erupted. "I just, I cannot countenance this!" she cried with the over-the-top passion you might expect from Joan of Arc at the stake.

"Why don't you take notes?" Daniella countered, calm and without missing a beat. "Sit by me so I can help edit. Linda, would you mind?"

"What?" Linda asked. The wine had made her slow.

"Switch places," Rachel hissed. Then, in an even lower whisper: "Anouk's tweaking!"

"Oh." With more effort and dizziness than she'd have liked, Linda got up. Anouk lifted her butt, scooted into the next chair, then—carefully—Linda walked around her and sat.

"Thank you," Anouk whispered. "Rudeness is very hard for me. I find it a kind of violence and I cannot abide it."

Gal watched all this transpire. Said nothing, just got more maudlin. She hunched over her glass, clutching it close as a faithful pet. What the hell was this about?

"Perhaps if Jackson had more business background," Daniella said.

Anouk jotted this, and seemed calm now that she had a pen in hand. "I saw her résumé. She's been a principal in Palo Alto for ten years, but she's originally from an outside town in Mississippi. Born in one of those flood towns. It's a marvel she's alive. Those kids are like fish in barrels. But I wonder if that kind of background doesn't attest to grit?"

"It's nothing against her," Daniella said, and Anouk kept jotting. They'd forgotten that the subject of the new principal's qualifications was invented and were taking it seriously. "I come from outside. But I'm not a principal. Does she know how to write recommendations?"

"Just because she's an outsider doesn't mean she can't write," Rachel said.

"I'm not elitist and I resent the implication," Anouk said. "I'm one-sixty-fourth Lakota and one-sixteenth Brazilian. I'm a firm believer in healthy genetic variation."

"Just throwing it out there," Rachel said. "In case you're taking notes on which people's abilities you question and which you trust. For, say, a statistical analysis at a later time."

"Should we write this not-elitist letter?" Daniella asked.

As was their clear intention, Gal had stopped listening. Though it was a brisk night, she wore no coat, just Omnium track pants and a short, tight T-shirt, and had bobbed black hair. She'd given up getting ActHollow's attention and was now focusing solely on Linda, whose nose and cheeks—her whole profile—felt hot under the scrutiny.

Unable to endure it, Linda asked, "Are my teeth red?"

Gal's brown eyes stared through Linda.

"Gal," Linda said, to snap her out of it. "I'm Linda. I'm wondering if my teeth are red."

"Can you hear what they're saying?" Gal asked in that breathy, baby voice. "I can't hear. I can't even hear what *you're* saying."

Linda scooted her seat closer. "Better?"

She nodded, her big eyes widening.

Linda gritted her teeth and pointed. "Are they red? I've just met these people. I don't want to make a bad impression."

Gal shook her head very slightly. As she spoke, she became less spacey and more present. "No. A little. But you're fine. That's what everybody here does," she said, regaining that cutesy, high-pitched voice.

"What?"

"They drink themselves shit-faced. Then they hug and fake-bond and pretend they're one big family. But none of it's real. Trish puked all night the first time she met these guys."

By now, Linda was three-plus glasses deep, which meant she was 80 percent shit-faced. There was no way to time-travel fix it now. "Their tolerance is that high?"

Gal nodded.

"They like wine because it's low calorie. Except for Anouk, who doesn't have to run, they don't want anything weighing them down at the big Thanksgiving race. They act like it's just for fun but it's not. Everything here's serious, except ActHollow. Even Trish knew, the clinic's a joke." Her face tightened, eyes squinting as if trying to hold back tears. "Charity. Starts. At. Home."

Linda felt the attention from ActHollow turning toward them. She tried to steer the conversation away. "Are you from here originally?"

"They're gonna eat you alive."

"What?" Linda asked.

Gal smiled, still sweet but also vacant, like Linda could have been anyone, including a cardboard cutout of a person. "I was lying. I'm not getting takeout. I knew they'd be here." Gal blew her nose with her cloth napkin, a meaty sound.

Linda looked over at the rest of them, who were pretending that Gal didn't exist but also listening, and she understood that the beef between them was big and ugly and the only reason they hadn't kicked her out was because they didn't want to deal with the wreckage of a screaming argument in the middle of the nicest restaurant in town.

There was something unstable about Gal. Something dangerous that couldn't be contained. "I'm not sure your sneak-attack approach is working," Linda said.

Gal kept going, hearing nothing but her own pain. "My wife left. Our kids are sick, so she gave up on them. She doesn't consider them hers because it was just my eggs." She volunteered this as if Linda had asked.

"That's awful if it's true," Linda said.

Gal let out a breath. "I'm a second marriage. I met Trish when I was sixteen, the cradle robber. I used to be friends with these guys. I lived in a big house. Now I have to leave Plymouth Valley. Because I wasn't the one with the job. When a breakup happens, the one without the job gets expelled. They're not even giving me the full year to figure it out. They're making me leave early because I'm trouble. I'm not trouble—they're trouble!" she said, her voice raised a few decibels.

Linda scanned the table. The rest were all watching.

Gal puckered her lips. Probably, *babyish girl-woman* had once been an effective life tactic for Gal Parker. But age and drink had tipped the parody scale from cute to obscene. "I'm okay about losing Trish. She stopped going down on me, so whatever. But I'm not okay about everything else."

"That's enough, Gal," Daniella said. "Get your food and go."

Though she heard, Gal spoke only to Linda, like the rest of them didn't exist. "They have so much. They're not the ones who have to sacrifice."

Linda had no words. It was all so bewildering.

"It's time for you to go," Daniella added, standing at last, preparing to usher Gal out.

Gal looked to Linda, her eyes wide. "Do I have to?"

What could Linda say? This wasn't her dinner party. It wasn't her town, either.

"They're making me do something I can't do," she pleaded. "And they say it's for the good of everyone, but it's not good for me or my kids. It *hurts* us. And how can I even trust they're right? They're crazy."

"Stop it, Gal," Daniella said, heading in Gal's direction. Then Rachel was standing, too. "Don't poison the well."

"Please," Gal urgently begged Linda, her words rushing together. "You're nice. You're so smart and nice. You're not like them. I can tell. Don't you know someone who can help me? A lawyer from the outside?"

"I don't know anyone," Linda said.

"Gal," Daniella said. "You have to go. Now."

Gal stood very slowly, as if still hoping someone would jump in and tell her they were just kidding. This shunning was all an elaborate test, and that test was over. They were sorry they'd put her through so much. She'd passed. She and her kids could stay. Congratulations!

"Gal," Rachel said, her voice hard. "Get out."

Unable to navigate the small space, Gal pushed the chair back as she stood. It toppled, legs up. There wasn't room for her to exit, or for her to bend down and right it. So she tried to climb over it. Her ankle got caught inside the metalwork aperture between spindle and apron. She kept going and the chair came with her, slamming the table from beneath. Linda stood, but everything was swimming. Crouching, she held the chair down by its stile and rear leg. Her efforts backfired. Like a bird, Gal thrashed harder. She lost her balance and fell.

She spun as she came down, landing in a straddle, right leg bent under her on the hard ground, the other still trapped. She might have twisted her knee, too. She didn't move at first. It was the kind of injury that hurts so much your body goes still in response, from the shock.

"Oh-my-God-are-you-okay?" Linda cried in a rush. The chair was still between them.

With a terrible grunt, Gal freed herself and started crawling, hurt left leg dragging and leaden.

"I'm so sorry," Linda said. Tears burned her eyes.

Oblivious to Linda's words, Gal kept going on hands and knees. She reached the door and went for the wood grilles to hoist herself up. But there wasn't enough purchase. She fell back down and crawled out.

• • •

The door stayed open to the hall, the sounds of chatter and music and metal on pottery pushing into their small room and echoing around. Rachel reached back and closed it. Everything got quiet again.

"Holy shit," Linda said. "I tripped her."

"She tripped herself, the goddamned oaf," Rachel said.

"Will she be okay?" Linda asked. "Should I go after her?"

"She agreed to the rules just like the rest of us," Anouk said. "But now that they stopped suiting her, she wants to tear it all down. I refuse to feel bad."

Daniella didn't flash one of her tight smiles and act like everything was perfectly under control. She looked just as sad as Rachel. "I'm sorry you had to see that, Linda. I let her stay because I didn't want her to cause a scene. You're new and you don't deserve that. But she always causes a scene. It's the one thing about her that's predictable."

Linda wiped her eyes. "She can't be twenty-five. She's a kid."

"We were all twenty-five. None of us acted like that or we wouldn't be here," Daniella said.

"Gal's got epigenetic trauma. The stress carried through to her children and made them sick. Anyone can see it, and it's not her fault. She can't help her lineage. Not everyone has a pure line. But what's happening to Gal and her family isn't our fault, either. We didn't hurt them," Anouk said, having raised her chin and lips from the protection of her shawl.

"Fuck. That was bad," Rachel said, her cheeks flushed and sweaty. She lifted her drink, knocked the whole thing back.

It was as if they were all coming down from a state of shock. The lights felt too bright, the sounds too loud. Everything was sharp and hard.

Daniella's voice trembled. "We can't help everyone. We have the clinic, and we have board seats to secure. We have a mission, and that's what matters." She ran her index fingers under her eyelids to dry them and keep the mascara from running. "Where are the entrees? I said they should take a leisurely pace, but this is negligent."

"What did she do to get kicked out early?" Linda asked.

"Gal?" Daniella asked. "She did everything. Every single thing."

"We tried to delay her eviction," Rachel said. She rested her head in her hands, pulling the skin back so she appeared wide eyed. "But she pissed everybody off."

"There's nothing that can be done for her kids, even though they're sick?" Linda asked.

Still looking down, Rachel flinched. A tear splashed. It was always the toughest talkers who were the most sensitive.

"You see how she is," Daniella said. "She fibs. She makes threats. We did try. We petitioned all the right people. She got in her own way. You throw her a life preserver, she uses it as a cinch to pull you overboard."

"Winch," Anouk corrected.

"I understand," Linda said, still shaky. "I'm not blaming you. It's just sad."

"Are *you* okay, Linda?" Daniella asked.

Linda looked up at the stained glass, which she only now realized was a caladrius, surrounded by green grass, a blue sky, and a godlike halo of cadmium-yellow glass slats. "I'm not the one who fell," she said. "But I have to be honest. This is the bat-shittiest job interview I've ever been on. You'd better give me the job!"

For a second, total silence. And then Rachel barked with laughter.

• • •

Their ordeal acted as a relationship accelerator.

The food finally arrived—family-style pasta and caladrius eggs served with a treat: four ounces of cow meat each from a fresh kill at Parson's Farm. Oh, she hadn't eaten beef in years. It was so good. They ate and drank even more wine—four bottles, all told. Linda did her best to pace herself, but the drinking was a tension release. She'd been carrying a lot lately, and it felt good to drop it on the floor.

Dinner plates were removed. After-dinner whiskey appeared, along with a chocolate brownie sundae, which they shared. Daniella and Rachel jousted spoons, and it reminded Linda of the easy friendships she'd had back home. More whiskey arrived. Anouk, drunk and loose, recited a poem she'd written called "The Inheritors." Linda especially liked the ending—

It is impossible to worship
A thing with feathers
that does not fly.
—A barricade
with capricious walls
—A gilded cage
without a key
For the princess
there's nothing left
but to dig
A city within a city
wrought of skin and bones.

"Huh. It's almost critical," Linda said.

Anouk's voice went low, and for the first time, Linda could see she'd been raised by a leader because she knew how to talk like one. "It's not worth our time to criticize the things we hate. Only the things we love."

There was clapping, and more laughing, and even shouting, and then, suddenly, the lights in their private room went bright so that the stained-glass bird shone like a visiting ghost. Drunkenly, they filed out, the last customers in the whole restaurant.

A moonless, cloudy night, made bright by streetlights. There were just a handful of cars in the lot. The flat emptiness of the midwestern terrain carried the sounds of their cackles and footfalls. Linda was giddy, the evening odder and more poignant than she'd expected. She'd forgotten how good it felt to laugh. "This was amazing," she said, working hard not to slur. She'd have added that she'd had fun, but given what happened with Gal, the sentiment seemed inapt. "I hope you have me back."

"Oh, we will," Daniella promised.

Linda clasped her hands and lifted her arms—giving herself the same champion shake that Keith Parson had done at the Beltane Crowning. "I rock! You rock! We all rock!" she said, feeling welcomed and understood, and also quite drunk, because *I rock* isn't something you say when sober.

As they were getting into their cars, she realized she'd forgotten her purse. She jogged back inside. The restaurant was fully lit. One of the dayworkers had tuned a longwave radio to news from outside Plymouth Valley. The announcements were familiar: there'd been an uprising against the West Virginia government, and a tornado had shredded much of Iowa. In brighter news, scientists had made further breakthroughs in nuclear remediation. Because of national security laws they weren't yet able to share their discoveries.

A handful of dayworkers mopped and wiped down surfaces inside the large church. It felt like being backstage at a play after the performance has finished. Someone had placed a cut pomegranate in a basket on the bandstand's Hollow altar just ahead of its Geiger counter. Photos of two children she didn't recognize were inserted into the meat of the fruit. Their shapes had been cut out from larger photos, the scissors overzealous, so that the kids were missing parts of arms and legs. The fruit juice had run upward via capillary pressure, staining the bottoms of the photos red.

In Linda's condition, it made little impression. Seeing double, she wandered into the small room where they'd met, which she realized was an old confessional with the screens dividing priest from sinner removed, to give it length.

She bent low. Spotted her purse under the chair where Anouk had sat.

When she came back out to the parking lot, the players had changed. Anouk was gone. Rachel and Daniella were standing on either side of Gal, who was swaying on her feet. Linda guessed she'd never gone home at all but had spent this whole time drinking by herself at the bar.

"The decision was made. It's done. It's over!" Rachel yelled. But that whiskey was starting to hit, so Linda wasn't sure. Maybe it was Daniella who was yelling.

Then, somehow, Gal was crying, and Daniella and Rachel were driving away.

Weaving drunkenly, Gal headed for Linda's car like she thought it belonged to her. She grabbed the handle and tried to open it: nothing.

"I think that one's yours," Linda called, pointing at the only other car in the lot: a clown-orange C class.

Gal tugged the handle. "I want *this* one!"

On jelly legs, Linda came to the fender. "Moot point. The engine won't turn with either of our blood alcohol levels behind the wheel."

Gal rattled the handle. Things were swerving, streetlights making trails. "Probably stop that," Linda said.

"I want to go home! To my real house!" Gal said, letting go. She wiped tears from her eyes with the back of her hand. But it was two sets of eyes. Linda squinted, doing her best to stay focused.

Behind them, the dayworkers headed for their bus. She considered asking them to make two stops before exiting town, but she wasn't sure whether this violated one of PV's many mystery rules. She pulled out her device. "Do they have ride services here? Do you know a number?"

"They don't care. No one cares," Gal said, her voice returning to that baby talk.

"But is there a number?"

"You just hit the red emergency button. They give rides," Gal said. Her arm looked freshly bruised from her fall. A splotchy purple welt had spread along her right shoulder and trapezius. Linda winced. Though they were covered, her knees had to be even worse.

Linda hovered her thumb over the red button. Calling Russell was the better move, but she hated to wake him. More to the point, she didn't want him to see her this irresponsibly drunk. It seemed like a violation of their partnership: they'd agreed to try hard to assimilate; she'd drunk her weight in booze.

"Red button," Gal said. "Press it, dummy."

"Are you messing with me?"

Gal shook her head. "That's all the cops do is give rides at night. It's all drunks and no crime."

Linda pressed the red button. Right away, a polite voice answered. "Would you like a car, Dr. Farmer?"

She didn't give her location. They'd found her through her device and were on their way. She hung up just as the dayworker bus pulled out. As soon as it was gone, the town went still. Sleeping. Like a clock whose gears have ground down.

"They said five minutes. Sit tight."

"But I'm not sitting," Gal said.

• • •

"People here are nice but they're not good," Gal mumbled.

They were in the back of a spacious police sedan equipped with device chargers and a screen. In the side pockets were Omnium shrink-wrapped toiletries like toothpaste and combs, plus a gallon-sized barf bag. Linda pulled this out, shuddered at the amount of alcohol necessary to fill it.

"No good. Meanwhile their dumb birds're barkin' all night and all day!" Linda answered. The whiskey had hit, and even if she'd tried, she couldn't have explained what she'd meant, because the birds didn't bark.

As the car traveled, the houses got smaller. Gal pulled out the toiletries on her side, tearing and tossing the Omnium wrap to her feet. She chewed on the toothbrush, broke the comb in half, then took the barf bag and slowly tore it down the middle. *Don't be a jerk*, Linda wanted to say, but decided not to engage. She rolled down her window. Crisp, cold air slapped her cheeks.

"Did Anouk recite her stupid poem?"

"'The Inheritors,'" Linda answered. There was a divider between the front and back seats, and the two cops didn't seem to have any interest in what was happening. This, Linda decided, was good.

"She's a penis face," Gal said. "Takes after her brother-baby-daddy. She wrote her own biography. That's why it's so long. It's longer than her grandfather's, and he invented Omnium. She writes all the brochures, too. That's why they're so useless."

Linda had the presence of mind to recognize that openly criticizing Anouk Parson was a very bad idea. "Penises are very unexpected. They're like if you're in the woods and a leprechaun jumps out."

"They act like they're on your side around here, but they're not," Gal said. It was as if they were having separate conversations with their ghost selves. "They used to watch my kids in the river. They'd tell me they saw them, that they were great swimmers. But the river's poison and I had no idea. Nobody told me. Can you believe that?" Gal asked, kicking the seat.

Linda was trying hard not to vomit. This drive was lasting too long, and they were headed in the opposite direction from her house. Why had she told them to drop Gal first? Why was she always such a goddamned martyr?

"It's hard to help people. You don't have to tell me. I tried with my kids. I made all the offerings on my altar and none of them worked," Gal said, seemingly in response to her own internal thoughts. "But what if Hollow's all a lie? Birds are just birds and kids just get sick?"

"What's Hollow got to do with sick kids?"

"You're a dummy," Gal said. "Dummy, dummy, dummy."

Linda felt the heave in her stomach, the deep pockets of sour in the back of her mouth. Dear God, they weren't here three months yet, and she was about to vomit in a cop car in the middle of the night.

The driver, a wet-behind-the-ears kid, pulled over. They parked in front of a small one-bedroom house surrounded by other small houses. A siren sounded in her mind: Had they left Plymouth Valley? Crossed the border? Would she be allowed back in? But then she saw the tall, unscalable wall just behind. This was the southwestern town limit, where retired people, floating temps, and the lowest-level executives lived.

Linda moved with deliberateness, performing her best approximation of sobriety. She was outside, even though this wasn't her stop. But moving felt good. She waved at the cops. For an instant, they looked too small and too human inside their metal chassis cage. Her mind played a trick, and the cage was made of caladrius bones.

"I'll walk from here! Thank you!"

The guy on the passenger side rolled down his window. He was young enough still to have a peach fuzz beard. "Are you sure, Dr. Farmer?"

Linda nodded, afraid to open her mouth. Acid had climbed up her stomach to her throat.

Gal was beside her, pressing a nauseatingly warm hand between her shoulder blades. "She's fine! She'll be fine. We're besties!"

The cops pulled away. Headlights shined down the empty street and were gone. Linda kept it in. She waited until everything was dark. Then came the heave.

• • •

"Don't *walk* home. It's so far! Stay here. I have a fresh sourdough. You need something to soak it all up."

Linda was standing over the scene of the crime—a grotesque replay of her evening's choices deposited on Gal Parker's narrow front lawn. She felt better, though. More present. "What time is it?"

"Too late to wake your hubby. Come inside. You can wash up in my toilet room," Gal said. No smart lights bloomed, so Linda could see only her silhouette. She was at her front door, using a metal key instead of her palm for entrance. Low tech.

Linda looked down the dark street. It stretched long and unfamiliar. She was tired and thirsty. How far was home? Three kilometers? More? A caladrius on the lawn had gone statue still as if sleeping, but its eyes were open.

Did these creepy fuckers sleep with open eyes?

Inside, Gal flicked a low-light lamp that colored the room a sickly brownish yellow. "Sit!" she said, and Linda landed on a funky plaid couch that was, somehow, warm. The air was cold. The house was cold. Almost as cold as outside.

"I'll just go check on the kids," Gal said.

Linda squeezed her hands into fists, her fingers swollen from dehydration. Small children whispered. She didn't hear what they said, only their sleepy kid voices, and Gal's surprisingly soothing words of comfort: *Rest, babies. Momma's home.*

Things weren't spinning anymore, which was good, but the room was wrong. There were crucifixes nailed to all the walls. Some hung upside down, others sideways. In the corner, on a midwall-height altar, was one of those Virgin Marys on the half shell. Stuffed bunny rabbits and bears were bent down in worship before it. But she was seeing it wrong. Had to be. It was some kind of play structure the kids had designed. Kids go through weird pagan stages when they're little. They're always making shrines in their pretend-play and would be all the more likely to do so in a town like this.

. . . Right?

There was medicine everywhere, too. Pills and vials, some empty and some half-full. Bleary, she lifted a used syringe and vial off the foot table. The contents were identifiable: Zovolotecan, a chemotherapeutic agent that had been prescribed a lot when she'd been in medical school but had lost favor with the discovery of more targeted drugs. The drug was made out to both children: Katherine Parker and Sebastian Parker.

She knew they were sick, but cancer? How could they both have it? She replaced the vial and syringe as Gal returned with a tray holding bread, plates, glasses, a bottle of aspirin, and a jug of water.

Gal poured the water, handed it to Linda with two aspirin. Then she sat across from her, in a grease-stained wingback chair.

"Feeling better?" Gal asked, newly cheerful and alert. But the whites of her eyes were veiny red.

Linda didn't feel better, but she nodded politely. "Do your children have cancer?" she asked.

"They're calling it idiopathic leukemia," she said.

"Both kids?" Linda asked as she gulped the water and aspirin. Something was wrong. It tasted like diluted alcohol. But it couldn't be alcohol. Who would do that? She put the nearly empty glass down. "Is this water?"

Gal lifted her own glass and sipped. "I spiked it with some grain to keep us from sugar-crashing. You'll have less of a hangover."

"Grain alcohol?" Linda asked. That wasn't possible. She'd heard wrong. "That's crazy. You're crazy. I could die."

"It's what we all do here. You don't know anything," Gal said with irritation.

Linda tried to stand. Her legs felt unsteady, as if their bones were a cluster of loosely tied sticks.

"Oh, fine!" Gal said. She jerked Linda's glass from her hand, returned shortly with it filled, along with a new jug.

"Water?" Linda asked.

"Water!"

Linda drank deeply, refilled. Drank two more like this. Went slow on glass number four, then peeled away a hunk of bread from the loaf. It was stale, a white funk about its crust. Maybe it had been fresh, but not recently. Linda ate around that funk, trying to soak the acid in her stomach.

Across, Gal watched. Her jagged, purple bruise had grown. It seeped across the goose-pimpled side of her upper arm. "God sent you," she said. "You're going to help me."

A laser of logic burned through the swirling dross. "I don't think that's true," Linda said, and then she couldn't remember why she'd said it. Couldn't remember what they'd been talking about. Then the laser was gone, and everything was churn, and yes, that first glass of water really had been diluted grain alcohol, because it was weaving into her bloodstream.

"You hate them, just like me," Gal's voice exclaimed, and though Linda was repelled by the high-pitched sound, she held tight to it. *Don't float away*, she thought. *Stay awake or something very bad will happen.*

"That's a staggering extrapolation," she answered, her words slurring. *Staggerin' strapolation.* This house wasn't just cold; the air had a spark of something. It was off, like someone bleeding out on a table after a gunshot. "Why's it so cold? Don't they maintain your solar panels?"

"I used to live in your house before Trish left," Gal said, as if in answer to the question. "I had a car just like yours. Everyone here is the same. They come for the same reasons. They stay for the same reasons. But it changes you. Every day you're here, you become something else."

Linda stopped chewing. "My house was your house?"

"Sunset Heights. Great view from the top of that hill."

Linda felt a swell of unease, but it was hard to remember why she felt it. On the floor, pieces of things: A xylophone without the mallets. A model barnyard missing the top of the barn. A doll wearing a shirt and no pants, her hair cut short. Those upside-down crosses.

"Since we're friends now, I want to be honest. I left my kids alone tonight. I leave a lot. Since Trish did what she did, it's too hard for me to look at them."

"Are they okay?" Linda asked.

"Plymouth Valley either digests people or spits them out."

"But they're warm enough?" Linda asked. She considered looking in on the children. But in her condition and at this time of night, she would only frighten them. And she'd heard them just before, doing their primary job, which was breathing.

"Cozy. Sleeping," Gal answered. "They're four and six, but they're super mature."

"That's too young to leave them alone," Linda said.

"Shut up, you dum-dum-dummy," Gal answered, terse, but without anger.

Linda chewed more bread, but it really tasted off. She was thinking of Poughkeepsie. Houses during the height of the bad times had smelled stale like this. Thirty years later, Poughkeepsie still hadn't recovered. Orphans had grown up and made more orphans. "I should go."

"Stay," Gal pleaded. "Just for a little bit."

Linda thought that seemed like a bad idea, but she wasn't ready to stand.

Gal came over and sat down beside her. She patted Linda's hand, and when Linda didn't react, she took and held it. She felt warm and sticky like an over-napped toddler. The digital clock on the wall read 1:34 a.m. In Linda's mind, that awful shadow, the hidden thing with beady eyes, was shambling a path up from the shelter, through broken Poughkeepsie and drowning Kings, to here, this room. It was stalking the halls, hungry.

"Same car. Same house. Same scientist spouse. We're so practically the same person that we should have the same name." Gal's eyes were bleary red. She leaned into Linda, pressed her soft cheek into the crook of her neck. Her body went limp, its hot weightiness pinning Linda to the sunken couch.

"I'm you. Let me be you?" Gal asked.

"Nah," Linda said. "Get off."

Gal squeezed her hand one more time. She was still close enough that Linda could see her clean, deep pores and smell her specific human scent: honey and stale hops, like the floor of a rarely cleaned bar. "They think I'm stupid, but they don't know," she said, back to that performative baby talk. "If I have to sacrifice, they do, too. It'll be their kids who suffer just like mine."

With the grain, everything was starting to spin again. In the sick, yellow light, all the broken things danced to a silent beat, the air bending and retracting with a *wonk wonk wonk*. "I don't like it here and I'm worried about your children. I want to go home," Linda said.

Gal's answer seemed to come from everywhere and nowhere, a disembodied voice: "You're not so pretty. I could hurt you, too."

She noticed, again, the rabbits paying homage to the Virgin Mary. Upon closer inspection, Mary's face was ground down and over the smooth white of it, someone had glued a beak.

With dim, dawning horror, Linda looked to Gal, whose mascara had run, chunks of putty-colored sleep caking the caruncles of her eyes. She grinned a terrible grin, and Linda thought, insanely, of that children's story about monsters on an island, with terrible claws and terrible teeth.

"I'm going to break this town and everyone in it." The walls closed in. The upside-down crosses and altar bent closer, like the air itself were buckling. She noticed that the pants-less Barbie's eyes had been scratched out, leaving two hollows. Gal was changed, too. She wasn't sweet or cute. She was rotten. "It's the only way, you rich, dumb cunt with your smart husband and your big house and your perfect life. My life. You took my life." The baby talk was gone. It was the voice of someone completely fucking different.

"I have to go," Linda said.

Gal's soft, full face scrunched with rage. Most people only ever made that expression in private, if they made it at all.

Linda looked for her purse and coat and oh, dear God, thank you God, they were beside her on this sunken, crumbly couch. "I'm sorry. I have to go."

"Everyone's *so sorry*," Gal answered in the semidark, her eyes half open, her skin ashen as lifeless wrapping. "Get the fuck out."

• • •

Outside, Linda couldn't find her device in her purse or pockets. Without it, she had no map. No way to call for help. *Just go*, she thought. *Run.*

Landmarks. The wall marked the westernmost part of town. If she walked east and toward the hillside, she'd find her way.

The streetlights had gone soft, making the hedges bordering most of the houses appear animated and alive, so she left the curb, went straight down the middle of the road, her shoes padding softly, her purse strung over her shoulder and tucked close. She looked back once at Gal's house. It hunkered glumly in the half dark, its old wood creaking and slanted, its dull façade a mean grit. A nightmare house.

• • •

An hour later, the houses were bigger and prettier. In the gloam, it was hard to tell which was hers. But this was Sunset Heights, the number was nine. Sunny was out of her shelter, her sharp beak retracting from a small burrow in the ground beside a slate stepping stone. She returned with a furry, moving thing clenched between her teeth.

Sunny chomped (a vole? a mouse?) until the poor thing went still. Jaw locked, the bird glared at Linda. Everything felt quiet. Like a lacuna in time, where all the world was frozen, except for Linda and this malignant witness.

"Go," she whispered, remembering, then, the shambling thing at the bottom of the shelter.

Sunny stayed. Her process was surprisingly graceful. She tore the creature in half, and it was gone in two swallows, her neck undulating.

"I'll go," Linda said.

Palm recognition took two efforts. Once inside, she headed for the kitchen, guzzled a liter of water like it was a two-ounce shot. Her headache eased like loosened shrink-wrap. She drank another half liter, and added some aspirin, calcium carbonate, and a sprinkle of salt. Finished that and poured one more half liter. Stomach sloshing, she carried it with her.

"Better," she muttered.

Up the stairs. In the dark, she didn't remember the location of the dresser or bed. She left her clothing in a pile, felt with blind hands until she knocked against the mattress, bruising her arm (like Gal. Same arm, same car, same house. Was that real? Had that happened?). She climbed in, where Russell was zonked.

Sleep didn't come. She was thinking of the nightmare house. She was thinking about all the lost people in the world, the disappeared people whose numbers were swelling large as the seas. It had happened with her patients. They'd come every few months, then they'd stop showing up, their devices disconnected. She'd lost acquaintances, too. One day, riddled with sham optimism, they were telling you about a job prospect or a move to a different part of the city that they were sure would reverse their fortunes, and the next, they were gone.

Thoughts spinning, she couldn't stand being alone with them. She shook Russell's bare shoulder. "I'm home," she said.

He pulled her in and kissed her. Water sloshing, head light and dizzy, it wasn't tentative. It wasn't shy. They made sloppy, unbridled love.

"Did it go okay?" he asked when they were done.

She'd tell him about Gal later. She'd tell him about the nightmare house, and the way it had reminded her of being a little kid back in Poughkeepsie, trapped in strange places without the agency or words to extricate herself. She'd tell him that she wanted to go back and check on those kids. For now, she said, "Complicated. But we might be able to stay."

• • •

Later, sirens rang out, but these seemed far west and outside the walls. She fell asleep believing their source arose from a distant tragedy, unrelated to her.

PRIMARY SOURCES: An Excavation of the Past

What people forget about those times before the Plymouth Valley disaster is that the fear was real. You could cut it with a knife. It wasn't just the nukes—those were too freaky to fathom. I mean, somebody zonked Iran. Like, erased an entire city, made half the country radioactive. We were all just waiting for the next one. That's some existential shit. But the everyday stuff was worse. You couldn't count on the weather or your car or your lights. If you lived in a basement in a waterfront city, you'd damn well better have an evac plan, or your whole family could drown. You know how people are nice now? All, *tra-la-la, let's cooperate*? Well, it wasn't like that then. We were too scared to be nice. We all knew something was coming—an earth-eradicating disease, or a nuke, or just famine, you know? One day we'd go to the store and there wouldn't be any food on the shelves. That happened. People forget, but it happened. Your money wasn't worth anything. Your bank wasn't a bank. Some days, no matter what you had to offer, you couldn't get clean water or bread. You know how, if you feed rats intermittently, they go crazy, because they can't stand not being able to predict what's going to happen? We were like rats. It was excruciating.

—Apple Rose Rodriguez, Milwaukee resident, 109 years old

—From FIRST-PERSON NARRATIVES FROM THE EDGE OF EXTINCTION, edited by Clementine Petty, University of the Great Lakes Press, 2118.

PART III

Passing

Something Has Happened

Through the early hours, the scent of burning hovered all through town, a cloudy layer of soot that floated between the mountains and blanketed the entirety of Plymouth Valley. But then the Bell Jar's particulate meter ticked into dangerous red. The system went into high gear. With a pneumatic hum, it suctioned the black clouds down from the sky, twisting them into a hundred thousand tiny tornados, then forcing them back out again, clean.

In the morning, Linda found her car parked in the circular driveway. A note on the windshield read: *Compliments of the Plymouth Valley Police Department. Hope you enjoyed your ride!*

"That's above and beyond," she said. Her hangover wasn't as immobilizing as she'd feared. The walk, water, and aspirin had done their work. She was ambulatory before noon. By then, she'd told Russell everything. "I think it was a success but I'm a little embarrassed. I was a real mess by the end."

Like always, after sex, they were sitting close, feeling close. "Don't be embarrassed. They drink a lot here. The wine's about three times more potent than the mead at home."

They were in the kitchen. She was trying not to be a cartoon of herself, but it was impossible not to hold her head, press down on the parts that hurt. Her temples pounded. "How do you know?"

"They drink at work. This cart comes by in the afternoon with cocktails. I suggested to Heinrich that they stop but he said it's the culture. It keeps people happy and working."

"Does their work suffer?" Linda asked.

He widened his eyes as if to say: *How would I know? They won't show it to me.* Then he lifted his mug of black tea, toasted it against hers. She looked at her own mug, wistful. Her stomach was too sour to drink it.

• • •

Having ended the evening on a blurry note, Linda decided to check in with the members of ActHollow that afternoon. She was getting into her car when Hip followed her out and stopped her.

"Can I come?" His shirt was buttoned wrong, his hair unbrushed, and he wasn't wearing his glasses. She felt a swell of sympathy for the kid. Except for rooting for a team he'd quit in ignominy, he'd had nothing to do all weekend.

"Sure!" she said, ruffling his hair. It was an intimacy he still allowed, unlike Josie, who'd banned spontaneous hugs upon turning thirteen.

As they drove, she noticed a smoky odor along Main Street but didn't think much about it. Back home, fires had happened plenty. Like city people accustomed to car alarms, this was so slight it barely registered.

They pulled around the storefront façades and into the lot. Unlike last night's cheerful crowd, the dozen or so residents waiting for tables outside Sirin's were somber. They spoke in hushed whispers or scanned their devices, their faces reflecting a purplish light. A few wore handkerchief masks.

As she and Hip headed for Lust's Bakery, they passed two weeping women clutched in a hug.

"I can't believe it," the younger woman whispered.

"It's unthinkable," the other one said.

Linda slowed her stride, trying to listen. Sleepy and oblivious Hip charged ahead.

Lust's was crammed with a half dozen customers. They quieted when the Farmer-Bowens entered. Hip went straight to the counter, looked at what was fresh.

One woman was still talking. She'd pushed her stroller sideways against the counter so her baby could look at the elephant ears and macaroons through the glass.

"How could she *do* something like that?" she asked the baker in neon blue Omnium slacks. Instead of answering, the man gave a side-eye in Hip's direction.

"Oh!" the woman yelped, and suddenly, the whole store was quiet. The baby's hand reached through the stroller's green hood and smeared the glass.

"Is everything okay?" Linda asked when their turn arrived.

"Absolutely!" the baker said. He was middle aged, with a handlebar mustache.

"Did something happen?" Linda asked. "Was there a fire?"

"They put it out," the baker answered, then bowed and did prayer hands. The mom with the stroller and a few others in the store bowed, too.

"Oh, that's awful," Linda said. "I smelled it, but I assumed it was coming from outside."

"Residential home, southwest side of town," he said. "What would you like?"

Linda ordered donuts even though she'd intended to branch out and try something new. She was thinking about Gal and her family, on the southwest side of town. "Whose house?"

"No one you'd know." He handed her three pretty boxes, each containing a half dozen donuts. Hip took these for her, plus the extra glazed donut she'd ordered, which he popped into his mouth.

• • •

"Will they like the donuts? Because they didn't at soccer," Hip said. They were in the car. She'd started the ignition, softer than a purr, and was still trying to figure out why everyone was so upset, and whose house had been on fire.

"I panicked. Should we get something else?"

Hip shook his head. It occurred to her that something specific was bothering him. The soccer game? His old team hadn't acknowledged him, not even Coach Farah. Later, when she'd tried to broach the subject with him, he'd acted like she'd been picking at a wound.

"What are the exact houses we're visiting?"

She named the residences.

"Okay," he said.

"You're still up for it?"

"Yes," he said, seeming very serious.

She plugged Rachel Johnson's house in the GPS and off they went.

As they drove, Hip babbled. "I sit in the back of homeroom, but Josie sits up front because it's alphabetical, but we got split. The teacher's a dayworker. He says we're spoiled, and we don't know anything, and his daughter Erin is six but is smarter than us. In Language and Literature, it's also alphabetical but Josie's not in that class . . ."

This went on. Back during the worst part of his sad phase last year, when she'd been very worried about him, Hip hadn't talked much at all. He hadn't eaten much, either. He'd spent most of his time in his room. His depression got so deep that she'd invented reasons to knock, afraid to leave him alone. This rambling was an improvement. Still, with her hangover, she was having a hard time feigning interest.

"Right," she said. "You sit alphabetically."

Rachel's house was a modern colonial bordered by a white picket fence with two A-class SUV hybrids parked in the garage. "Okay," Linda interrupted. "I'm just going to run out. You mind waiting in here?"

He thought about it and as he did so, red bloomed along his cheeks and neck. He had Russell's blond hair but her brown eyes. He was short like her, too. "Do you know Cathy Bennett?"

"Is that Daniella Bennett's daughter? The one in your year?"

"Can I say hi?" he asked in a rush. "I want to say hi to her. If that's okay. But don't make a deal about it. Don't say anything about it."

So, not about soccer. Linda felt a warmth toward this Cathy girl, though she'd never met her. A protectiveness toward Hip, too. Her son didn't say *hello* to girls. Hip was scared of girls, except for his sister.

"I hadn't planned on going inside any of the houses. I was just going to leave little gifts."

"Oh," he said. The red deepened to the color of an overripe strawberry.

"But sure! Let's do it!" she said.

"Okay," he said, letting out a ragged, terrified breath. "But you can't say anything, Mom. Not a word!"

• • •

A caladrius peered out at her from its shelter as she headed up Rachel's walk. It had flipped its bowl full of dried mealworms, which she knew from her own bird meant that it didn't like the meal and wanted dried jerky.

At the door, she considered knocking rather than leaving the food and note on the stoop, as she'd intended. For one, the donuts would get cold. For another, it would be nice to see Rachel again. She didn't think Rachel would mind a quick hello. She banged the brass caladrius knocker.

"What is *that*?" a deep alto inside the house asked. After a few seconds, a slender Asian man opened the door. Young and fit, he wore a tracksuit made of Omnium and appeared both harried and irritated.

He looked Linda up and down, seemed unable to categorize her. "She's been home three days in two months, and we get a pooping pastry delivery? What's wrong with her?"

"Sorry!" Linda yelped, lowering the small, warm box. "I'm not a delivery person."

The man leaned into the doorway, awaiting further explanation. Deeper in the house, she heard the warble of children.

"I went out with Rachel last night, if this is the right house?" Nervous, Linda blanked on Rachel's last name: *Johnson*, that was it.

"And you're standing?" The man spoke with heightened enunciation. Definitely a long-term local.

"Aspirin was involved. Is she here?"

"No. Something came up."

"I'm sorry. You're obviously busy and this is a bad time," Linda said.

"But is something wrong? Everyone in town seems very upset today. Does it have to do with the fire?"

"Where have you been?" he asked. "Of course it's the fire!"

She waited. He didn't elaborate. "What happened?"

"Don't you know?"

She shook her head. The kid-chirping inside the house got louder. They sounded like preschoolers. From experience, Linda knew that you could leave that age group alone for five minutes, and after that you were taking a risk. Maybe they decided to help you clean by covering all the floors with water. Maybe they mashed Play-Doh into the carpet, or one sibling pushed the other off the couch, and suddenly everybody was hysterical.

"You're the new people? The doctor for the clinic?"

"That's me. What's going on?"

A kind of curtain drew at this news. A closure. Outsiders. She was an outsider. He stopped leaning, stood straight. "Hard to explain. Did the interview go okay?"

"I think so. I hope so. Hence the donuts."

From his body language, she saw that he wasn't irritated anymore, at least not at her. But his resting face was a frown. "Good. We could use that. Rachel and I have been trying to make a lot of changes around here. A doctor for the clinic is one of them."

"Put in a good word for me?" Linda asked.

He smiled just slightly, and then the smile was gone.

"I'm sorry. But I'm a curious person. Was anyone hurt in this fire?" she asked.

"You don't know them," he said.

"Oh," Linda said. "I might."

"No. You don't. It's sad, though. A tragedy."

She waited, hoping he'd say more.

"Did you know I've never been outside of Plymouth Valley? Not once in my life?"

"I'm not sure I follow," Linda said.

From inside the house came more squawking. A laugh and a shout. Linda got beyond her own nervousness and noticed that the poor guy looked exhausted. "I'll just keep these," she said, holding the donuts and handing him the note. "I'm sorry to interrupt your Sunday. Let her know I stopped by?"

He eased up and laughed at himself. "Kai Choi Johnson. I took her last name for the clean slate. Clean slates are a little naïve, though. Perhaps you can tell that I'm having a bad day. And maybe an existential crisis."

"Seems to be going around."

He didn't take offense and instead grinned. "I draw up the budgets for ActHollow so we might be working together. It's been a long weekend for me. I've had the kids since early release on Friday and our sitter quit—the dayworkers keep leaving PV Extension lately so it's almost impossible to find a decent nanny. So, it's just me. And then with the fire, Rachel had to leave at the crack of dawn. I didn't even get the chance to go for a jog this morning."

"Linda Farmer," she said. "I know your pain. I've been there. Remember, when in doubt, planting them in front of a screenie while you nap is your friend. You sure you don't want the donuts?"

He shook his head, gentler now. "I overeat when I'm tired. I'll go through the whole box. But thank you."

• • •

Next, the Parson family's mansion. She turned onto a private road along the northeastern edge of town. Apparently uninterested in the cause of the no-longer-lingering smoke, Hip played soundtrack. "It's important everyone takes Civics class. I wish they'd done it back home. People would have cared more about supporting our democracy instead of being mad it wasn't doing enough for them. It's not capitalism's fault. It's the consumer society. Consumers can't do anything except complain. It's all they're taught to do. That's why they can't handle democracy. They won't work for it. PV's Civics class is awesome. They're teaching us that taking really good care of yourself is part of the social contract. If you're not doing okay, then you're a liability. You won't be able to take care of anyone else. So, if you're a parent with asthma, you're morally obliged to live in a place with clean air or you aren't going to be any good to your kids. Cathy Bennett said it's like putting your air mask on first when you're on a plane."

"Right," Linda said, no longer paying attention. "Breathing's important." This fire must have been bad, or else it wouldn't have dragged Rachel out of bed at dawn. People in town wouldn't have been clutching one another like tragedy survivors.

What had happened? Why, in this deep and sinking way, did she feel like it had something to do with Gal Parker?

The Parsons' security gate was crewed by two armed officers. As soon as she stopped, she regretted it. This was the founder's house. Royalty, practically. What was she thinking, just driving up?

But then a security officer in a green shirt was at her window. She wore a sidearm, like many of the police there. According to the pamphlets, they were the only people permitted guns. "Who are you here to see?"

"Anouk Parson. But I don't have to see her. I just wanted to drop off some donuts . . . They're fresh. They're still warm."

The guard pointed. Having seemingly passed an invisible test, she didn't radio to anyone. "Guesthouse four. It's the one with the thatched roof and black beams. You can leave it there."

Linda drove past the mansion, a giant Greek Revival with a wraparound porch, then took the road back, crossing a narrow bamboo bridge that opened to a clearing. Guest cottages one through three were of that same Greek Revival architecture: tall columns and external staircases that kissed at the center. Last, pushed against the hillside, she came to something different: a small bungalow with a rounded, fairy-tale roof whose white plaster façade was splotched with random bits of rusticated masonry.

Outside the tiny house was a penned-in flock of caladrius. She'd never seen so many together. They acted wary of one another, each taking up its own separate space. One was divided from the rest by mesh wire. It had been pecked, its hind plucked bald and scabby.

Newly energized by the prospect of the mysterious Cathy Bennett, Hip got out, bent down, and petted the injured one. "Hey, there. It's Uncle Hip!"

The bird limped in his direction.

Linda looked through the cottage window. The main space was a studio with a writing desk. On the floor was a simple mattress, unmade and exposed. Did Anouk sleep there? It seemed odd, but not impossible.

Before she could leave the box and note, the door swung open. It was Keith Parson in his Beltane Crown, his body so bulky it filled the entire frame. He cut a scary, intimidating figure. Jesus, his neck was practically as big as his head.

"Hi! Is Anouk here?"

"It's a bad time. Mommy's with Granddaddy," Keith answered in that same, perfect accent as Anouk's. Mommy? Granddaddy? Suddenly, it was a lot easier to picture Anouk, the richest woman in town, sleeping on a mattress in a dirty, cluttered room.

"I'm Linda Farmer. I'm a friend. Is something wrong?" Linda asked, holding out the donuts.

Keith opened the carton and bit into a chocolate glazed while they were standing there, Linda still holding the box. "People bring sourdough."

"What?"

"When you visit, you're *supposed* to bring homemade sourdough. Something that takes effort. No one brings this sweet crap," he said, even as he chewed. His crown was too small for his head. It made him look crazy. "Donuts are for babies and outsiders."

Linda bit back her first response, which was to tell him to spit it out. There were plenty of people in the world, herself included, who were hungry right now, and loved donuts. "I'll remember that for next time. Thank you for the advice. And congratulations. I saw your crowning."

Keith smiled. Bits of chocolate donut stuck to his teeth. "How old is he?"

"What? How old is who?"

Keith pointed his chin at Hip, who'd somehow tamed the picked-on caladrius. *Hey, guy*, he was saying as he petted its back, *you're a good guy!*

"Fifteen," she said.

"You have any others?" he asked. She didn't like his tone. It was predatory, somehow.

"He's a twin."

"Huh," he said, taking another bite, his mouth open. "Are they strong? Good genes?" The crown was definitely made of bird bones. Some were white, others ivory tinged with yellow and brown. She could make out the vertebral column and a wing along the cap.

"Right. Lovely meeting you. Could you get the rest of the donuts to your mother?"

He looked her up and down in an angry-sexy way. The *I'm considering screwing you, but I want you to know I could do better and you're too old* look that she'd gotten a few times over the last couple of years and had never appreciated.

She headed back. Hip joined her. The bullied caladrius tried to follow and come home with them, pushing against sharp mesh wire. She considered the possibility that the injured bird was special and especially sweet. The more likely possibility was that her son was special and especially sweet.

"That was the Beltane King, wasn't it?" Hip whispered once they got in the car.

Linda let out a sigh that meant *yup*.

"He's weird. Josie should kick his ass."

They chuckled.

"We could kick his ass," Linda said.

"Oh, no," Hip answered, deadpan. He'd righted his shirt and was running his fingers through his hair. "I'm a lover, not a fighter."

As they passed the mansion on their way out, she saw Anouk standing beside Rachel Johnson, John Parson Junior, the handsome man from the crowning, and beady-eyed Jack Lust, all five deep in conversation. The old man gesticulated, his skinny arms shooting out. The others tried to calm him.

Linda slunk down, hoped no one noticed her.

• • •

On the way to the next house, they passed Caladrius Park, where she noticed several people openly weeping. Worry gnawed a hole in her stomach and she tuned to PV radio just as an announcement was ending: "Terrible tragedy, folks. They're in God's hands now." Then, classical music started to play.

"And the beam Josie and I hide behind at lunch smells like old food—" Hip said, either oblivious, or so accustomed to radio tragedies that none of it registered as unusual. She rolled the car to a stop. His voice switched from monotone drone to nervous croak. "Is this it?"

Daniella Bennett's house took up an entire Plymouth Valley block. Stone angels with caladrius wings presided over a gaudy reproduction of a southern antebellum mansion.

"Cathy Bennett's house?" Linda asked. "I imagine so."

He pressed his index finger to the bridge of his nose, forgetting that he wasn't wearing his glasses. It occurred to her right then that he'd left them home on purpose.

"Ready?" she asked.

His body stiff, limbs seeming locked, he opened the door and started walking without answering. She got out, closed her door and his, which he'd forgotten to shut, and rushed to catch up.

"We're here for Daniella Bennett," Linda said once the servant, wearing a black butler's uniform, answered the door. She'd decided to give Hip the chance to ask for Cathy on his own. The kid was so shy that he often gave her a case of sympathy anxiety. In shops he didn't always ask for help. Instead, he stared at the thing he wanted. Unless some attendant came along and talked softly to him, he eventually walked away, defeated.

The butler seated them on a shallow parlor couch upholstered in red velvet. Thinking about the night before with Gal, and the mood in town, and the scene in front of the Parson house, Linda kneaded her hands, and now they were both nervous.

"If she's not home we can come back. But you should ask after her as soon as you get the chance," she said to Hip, just as a girl who had to be Cathy strolled through.

Hip blushed, died a small death.

Cathy froze. She wore a hooded onesie pajama with sunflower petals, all messily handsewn: soft Omnium and bamboo for the body, glazed paper for the petals over the hood. She was a pretty girl, but small and mousy. Nothing like her mother.

"Hi!" Hip said, his voice low and flat. He'd probably intended to sound cool but it came off sullen, like he'd been dragged here against his will.

Cathy yelped. There was an unexpected visitor in her home, and this visitor was a boy from school with a peach fuzz stubble. She rushed out of the foyer, back in the direction from which she'd come.

Linda said nothing. Her timing hadn't been good. Apologizing would make it worse.

"She interns at the Fabric Collective," Hip said, low. "She told the class she wants to be a clothing designer, but except for the person who founded the store, that's not golden ticket track. They do some kind of side job in the back room. They won't let Cathy help because they say it's a Hollow secret. It's not fair. She's so talented."

"She'll figure it out. Her outfit is great. She seems great," Linda answered, though in truth, the outfit seemed ridiculous.

A second later, Daniella arrived. Appearing under-slept but not hungover, she wore a dark blue robe cinched tight.

"Oh, Linda," she said in her calm, lush voice. "I was going to call but I didn't want to be a pest. How are you?"

"Great!" Linda said. "We're both great! I just wanted to follow up and thank you for last night."

Daniella laughed. "Totally unnecessary but much appreciated. You must be very resilient. I feel like I got hit with an anvil!"

"That, too."

Daniella looked down to the couch as if to join them on it, but seemed to have too much storming inside her to do so. "Has anyone told you what happened?"

Linda felt an unraveling in her queasy stomach. "No. What happened?"

Finally sensing something was off, Hip straightened and moved closer. Like his dad, he was protective.

"Cathy?" Daniella called.

As if she'd been listening around the corner, the girl appeared.

"I want you to entertain Hip for a little while. Is that all right with you, Hip?"

"Yes, ma'am," Hip said. Linda wouldn't have guessed he knew the word *ma'am*. But there you go.

"Show him your room."

Cathy scuttled up the stairs, fast and without looking back. Her little petals rustled. Linda nodded to let Hip know that whatever was happening, the grown-ups were in charge and she didn't need his help. He could go. He got up and followed, his movements jerking and self-conscious, as if his whole body were eyes, trained inward.

Daniella and Linda waited for their children to be out of earshot. Soft, Linda said, "He's a gentle person. She'll be totally safe."

Daniella cracked a smile. "I hope not. Cathy could use an adventure."

"But I'm the mother of a son. So, I want to make it very clear. I've raised him to have respect."

"Mine's lovely, too," Daniella said. "It's unfair that the lovely ones have the hardest time."

"Yeah," Linda said. As a little kid, friends and school had come easily for Hip. It was around the time he turned eight years old that the trouble started and his self-esteem nose-dived. *Why do you talk like a grown-up?* the kids had teased when Josie wasn't around to defend him. *Why do you dress like an old man? What's wrong with you?*

It got worse when he hit puberty. No friends except for the ones Josie shared. His depression had been deep. She'd been so scared for him. Even now that the cloud had lifted, she was still scared for him.

"Cathy has anxiety," Daniella said, her voice low so the kids wouldn't hear. "An attack can wreck her for days. She panics during tests. She panics if she doesn't like her lunch because she doesn't want to eat it but she's afraid to hurt the cafeteria people's feelings. She panics at the idea of not getting a golden ticket. It keeps her up nights . . . Linda, my husband's the CEO. Does she really think we're not going to pull a few strings? We've put her on every kind of drug but none of them help. Everyone knows that she's frail. Her whole class treats her like she's made of glass. I'm a mutt of a woman and I gave birth to a pug."

It was funny, but also mean, like spreading your kid out on an operating table and dissecting their flaws for an audience. "They'll turn out. The gentle ones always cook a little longer, but they're worth the wait."

"Will they, though?" Daniella asked. "Turn out?"

Linda shrugged. "I mean, what's the point in thinking otherwise?"

Daniella chuckled, then squeezed her temple. "What a headache. So, what happened last night? I heard from Cyrus Galani that you didn't go straight home. You must be exhausted."

"Cyrus Galani?"

"The on-duty patrol last night. I don't know what we were thinking, Linda! Can you ever forgive us? I didn't remember you were still at the restaurant until I got into bed. I had it in my head that you'd already gone home. My car's the newest class—you don't even have to be conscious to kick in the autopilot. We should have been the ones to give you a lift!"

Linda waved her hand. "I was fine. I'm just hoping it's not a mark against us, that I indulged so much I needed a ride."

"It's a heavy drinking town. They're planning to make all the cars autopilot soon. But how are you feeling today?"

"Fine?" There was something Linda didn't know, hadn't been told. A lot of things, in fact. That was obvious. But since this morning at the bakery, a suspicion had been growing in the back of her mind. She'd kept it there in the dark, like a mushroom. She was thinking about that fire, and about Gal Parker. She was thinking about those sick kids.

Daniella let out a long breath. "I want you to brace yourself."

Linda's heart pounded. "Okay."

"Gal and her kids were hospitalized."

Linda felt light-headed. "Why?"

"A fire very early in the morning. The solar panel's converter tripped."

"What's that?"

"I don't know. Whatever it is, Gal rigged it."

"Rigged it?" Linda's stomach caved in on itself. She felt undone and reversed.

"Those houses on that side of town are wood. They're slated for rebuilds. Apparently, it went up in a snap."

"The kids? Is everyone okay?"

Daniella squeezed Linda's knee. "They're alive."

"Oh, thank God."

"She gave a statement. Gal, that is. Apparently, she planned to go up in the fire. Kids, too. But once the fire started it got too smoky and she ran out. Just, instinct. You're in a burning building, you leave it. And then, she ran back in and dragged them out, too. One at a time. Wrapped them in blankets so they didn't burn. She burned, though. Lloyd called from the scene. When he got there, the kids were laid out on the lawn, two separate bundles."

"How bad?" Linda's voice cracked. She was crying, eyes wet and chest heaving.

Daniella gave her a steely look. "Don't you cry, or you'll get me going."

Linda tried to stifle herself, crossed her arms like a containing gate. Daniella waited. "Sorry." Linda sniffled, looking at the crown molding in the ceiling, the gold wallpaper trim that was maybe pretty, maybe tacky, maybe both.

"It's my own problem. I hate crying. But please stop doing it."

"But the kids, are they okay?"

"They're in the ICU," Daniella continued. "Or maybe critical care. I'm not sure I understand the difference. Whatever it is, Lloyd spoke to your Dr. Chernin. They're expected to survive. *Fully recover* were Chernin's exact words."

"Oh, thank God," Linda said, her breath hitching, but the crying done. "And Gal?"

"She's hurt."

Linda pictured Gal as she'd left her, a furious husk of a woman. "How hurt?"

Daniella shook her head. "I don't know. Third-degree burns? First? Whichever the worst kind happens to be."

"Third," Linda said, so full of emotion that she was standing. "Should we go see her?"

Daniella pulled her back down. "PV takes this kind of thing very personally. She and her children will be cared for by people who know them."

"I can't believe this. I was there. I was in that house," Linda said. "It was cold. I asked her if her solar system needed repair."

"What did she say?" Daniella asked.

"She said she was going to hurt people. She was going to break this town." Linda remembered the messy house. The worship totems. The medicines.

I'm you. Let me be you?

"There wasn't a babysitter," Linda continued. "The kids were alone the whole night. Nothing was packed, even though they were supposedly leaving town. She said she was going to turn up the heat. I thought, figuratively. She was going to get even more aggressive with you all. But she meant literally. She turned up the heat and set her own house on fire."

Daniella picked up a donut, held it by her thumb and index finger. Everything she did was graceful. "It's not your fault. Who would imagine that?"

"Me," Linda said. "It's my job. When I suspect something wrong in a home with minors, I'm legally obliged to report it. At least, I was obliged in New York. But I was so tired, and I'd been drinking so much."

Daniella took a bite. "I never eat these. The sugar," she said, without looking into Linda's eyes. "Feeling bad doesn't fix anything. There's no point."

Surreptitiously, Linda wiped her eyes. "But why would she do such a thing? Why hurt her kids when this town and the ex-wife are the things she's mad at?"

"Spite," Daniella answered, and Linda thought it was the meanest, worst word she'd ever heard. *Spite. Spite. Spite.*

"Don't cry. Eat your fattening donut. I can't be the only one."

Linda took a bite, the first bit of food she'd had all day, and realized she was starved. They ate quietly and without plates. Linda held the donut over her hand to collect crumbs. Daniella did the same.

"Should I call the police and give a statement? I must have been the last person to see her."

"If it makes you feel better," Daniella said. "But they have her confession. They've already analyzed the converter."

"What'll happen?"

"If she's strong enough to stand trial? I don't know. We're not equipped for attempted murder. We don't have a jail. My guess is they'll extradite her to the New York court. We use that one or the one in Chicago."

"I guess now I know why everyone in town was so upset today. I asked but no one would tell me."

"They love their secrets. Even things that don't need to be secrets," Daniella said.

"They took it hard," Linda said.

Daniella nodded. "Those Parker kids were born here. We all know them very well. Don't be surprised if people are on edge for a while."

"Of course," Linda said.

"New patients might even show up at your hospital, too. Psychosomatic illness happens a lot here. We're all so safe that I think it weighs—the guilt. Some people haven't lived. They're drawn to vicarious tragedy. Do you think that word comes from *vicar*?"

"I'm just sorry all this happened," Linda said, stanching another wave of tears.

"I'm sorry, too," Daniella said without looking at her. "Don't think I forgot that she was screaming at us to help her last night. You're not the only person who feels bad. But let's make a deal. I won't blame myself and you don't blame yourself. She did this. She planned it long before last night."

"It's just so barbaric."

"You have to understand this about me if we're to be friends, Linda," Daniella said, rubbing her thumbs along the rest of her fingers, to wipe away the donut crumbs. "I don't dwell. I don't like being around people who dwell. It's just being sad for no reason. We've discussed this, and now it's done. I won't discuss it again."

"Okay," Linda said. "Sorry."

"Don't be. Just let's not talk about this again."

Linda nodded.

Then Daniella laughed, her seriousness gone. "I'm the one who should be sorry. I invite you to a little get-together and you wind up traumatized."

• • •

They changed the subject. Linda learned that ActHollow had agreed to move forward with her candidacy. Rachel would contact her with more details.

"Thank you," she said. "I'll do everything I can."

"I know it," Daniella said after giving her a hug. "We outsiders are the only people who make this town run on a schedule."

Soon, it was time to leave. Daniella called to the kids. On the landing halfway up the stairs, Linda spotted a Hollow altar. It was about twice as big as the one at 9 Sunset Heights. Something wet and red was inside. At first glance, it appeared to be a grisly set of animal intestines, but then she understood that it was boiled cranberries strung together and piled high.

By the time the kids headed down, Hip seemed much more at ease. He and Cathy walked close together. When she stumbled at the landing, he caught her.

"Whoa," Daniella whispered into Linda's ear. "That's the cutest thing I've ever seen. And a little bit hot. I wish I was fifteen again. I'd do it so different."

"Wouldn't we all," Linda answered.

• • •

On the ride home, Hip's babbling suddenly made sense. Turned out, Cathy sat across from him in half his classes: on the first day, she'd smiled at him. He'd liked her ever since.

"She's vegan, too," he said. "And I'm vegan. But we agreed it's okay to eat caladrius. Not doing that would be wasteful."

"That's great, honey," Linda said. Had Russell acted this lovesick when they'd first gotten together at Sluggs? Probably. They were sweet, these men in her house.

Instead of going home, she headed southwest, following the landmarks she'd spotted the night before. Gal's block was closed off, a tan sedan parked horizontally in the middle of the street.

Hip sat straighter when he realized they were in a place he'd never been before, and not on their way home. The area gave off a wet, wan smell, like morning at a campsite after the fire.

"I need to see something," she said as she got out.

Hip started to ask a question but it died on his tongue. The house next door was still standing, unsinged. The shell of Gal's house remained. But its north half was charred black, the roof above collapsed.

Linda went off the path and onto the dead, trampled lawn. The caladrius was still in its shelter, talons poking out. It had been sleeping last night, eyes open, she remembered. On the ground, beside stale vomit, she found her device. Her texts populated the screen in the order of newest to oldest:

Daniella:

Something happened last night. Call me so I can fill you in.

Anouk:

My fellow scholar! Please read and let's discuss. I'm DYING to talk inherited trauma. If we can rout it, we can solve childhood illness.

www.moderneugenicsproject.org

Gal Parker:

UR listed so don't be mad Im txting. I just ospit say Im sprrt I was meen. I'm not weel.

Empathy

By morning, Plymouth Valley's landscape was changed. In front of nearly every house, sets of red candles joined by black ribbons had been burned to their nubs. They stuck to front curbs, the wax pooling out. Occasionally, in red chalk, someone had written names: *Sebbie, Katie*. This had happened in the night, probably while the Farmer-Bowens had eaten dinner or slept.

"What the hell is this?" Josie asked. They were driving along Sunset Heights in the direction of the school.

"I think they had a prayer vigil for those kids I told you about," Linda said.

Car line was usually a quick in and out; every parent knew their routine. Today, the line wound down from the school for about two blocks. "Can you guys get out and walk?" Linda asked.

"I have all my PE stuff, which I usually wouldn't but you took forever to clean it," Josie said. She was cranky about what had happened to those kids, probably a little freaked out, too.

"Josie, get out of the car," Linda said.

"I can't!"

Hip was already out the door. He'd taken Josie's backpack with his own. "Come on," he said.

Josie took her time. The gap between Linda and the car ahead got to be three car lengths while Josie unbuckled, tied her shoes (which she'd untied in the car for some reason?), arranged her soccer bag and lunch. The car behind Linda pulled up beside her. The window rolled down. A smiling brunette called across. Her elementary-aged son was in the passenger seat, drawing on the dashboard in crayon. "Hi! You're holding up the line!"

"Yeah," Linda said. "Monday morning."

"But now I have to pass you," the woman said, still smiling. Her son smeared black crayon scribble over the vinyl vent, then stuck his tongue out at Linda, revealing a red-striped median, as if he'd eaten candy suckers for breakfast.

"You do what you gotta do," Linda said.

The woman's jaw went slack, like what she was hearing was insane.

Josie finally got out of the car. She and Hip started walking. "Have good days!" Linda called.

Hip waved. Josie shrugged, an embarrassed apology for causing trouble with the car line police. Linda shrugged back, to let her know not to worry.

The woman stayed beside Linda, dumbfounded. "You can pull ahead," Linda told her. The boy pressed his black crayon so hard it broke. What kind of jerk lets their kid draw all over their car?

"But now you're not even doing car line," the woman said.

Linda lost patience and rolled up her window, pulled ahead and around. She found the root of the bottleneck: two parents had come to a full stop and gotten out of their class Cs—solar-powered sedans without lithium batteries. She caught the tail end of a tirade: "The right of way!" the tall guy shouted. His neck veins bulged with rage. They were standing close with puffed chests.

There may have been buildup. Tells Linda hadn't noticed. But like all violence, it seemed to happen out of nowhere. The short woman swung, her fist half-open like a claw, landing hard against the tall guy's chin with a *swaack!*

The tall guy staggered, cradled his jaw with the heel of his hand, eyes meeting his assailant's: "You can't do that outside a festival!" he cried, incensed and on the verge of tears.

Outside a festival?

The woman was too charged up for words to land. She quivered like a fallen wire after a storm, rearing for another swing, this time with a real fist, metal rings and all. Linda wanted to insert herself somehow, to stop it. But also to run from it. Inconceivably, she did neither.

But then, the crossing guard drew her lips against her teeth and hissed: *SSSSSSS!*

Like thunder, the sound rolled. Through open windows all around, in the cars that were luxury A class and B class and C class, everyone hissed: *SSSSSSS*. Linda found herself hissing, too. It felt good. It felt like *doing something*.

The sound seemed to remind the combatants of the time and place: eight in the morning, in front of the local school. Sheepish, the tall man retreated to his car. The woman dropped her fist.

Almost at once, the witnesses stopped hissing, including Linda.

She was still in a state of surprise, her heart beating fast, when that same mom with the obnoxious crayon kid tapped politely on her horn. A line had formed.

• • •

True to Daniella's word, the hospital was busy, its typically empty parking lot completely full. Between driving around, looking for a place to park, and the fight in front of the school, she was five minutes late. She'd planned to check on the Parker family, but there wasn't time.

Though the ER hadn't admitted any true emergencies (gunshots, cardiac arrests), orderlies and nurses rushed to take vital signs and settle faint-feeling patients into beds and wheelchairs. Ringing devices in reception and triage played a jarring soundtrack.

Nine kids showed up before lunch. Most had nothing but phantom aches; Linda prescribed fluids and a return to school. Another needed a shot of one of the newer antibiotics. "Out of curiosity, can I ask why you didn't take him to his pediatrician?" Linda asked the mother of the kid with strep.

"The line's around the corner. I couldn't get an appointment!" the mom answered.

Just before Linda's shift ended, that same woman from Lust's Bakery showed up, pushing that same stroller, screaming, sticky-handed baby inside. The baby's stomach hurt and the under-slept, messy-haired mom, Tania Janssen, was bawling. "It's cancer!"

Linda felt the baby's belly. The child was otherwise healthy and had no bruising or marks. But Tania was convinced this was cancer, so Linda ordered an abdominal CT and bloodwork, both of which came back clean.

Tania was not mollified. Wanting to right the wrong she'd committed with Gal, and pay better attention, Linda pulled up a chair. "Babies aren't good at distinguishing discomfort from pain. They scream about both like it's the end of the world. And if you don't mind my saying, I can tell she's been keeping you up nights. You're exhausted."

Tania burst into tears. "You don't know. It could happen. She could get sick."

"Anyone could. But she's not sick now, Mrs. Janssen. Have the pharmacy print up some polyethylene glycol. If it gets worse, come back. I'm here for you."

Tania looked at Linda like she was the dumbest woman on earth.

"What am I missing?" Linda asked.

"You're new. You don't know anything," she said as she snapped her baby into the stroller.

"I have a medical degree and fifteen years of pediatrics under my belt. I know some things. What are you worried I'm missing?" Linda asked.

"Anything! You don't know anything!" Tania huffed, new tears emerging from the corners of her eyes as she walked away.

When her shift ended, Linda offered to hang around for a few hours and help out, but the doc on call was the guy whose shift she'd taken, and he didn't want her around. After that, she checked the Parker family's status on the floor console. The good news: Katie and Sebbie Parker really were in step-down, which meant their injuries were minor. The attendant photos of them showed a pair of adorable kids with straight black hair and big brown eyes. Less great: Gal was in critical condition. Linda stood at the console looking at room numbers, considering visiting, when her device pinged with a text from Rachel Johnson, asking her to come over right away.

• • •

"I ordered krill. It smells, but everybody likes it. Are you in?" Rachel Johnson asked when she opened her door. She was still in pajamas, her hair pulled tight in a ponytail, her feet in slippers. A powder blue suitcase nested just inside the front door.

"Yes!" Linda was starved. She'd been running around the hospital all morning. "Are you going somewhere?"

"Hellz no! My trip to Vegas tonight got canceled. Too hot to land. Thank God. I've had at least a hundred flights this year. Ignore my dissolute condition. I'm taking a personal day because my ears haven't stopped popping."

They were standing inside an oak-inlaid center hall with a winding wooden staircase that went up three flights. Beams of light crossed, illuminating a red velvet parlor couch and a sunken sitting area to the right. Crayons and toys were scattered all over.

"I have a red velvet couch, too," Linda said. "It's a weird choice."

"Daniella decorates a lot of the houses around here," Rachel said, pointing out the gaudy gold paint on the far wall that matched the furniture's gold trim. "It was her side hustle before ActHollow. Everybody's sitting area looks like a cathouse."

"But a classy, put-yourself-through-college cathouse," Linda joked. "Not the sex-slave-refugee kind."

Rachel eyed her with amusement, started left behind the stairs. They passed a Hollow altar carved in a semicircle, a discreet foot and a half long, foot wide, and foot deep. The strung cranberries had dried without being replaced. She hadn't seen that yet. Most places kept them very fresh.

They landed in the kitchen, where they sat at a small nook table. Wordless, Rachel got plates while Linda pulled sandwiches from the Sirin's takeout bag. Though Linda's visit with Daniella had been friendly, she'd never forgotten her place as subordinate. In Rachel's house, there wasn't so much ceremony.

On the table was a large stack of paper files, which Linda knew were meant for her to take. She was eager to read them. The nearby counter was kid-messy; drawings and report cards were magnetized by alphabet letters to the refrigerator door. She spotted a tangled Slinky, stretched long as if undergoing corrective surgery, and several pairs of small shoes, all seeming to have been tried on and cast off during the morning rush.

"How old?"

"Three and five," Rachel said.

"The magical thinking years. Mine believed in fairies. They were always looking for them under plants in Kings' Park."

"Some people never outgrow that phase," Rachel said. "Kai, for instance. He wants to leave PV."

"Why?"

Rachel raised an eyebrow, lips sealing tight. She had great facial expressions. They were both comic and illustrative. "He feels trapped."

"Huh," Linda said. "He might change his mind once he tries living out there. Does he have a plan?"

"Man's never held a greenback. Never done a load of wash. Never used a key, driven a car, or cooked. He's the son of a board member, grandson of a board member. When I came here, they were in the process of kicking him out. He didn't like any of the jobs—kept screwing up on purpose. Didn't like PV or Hollow. Was in a rebel phase. But then we fell in love. My hazing stopped because I was with him. Everybody was happy, until we stopped being happy. I moved out of the bedroom this weekend."

"I'm sorry."

"Don't be. Or, okay. Thank you." Coolly, Rachel appraised her sandwich, gave it a withering look, like it had disappointed her, and sipped her mead instead. "He kept the master bedroom. I'm stuck with the guest room. What kind of man won't move out? I'll bet he's never slept on a couch in his life."

"It's a myth. None of them do," Linda said. "They've all got crap backs."

Rachel liked this answer. She grinned, those eyeteeth protruding. "Mead?"

"Nope. I'm never drinking again."

"Sorry about leaving you with Gal, by the way. I didn't think you'd wind up hanging out with her. I thought you'd just go home. You weren't looking for dirt, were you? My advice is stay away from that woman."

"Dirt? No. Something was obviously going down between all of you and Gal, but I have no interest in knowing it. I'm just trying to get by around here, Rachel, and drama's not my favorite subject. I was planning on going home but I was too drunk to use my car, and it seemed wrong to just leave her there, so I called us both a ride."

"Shit," Rachel said. "I forgot. You have a B class. We'll have to fix that." She finished her mead and poured more.

"Do you have any news of Gal or what happened?"

"It's early so things are up in the air. I just heard this morning that the ex-wife, Trish, is going to take the kids—Katie and what's his name? Sebastian. They'll go to Palo Alto. Trish is a real piece of shit. Lowest of the low. But not even she expected Gal to do anything like this. It's harder to know what to do with Gal. We might let the court system know what happened. But we might just expel her like we'd originally planned. Whatever we do, we'll do it quietly. Everybody around here's pretty worked up. I'll bet the hospital was full."

"It was," Linda said.

"Figures. They can't even let a tragedy happen without wrapping it around themselves, making it their own . . ."

"Daniella said it's empathy."

"I didn't see them knocking on Gal's door or offering legal advice before this happened. If it's empathy, it's the convenient kind."

"A lady in the ER was convinced her kid had cancer. She wouldn't believe me when I told her the kid was healthy. I thought it had something to do with Gal's kids. Do you happen to know their diagnoses? She said it was a cancer called idiopathic leukemia and they both have it."

"I stay out of Gal Parker's business. But these residents"—Rachel shook her head in slow disgust—"they glory in this crap. Listen, if you're having a hard time, and then I decide I care so much about your hard time that now I'm having a hard time—that's not a useful reaction. Daniella's much more forgiving of these dilettantes than I've ever been."

Ever consider joining your husband and leaving PV? Linda thought. *It doesn't sound like you like this place so much, either.* But this was too personal an observation to make. "There was a fight at school drop-off this morning. Two parents. A mom hit a dad—this awkward claw punch. The dad was all—*that's not allowed except at a festival!* Then everybody started hissing and they both backed down."

Rachel sipped more mead. "The hissing. They do it to show disapproval. So weird."

"Where does it come from?"

"The birds? Damned if I know. Real fights hardly ever happen around here. They're just worked up about that fire. It'll die down once everything's resolved."

"They seemed bad at it—fighting. I thought the mom was going to apologize while also swinging. Or cry while swinging."

Rachel grinned sidelong.

"I'm going to hell for making fun of people for being bad at fighting."

"Take me with you."

"But are people allowed to punch during festivals?"

"What?" Rachel asked. "Oh, no. I doubt it. If it happens, it's in some kink room at the Winter Festival. Oh! Yeah, there's also boxing as one of the competitions at Beltane. But that's strictly volunteer and practically nobody volunteers. Keith Parson has held the title since he was fifteen and nobody wants to fight him."

"Is it me, or is he an odd duck?"

"He's a lot of passionate intensity and fucked-up conviction," Rachel said.

"That's spot on," Linda agreed, and they both chuckled as she pressed her hands over the papers. She already felt proprietary. "Here's a weird question. Did my house used to be Gal's house?"

Rachel thought. "No. She was in your neighborhood, but I think next door."

Linda made a sound of relief. "She told me my house was her house. She told me Russell has her ex-wife's old job."

"What? No. Same department, but different. Trish wasn't numbers. She was a biochemist."

"Oh, wow. That's a real mindfuck. I felt so bad. Like I was replacing her."

"I told you. She bites."

"I'll stay away, then. But ouch, the whole thing's awful."

Rachel nodded, her ponytail swishing. "The crazy part is, she used to be sweet. When she first got here, she was like clay. Whatever you told her, she did. Whatever anybody wore or said, she wore, she believed. I've always thought this place was wrong for her. She couldn't handle it. She worshipped Trish and those kids. They were her baby ducks. She used to sew all their clothes and she was better at it than the weird-ass people who run the Fabric Collective. Her kids were the smartest-dressed babies in town. But then Trish screwed her over, her kids got sick, and everybody dropped her. She lost herself."

"That makes me sad," Linda said.

"Yeah. Me too. But enough about Gal. I can't take on any more people's problems." Rachel tapped the pile of papers. "It's all there. The applications for use, the budget, the schedules, the volunteers, the inventory, everything. Does Friday work for a tour? I might be out of town but Daniella and Anouk can do it."

Linda's heart double-beat. "So soon! That's great! I'm so glad!"

"When you find out what a heavy lift this is going to be, you might change your mind."

"No. I like work. I'm happy."

Rachel finished the last of her mead, looked around like she wanted to get up and pour more, but Linda's presence prevented her. "Listen, I don't invite just anyone over. In this town, houses are private spaces."

Linda waited.

"I think I might like you. You're kind of a clown, but you're real. So, here's some advice. Everything here's on a trial basis until you get your golden ticket. You might not like this job. It might not be a fit. We might not think you're right for it. My advice is to be open to that. Daniella or Anouk might move you around to a different responsibility. If that happens, you'll smile and say thank you. Even if you wind up manager, this isn't your show, it belongs to ActHollow.

"If you don't know the right people, your husband won't get past his first review. They don't take spouses seriously, either. Chernin'll string you along at that hospital with one shift a week, but it would take a hundred years before you got a golden ticket on your own. He's notoriously bad about helping people get in. If you're with ActHollow, that changes. ActHollow'll be inconvenienced if your husband's review goes badly because his department sabotaged him. People get in trouble when we're inconvenienced."

Linda nodded to show she understood.

"You know there's a board, right? Parson's chairman, but it's also Jack Lust and Lloyd Bennett, a bunch of other guys you probably won't ever meet, and me. I think we told you the other night that I'm up for a job with more responsibility. I intend to make substantial changes. This place will be better than it's ever been.

"Daniella's married to the CEO. Anouk's dad is chairman. They work behind the scenes. We're a block, the three of us. Our votes count. People respect us. Everyone here thinks perfect grades are what matters for their kids. Grades mean nothing. What matters is what you do on the side, and the people you know. What matters is the hustle. ActHollow is your hustle."

"Thank you," Linda said. "I appreciate that you're making the effort to talk me through this. I can intuit it, but things always feel more secure when they're explicitly expressed."

"They're short on frankness here. Everything's an open secret, but then you actually say the secret out loud and it's like you committed a felony."

"How long has it been since new people came?"

Rachel closed her eyes, thinking. "By marriage and transfers, we get a few every year, but a new family with no company town roots? You're the third since I moved here."

"What happened to the other families?"

"They got kicked out."

"Huh."

"So, take the job," Rachel said.

"I never needed any convincing."

• • •

Late that night, she and Russell sat on the porch steps, knees touching. Fall had truly arrived, and the days felt shorter. They'd done this years ago when they'd been students, on the fire escape of a tiny apartment, oversexed and freshly in love. Before kids and bills and more responsibility than either of them had been able to handle.

The events of the past few days and weeks and, hell, months conspired. She started crying. Russell took her in his arms.

"It's not your fault," he said.

"I could have stayed. I could have helped."

"She poisoned you, Linda. What if you'd passed out, and you'd burned with the house? I thank God you left."

The times in her marriage that she'd needed him, he hadn't been around. He'd been working, too busy to notice, too overwhelmed to take on her emotion. But he was here, now, and she was glad.

It was then that their devices both sang at the same time. Linda read hers:

> This is Heaven Gelman from the Beautification Society. We had a misunderstanding last week! I didn't know you were friends with Daniella Bennett! You can help any time you like. Please come to our next meeting! ☺

"What does yours say?" Linda asked.

"It's from Nanny. The complete files containing all the data I've been asking for. They say they just found everything. They didn't know they had it . . . and their wife is wondering if you could put in a good word for her with ActHollow. She wants to be their secretary."

Resident Guidebook for Greater Plymouth Valley

Festivals and Traditions:

Just as people hold certain values dear, so must a corporation.

The festivals and traditions of Plymouth Valley are collectively referred to as Hollow.

Hollow is a set of shared beliefs and activities exclusive to BetterWorld's Plymouth Valley.

When our founder John Parson Senior built PV, he knew that this experiment of community was special, just as the land, shelter, and newly revived caladrius were special. Every year that this town continues to thrive, we pay homage.

Plymouth Valley celebrates four important holidays:

1) **Beltane**—The dark is over! Beltane celebrates spring's longer days, ripe harvests, and warm sun. The event takes place on the north field, complete with maypole dancing, a talent show, and a bonfire. Each year, children suffering illness receive black ribbons in the hopes the collective will cure them. An adult Beltane King is chosen.

   Beltane Crowning—this is new! A celebration of our annual king, with a show of speed, a crowning, and libations.

2) **Samhain**—Get out your party hat! If you're in town, count yourself lucky! Samhain is consistently voted our most popular holiday.
   - By law, houses must offer treats for young children between the ages of 0–13 during the afterschool hours. Otherwise, tricks are ENCOURAGED! 😄
   - After sundown, all PV residents over 13 years of age are invited to attend our haunted maze in the Labyrinth beneath Caladrius Park, followed by an outdoor feast and bonfire for survivors. (Just kidding. Everyone survives!)
   - In Hollow tradition, a pecked caladrius is sacrificed at midnight. This is our way of respecting the mercurial

nature of luck, and the bounty of our good fortune. We appreciate that not all who deserve to survive will do so.

* Costumes are required. Those with heart conditions, please register with the PV police department, and please do not go through the maze alone!

3) **Thanksgiving**—In PV, this holiday is especially important. We acknowledge our roots, and the greater power that brought us all together.
    - We start the day out with a race because EVERYONE between 13 and 90 years of age has to earn their dinner!
    - We feast after the race. Each of the three parks is equipped with heat lamps and good cheer. Tables are assigned according to tenure and track.
    - Our main dish is caladrius. Though we honor these birds, we must also accept that the town cannot support an unlimited number. All resources are finite.
    - Starting Thanksgiving, Sirin's Bar and Grill closes at 10:00 p.m. on weekdays, midnight weekends.

4) **Winter Festival**—the Plymouth Valley Winter Festival is a three-day party! During the shortest, darkest days of the year, we all need to let off some steam. This is a resident-only holiday.

* All Hollow traditions are hosted by resident volunteers. Contact the Beautification Society to learn more!

The Reviews Are In

Acceptance happened so fast and with such little fanfare that it almost seemed to the Farmer-Bowens that they'd never gone through a hazing at all.

Hip and Josie had friends and things to do. Russell got invited out to lunch with his team. After reading all the files, he petitioned the judge for a delay in the court case while he ran new trials. People who'd formerly been aloof, like the Roc soccer team, now clapped backs and invited them to pregame brunches. They acted as if they'd always been this hospitable, as if they'd been friends all along.

October 18 arrived, and Linda met with Zach, though it was no longer necessary. He told her their progress in this town was great, which he'd expected, because he was a great judge of character. "On the off chance my husband's testimony doesn't win the court case, for how long will we be allowed to stay in PV?" she asked.

"Don't worry about it," he told her. "I've only heard wonderful things about all of you." Then he did prayer hands.

With a house so big, and Linda now working two jobs, she could no longer push the start date for the housekeeper, Esperanza Lopez. Having been in PV's employ for the entirety of her career, Esperanza required no instruction and though she was often in the house, she avoided direct interaction with the Farmer-Bowens. Quickly, the house gleamed.

Sunny got bold and started waddling out from her shelter to beg at their front door most mornings for food. She wouldn't eat dried insects anymore, only jerky, which she dragged back to her shelter like a dragon guarding its treasure.

Through ActHollow, Linda learned that the Parker children were flown out to reunite with Trish in Palo Alto. Gal remained in the hospital, her health tenuous. Inpatient recovery would take months, delaying her eviction. The board had considered ousting her without treatment, but by one vote, the members decided she could stay.

Many times over the following weeks, Linda was tempted to visit the ICU. The details of that night weighed on her. What had Gal done and why—*why?* But then she'd remember Gal's grin, that husk of a person on a couch, and the terribly sweet sounds of young voices like stacked, abandoned dolls in a toy house. She'd think: *I'm not ready.*

• • •

Soon, life was going better than she'd hoped.

"Hi, Sally! What's new?" she asked the border guard, Sally Claus, a cheerful thirtysomething with prematurely gray hair that shone a pretty silver. Linda handed over the list of supplies she was transporting to the free clinic, and Sally, holding a steaming tea, searched the trunk one-handed to make sure the list and the physical contents aligned.

"Looks good, good-lookin'!" Sally announced. They high-fived, which they'd done on that first day out of spontaneity and now did every Friday. Then she went back to her booth, drew open the border wall.

The drive out of Plymouth Valley and into the clinic in PV Extension was a quick half kilometer. She passed small trailers and slab houses along the way, most of which belonged to dayworkers. PVE's fortunes had declined along with the fortunes of the town it serviced. Rusted trampolines, slides, and swings dotted front yards.

The area had been plagued lately by dust storms, and visibility today was tough. She drove slowly and listened to *News in a Minute* from a station out of Rapid City. PVE had good reception. They headlined with the good stuff: Oregon had ratified its state constitution and tornado mitigation efforts had saved Des Moines. On the East Coast,

New York's governor had announced a run for presidency. Along with the DA, she'd been responsible for indicting the heads of the Health Department, the Department of Consumer Affairs, and the Department of Education for corruption. She was ahead in the polls, but, because of gerrymandering, would need a popular vote of 70 percent. Right now, she had 65 percent.

The bad news: a new and aggressive strain of leprosy was spreading through Florida, a nuclear reactor outside Paris had leaked, and unemployment was at an all-time high of 29 percent.

In the short time she'd been living inside PV, she'd begun to see the outside as scarier and more chaotic. How had she tolerated so much noise and misery for so many years?

She pulled into her spot behind the one-level stucco building, which had once been a convenience store. FREE CLINIC was written on a small billboard in bold letters out front, beside the caladrius shelter Anouk'd insisted on installing.

But they can't tolerate the air out here, Linda'd said. *What's the point of a shelter without birds?*

When Caesar left Rome, he carried its dirt in his pocket, Anouk had replied. *Where he went, Rome went.*

Well, okay.

As soon as she got inside, a day-nurse and an admin greeted her. These were rotating volunteers who came as their schedules allowed. "Any new appointments?" she asked.

No. Just the four from the roster she'd checked last night. There was a reason she came only on Fridays. Still, four patients were better than last week's three, and the previous week's two, and her first week's zero. This was progress.

Her morning patients came with the typical ailments like asthma and generalized fatigue. For the first, she gave company-mailer samples of alveolar macrophage down-regulator, as the three-dimension drug replicator the clinic had been promised still hadn't arrived. Her afternoon patient's problems were more complicated. Brought in by his father and his grandmother, six-month-old Carlos presented with lassitude and fever.

The family was repelled by the pomegranate- and stone fruit–filled altar Anouk had placed in the examining room. "Dios mío," the grandmother said as she made the sign of the cross.

"Weird, right?" Linda asked. "I'm new, so I don't know much about it. Plus, I'm lapsed Catholic, which makes me immune to all other religions, or whatever Hollow is."

The dad, Danny, had callused hands and a scarred, lived-in face. He didn't react to her joke. Linda had the feeling he found her frivolous and possibly stupid.

"Yes, but it's an insult," the grandmother said.

"I don't think it's personal," Linda said. "Can you ignore it?"

The youngish grandmother gave her the stink eye. Linda didn't read it as unkindness, but disappointment. The kind of look you might give to a neighborhood kid who litters, or your friend at the grocery store who doesn't return their cart. "An insult to God," the grandmother repeated.

"Right," Linda said. "Sorry. It's not up to me."

A doctor in Sioux Falls had diagnosed Carlos with a bacterial infection, but after six weeks of antibiotics, the kid wasn't any more energetic. He was slender, his hair not yet grown in, but he still had a thick down over his face and neck that indicated he wasn't thriving. His eyes didn't track her movements, either. "I think you're right," Linda told them. "There's something more."

Here, at least, their luck was in. She'd finagled a blood analysis machine as a donation just last week. Chernin had combined two departments, making his second machine redundant. It had been headed for storage. Still, she'd had to fight for it, presenting a strong argument before Chernin agreed. The guy was an odd duck.

The analysis took only a few seconds. The child's WBC and RBC counts were irregular and mutated. In particular, his monocytes and platelets were a mess. This was cancer—a kind she'd never studied before. "I'd like to send this to the lab in PV. I think they'll have more data than I do," she said.

Father and grandmother conferred in excited whispers. Linda interrupted to show them her screen, let them see every note she'd taken along with the statistics on pediatric leukemias. "Intervention now's really important," she said. "Take the help. It's free."

Danny crossed his arms. "I don't want to insult you."

"You can insult me."

Carlos lay on his back, too still.

"The people of the valley . . ."

"What?" Linda asked.

He looked at her straight on. "They lie."

She printed up the blood report and all her notes. Tried to hand them to him, but he wouldn't accept the papers. The grandmother snatched them, secreted them into her purse beside an empty soda bottle and a Hershey Bar wrapper. All the while, Danny held his son's belly, which seemed especially sad to Linda, given the child hadn't the strength to roll. "I don't know what you've experienced before. I told you, I'm new. I promise I'm not lying. Go. Get a second opinion. Then come back. He needs treatment."

"I don't like owing the valley people."

"Just come back," Linda said with exasperation. She saw them off, letting them know they didn't need an appointment. Just show up any Friday.

At the end of the day, she looked at her schedule for next week. Six patients in all.

Progress!

• • •

Saturday was a big night in the Farmer-Bowen household.

Around five thirty p.m., Cathy Bennett dropped her bike down onto their front lawn and left it there. The fact that it didn't need to be locked—no one would possibly steal it—still surprised Linda. Rocking another onesie pajama, this time with a fringed collar made from what looked like recycled tires, Cathy appeared at their front door.

"Hi, Cathy! Come on in!" Linda said.

Cathy blushed, her gaze pointed between her funky, handsewn house slippers. "Hi, Ms. Farmer. Bowen. I'm sorry, *Dr.* Bowen," she mumbled, lathering herself into a high-pitched panic. "Dr. Farmer!"

"Honey, it's Linda." Cathy looked like she might cry, so Linda put her hand on the kid's shoulder. "Or whatever you want. Just glad you're here." Then she stepped aside so Hip could greet his guest.

In the time they'd been a couple, he'd gained confidence. He stood taller and his voice had lost its questioning lilt. He liked taking care of her.

"My mom made onion dip," he said, which was true. She tried to keep the fridge packed with every possible temptation. It seemed to be working, as Hip's appetite had remained strong.

Soon after Hip and Cathy disappeared, Josie came down in her heavy, knee-length coat. She'd become friends with a large crew of kids who traveled in a happy, clean-cut pack. They roamed the streets, goofing around in night parks, visiting one another's houses, and generally looking for mischief, but finding none. The group was composed of the soccer team, the spring swim team, and the debate club—the ambitious kids who'd been marked as the most likely to succeed there. They didn't seem to have silly bones, like Josie's old friends in Kings. Nobody ever laughed until they cried. But they were upstanding and it was a relief that Linda could let her go out at night and know she'd be safe.

Josie opened the front door and there they were, a crew of about ten kids that would snowball into twenty or more over the course of the night. She walked out, engulfed.

Linda and Russell were last. He came down the stairs all dressed up and offered his arm. "Ready?"

• • •

Their first stop at Sirin's was at the soccer parents' regular table in the main room, where they were greeted with hoots, hollers, and hugs. The big topic was the new principal, who everyone felt needed more training. "It seems soon to cast judgment," Linda said. "Shouldn't we give her a year to get her footing?"

"We don't have a year! BWU essays go out in the winter," Farah said. "These towns are drawing wagons. If kids don't graduate from honors track, they'll never make it. Think about all those poor high school seniors whose futures are on the line. This has to be resolved now."

"Outsiders are good for shaking things up, but they're clueless. You can't hire an outsider as a principal. It's irresponsible," Ruth Epstein said. Then she remembered that Linda and Russell were new. "Not you guys!"

"Are you coming to the pregame tomorrow?" Amir asked Russell.

"Looking forward to it," he said.

Russell stayed. Linda moved on to that same back room from the first time she'd met ActHollow.

"You've arrived!" Anouk called with flourish. She draped her scarf as she did this, a little for humor, a little pure arrogance.

Like every other Saturday they'd been having these meetings, Linda gave them a breakdown: the on-site X-ray machine needed a regular technician, and they were still waiting for the MRI and drug printer. She also wanted oversight for her position. All doctors need fellow doctors with whom to review their cases. It's often in the troubleshooting that better answers appear. She was confident, her tone definitive in ways it wasn't at home or socially. She knew how to run a clinic.

"You don't need oversight," Daniella said. "You're a marvel."

"This isn't a cowboy field," Linda answered. "The best doctors have colleagues."

"Point taken. We'll send out a call," Daniella said.

Kai read the budget. He'd been coming to meetings again. He and Rachel still lived in the same house but took separate cars and sat apart. They seemed to enjoy antagonizing one another, in the way that people with strong feelings, who aren't yet willing to give up, tend to do.

"We've underprojected expenditures this month," he said. "Which would be great, if we also hadn't projected twenty patients a week."

"So, basically, the only thing we need is patients," Linda said.

"I didn't guess that would be our problem. Their population's not much lower than ours and they don't have any doctors. I thought we'd feel terrible, having to turn them away," Daniella said.

"Town relations haven't been very good, have they?" Linda asked.

"It's Hollow," Rachel said, eyes swollen with exhaustion. "They think it's evil magic." She'd just flown in from Beijing. It could be eight in the morning, or eight at night. She was probably so turned around, it made no difference.

"Not to press a point, but any chance we can back off from the Hollow stuff, at least until we gain their trust?" Linda asked.

"Where Caesar goes, Rome follows," Anouk answered.

"Right," Linda said. "You're the boss."

Meeting adjourned, they packed up and joined the large front table for dinner. This was composed of a rotating group of the most important people in PV, most of whom were on BW's board. The waiters came often, and the food was preselected. First course, already being served, was seared sea anemone.

Linda'd gotten to know Lloyd Bennett, the handsome man from the crowning. She found him charming. What she liked most about him was that he often sat next to shy Colette Lust, Jack's wife, and included her in conversation. Ever consistent, Jack stone-faced everybody. He also had the bad habit of looking Linda's figure up and down whenever they met, and seeming, every time, unimpressed.

The evening passed fast. Anouk announced that her next poetry collection was about epigenetic trauma: *It's such a sad world out there, so full of people on the outside whose genes have accumulated so much damage. People blame chemicals for their cancers and asthma, but it's really stress from abuse and bad parenting. I want to honor their unavoidable suffering, and also honor the pure genes of Plymouth Valley, which will lead the way to the future.*

Everybody paused at this pronouncement, most in horror. Then they all made prayer hands, even as they looked at one another with wry, disapproving expressions, and it occurred to Linda that prayer hands could be sarcastic.

Before the night ended, Russell's boss, Heinrich, gave him a compliment: *You handle your team very well. They're not an easy group, especially Nanny.*

Russell beamed.

• • •

Linda was sitting across from Russell, eating toast. He'd been tossing half the night. "That judge is gonna give you the extension," she said.

The bespoke number from the Fabric Collective hadn't yet arrived, and in the current suit he'd brought from home, he looked a little like an undertaker. It had somehow shrunk, hugging his upper wrists. He did not seem aware of this, and she had no desire to tell him. This was his only good suit. He couldn't very well show up to virtual court in bright blue Omnium.

Today, the judge would give their decision on whether to postpone the trial.

"You never know," he said. "They gave me every possible file. But there's still some stuff that doesn't add up."

"Like what?" she asked.

He raised his eyes. "I don't know! That's why it doesn't add up!"

• • •

Daniella, Anouk, Rachel, and even Chernin had assured her that he'd get the extension. After work and feeding the kids that night, she dressed in something slinky (and a little lumpy) for the occasion, and ordered a spanakopita, his favorite.

The clock ticked past eight and into nine. She texted a few times and called twice. *All good!* he wrote back, which wasn't an answer, but okay. At midnight, she peeled the phyllo from the top of the dish, having eaten it layer by layer, so by the end it looked like an open-faced spinach melt. An hour after that, she left it there, cold and gluey, and went to bed.

She woke a few hours later when he flicked the bright overhead light. His tie hung loose around his neck, his jacket gone. She'd later find out they took it from him, cut it to pieces. He'd helped. This had been very funny, apparently. They'd all laughed at his cheap suit, then destroyed the cheap suit.

He swayed on his feet.

"What happened?" she asked.

"I got the extension!" he said. "They took me out to Sirin's. They made a big deal about it. They were all there! Everybody from my office!"

"Wow! How fun!" she said. She tried not to show her hurt. This was his big moment. He could celebrate it however he pleased. But it felt very bad that he hadn't wanted to celebrate it with her, and it reminded her of their life back in Kings.

When she met him, he'd been getting two PhDs at the same time. One in toxicology, the other in statistics. She'd liked that about him. It had made her feel safe. In a world chock-full of people who'd given up, that kind of industry had smacked of optimism.

But after the kids came along, he went into a panicked overdrive, coming home after she fell asleep, going back out again before anyone in the house woke up. This went on for years. When she complained, he promised that it would be worth it. One day they'd have a nice house in Jersey.

But this apartment is fine, she told him. *What we have now is fine.*

With all these cuts and reorganizations, it might not last, he told her. *The only way to keep what we have is to get so far ahead they can't catch us.*

He'd deserved the position of department head at the EPA. He'd deserved all the salary increases he'd asked for. But though they'd always been happy to give him more work and responsibility, he'd never gotten those promotions or raises. It had never made sense to her. He hadn't joked around with his staff or invited them for dinner. He'd never been a social animal, but he was perfectly nice. Funny, with a biting sense of humor once he loosened up. What more had those people wanted from him?

"They told me I'm on the right track," he now said, then softer: "They answered a lot of questions I've been having about these Omnium studies."

"Were you right? Was there something they weren't telling you?"

"It was nothing like I thought. They keep their records differently. They showed me, and it all made a lot more sense," he said, getting into bed. "I'm tired. I love you."

"I love you," she said.

• • •

Probably because he was drunk-snoring, she couldn't fall back asleep that night. She wandered the main floor of the house. It felt different at night, foreign. Sunny was easy to see, her white feathers glowing in the moonlight as she foraged for burrowing creatures across the drought-resistant Kentucky bluegrass.

Linda ate some gluey spanakopita, picking away pieces of the dish from the pan with her pincer fingers. She opened the package containing the most recent altar offering: a bruised red fruit. The insert described it as a pomegranate.

She copied what she'd seen in other people's houses and cut it in half, then placed it directly in the hall altar, below the Geiger counter. Small, fetal-like seeds stuck to layers of white rind. Red juice bled down from the burst parts.

A kind of nighttime logic overcame her. She prayed, like she'd done when she was little, and it was not clear to her to whom she was praying. "Thank you for helping us settle in. Please let Russell win his case. Please let things go on as they've been going. Please let us stay."

Who's the Big Bad Samhain?

Put your hands together and clap, 'cause it's Samhain!

According to the Plymouth Valley Chamber of Commerce, all residents can expect pumpkin deliveries by this Friday.

Need more lights? Want a smoke machine and some scary blow-up monsters? Call the volunteers—we've got plenty and are happy to help you set up.

Some reminders: All residents are required to hand out treats from 4–7 p.m. Otherwise, expect some naughty tricks!

The Labyrinth is open from 8–10 p.m. at Caladrius Park. This year's serious. Beltane King Keith Parson plans to scare your pants off, so enter if you dare!!!!!!!!

Samhain

During the week leading up to Samhain, PV radio tittered with excitement. The hosts of *NewsHour*, a dinnertime weeknight radio show, fielded tongue-in-cheek call-ins over whether the Beltane King would frighten someone into a heart attack, as he'd apparently done the previous year. "Oh, it *will* happen!" said a milky-voiced Southeasterner. "I *know* it!"

"Would you bet your beef ration on it?"

The lady paused, and Linda pictured her sitting on a porch on Gal's side of town, a retired octogenarian who still remembered when Sirin's had been a church, and the northern farm had been flat plains. "No. I don't think I would bet that," she said, scandalized by the question, and with her answer to it, too. "I love my steak!"

Samhain was a big deal. The Beautification Society turned the Labyrinth into a haunted maze. Then, the Beltane King and scores of volunteers dressed up and scared people inside it. During the weeklong lead-up to the holiday, volunteers posted photos all over town of Keith wearing an eerie all-black costume. He'd made it himself, apparently, and was supposed to be the personification of *death*. Linda would be walking along Main Street or parking at the hospital or waving to Sally, and there he'd be, thick necked, that pitch-black costume over his face, wearing a crown of bones.

"Who had a heart attack?" Linda asked. She and Rachel talked a few times a week. Sometimes it was about the clinic, but more often just to touch base. Rachel was her best in the mornings and Linda always tried to catch her then.

"Some old guy with a bad heart. He was like a wrinkle bag, so I'm going to guess he was over a hundred," Rachel said. "I could have stashed three bottles of mead in those folds. Crazy part is, he lived. He's still alive. He's probably going back for more this year. Listen, the people here build this thing up, but your street in Kings was probably scarier. It's a thrill for people who've never had anything bad happen to them. For the rest of us, it's entertainment."

• • •

By the morning of Samhain, every house in town was festooned with lights, billowing vampires, zombies, and cornucopias. The Farmer-Bowen house had accepted all offers of help and decoration, meaning the whole thing was ablaze with lights, blow-up night crawlers, and graveyards. Even Sunny's shelter had a headstone over it.

Linda's friends had made all kinds of costume suggestions: zombie (Rachel), one half of a historical couple like Marie and Pierre Curie (Daniella). Anouk was very clear that she should not be a caladrius, which carried too much Hollow significance. After much consideration, Linda went with her old standby: sexy black cat. She wore a stretch black leotard, applied eyeliner for whiskers, and pinned a black yarn tail to her bottom.

All afternoon, she answered the door to adorable children and their equally adorable parents. Several neighbors came inside to chat. A few expressed admiration that she'd become an integral part of Plymouth Valley so quickly.

"You're on the fast track to a ticket," Kim Jackson, the PV K–12 principal, told her.

"Are we?" Linda asked.

"Absolutely!" Kim answered. "I'm from Palo Alto. We had a lock there. Twelve more years and I'd have gotten a golden ticket. But when this chance to live in PV came along, I grabbed it."

"Is PV that much better?" Linda asked.

"The other towns have no culture. It's all work all the time. This place has a sense of fun. I hope we get to stay. They're sending me to Boston for a week of recommendation-writing training. But I don't know if it's enough. Would you have lunch with me sometime?"

Linda noticed that (a) Kim was very nice and (b) no one else was talking to her, or to her family. Though she'd been in this town longer than the Farmer-Bowens, she was still getting hazed. "I'd love lunch."

Between meeting, greeting, and handing out candy, she and Russell took turns helping Hip with his costume. He was going as the diminishing plastic island in the ocean, but the soymilk containers kept falling off, and so did the trash bags. Linda glued more precisely, held the plastic pieces to the glue for a longer time, to let them adhere. Russell drew on the cardboard sandwich board base in Sharpie, labeling each thing, so people would know the kid was Plastic Island and not a random pile of garbage. Despite all this effort, he nonetheless looked like a generic pile of garbage. "I can't leave the house like this! I look like the stupidest loser in the world!"

Russell, having spent a lot of time on that Sharpie sign, left the room in annoyance.

Linda stayed. The hormone-incited pity-party ended after about five minutes, leaving her the remainder to fix the label so PLASTIC ISLAND read more prominent. "Is it really almost gone?" she asked as a means of distracting him.

"A tenth of what it used to be, because of Omnium."

"People here are so proud of Omnium. They're gonna love your costume. What made you pick it?"

"Cathy says Omnium's changed everything. I want people to know I believe in this place. That I'm on her side. She gets nervous. But it's not her fault. It's hard for her because the job she wants doesn't give a golden ticket."

"You like it better here than New York?"

He was surprised by the question. "The air's clean here. That's all that matters."

Then she went to Josie's room, to discover that Josie'd ignored the

Salem witch trial judge's robe and wig Linda had ordered for her and instead turned her soccer uniform inside out, because serial killers *look like normal people*.

Linda wanted to object. It was Samhain! Everyone was dressing up! But the girl was turning sixteen in February. The last thing she needed was a mom who picked her clothing. "You sure you don't want to be an evil judge?" she asked.

Josie tugged her jersey, nervous. "I can't. They told me to wear this."

"They assigned it? Who?"

"Them," she said. "Arnie Nassar. He picks what everyone's going to be. It's a whole thing. It's fine."

"Takes the fun out."

"Fun-suck vampires," Josie agreed.

Linda had hoped that by now, Josie would have found a close confidant among her friend group. But it was a revolving crowd. During dinner and at night, she texted until Linda took away her device. It wasn't happy texting. It seemed desperate. She'd never known Josie to be so eager to please. Linda tried not to worry. Josie was the kind of person who got through hard times. She bounced.

"Maybe it'll be fun, anyway?"

"Maybe," Josie said, then smiled a fake, trying-too-hard smile.

• • •

Night came. The family headed out.

At Caladrius Park, a set of badged PV police, dressed up as ghouls, guarded both the Labyrinth entrance and its exit on the other side—sets of stairs made to look like mouths.

"Scarier every year," someone said.

"Too scary. I'm not going," someone else answered.

Josie found her gang—a gaggle of boys and girls and thems. She faded into the group without saying good-bye and was the first of them through the mouth, down the maze.

Hip found Cathy Bennett. He didn't wave at first, just admired her. Their eyes caught, and she did a silly, self-conscious jog in his direction, arms flying out and flapping like wings. They kissed in greeting.

Overlapping lips. It was love. At least, on Hip's end, it was love. Was fifteen too young for this intensity? Probably. But when is anything ever more intense than when you're fifteen?

Cathy's costume was a yellow canary. She looked both spectacular and thirty years old. Daniella had used fabric glue to cover a yellow leotard in feathers. Her plunging neckline exposed budding cleavage, and her face was specked with silver glitter. Cathy had wanted to go as Emily Dickinson, Linda knew, but Daniella hadn't allowed it. *It's not like I have anything against lesbians. I like lesbians*, she'd explained to Linda in whispers on a call. *It's the depressed personality. Jesus, that woman was a sad sack.*

Hip registered her discomfort, gave her his jacket, whose back read PLASTIC ISLAND. She zipped it to the neck. They walked to the side of the entrance, where Cathy leaned against a tall hay wall that messed her hair. Hip leaned in front of her, his arms on either side. Neither of them was going in. Last year, Cathy'd been scared badly inside this maze and had vowed never to enter it again. Hip had decided to keep her company.

Linda tugged Russell's shirt, so he'd look in the young sweethearts' direction. How was it possible that the same boy who'd been crying about the way the plastic hung from his costume just two hours before could be so upstanding?

"Good for him," Russell said with amazement. Then he took Linda's hand, kissed it.

Pretty soon, their friends appeared at the edge of the park. The group included Heinrich; his husband; their daughter, Sally, who guarded the border; some coworkers; plus the ActHollow crew and a few of Rachel and Lloyd's friends from legal. Anouk and her family weren't among them, but Linda'd heard they didn't typically participate in festivities; they presided over them.

"Did they meet up before this?" Russell asked.

The boisterous group approached, and it was clear they'd been drinking. Russell started for Heinrich and the rest. Linda weaved, hugging her hellos until she found Daniella, Rachel, and Kai. Rachel was red eyed from either emotion, drink, or both.

"Everything okay?"

"It's always okay. Everything's always okay in paradise, didn't you know?" Rachel asked.

"Someone spiked Rachel's mocktail with about five shots of absinthe," Daniella said, then they all looked at Jack, who was talking to some board members nearby. Wearing his usual tight black suit instead of a costume, his demeanor was excessively relaxed. Slothful, even.

"Who would do that?" Linda asked.

"There's only one person," Kai answered. "The better question is, she must have tasted that something was wrong with it. So why did she drink it?"

"Because I'm tough, that's why," Rachel said. "He has no idea what I come from. He needs to understand that whatever he throws at me doesn't matter. I can handle it."

Kai's eyes watered, and Linda realized for the first time how deeply Kai Choi Johnson loved his troubled wife.

"Sorry if we kept you waiting," Daniella said. "We were at the Parson Mansion for a little PV business."

"They're making their list and checking it twice," Rachel said.

Daniella squeezed Rachel's arm, hard, in a way that clearly meant *stop talking*.

"I need to get home to the kids," Kai said.

"She'll be okay. I have her," Daniella said.

Their group of about twenty-five people amassed. Lloyd Bennett got out in front of them all. "Tallyho!" he called, and in a line, they entered the mouth.

Linda, Daniella, and Rachel lingered. "Do you want to do this?" Daniella asked.

"The top contender for CEO has to show her face at all these things," Rachel answered. "Of course I'm doing this." She straightened like the very model of sobriety, walked between security officers and down the stairs, into the maze.

Daniella turned to Linda. "That answers that."

• • •

What Linda had neglected to tell Rachel on their call was that while she'd seen a lot in her life, and been through more, these experiences had not served as inoculation. She scared easily.

They got to the landing, where the Labyrinth began. It was cold and dark. Overhead speakers played spooky music. She heard they'd shortened the route to a single kilometer rather than the full three, and they'd locked the inner shelter as well, so no one could cheat or get lost.

The ceilings had been lit with ultraviolet lights, making teeth glow. Haystacks lined the walls, but these made narrower paths than she remembered. She had the idea that there was extra room on either side for volunteers to assist stragglers, or else jump out and scare people crapless.

By now they'd passed two intersections. Linda looked back, trying to remember from which way they'd come, but the walls were moving. She reminded herself that while this place was scary, it was also wondrous. Magic, even, in that human, awe-inspiring way that the ancient pyramids and modern medicine and functional governments feel like magic. Humans had made this awesome thing.

"What's he do, the Beltane King?" Linda asked.

"Keith? He likes to grab people and shake them until they cry. Chances are, it won't be you," Daniella said. "But isn't the risk a thrill?"

"Yes, he's insane, and that makes it SO MUCH FUN!" Rachel shouted from up ahead.

Every fifty strides or so, they passed under a hyperfocused speaker. They heard creaking doors, singular and eerie, then at the next stop, a weeping, ghostly woman.

Linda tried to discern Russell in the pack ahead. But they were just a blur, drifting farther and faster. A wall moved and he was gone.

Deeper. The rows darkened. So did the music. They couldn't talk. The music beat in her chest, loud. It pulled her out of time and made her feel trapped in her own skin. She had a brief, mad thought that there was something down these tunnels with all of them. Something amused by their pale imitations of horror—and insulted by them, too.

Something old that should never have been dug up.

"I am *not* a fraidy-cat," she shouted.

"Oh, I think she is," Rachel said. There was a hint of mean happening, here. Rachel could be mean.

"Are you scared?" Daniella asked, bellowing to be heard.

They turned, or maybe the maze curved. The crowd ahead and behind were gone. It was suddenly just the three of them. They came to a four-way intersection.

They went left. Loud speakers, flashing lights.

In the dark, something lurched. The music got staccato, reminding her of stab scenes from old screenies. The lurching thing limped on a stiff leg, pulling himself with the good one. A chain connected its wrists. She didn't think it was Keith. Probably, a volunteer actor. Of course a volunteer actor. Who else would it be?

"I'm not usually scared in real life," she said as she froze and would walk no farther, loudly answering a question whose time had come and gone.

"She's scared!" Rachel shouted, her voice compassionless as a toddler's. She was blitzed out of her mind.

About three meters out, the lurching thing reared, standing tall, and scream-howled. Rachel laughed. Linda's stomach dropped. His lurch and limp gone, he charged full speed. Being good at his job, he picked the person who was terrified. He rushed at Linda, suddenly standing over her, heavy chain links rattling. In her mind, the sound carried, resonating through every hall, waking all the monsters that lived down there.

Time slowed. She understood that she was attending a fun festival in a wealthy company town filled with pleasant people who made a ceremony of everything they did, because they had nothing of true importance on their minds. Still, she also thought that this wasn't an ordinary festival at all, or an ordinary tunnel. Monsters lived here. They weren't human. This place wasn't human. And if you lived here long enough, you became inhuman, too.

The man bent down over Linda. He smelled clean, like toothpaste. Up close, his face was clear, his brown eyes bright. This wasn't a monster, she rationalized as she tried to squeeze her ears shut from the inside. It was someone she'd met or would meet on Main Street or at the hospital. He was *not* going to murder her.

"Beware, the sacrifice!" he called in a distinctly human voice, then scrambled past them down the hall.

When it was over, they found themselves standing between speakers in the relative quiet. Daniella and Rachel fell into each other with laughter. The laughter was infectious and Linda laughed, too, only it was cry-laughing.

"You guys, I just peed my pants," she said.

"Did you?" Daniella asked.

"—Dirty Kitty," Rachel said at the same time.

"Almost. A little bit. Was that like what Keith'll do?"

"Oh, no," Daniella said. "He's much worse."

They went right. Sprayed in shining red against the hay: *Beware the sacrifice.*

A breathing thing came up from behind. She whipped around to find a very convincing zombie, like one you'd see in a nightmare. Teeth impressions coated in congealed blood marked its abdomen from where it had been made zombie, and blood glistened on its mouth and chin from a fresh feed.

Registering her fear, but doing the opposite of the last guy, he said, "Excuse me," very politely, and lurched down the row. This time, Linda laughed, even as she held her heart, and noticed the sticky corn syrup blood he'd left on her arm. "Do men dressed like ghouls pop out and grab you the whole time? What the hell? No wonder Cathy won't go inside!"

Instead of answering, Rachel bent down, hands on knees. Gently, Daniella grazed her back with red-painted fingernails, a contrast to her white angel costume.

Rachel vomited. Linda saw her retching, shoulders widening and contracting, between flashing black lights. "What if I get in there and nothing changes? Why don't we just admit nothing ever changes?" she mumbled, then pulled out a handkerchief that glowed under the black lights and wiped her mouth with it. She was wearing soldier camouflage that was two sizes too big.

"You've got to stop doing this to yourself. It's not just your reputation on the line here. This affects all of us," Daniella pleaded with her friend. It was the most genuine emotion Linda'd ever seen her express.

"Let's just keep going," Rachel said. "It's the flashing lights."

"I know the back way out," Daniella said. "Where the staff comes through."

They moved forward. Science fiction music played. The kind of eerie stuff you hear upon approaching a black hole or alien ship. They went right, the opposite direction of the crowd ahead of them. A mannequin attached to a zip line plunged overhead. All three yelped, dropping hands and jogging ahead.

They came up behind a large group, all in plague costumes. A zombie volunteer waved her arms and fake-bit the lead plague victim's shoulder. Another arm reached right through the hay, and grabbed the second in the group.

Linda held her heart and pushed down on it like it was an excited animal in a small box. She didn't like being scared, she decided. She wasn't ever doing this again. She turned to say this, but Daniella and Rachel were gone. They weren't behind her. They weren't ahead. She jogged down the row, passing the masked people and the zombie, wrenching her leg away hard and fast from the hand that had reached to grab it.

She turned left, entering an empty row. Percussive music built, pushing her forward like a hand on her back. Then, she was at the mouth of a great room where the music crescendoed. Lit up along the back stone wall was a massive altar. People knelt on long slats of wood that looked like prayer pews.

A bad thing was here. She could feel it, watching. A bad thing that had been woken and was waiting. She remembered, then, the thing from the shelter on her tour that Zach had told her was a large caladrius. But *remember* wasn't the right word. It surfaced from her consciousness like a floater full of gas.

The people ahead of her filed out the far doorway, their mouths red now, their hands slick and red, too. Fear crept inside Linda like an animal with its own will.

Up ahead, a space opened. It came too soon. She was scared. She wanted to be home. But where was home? Nine Sunset Heights? Kings? The crowd behind pushed her forward and she knelt, nearly weeping. Against the stone were bones. No, not bones. Skulls. Rows and rows of skulls. Hundreds of them, the bones cleaned and smoothed.

A joke, she whispered to herself. *Samhain decoration.* But like the bone crown, they appeared real.

Above the skulls was a hearthstone outcrop from which red slow-dripped. She peered directly overhead, couldn't discern what hung there. She glimpsed just its side—no face or legs. Her guess was a slaughtered animal. But its pelt was thicker than fur and dirty white. Wool? A lamb?

An insult to God, she thought. Did she believe in God? Yes, maybe she did, because she could discern its absence. God existed, but not here.

Beneath the carcass was about a foot of stacked skulls, sopping and dissolving in the blood. Dissolving? How were they dissolving? What the hell was happening?

Hands on either side of her reached out along the row where she knelt. They took the skulls. Were people eating them? Yes, they were. They were eating blood and bone in a makeshift church built inside an underground labyrinth, and God didn't like it one bit, but the monster was happy. The monster was loose.

She'd never sleep tonight, never feel safe in this town, unless she stayed right now, and checked. She pulled free a skull from the stacked pile. It felt grainy and loose in her fingers, not like bone. She copied the rest and set it under the dripping red, which was too thick and sticky for blood.

She knew by then that this was a trick. A joke. But her body didn't believe it.

She ran her finger along the red and tasted sweet syrup on the tip of her tongue. She licked the skull: granulated sugar. As if to conquer the thing, she took a giant bite.

"Ha!" She laughed, loud and with a full mouth. "You guys are pranksters!" Familiar faces turned from kneeling positions, their expressions bright with amusement, but they didn't break character.

So, it really was just for fun. No monsters. No madness. Nothing loose.

How had she imagined such absurdity?

She got up off her knees. Most people took the right turn out of the skull room, but it was loud in there, lights flashing. She went left and caught her breath. As she walked, she found a large spyhole in the hay wall. She looked through, making sure to stay far enough from the aperture that a hand couldn't grab her.

On the other side, more maze.

A bunch of teens stood in a half circle, passing several flasks between them. The polite zombie from before was trying to scare them, grabbing at their arms and snarling. *Dude, it's like he shit his pants and made it a costume*, one said. *Man, he smells like he's dead*, said another. The zombie broke character, dropping his arms to his sides and standing tall. He looked at them for a beat or two, then lurched in another direction, to try to scare some people it might actually be fun to scare. The kids made soft laughing sounds that Linda's adult mind interpreted as contrition. They were at an age where they still didn't understand that they had power. That adults cared what they thought, that adults' feelings could be hurt.

She saw, then, a soccer shirt and Josie's inside-out number: 14.

"Oh," she cried in deflated surprise.

Josie heard, somehow, even though the music was still loud. She looked around in all directions.

Linda chose not to call out to her, embarrass her. She made a left, and then another left, thinking it would lead her to the group of teens, but somehow, it led elsewhere. This was impossible. This had to end. It wasn't fear so much as adrenaline drain. She was exhausted. Her sexy cat outfit wasn't nearly enough clothing.

Something leaped out. Its costume was a black, skintight suit, the ill-fitting Beltane Crown upon its head. *Boo!* It laughed. Keith's voice. He jigged left, blocking her passage.

He'd caught her alone. She should have guessed he was the type to delight in sneak attacks.

"Let me go, Keith," she said. "I know this is your job and I want to play along. But I'm done. I can't."

She went right. He jigged and blocked her. Through his skintight suit, he had an erection.

It occurred to her that he could do whatever he pleased. There weren't witnesses. Even if she told people and they believed her, this was a Parson.

"Please," she said. Her voice came soft. Begging. It shocked her that she was the kind of person who would beg under such circumstances.

The smug son of a bitch lunged. It happened so fast she didn't scream. His ropelike arms circled her shoulders, drew her tight to his broad chest. She was pressed against him, hearing his heart beat fast and uneven. How had this happened? Why had she talked to him? Why hadn't she run?

"Beware the sacrifice," he cooed in the kind of lulling voice a certain kind of creepy guy might use during foreplay.

She dug her elbows into his chest. No effect. He was solid as a mountain. His suit was so glossy and shining that she saw a reflection against his face. She saw herself, a frightened woman. But there was something dirty white behind her. It was moving closer. It was huge.

Her imagination, surely. It often ran away with her. But she remembered the shadow. The monster in the Labyrinth. The reflection came closer: a graceless, slow-moving creature.

"Today, it's me. Tomorrow—" he shouted so hard her eardrums sang. The white was getting bigger, coming closer. "It's y—!"

She kneed him in the crotch, a delicate squish. He let go for only a second. Enough time to break away.

She didn't look back as she ran, though she heard his pain-moan. She didn't care. Her last burst of adrenaline burned explosive, like a struck match. It honed her instincts: 99.9 percent chance Keith Parson was a harmless weirdo who took the Beltane King thing too seriously; 0.1 percent chance he was a maniac in cahoots with the scuttling, hungry thing that lived down here, and in her nightmares, too.

She followed the crowd, thick now, all heading in the same direction.

"Linda!" a voice called. Daniella and Rachel were standing in an alcove, waiting for her.

"Where'd you go?" Linda asked, loud and angry. Too loud and angry: it wasn't smart to show temper with Daniella. It wasn't smart to show temper at all, at least not in this town.

"We were inside the galley here. It was right next to you. We were calling, but you didn't hear," Daniella said. "You panicked."

"Note to self: if I ever want to make Linda lose her shit, bring her to a haunted labyrinth," Rachel said, dry. Later, Linda would think: *For Rachel to be this drunk, but to sound this coherent, she wasn't just a seasoned drinker; she was a longtime alcoholic.*

Linda took both their arms and squeezed, glad for the substantial *thereness* of them. She hugged them hard, stanching tears so Daniella wouldn't get angry.

"Oh, honey. I'm sorry. Was it that bad?" Daniella asked.

"It was everything. I don't have words for all the things."

"You need a drink," Rachel said.

"I could have a thousand and I don't think I'd feel it," Linda said when she finally let go. "You guys—I think I just decked the Beltane King!"

Their eyes goggled.

"Little you?" Daniella asked.

"Most people have fight or flight. I have fight, then flight."

"You got away from him?" Rachel asked, equally incredulous.

"I kneed him between the legs and bolted," she said like it was funny, but it wasn't funny. It was scary. She wanted very much to cry.

Daniella burst into laughter. "But he never lets anybody go until they cry! Bet he's fit to be tied! Or having a fit?"

"Holy shit. You're my hero. He's had that coming for years."

"Like *kneed* him," Linda said, miming it now, with her knee.

At first, they tittered under stifled grins, all looking away from the other to prevent contagion. But it didn't subside. Rachel was the first to crack, eyes teary with pent laughter. She brayed. Then all of them were laughing so hard they were holding their stomachs.

"This is my favorite Samhain that's ever happened," Rachel said.

"Me too," Daniella whispered. "I hate that guy so much."

This brought more laughter of shock and delight.

"I was scared I was the only one," Linda said. "I thought people thought he was normal!"

More laughing, and leaning on one another, and finally wiping their wet eyes, spent.

It didn't take long before they found the exit sign and climbed the steps out. The egress opened at an obtuse angle, allowing a panoramic view of the park above, which came suddenly. Russell was out there, along with the rest of their friends. It was bright and it wasn't scary.

She could see now that, yeah, Josie had been part of that group of teens. She was with them still, her shoulders hunched, seeming not quite a part of the crowd, but on the periphery of a very tight-knit group. She clocked Linda, acknowledged her with a pleading glance that indicated: *Please—I know I was wrong—but don't bust me in front of these people.* Linda shook her head with exasperation, extended her hand palm-up to indicate: *Go finish your night.*

The three women joined their larger crew, who erupted with stories of who'd been scared, who'd laughed, who'd hidden their faces in their hands and begged for it to be over. With Daniella's prodding, Linda told how she'd escaped Keith. She was tentative when she started, but off their expressions, their interjections (*Holy cow! I'd have lost my mind*; *Don't mess with Linda—she knows jujitsu!*), she was laughing. It wasn't a scary story anymore. It was a funny one. They were all laughing all over again, hard as burst hydrants. She couldn't remember a time she'd been so relieved.

"Do you think Keith'll be mad? Or Anouk?" Linda asked after they'd all recovered and were heading for the bar.

"It's the game!" Lloyd reassured. "You played it. No one can hold that against you!"

More happened. There were drinks and food trucks and meeting new people and laughter, so much laughter. They all felt like courageous survivors. And they were, weren't they? By birth or cunning, they'd each gotten out of something very bad and arrived safely here.

After the maze was cleared of stragglers, John Parson got onstage to say that the night was for honoring the dead residents who'd sacrificed so much to build this town. "May we never forget," he called, and the crowd responded: "We will never forget." Then Keith Parson, fully costumed, set a sick caladrius on a chopping block—it looked like the pecked one from outside Anouk's cottage—and severed its head with an axe.

The act was an apt and violent punctuation to a wild night. Intuitively, she understood that it acknowledged that not everyone was lucky. Not everyone got to live in PV. If she'd tried to explain this to someone back home, she didn't think they'd have understood.

It was something you had to experience to understand.

November

The jack-o'-lanterns came down and the lights, scary sound effects, and synthetic rubber masks got put away until next year. In their place, the Beautification Society delivered front-door corn husks. Pomegranates got rotated out in favor of hard-boiled eggs, dry beans, and seeds for the late-autumn season. In a neat, aesthetically pleasing way, Hip took over the job of stocking the altar.

Dayworkers raked the wild red piles of leaves at the edges of houses, transporting them to the northern farm as compost. By the end of the first week of November, a light frost webbed the windows and browning lawns. Days got shorter. Winter coats appeared.

Russell's delayed court case arrived. With his new data, he testified in Omnium's defense and won, much to everyone's relief. Then he started on a new case, and they understood that this would continue: there would always be cases to try, information to retrieve despite difficult obstacles, victories to grasp. His performance would never stop being judged. But at least now, they'd passed the first and most difficult gauntlet: finding their side hustle and learning how to navigate the people of this town.

Josie's team stayed in third place, but her footwork improved and Coach Farah moved her to left forward, where she belonged. She still wasn't *happy Josie*. Linda didn't know how to fix that. Then again, maybe it wasn't something that could be fixed. Sometimes you're not happy. Some years you're with the wrong people until you find the right ones.

Hip spent most of his time with Cathy. He'd supported and taken on her cause: lobbying for golden tickets for everyone born into PV. "It's not right that Cathy doesn't feel safe in her own home," he told Linda one afternoon. "If you're born here, you should have the right to stay here forever."

"What about outsiders, like us?"

He nodded at her, like this was something he'd already considered. "It's smart for us to be patient. We have to work on one issue at a time. I'm trying not to be selfish. Selfish people aren't what this community needs. If we ask for golden tickets early, it'll just alienate everybody and remind them we're outsiders."

"Without a golden ticket, do you feel safe?" Linda asked.

Hip looked at her with surprise. "Of course! I live *here*!"

• • •

Mid-November, Linda had some time on her hands and stayed late after her shift at the PV Hospital. Thinking of Gal, but still unready to visit her, she researched the cancer Gal had claimed both her children were afflicted with: idiopathic leukemia.

There wasn't any record of the disease in the main BetterWorld search engine, but that didn't mean much. Every private corporation had its own engine, as did every country, and these didn't typically assimilate data from outside sources. She tried the medical school consortium but her Downstate password had expired. She tried the Bed-Stuy Children's Clinic's files and couldn't connect.

She did find an article in the *Journal of Pediatric Oncology* published a year earlier, in which the disease was considered difficult to treat because diagnosis took so long. Etiology was unclear. It was higher in the presence of toxic exposure. The Review section highlighted a geographic information systems analysis that pinpointed hot spots all over the globe. These hot spots tended to center in poor, rural communities. The disease itself was strange, affecting monocytes, platelets, and red blood cells alike. Several immunotherapy drugs were recommended, but not Zovolotecan—the chemotherapeutic agent Linda had seen on Gal's table the night of the fire.

Though most of the articles were locked, physicians had written open letters in several issues of the *Journal of Pediatric Oncology*, vouching for the increased presence of idiopathic leukemia and the lack of standard treatment. Doctors all over were frustrated, trying to find a cause or consistent pathology. Some claimed that idiopathic anemia wasn't a single disease, but a term for a host of illnesses. These included leukemias and complex autoimmune diseases like aplastic anemia. Clinical trials were taking place at the Cleveland Clinic and at the NIH Clinical Center. Similar trials were also happening in Cork, Ireland, and Beijing, China, though because of global data-sharing restrictions, their methods were unknown.

She wrote a note to Chernin, asking whether PV had sanctioned Zovolotecan's use for idiopathic leukemia, and what insights he had on the drug's efficacy. Then she wrote to her old boss, Fielding: *What do you know about this disease? Is Zovolotecan a common treatment, and do you have any idea what causes it?*

Then she read the report on Carlos's blood panel, which had come back inconclusive. The PV oncologist who'd signed it suggested more tests. For the third time in as many weeks, she called the number Danny Morales had written on the intake form and left a message: *Please come back. This isn't something that can wait.*

• • •

That night, they went to the talk hosted by the Plymouth Valley Chamber of Commerce. Most residents didn't bother attending, but as newcomers Linda and Russell found the talks helpful.

Only about thirty people were present. Sally Claus, the border guard, and Henry Pratt, the chief of police, opened with a Samhain debriefing. Then the procedures for reserving vacation spots, school pickup, sending mail, and the like were discussed. Volunteers with at least five years of PV residency were wanted for the Thanksgiving and Winter Festivals. The main PV access road was now going to be guarded by extra police, as unhoused dayworkers had been sneaking into the Labyrinth and setting up camps instead of going home at night. In addition, the stop sign on Maple Street had been defaced on Samhain night. They had identifying footage, but preferred the culprit surrender first. Punishment would be community service. Finally, they announced that two babies had been born this month, both healthy girls and welcome additions to Plymouth Valley.

• • •

After her shift at PV Hospital the following week, Linda stayed late again. Chernin never replied to her question, but Fielding did:

Hi, Linda!

So good to hear from you. Have you picked up golf? I hope not! Anyway, life here is deplorable and your patients miss you. I do, too.

Regarding idiopathic leukemia, I've never heard of it. It sounds more like a legal term than a medical one. Research institutes and hospitals have lately lost access to Med-Nex, which is where I'd be able to find your answers for you. But like my old friend Joseph Mitchell, I had some insomnia the other night and did some extra research. There was a lawsuit pending against BetterWorld by the European Chemicals Agency for its role in causing Waldenstrom's Macroglobulinemia as a result of Omnium degradation. In labs, the reaction between GREEN and Omnium is clean. But when GREEN attaches to reactive substrates like chlorine, it could potentially release an unstable benzene ring and PERC in the waste (they call it sludge?!). If you remember your organic chemistry, those can be highly oncogenic. I'd hoped to find more about this condition internationally, given Omnium's mostly made and broken back down in Asia, but those databases are locked down. What I did find is that there was also a case against BetterWorld and the government of the Republic of Ireland, likewise claiming the Omnium mill there caused blood diseases and birth defects. It was dropped a few years ago, with the republic receiving north of three trillion dollars in damages.

Zovolotecan—As you know, it's a chemotherapeutic agent, and could make sense for treatment of either a leukemia or an aplastic anemia, though it's a very old drug. The new class is much better and has less side effects. Whenever a young patient has an aggressive disease like this, marrow transplants and radiation are also indicated.

Would be great if we could get the consortium of universities back up and running. At the risk of sounding like a conspiracy theorist, it's very convenient none of us can talk to each other, but these giant corporations mine every bit of data we surrender. For all we know idiopathic leukemia isn't rare at all.

As for me, I'm fine. I'm down to working only two days a week, as I get tired. I enjoyed doing this sleuthing for you, as lately my mind has not been as sharp as I'd like and this mystery acted as a whetstone. In that light, take my findings with a tablespoon of salt. I have become forgetful, and this letter took me longer than it should have to write. I hope we meet again, Linda Farmer-Bowen. I have always found you to be an impressive person.

Anyway, consider the above the ravings of an under-slept old friend who misses you quite a bit.

Sincerely,
Carole Fielding, MD, MPH

Linda read the letter more than once. The first time, she couldn't focus. Fielding had been good to her. Like a parent, in many ways. It was hard to imagine the woman in a sickbed. In the entire time Linda'd known her, she'd taken every lunch break standing up.

What should she do? Should she fly out? Would she be allowed to leave PV for such a reason? Fielding had a daughter who lived with her. She was cared for. And Linda'd seen plenty of death. She didn't think she could handle losing one more person she loved. Still, she shot off an email to Leticia, the receptionist: *Let me know when things are going south with Doc Fielding. Please.*

Then she closed those feelings away. Moved on.

She looked up idiopathic leukemia again but found no cases in PV's system. She looked up leukemia, non-Hodgkin's lymphoma, and

Waldenstrom's. Those weren't present, either. How was it possible that not a single resident in any of BetterWorld's eighteen company towns had been diagnosed with blood cancer? She printed Fielding's email and handed it to Russell that night.

"Does this make any sense to you?"

He spent about ten minutes reading it over, which was a long time for Russell. As he read, he paled, eyes blinking.

"What do you think?"

"There's no way Omnium makes people sick. I like Fielding, but she was always a conspiracy theorist. And there's no PERC. Tetrachloroethene was outlawed in the United Colonies decades ago."

"I know," Linda said. "And I know neither Omnium nor GREEN has those chemical components. But maybe she's right. Maybe in the presence of chlorine, like you might find in a landfill, something different happens."

"Those disposal sites are clean," he said, handing the paper back. "And we definitely paid off Ireland, but that's because their standards on causality are so different. You don't have to prove anything. It wasn't worth the court fight. Easier to pay them off. You know she's sick, Linda. Stage four lung cancer. I hate to say this, but that tumor might have traveled to her brain."

Linda looked down. Tears came.

"Oh, honey," Russell said. He hugged her.

Her voice came out muffled. "I know. The brain is usually the first place it travels. I hope that isn't what this is. But then again, I do hope. Because either way, this is a very upsetting letter."

"Tell you what. Let me have a look. I'm already researching idiopathic leukemia for you. I can poke around a little on this biochemistry stuff, too."

"Thanks," she said. "And sorry to be laying this at your feet."

"Don't be sorry. We'll both feel better once we have the numbers. Then you can tell Fielding to receive a kick in the balls from me."

CHAPTER 5: Plymouth Valley Case Study: Hollow

The events leading up to the catastrophic disaster in Plymouth Valley are indicative of a culture in decline. Imagine the Mayans upon year thirty of drought. Their people were starving in the streets, and their science had no explanation for it. They turned to their gods. We can see this throughout the mini ice age when Rome and the Incas finally collapsed. We can also see it toward the mid-to-late twenty-first century.

What's interesting about the Plymouth Valley Hollow movement is that its birth was contemporaneous with like movements throughout company towns across the globe. These started as pseudoscientific ideological clubs—a source of bonding and civic pride and an occasional tax dodge. Over time, religious elements burgeoned.

—From THE FALL OF THE ANTHROPOCENE, by Jin Hyun, Seoul National University Press, 2093.

Giving Thanks

The Tuesday before Thanksgiving, Linda's front bell rang. She opened it to a young, pimpled man in a PV police uniform. He was familiar. Maybe she'd seen him at the Samhain festival, or perhaps he'd spoken at the Chamber of Commerce meeting.

"Mrs. Farmer-Bowen?" he asked. His voice was deep for someone so young.

"Hi! Do I know you?"

"Cyrus Galani. Most people do. I grew up here, so. But yes, we did meet a few months back."

"When was that?" she asked, leaning into the doorway. "I know you, but I can't place it."

"You needed a ride," he said. "You were feeling poorly."

"The night I was with Gal Parker! That was you!"

"Awful night," he said.

"Yes," she agreed. She didn't often get to talk about Gal Parker. Though this town could be incredibly gossipy, Gal and her kids were off limits. It was as if they found the memory of the whole event too painful to contemplate. Even blunt Rachel had closed the lid on all conversation relating to Gal. *Woman, you gotta shut up about this. It's too sad. I can't take it* had been her exact words.

"Can I ask you a question about that night?" Linda asked.

"Of course."

"Did you have any idea she might start that fire?"

"Absolutely not," he said with wide-eyed sincerity.

"Me neither," Linda said. "I feel a little dumb every time I remember that car ride. That whole night."

Cyrus said nothing, probably because he was a wet-behind-the-ears kid unequipped to handle a middle-aged woman's emotions. Linda laughed at herself. "Can I get you something? Tea? My housekeeper made a sourdough. I'd take credit but who'd believe me? They're impossible to get right."

"No, thank you. I'm here on business."

She waited, thinking he was probably making the rounds, asking for volunteers. Assembling the race route and banquet tables for Thanksgiving was probably a lot of work.

"You heard about the stop sign that got smashed?"

Linda puffed air into her cheeks. Not an auspicious question.

He produced his device and handed it to her. On-screen, she saw a still photo of Josie wailing on a stop sign with what looked like a flour-stuffed sock while her crew of about twenty kids watched.

"This is your daughter?" Galani asked.

Linda had been taught from a young age, by a town full of people who did a lot of illegal drugs, to never admit to anything, and to always get a lawyer. "Hmm," she answered. "Is that a flour sock?"

"I don't know," Cyrus said. "What's a flour sock?"

It's when you wet flour inside a tube sock and swing it like a weapon, she might have said. *For Halloween pranks. Not exactly wholesome, but a far cry from a knife or gun.* "I don't know," she said. "I saw one on a screenie one time."

Cyrus pointed at the inside-out number fourteen on her shirt. "This is your daughter, Josie Farmer-Bowen."

"Can you actually break a sign with a flour sock?" she asked. "That's what this is about, right? The sign?"

"She defaced it," he said. "This is Josie?"

"Oh," she said, squinting. "I can't tell. I hope not!"

Cyrus gave her a dirty look. "It *is* her. The department agreed that her punishment is community service. She'll set chairs up all day on Thanksgiving."

Linda didn't know what to say to that.

"She reports to the station first thing in the morning. She can appeal this decision on the basis of her innocence, but to do so, she needs to report to the department or face charges of contempt."

Cyrus handed Linda a short blue piece of paper. *Summons*, it read along the top. She took it from him, flashed back to when she'd first met him in an empty parking lot. Gal had gotten in first, lying flat on the seat and sliding herself over on her stomach like a weirdo. Linda had gone next, holding fast to the side as she'd lowered down, to keep from falling. He'd nodded ever so briefly, then looked straight ahead as if to say: *Don't worry. Your level of drunkenness is none of my business.*

"I'm sorry," she said. "I don't know what to say. You've caught me off guard."

"They all go through this," he said.

"Rebellion?" she asked.

"No. They all hate Plymouth Valley. I went through it, too, and not very long ago. But they get over it."

"I don't think she hates it here," Linda said. "She's on the soccer team and she gets straight As. She's not a troublemaker. She doesn't have dark-enough feelings to make trouble."

He fiddled with his device and started playing something on the screen: the footage of the stop sign attack. "Look at this."

Linda's center of gravity went low. She'd seen Josie have tantrums as a kid. Seen her throw ceramic dolls, mash wet paintbrushes against her own artwork because it wasn't perfect, *lose it* right before a big soccer game, punching pillows in her room to relieve the tension. But that had always been contained and at home. Outside, she'd always been charming, cheerful—a delight.

In the video, Josie was screaming, whaling on the sign, like something savage.

• • •

"Oh, honeys," Daniella Bennett whispered to her stepkids an hour later. "You're safe now."

The stepkids had just flown back from visiting their mother, who lived in Denver. There'd been a shooting at the restaurant where they'd gotten dinner. They'd seen their first dead body. Linda listened from the parlor while Daniella helped them unpack upstairs. They were in their late teens and early twenties and Linda was surprised by how patient her friend sounded. She wouldn't have assumed that. Daniella could be mercenary. It was nice to overhear this soft side.

The altar at the top of the hall was filled with six powder blue caladrius eggs that emitted a light sulfuric scent.

Eventually, Daniella came down the grand stairs, gathered Linda, and brought her into her private study.

"I'm sorry they witnessed that," Linda said.

Daniella flopped into her red velvet fainting couch, raised her arm over her forehead. "They're wrecks. I had to call Chernin for sedatives. It's lucky he's so loose with them. By the time I was their age, I was working twenty-hour days as a hostess at a social club. Not much surprised me. You see many dead bodies as a kid?"

Something about the very tackiness of this office made it easy to relax. Linda melted into the sofa, legs spread. "Between the junkies and the climate refugees, floaters were always washing up along the Hudson."

"We were grown-ups," Daniella said. "We don't cry unless we're physically hurt."

"Or so traumatized we no longer have access to our feelings, so when bad things happen our first reaction is to say it's no big deal and get mad at people who try to make it a big deal."

Daniella flipped Linda the bird. "My shrink tells me I resent the better life I'm giving them. Apparently, every time I'm disappointed they aren't tougher and more resilient, it's really my own resentment. I'm perpetuating a cycle of trauma. Or perpetrating. Let's say perpetrating. I prefer that spoonerism. Do you resent your children's better lives?" she asked.

Linda guffawed. "Absolutely!"

Daniella cracked a smile. "These PV shrinks are messed up. They raise children who bite and draw on walls, and I'm supposed to take their advice? Then they're surprised when a whole generation turns out like Keith Parson."

"Can't you get a shrink from outside?" Linda asked.

Daniella shook her head. "No money to pay them."

"You don't have anything tucked away?"

"Lloyd does. But I've got no idea where."

It was an insight into Daniella's marriage that she hadn't expected. She'd assumed, given how in love they seemed, that relations between them were equal. "Oh. That's unfortunate."

"My kids are turning soft," Daniella said.

"You can't judge that yet. They're not done cooking."

"Hollow's supposed to address it a little bit. The competitions and maze and race—it's survival-of-the-fittest role-play. But I don't know," Daniella said.

"We could give them combat lessons," Linda joked.

Daniella laughed. "Can you imagine Hip trying to slug someone? That fey thing would hurt himself!"

Linda squirmed. It never paid to disagree with Daniella. Still, it was a shitty thing to say. "It's still better than New York. They weren't allowed outside the apartment at night. Josie played soccer with a particulate filter because of the pollution. With bomb threats and strikes, I had to keep them home from school half the time. There's a reason you never see them on bicycles—that I have to drive them to school. They can't ride. New York didn't make them street tough, because I never let them out. You could say both places are cages. The scenery here's better."

"That's why I like talking to you," Daniella said. "Perspective. You're so smart, Linda!" This was Daniella's superpower. Sometimes she didn't have time, or she wasn't in the mood. But sometimes, like then, her light of favor shone, and despite the way she'd insulted Hip just seconds before, her praise still gave Linda an adrenaline rush.

"I try."

Daniella indicated the kids on the second or third floor by pointing her chin. "It would be more rewarding if they didn't hate me. They think I took their mother's spot. But their mother was useless to Lloyd. A total liability."

"Kids are dummies," Linda said, though she felt a pang of sympathy for wife number one.

Daniella laughed.

"Want to see the pamphlet?" Linda opened her folder, passed it to Daniella.

The pamphlet Anouk had composed to attract more PVE locals to the clinic was tone deaf. It bore the same cover as the Plymouth Valley Resident Guide: a bunch of kids colored in with crayon. Inside, in all different colors and kid-like writing, it read: *The best health care in the world! We're a one-stop shop! Our staff is second to none! Come, let us help you!*

"It's not actually a one-stop shop," Linda said. "I already had to outsource a kid last week because we don't have an ortho. And even if my patient with the blood cancer comes back, I won't be able to treat him. I won't have access to the drug printers."

"It *will* be true," Daniella said.

Linda made a face.

Daniella laughed. "Let Anouk have her day. It's a lovely pamphlet and the thing to do is hand it out and get more patients so we get more funding for all the things you want. The thing to do is to say thank you. She's massaged her father's ego all year to keep this thing going. And let me tell you, Jack's no dreamboat, either. If he could figure a way to embezzle it, every clinic dime would go to a pool in his backyard."

"Jack's that bad?" Linda asked.

"Do you get a *good* vibe?" Daniella asked back.

"No. Not once have I gotten a good vibe. I still have nightmares about our pre-interview. He was so creepy. And what was that all about with the absinthe? Did he really sneak that into Rachel's drink?"

"Not him. He's too smart for that. I'm sure he called in a favor and put someone else up to it. Parson's getting old. Anouk and Keith aren't suited to lead when he's gone. There's a vacuum. CEO, chairman, and the rest of the board have to come from in-house. Hollow makes our town just too idiosyncratic to accept a transfer from any other settlement. Lloyd's ready to lead. But he needs reliable people under him.

"Before me, Lloyd was on a road to nowhere. I got him where he's at. With Lloyd moving to chairman and CEO opening up, I suggested Rachel. She's my candidate. Lloyd trusts me. I got his backing. Anouk's behind me, too. But Jack also wants the CEO job. There's a faction that supports him. They love him. What's to love? I think it's daddy issues. He wants to double down on Hollow, close this place like a tomb. He's not a believer like the Parson family, who started Hollow. He just understands that it's a good way to control people. He's been Parson's earworm, telling him that choosing Rachel betrays the principles of Hollow. He's good at getting hooks into people. The absinthe—he wanted to get her publicly drunk. He plays dirty."

"That's cutthroat," Linda said.

Daniella leaned forward. Lowered her voice. There was anger there. "She was dry for years until they started working together. He's the one who got her back boozing. And it's even dirtier than that. He was sneaking it into her smoothies. By the time she was openly drinking, it had been months. Nobody could do anything about it."

"Jesus Christ," Linda said. "No wonder Kai's so worked up."

"She's been good all month—since Samhain. Have you noticed? We're hoping it sticks."

"I'm glad to hear it, but Jack should be in jail."

"Ruining a person isn't illegal, unfortunately."

It's a specific and grave sin to mess with someone's sobriety. Tears swelled in Linda's eyes. Daniella saw and slowly shook her head, her gaze steely.

"Right, I forgot," Linda said, clearing her eyes. "No crying. See? I'm not crying."

"Good." Daniella sat back, luxuriated like a pinup girl on her fainting couch, serious conversation over. "Anyway, stop making me explain things to you. I know what I'm doing. Take the pamphlets. Let Anouk put her name on something. She's earned it."

"I will. You're right," Linda said, still in shock.

"One-stop shop is phase two," Daniella said.

"Done," Linda agreed, standing.

"And keep some compassion for Anouk. She's between a king and a tyrant."

"Okay. And thanks for everything," Linda said. "I'm not sure I ever did thank you properly, but you've really saved me in this town."

"Aw," she said. "You're so sweet. See you at the fun run. Bring your serious sneakers, because these people do *not* play."

• • •

That night, Linda knocked on Josie's door.

"What?" Josie asked on the third knock.

Linda found her sitting at her desk. She had no screen lit, no earphones inserted, no books opened. She was looking at the dull wood. The obvious dawned on Linda: her daughter was depressed. It was a shock. She hadn't imagined Josie constitutionally capable of depression.

"Plans tonight?" Linda sat on the bed Esperanza had made with tight, hotel-like efficiency. She'd pregamed this conversation, decided in her mind what she wanted to say: *Lower your profile. Get away from these kids. All you have to do is survive the next two and a half more years and you're in BW University—a free ride!*

Upon seeing Josie, she decided not to say any of that.

Her daughter stayed in her desk chair, showing Linda her profile. Her room was large, with wood floors. Her half-filled dresser was equipped to store more than she owned, and upon her vanity were bottles of perfume and sundry makeup that she'd acquired over the years but had outgrown. She hadn't culled anything from the move, had simply packed and unpacked with no organization.

"Well?" Linda asked.

"I dunno," Josie answered.

"You go out a lot, and I never know where you go," Linda said.

Josie's strong, broad shoulders rose close to her ears, then dropped in a shrug.

"I figured: It's so safe here. What could I have to worry about? Plus, I didn't want to salt your game. It's hard being new, isn't it?"

"No," Josie said, soft.

"That's true. It's hard for some people. But you're so good at making friends. People love you."

Josie's shoulders went up again, this time staying there. When she

was little, Josie'd had a lithe, graceful body. And then puberty
she thickened. Linda had mourned that swanlike neck, thos
wheels and backflips. But she'd come to understand that the ch
was natural. Desirable, despite what the billboards tell you. This
a young woman, heading toward full bloom.

"Could you turn around and look at me?" Linda asked.

Josie turned. Her eyes were red.

"Oh, honey. What is it?"

Her daughter seemed surprised by the question, and Linda pointed. "You've been crying."

"Oh."

Not for the first time, Linda asked, "Please. Tell me what's going on with you."

Josie's eyes watered. More tears fell. She did that thing kids do, where all the emotions come to the front, and she was afraid to talk, lest the exhalation of breath break a dam inside her.

"Come here."

Josie shook her head, stayed wiping her eyes, her body tense and pent up.

"Can't you tell me?" Linda asked. She had so many questions, but they all came to this: *Don't you see this is better than back home? What's happening to you?*

"It's nothing," Josie said. "Just long days. There's so much work."

"Yeah?" Linda asked. This was not the answer she'd expected. "How much?"

"I have to catch up. Everybody's already taken these college classes in middle school. Then they take them again in high school. But I'm taking them for the first time. It's four or five hours of homework a night."

"God, that's too much," Linda said. "Just get Bs."

"But I have to get As!" Josie answered. "I can't be remediated. Those classes are for the loser kids."

"Well, not *losers*," Linda said. "Hip's not in advanced math or history."

"Then I guess he better marry Cathy, because he's on the wrong track for the honors program at BWU. He won't get a company job."

"I don't think it works exactly like that. But even if it does, is living on the outside so bad?"

Josie looked at her with horror.

"Okay, it's bad. Because you want a company job, and you want to live in a town like Plymouth Valley. Is that what I'm hearing?"

Josie looked at her with exasperation. "I don't *want* it! I have to. There's nothing outside. No place to go except a company."

Linda spoke softly. "You're a competent person. You could find places that are still healthy, where the air's still clean. They do exist. Out of anyone, you could make that work."

"You couldn't," Josie said.

Heat rose along Linda's neck. "True."

"You dipped out like Kings was on fire."

"We did, didn't we?" she answered. "I thought this was the best option."

They were facing one another. Linda on the bed, Josie in her chair. She was taller than Linda, and more robust. The fact of your child's ascendance is surprising, long after it's begun.

"Is that why you're so angry?" she asked.

Josie grimaced in obvious anger. "I'm not angry."

"Okay. Do you ever talk to Angela?" Angela was Josie's best friend from home.

"The signal's crap. You know that."

"I'll bet you miss her."

"No," Josie answered. "She's not going anywhere. I'll probably never see her again."

"What about these new friends?"

"They're not friends. We share air."

Out of ways to lead into this delicately, Linda took Josie's chin in her hand. Josie tugged back and out of her grasp. "A police officer came to the house today."

Josie crossed her arms.

"He showed me a video of you tearing up a street sign. You weren't yourself, Josie."

Josie stayed looking down.

"Officer Galani wants you to go to the department on Thanksgiving and set up chairs as community service."

"Oh," Josie said. "Maybe that's why no one's talking to me lately."

"I don't follow. Your friends aren't talking to you?"

She was locked tight, arms crossed and looking away. Linda was reminded of the monkeys that speak, hear, and see no evil. Linda'd always thought the monkeys meant that if you didn't engage the evil, it didn't exist. It occurred to her for the first time that the opposite was true. It meant evil was everywhere. Inescapable.

"Did they put you up to it? They're afraid you'll tell on them?"

"No. They were fine with what I did. But they probably don't like that I got caught. People around here don't like trouble. They don't like being friends with anyone in trouble."

Linda felt sad to hear that. She'd wanted to believe it had been someone else's idea. "How can they not be talking to you? You've been going out, haven't you? I know you got a ride home today."

"It doesn't mean they talk to me."

"Why else would they give you a ride or hang out with you if you weren't getting along?"

"They're polite, Mom. It's their thing."

"That sounds more complicated than it ought to be."

Josie stayed looking at the floor. "You know Jeanette with the different-colored eyes—one's blue and one's brown?"

"I do." Jeanette was striking, refined, always had some hot companion's arm wrapped around her.

"She said she like-liked me," Josie said. "On Samhain."

Like-like. So, this expression was still used. "Did you like-like her back?" Linda asked.

Josie shrugged. "I said I did. I've never had somebody. The rest of them have all dated somebody. They've done . . . more."

Linda listened. Wanted so much to offer advice. "So, were you a couple?"

"I *thought* so," Josie said, "but it was a joke. She was only joking."

Linda felt the contents of her stomach bubble. Oh, the humiliation of the fake ask-out. "Then what happened?"

"She laughed about it. They all did. So, I laughed."

Linda wanted to tell her daughter to punch their dumb goddamned faces. As if reading her mind, Josie added, "It's that or be alone."

"Can't you hang out with other kids?"

Josie sneered. It was ugly, and it made Linda sad. "They're losers. They get teased so bad. You sit alone, you get teased. You sit with the wrong group, you get teased. I'm in with the *right* group. All I have to do is make it two and a half more years here, and I can leave, Mom. I'm at BWU and fuck them."

"Yeah," Linda said, tears coming to her eyes. "What about Hip? Does he get teased?"

"He would, but he's with Cathy and she's untouchable."

"Right," Linda said. "Because of her parents. You feel pretty stuck, don't you?"

Josie shrugged, like Linda had no idea. Like she was some kind of moronic alien life-form. "I feel stuck, too," Linda said, the words surprising her as they came out.

"You do?"

"It's so stifling," Linda said. *Stifling*. She'd thought the word, but she'd never allowed herself to consider it. She'd pushed it down like a weighted floater in the Hudson River.

"You feel trapped, too?" Josie asked with surprise.

"I'm not myself here. I'm this pleaser . . ." Linda said, realizing for the first time that what she was saying was how she really felt. It had been like a pill stuck in her throat for months, unwilling to dissolve. "I don't say what I think. I just agree . . . I'm not even sure I like the person I'm becoming."

"So?" Josie asked.

Something was happening, here. Linda could feel a wall in Josie coming down. She wanted very much to say the right thing.

"So, I don't know," Linda said. "You're not alone."

"I am, though," Josie said. "Can you go away?"

• • •

That Wednesday was a half day. Linda met Russell at his office for the department party.

Each staff member brought a plus-one, so there were twenty people in all. Streamers and paper caladrius sat on desks or hung from ceilings. Trim, young dayworkers with their hair pulled back passed hors d'oeuvres. Linda had been seeing the same crowd for so long that these fresh faces felt new, like a date night.

"Delicious cocktails," Russell said.

"But also fussy. Like a tuxedo shirt with ruffles," Linda answered.

"Or a bonsai plant."

"I hate bonsai plants. I mean, what the hell?"

"I love them. I mean, what the hell?" Russell said, which was funny but also true. He loved bonsai plants; she found them horrifically controlled.

An hour in, with the help of his assistant, Heinrich climbed up onto the desk outside his office and made a speech about what a great job they were all doing defending the company. Their sister town was making great progress on another new synthetic that was set to launch the next year. Science was leading the way, and there was no stopping it. "In Plymouth Valley we trust!" he cried. Then everyone toasted with their absinthe-dipped pisco sours.

Linda pointed out the altar to Russell, upon which someone had broken raw eggs, so they were exposed and rotting. The ventilation was so efficient that they were hard to smell. "What and why?" she asked.

He kissed the back of her hair. "Let's enjoy the mystery."

She went over to the altar, inspected the three eggs. In each, the clear albumin had congealed. Green mold ran in veiny lines all through. Words were scratched into the wood over which the eggs rested:

Beware the Sacrifice

Russell joined her, his arm around her waist. "If we ask someone, they'll tell us it's nothing," she said. "Just for fun."

With hesitation, he stated like a question: "Maybe it is nothing? Or at least, not our problem?"

The party, though cocktails and not dinner, lasted four hours. The twentysomething assistant got happy-drunk, a middle-aged lady fell asleep at her own desk, and someone's wife puked, which Linda discovered because she entered the bathroom when it happened.

Linda was washing her hands, thinking that the stalls there were the same size as the ones at Sluggs, where she'd taken Russell so many years before. They'd been so young back then. In old pictures, their faces looked as unformed as dough.

She heard gagging. She bent down, saw kitten heels pointed at the toilet. "Are you sick?"

More gagging.

"Can I get you some water?"

"I'm totally okay!" a cheerful voice answered.

Linda came out. The woman did, too. Then Linda laughed. "It's you!"

It was Tania Janssen, the woman from the bakery, who'd come to the PV Hospital with her baby after the fire, worried the child had cancer.

Linda went to the sink, poured water into one of the glasses against the backsplash, and handed it to her. Tania swished and spit. Water ricocheted. Linda pretended not to notice that it had landed on her hand and blue silk party dress that she'd only just gotten from the Fabric Collective.

"Is everything okay?"

Tania shrugged. "I've got a PhD in this stuff, but I gave it up when I got pregnant. I never liked the work. Numbers. Who cares! I get so bored at places like this. These nights never end. You'd think we could play cards or go for a walk or something. Maleek usually keeps me home. I'm an indoor cat."

Linda nodded with understanding. "It's too much booze and it's bad getting drunk but it's worse building the tolerance and getting used to it."

Tania smirked. "The baby's fine, by the way. My mom's watching her. And I'm not worried she'll be sick. At least not this year."

"This year?"

"The Parkers already got sick this year," she said. "After the fire, I thought they might die, so then it would have been some other kids forced to hold black ribbons at the Winter Festival. But they didn't die."

"What?"

Tania took the glass, flung it inside the stall, where it shattered against the seat. Glass projectiled back, slamming Linda's legs without breaking skin.

It felt surreal. Impossible. "What the hell are you saying? Why did you do that?"

"Oh, that's right, you're new," Tania answered. "Don't worry. Someone always cleans it up." Then she popped a breath mint and walked with drunken precision back into the bustling party.

Linda stayed a minute in the solitary bathroom. She didn't dry her legs. Drips ran down. The wash sinks were three side by side. A mirror along the wall traversed their expanse. She saw herself. A pretty woman in blue silk and done hair whose grays she'd recently dyed back to brown. A rich woman, who'd lost weight but nonetheless grown soft. Linda could see this in her own expression, which had lost all certainty.

She headed back out to the party, opening the door to laughter and music. She didn't hear it. She was outside it all, watching open mouths and red lips and glinting teeth. People with glasses of imported wine toasted rotting eggs on an altar for a god she did not know. She saw her husband among his friends, looking happy and accepted, his eyes following every movement, every word issued, in what appeared to her like submission.

• • •

At first light Thanksgiving morning, Linda drove Josie to the police department.

"Next time you beat up a stop sign on Samhain, I guess you wear a mask," Linda said.

Instead of chuckling or rolling her eyes, Josie started crying. Lonely crying, where just her eyes were wet and she was trying her best to hold it in. Linda pulled into the police department lot, put the car in park, and waved her hands at the outside—the police department, Plymouth Valley, the nice houses and shops, the pleasant people. "None of this is as important as you are. You know that, don't you?"

Josie's voice sounded low and old. "What does that even mean?"

"I mean, relax. Don't take this all so seriously."

"That's what I thought you meant," Josie answered, disappointed.

She'd failed to answer the question correctly. But Josie didn't explain. Instead, she got out of the car, her broad back hunched.

It took Linda a second—sometimes the right thing needs to percolate before it becomes apparent—then she followed Josie inside. She found Officer Galani standing with Josie and two other kids who looked to be in their late teens. A skeleton crew was working reception and the desks in the back. Thanksgiving decorations had been tacked to the walls: folded tissue paper caladrius ornaments, a host of white feathers stuck into an apple on the altar.

"Great!" Galani called. "We're all here. Today's going to be fun. So many chairs to arrange!" he announced with mock enthusiasm—the way everybody talks to teenagers, like they're hip to the fact that kids hate adults, which is what makes the power structure so especially funny. The kids looked at their running shoes, glancing occasionally at one another.

Linda's worries eased. Okay, nobody was going to question Josie about what had happened. She wasn't going to get in extra trouble, or need a lawyer, or get yelled at. In fact, this kind of punishment made sense. It would give her a sense of closure and community, without belaboring the crime. Kids get in trouble. They do dumb things.

"We're good, Mom. She's in good hands," Cyrus said.

Linda moved to kiss Josie's cheek. Josie backed up to avoid her.

"Call me if anything comes up. I'm always here."

• • •

About an hour later, the remaining Farmer-Bowens were dressed and ready to go in new sneakers and warm, breathable jackets. Hip took the back of the car. "Did you know that corporations have the same rights as human beings?" he asked.

"Yeah," Linda and Russell both answered.

"Cathy's dad says corporations are more trustworthy to work for the common good than regular people."

"They probably are," Russell said, though he wasn't paying attention. He was following a text chain that had been going around his office, half work related, half fun.

"Bee Ess," Linda said. "A corporation marketed Glamp to everybody without health insurance on the East Coast."

"Cathy's dad says they do bad things because everybody does bad things, but the sum value is positive. Through the lens of history, the sum value's all that matters."

"I love Lloyd Bennet, but that man needs to get out more if he really believes that," Linda said. They were a kilometer from the race and already parking was limited.

"Do you think Josie'll be able to come later?" Russell asked.

"No idea. But she's got her device. She'll let us know. Did you talk to her?" She'd asked Russell to check in with Josie about what had happened with the stop sign and had reminded him twice.

"Hm?"

"Did you talk to her?"

"I've been getting home too late. Not yet."

She pulled into the Caladrius Parking Lot, and the three of them walked toward the crowded starting line for the race. Halfway inside the park, Hip found Cathy in a pretty wool cloak and tennis shoes, an inauspicious combination for a race. Linda expected they'd walk the whole thing, chatting about existence, philosophy, and the great corporation.

Russell found his crew: Heinrich, Lloyd, and the rest. Linda joined Daniella and Rachel up closer to the start line.

"I'm just glad we'll have less of these fuckers running around, eating my garbage," Rachel said, low. True to Daniella's word, she appeared vigorous and sober. The lines Linda'd gotten used to seeing under her eyes were gone. She looked ten years younger.

The Plymouth Valley Anthem, a song to the tune of "The Merry-Go-Round Broke Down," began to play. "I haven't done this in years," Linda said.

"Don't worry. Nobody here's looking to break a record," Daniella said.

The crowd of about 3,500 jogged in place and stretched hips, thighs, and calves. At least a hundred penned-in caladrius clogged the podium, bumping around and gnawing the inedible wood stage. Dumb little monsters.

"You know, I saw this once before at Anouk's house—caladrius penned together. But I thought they were solitary. I was told if they're kept together," Linda said, "they'll fight."

"It's not indiscriminate. Discriminatory? They gang up and pick on one," Daniella answered.

"It's community building," Rachel joked.

"Plymouth Valley," Anouk called from the podium. "We're here today to celebrate community. Let's all give each other a sign of goodwill and peace."

The crowd became a sea of gratitude prayer hands. Linda bowed to the person closest to her. The call was "May the wind be at your back," and its response was "May you never come in last."

This was not done with amused smiles. It was serious.

A man to Linda's left offered his hand. She shook it, noticing only then that it was Percy Khoury. He wasn't wild eyed like he'd been at the hospital and the soccer sidelines. Now, he appeared sluggish. She suspected lithium. "May the wind be at your back," she said.

His eyes flashed with recognition, and she may have been wrong, but she thought she saw kinship there, too. "Beware the Great White," he mumbled.

"What?" she asked.

But he'd turned to Amir Nassar. "Never come in last," he mumbled, back on script.

Up ahead, Kai Johnson left the group of men he was with, including Russell and Jack, and walked back to Rachel. "Jack's up to something. Run hard. Don't stop. Make it a personal best," he told her.

"I've got CEO in the bag. You worry too much," she answered. Then she kissed him. They held one another. It warmed Linda's heart.

"And now!" Anouk announced: "The Beltane King will do the honors."

Keith Parson emerged from behind his mother, his costume that same skintight black jumpsuit, only he'd removed the mask. His movements were loose, like a cartoon jester's, and she remembered his shamble back in the tunnels.

"On your mark." He didn't shout, but his deep voice carried. "Get set." His eyes surveyed the crowd. Linda felt her shoulder with her hand. It had ached for days after pushing past him. His eyes found her. They stayed on her. They weren't happy.

"Go!" he shouted.

It took a few moments before there was room to move. They were separated by heats, each wearing chips that activated once they crossed the starting line, for an exact race time. Suddenly, there was room. The three of them were jogging. Slow, at first. Anouk waved as they passed and they waved and hooted back. The road opened. Daniella and Rachel shot out. Linda sprinted to keep up.

Uh, oh.

Daniella and Rachel weren't an anomaly. Everybody was running fast. Top speed. Didn't they know this was a 5K? Were they really going to hold this pace for the entire race?

Linda panted, pushed herself. Her lungs burned. It wasn't fun. It was hard. They passed the one-kilometer mark, where she noticed the map. It looked a lot like the Labyrinth below—turns upon turns that made a perimeter.

The sound of thousands of runners, shoes slapping, is a mix between rain and applause. You feel it coming up from the road and through you. The sound drowned under her heartbeat, her panting breath.

Going south, they passed the two-kilometer mark. Vaguely, she recognized Gal's side of town, but this knowledge went nowhere, because all conscious thought was this: *I can't do this. I can't keep up.*

They rounded a corner. Her knee twinged. Her untested sneakers pinched. *Guys, won't you slow down?* she wanted to ask. *Isn't the point of this to do it together, not to come in first?* But probably, like most things around there, she had that wrong. The point was the performance: to come in first, to show strength, or not run the race at all.

Winding, winding. They approached Gal's house. It had been repaired, the back half rebuilt and painted fresh. A hatchback was parked in the driveway. Linda felt her scalp recede over her skull, her hot limbs break into goose bumps: that was Gal's car from the lot that night of the fire. Was she home so soon from the hospital?

"Have either of you visited Gal since the fire?" Linda blurted, loud and for everyone around them to hear.

"I've been busy opening a clinic," Daniella answered.

"Right." She knew they wanted her to stop talking about Gal. They'd both made this clear. But a bad thing had happened and for reasons she could not fathom, that thing had gone unresolved. Had Gal really set her own house on fire just for spite? Were her children okay in Palo Alto? Was she ill? If so, should she be allowed out in the world, where she might have more children and commit the same crime twice?

This worry inside her had been a low-level noise for a long time. She was pretending everything was fine, happy as could be, but she wasn't sleeping. She wasn't eating. This had occurred to her only when she'd talked with Josie about the street sign. When she'd admitted that she wasn't sure she liked herself around these women. An agreeable milksop. Jack Lust's wife, Colette, part 2. "I ask because I've been doing research on idiopathic leukemia. I want to make sure her kids are getting the proper treatment in Palo Alto."

"They have doctors in Palo Alto, moron," Rachel said.

"*Moron*'s strong," Linda panted. She could hardly put one foot ahead of the next. They were toward the end of the block, running north along the wall.

"I don't know why you worry about Gal Parker when your own daughter needs you," Daniella said. She wasn't panting. For her, this race was a ride on a slide.

"What?" Linda asked. Her voice broke with a high-pitched squeak.

"She vandalized PV property."

"No, she didn't!" Linda said, which was a stupid and untrue thing to say.

"Liar," Daniella said.

Linda'd always assumed the expression *knife in the back* was figurative. But right then, she felt a sharp and penetrating pain, as if she'd been stabbed from behind—from a place without eyes to anticipate.

"Linda's daughter's a thug," Rachel said, jokey and mean.

Daniella laughed. "But what's a thug, anyway?"

Linda stopped. She had no gas left in her tank. The other two slowed, but not much. Their red, adrenaline-fueled faces craned back as they ran.

"Don't come in last," Rachel called.

Then they were far ahead. In the distance, Linda heard Daniella crack a lighthearted joke, like everything was just fine, and no one was cruel.

Her eyes brimming, Linda tried to make her way to the side of the street. A man collided with her, knocking her down, then scrambling back up without a care for her, and running away at top speed. She was on her knees like a stone in a river. Racers passed all around. Trapped, she protected her head with her arms. Nobody stopped or offered help or even asked: *Are you okay?*

They were a monolith. A dead titan. She felt, suddenly, that she was underneath it. Couldn't possibly find a way out.

But she had to stand. She'd get hurt if she didn't. She'd come in last. And it was very, very important not to come in last, or you might get a black ribbon. You might get left in the tunnels at the Winter Festival. *Beware the Sacrifice.*

All these feet, coming at her. "Get out of my way!" an indignant voice screamed. She stayed on her knees and crawled, her hands getting stepped on, her stomach kicked with a hard foam sole. The pain shocked her with its bright intensity, radiating through her abdomen like a star. She kept going. And then, she was standing on the side, the race going by all fast and blurry—the polite and polished and pleasant in their beautiful exercise suits and their beautiful bodies. Palms bleeding, she wept.

Around the corner came Lloyd Bennett. Her heart lifted like helium. Friends. There was Russell! Even a block away, his group was loud talking, trying to appear impenetrable beneath their exhausted pants. They were coming.

"Russell!" she cried.

He jerked, recognizing her voice. She saw it. But her call had been soft, and this race was loud. He didn't look for her. He kept going. A bastardization of an old proverb occurred to her: *If you fall during a race and your husband doesn't see you, did it happen at all?*

Warm blood trickled down her knees. Signs showed the winding race path to the park three kilometers away. "Get out of the way!" someone shouted, though she wasn't in the way; she was on the side, not running.

Fuck it. She walked back in the direction she'd come. *Fuck this race.*

Even with the one-kilometer lead, most of the people she knew had beaten her to the finish line, including Hip and Cathy. Feeling meek, she stayed at a distance as the rest gathered to watch the last runners. A group pushed through the finish together, all in their eighties and seeming greatly relieved. Then a few more—Dr. Chernin rushed past, pushing Louis in a racing chair. Sweaty, eyes haunted, he didn't stop for another ten yards after the finish line.

"The last two!" Anouk shouted.

About twenty yards from the finish came an old man who had to be in his eighties, neck and neck with a heavyset young man no more than sixteen, who was limping, having fallen and sprained his ankle. It was goiter-sized and had bled through his white sock. People all around Linda were mesmerized. *Oh no,* someone beside her whispered. *Who let him get that fat?*

Someone else answered: *It's not right! It's not fair! He's too young!*

The old man approached the finish line. The boy was behind him, dead last with no chance of catching up. You could have heard a pin drop.

I can't watch. I can't bear it, someone whispered with such heartfelt pain that Linda felt pain, too.

At the last second, the old man stopped. The teen limped ahead, gasping in pain, his mouth gaping in surprise as he passed the man and finished the race. The audience cried out, laughing and cheering. The old man mugged for all of PV as he crossed the finish line. A kind of *Who, me? What an honor!*

"And the last of us shall be the first!" Anouk announced.

The old man climbed up the steps. She presented him with a medal on a black ribbon. "The honors!" she announced as she stepped out of the way, and Linda saw that on the podium was a butcher's block.

The old man showboated. He commanded the audience's attention, had them laughing as he pointed at each of the caladrius onstage and counted eeny-meeny-miney-moe, at last landing on the closest one. This he gruffly lifted, placed on the block under a neck strap, and slammed down an axe.

The crowd was so thick that Linda didn't see the bird lose its head. She only heard the cheers. "And as the last of us shall be first, we take and we receive, and we are grateful," the town, all of Plymouth Valley, replied, in unison.

Quickly, the crowd dispersed, venturing to their assigned tables. She moved slowly, feeling out of time, as a group of elementary school kids sang harvest songs about bounty, John Parson's great town, and the culling and hoarding of crops.

At last, she found her table. Daniella, ActHollow, and their spouses had taken a far end, and it was packed. Along the length of the table were Heinrich and Russell's work people. She bent down beside Russell. "Hi," she said, feeling meek and, for reasons she could not explain, ashamed.

"Oh, hi!" he said, pleased to find her. "How'd it go? Oh! No! What happened to your knees!"

She shook it off. If she explained, she might start crying. "There's no chair for me," she said, voice quivering.

"There's not?" he asked. "I'd have saved you one, but I assumed you were eating with your crew."

"But it's Thanksgiving."

He shrugged, sheepish. "There?" He pointed. At the opposite end of the table were four empty seats. "Do you want me to get up?" He was in midconversation, enjoying himself. Yes, of course she wanted him to get up. But not if she had to insist on it.

She headed to the empty seats, claimed one. Caladrius was served. It looked a lot like wild goose, the meat mostly brown and fatty. Her portion was a very long thigh and a thick breast, along with yams and spinach. She didn't lift her fork. She'd eaten caladrius a few times since arriving in this town and though the taste was fine, like goose, she'd never enjoyed the experience. You don't eat what you hate.

She sat by herself for a good twenty minutes, until Hip and Cathy joined her. The fourth seat was probably meant for Josie, who texted to say that she'd be setting up chairs at different parks all day and most of the evening, too.

Linda couldn't put her finger on the exact problem. There were so many inconsistencies. So many strange behaviors. But she *could* name the feeling: loneliness.

She spent the entirety of the meal trying not to cry. At the opposite end of the table were the members of ActHollow, who'd waved once, cheerful and pleasant, and then resumed their separate conversation. As she sat quiet in the din, she remembered Gal watching them that first night. A woman on the outside, looking in.

John Parson's Journey!

John Parson built a tunnel.

John Parson built a manse.

John Parson came to live with us

on this Labyrinth prance!

**Sung to the tune of "The Merry-Go-Round Broke Down"*

The Itch

When your mind isn't protecting you enough, your body takes over and shuts down. There'd been too much adrenaline. Too many stifled emotions, half-realized epiphanies, that had quietly lacerated her from inside. Too much ahead, she suspected, that would be much worse.

At home that Thanksgiving night Linda felt an overpowering heaviness. She did not undress, but collapsed into bed. In the calm, floating drift before sleep, it came to her that all of this was a game. The price of living here meant playing. She was expected to drop the subject of Gal Parker and move on with her life. She was expected to make the clinic look good and to raise her kids and to canoodle her husband. She was expected to continue being a member of ActHollow by doing exactly as told. She was expected to be the woman in the mirror—pretty, appropriate, and yielding.

For the sake of her family, for the sake of peace in her life, she wanted to be the kind of person who went along. But there was a monster underneath all this. An ugly thing that breathed and watched. A hungry thing.

Morning came in a blink. No dreams. No thoughts at all.

She left the house before anyone was awake. Despite the holiday, the clinic was open. She forgot to make small talk with Sally, to ask her what was new. Like a robot, Sally continued with the script despite the omission. She checked Linda's car like always, and told her, "Looks good, good-lookin'!"

Seven patients were scheduled. Linda gave up swallowing her

unease, or logic-ing it away. Between her first and second patients, she called the PV Hospital and asked after Gal Parker. It turned out Gal had been released a few days earlier. "She's got lots more treatments left," the nurse said. "We'd have kept her here until she finished, but everybody was tired of looking at her. All she does is complain that she couldn't see her kids. But she had it coming."

So, Gal really was back home, in the very house she'd set on fire.

Linda left the clinic late that night, her assistant and the X-ray technician having gone home to spend the remainder of the holiday with their families. As she headed for her car, she noticed that the back wooden wall of the caladrius shelter had been smashed. The two-by-fours were broken inward, as if a vandal had struck them with a blunt object. She pulled the slats free, leaving a craggy hole so that the shelter was exposed on two sides. The wood had been cleanly broken. This hadn't been done with a foot or a fist. So . . . an axe?

• • •

The Saturday after Thanksgiving, a shipment of caladrius feathers and leather arrived on their doorstep. The leather was rough and still wet from salt curing. Bird skin, it was thin and fine.

Though it was announced that 60 percent of the caladrius population had been culled, mostly for dry food storage, Sunny had survived. According to one of the pamphlets, residents were supposed to clean caladrius shelters every year after Thanksgiving. The job could not be outsourced to dayworkers. Wearing soccer goalie gloves, Linda went into Sunny's shelter for the first time. She found a mound of tiny bones. Sunny'd licked these clean, practically polished, and divided them from the fur, which she'd used to insulate her shelter. Upon realizing Linda'd gone in there, she followed, hissing: *SSSSSSSSSSS!*

It was dumb. Linda was hunched inside the small shelter, trapped by a flightless bird that must have gained at least three pounds since June. "I don't want your pile of garbage, garbage lady," she said. Sunny opened her sharp-toothed mouth as if to bite.

"Try it, little witch, and nobody's feeding you."

Maybe she sensed Linda wasn't in a patient mood, could read

from her muscle twitch that she'd have been happy to kick her. Sunny waddled aside.

Around dusk that evening, Cathy Bennett's stepbrother dropped her off. She and Hip had gotten more than a thousand signatures supporting golden tickets for all born citizens. They planned to spend the evening making calls, explaining their case, and getting at least fifty more. Eventually, they'd ask for an audience with the board. Daniella had told them that when Rachel became CEO and Lloyd chairman, they'd be receptive.

Cathy beamed lately. Linda'd never seen her so radiant.

"You know, this doesn't help the Farmer-Bowen cause much," Linda'd recently told Hip.

He had nodded at this, like the idea was neither new nor interesting to him. He no longer brooded like he used to in Kings. The things that used to concern him (how he measured up against his sister, his weight, his performance in school, whether the United Colonies would last into his old age) had fallen away. All he cared about now was making Cathy happy. "I'm not in it just for the now. I'm in it for the long game, Mom."

"You're a good boyfriend," Linda told him, because it was true. Though she was beginning to think the relationship was uneven. Cathy snapped, Hip asked how high he ought to jump. Hip snapped, the sound echoed.

Soon after Cathy and Hip disappeared, Josie headed out the door to meet the crowd of kids waiting for her. "You don't have to go. You can stay home," Linda said.

"I know," Josie answered, soft and meek.

Dinner at Sirin's went how it always went: jolly and silly. But she'd gone to enough of these evenings that their novelty had scraped away. They were beginning to feel like a performance: *Here are the important people. Look how much fun they're having! Do what they do. Act how they act! Or else you'll get kicked out, you poor son of a bitch!*

As if there'd never been any tension during the Thanksgiving race, Daniella acted just the same. Rachel and Kai sat close and held hands. Jack seemed displeased about this turn of events and was especially mean to his wife, Colette, telling her she was no good at spreading butter on bread, sneering at her choice in mead, and ignoring her when she asked him to scoot down a little. Lloyd came to her rescue, offering to switch seats because he worried she was being affected by a draft. He entertained her with stories about a town in Florida he'd visited, where the rule of government was decided by a divining rod. "You'd think it would be a mess. But it's actually worked for them. That's the crazy part."

Linda drank more than usual. It made everything feel further away. She had an itch inside her that she wanted very much to scratch.

• • •

"I wasn't able to find much on idiopathic leukemia," Russell told her later that week. "The hospitals aren't sharing information. And you're right, BetterWorld categorizes illness differently. You have to look under *spontaneous mutation* or *immunologic auto-aggression* to find anything, but once you get there, the numbers align. The incidence of leukemia and lymphoma in this town is something like .01 percent, which seems to be a little less than on the outside, though it's all guesswork."

He handed her the materials he'd printed out, along with Fielding's letter.

"Anything about chlorine and benzene?" she asked, running her thumb over Fielding's name. She and Fielding had been exchanging emails once a week. Fielding's grammar was going. Her sentences weren't making much sense, either. A normal person would print them all and keep them in a special, cherished file. Linda didn't want to do that. Such an act would be an admission that these letters were finite.

"Nothing of note. There's no reaction that I'm seeing. No benzene or PERC. I know Fielding mentioned them, but running GIS on this end, there's no idiopathic leukemia clusters on record. I honestly think that tumor's spread to her brain."

• • •

December meant flu season. Her work picked up. Between the hospital and the clinic, she was seeing at least twenty patients every week.

She enjoyed the ride to the clinic, listening to news from the outside. Despite the global information embargoes, an international consortium of scientists had gotten together and made their own network. Threatened with espionage charges by their home countries, they'd encrypted their exchanges and had so far eluded detection. Some people thought this was treason—the scientists would get together and hold the world for ransom. Linda thought it was Promethean, but probably doomed. People had been trying to halt the Great Unwinding for a very long time, and so far nobody'd found traction.

• • •

Mid-December. In tranquil Plymouth Valley, everything but the weather stayed exactly the same. Small wood fires burned at night in houses, their chimneys billowing gray smoke. Caladrius retreated into their warm houses and snow fell and piled. It was fluffier than eastern pack; you could see the individual patterns of flakes as they drifted, at first melting on blacktop and then collecting into a perfect crust of white.

An itch, an urge to scratch.

As a kid, she'd lived by the river. She'd been born the youngest of four. By then, her parents had been old. She'd had more freedom and almost no supervision. She'd ditched summer camp at the community center and gotten lost in the woods, then found herself again.

And then, practically overnight, Glamp took over their lives, and the school, and camp, and the town. At first it was the miracle drug everyone loved, and then it was the outlawed drug that everyone still loved and took but didn't talk about. They kept it in hidden purse pockets and locked drawers and glove compartments. She'd tried it. Even now, she didn't like to admit that, but yeah, she'd spent a few months crushing and snorting it. She finally learned, then, the joy of secrets. They nest inside you, and make you feel less alone. At fourteen, she lost her virginity to a thirty-year-old pharmaceutical rep in the back of his car.

When her mom got hospitalized with heart failure, that high, absent feeling lost its appeal. She kept sleeping with friends and strangers.

It made her life feel less empty. Then she met Russell. She'd never felt understood by him. He didn't seem to get her moods, or to know why she liked having friends for dinner, or her interest in working at a free clinic. Having come from parents who fought when they talked, who'd aired grudges like laundry set to dry, he'd craved peace. For that reason, he wasn't curious about people or what made them tick. But he'd loved her. She'd felt that love. It was certain and unwavering—the pillar she'd been searching for since she'd first started wandering those woods.

Even during their bad times—when he'd left her alone with the kids, when she'd begged for help and he'd agreed, looking her plainly in the eyes, then gone back to work as if the conversation had never happened, forcing her to sideline her medical career so that it eventually became more of a hobby than a profession—she'd always known he loved her. Even when, fed up, she'd asked for a divorce, it hadn't been because she hated him, as happened to so many couples she knew. She'd been bluffing, hoping to force a little more equality. That time, he'd been good. He'd promised to change and actually changed, going so far as to come home for dinners and show up for his first parent-teacher conference. But he'd soon backslid, and by then she'd been worn down. The kids would be home for only another few years. Logistically, divorce wouldn't help her situation. She'd wind up having to do more on less money. She let it go, even as she'd wondered: What was it like, inside other marriages? Did this happen to everyone, only they didn't talk about it? Or despite her outward bravado, her competence, was there something deeply wrong with Linda Farmer?

Had her own falling-apart family of origin been the thing to make her cling to Russell that much more tightly? She didn't know. All she knew was that for a long time, she'd told herself a story about how her life could have turned out tragically, how Russell, in his unwavering stability, had saved her. He'd been the reason that she'd escaped the rest of Poughkeepsie's fate. But she saw now that she'd given him too much credit. Some people have Glamp-shaped holes in them. Either they're born with that hole, or something cruel carves it into them. Her own emptiness could never be filled by something like Glamp.

Always, she'd been someone who needed to understand *why*. Why had her family succumbed? Why had the manufacturers marketed it? Why had the distributors and regulators agreed it was safe? Why weren't they all in prison now? Why had her family chosen it, over her? She'd looked on at the wreckage of Poughkeepsie, and hadn't wanted to drown in it; she'd wanted to pave it. To undo it, save it.

• • •

One December morning after drop-off, she drove to Gal's house. Gal's car was parked in the driveway. A light was on in the den, the place with the couch where Linda had once sat. She noticed the ash tree, leaves heavy with snow. Someone had wrapped its trunk in black ribbon.

When she got home, she checked her email and saw a note from Leticia. Dr. Carole Fielding had died. Her daughter had her cremated, no funeral. Without reading any of it, Linda printed up all of Fielding's correspondence then, and put it in a special envelope marked CAROLE.

Then she went outside.

The air was bitter, its sting pleasant on her lungs. She tried to think of who to call, to tell what had happened, but Russell didn't typically answer his device during the day. He wouldn't know what to say, anyway. She'd feel him on the other end, trying to come up with something pacifying, so he could go back to work. Neither Rachel nor Daniella would be interested. Probably, they might even ask her why she'd called them, as her sadness was ruining their day. She thought of Hip, who would hijack the conversation with talk of Cathy and golden tickets. She thought of Josie, to whom she'd always been so close. But Josie wasn't Josie anymore.

She walked in just her sneakers through the snow, her feet crunching through the top, thick layer and sinking down midcalf. It felt so satisfying. She kept crunching, all over the lawn, until her feet were numb from cold. Until half the yard was packed-down footprints. She looked over her work and saw that she'd made a giant spiral—a circle getting ever wider.

The itch, the urge to scratch.

"Fuck you, Russell. That letter was lucid," she said.

The Scratch

The PV library was a one-level box-building with an alcove devoted to Plymouth Valley and its history. The next cold morning, Linda headed there.

"This is all the material we keep offline. You should be able to find what you're looking for. And if you can't, I have no idea what you're looking for," the friendly librarian told her.

The room was formal, with wooden banker's chairs and a long square table surrounded by books with hard spines. Linda went first for the pamphlets fanned out in a display. These were folksy, and definitely written by Anouk. On the backs were cartoon mythological birds hanging out together: a gryphon, a roc, and a phoenix. In the center, a giant caladrius. The thing was as big as a moose, dwarfing the rest of them. These creatures were enfolded in one another like best buddies.

Thinking of idiopathic leukemia, she went next for the science section. Looked for books relating to health, toxicology, psychology, and cancer. None were present. So much for that.

In the history section, she leafed through a leather-bound book with gold-embossed writing that described the construction of the tunnels, subsequent Labyrinth, nuclear reactor, and purified air dome—engineering feats that many other company towns had since imitated. In the founding history, she noticed a mention of sickness in Plymouth Valley called *the blight*:

The Blight

In the early years, Plymouth Valley's populace was infected with a blight characterized by loose bowels, dizziness, and night sweats. Several children failed to thrive. The blight was short-lived, and by the town's second decade, all reports of this type of illness had ceased.

She looked for more on this blight. Found nothing. She checked the dates on when the Omnium Mill had been built—1984—and when it and its waste-processing center, both located along the river, had been decommissioned: 2001. Possibly, that tracked.

Tucked inside this book was another pamphlet, black on both sides, and without illustrations:

The Plymouth Valley Winter Festival

It is the intersection of luck and diligence through which we find success. But outside these fortress walls, even the strongest, most exceptional people do not always survive. As it has always been with the greatest of empires, we owe our bounty to our industry and to our sins. To perpetuate our survival now and always, we pay homage with a sacrifice to the Great White Caladrius.

Beware the Sacrifice

—John Parson Senior, May 2024

She headed back out, indicated the relevant section of the history book to the librarian back at her counter.

"Can you tell me anything about this blight?"

"Huh! I've never heard of this."

"No?" Linda asked.

"Never!" she said.

"Do you think there's any other place I could look for information?"

The librarian pointed back at the room from which Linda had

come. "It would be in there, if anywhere. It couldn't have been that serious. I'd have heard of it."

"Oh," Linda said. "Thank you. One more thing—what do they mean by a sacrifice to the Great White Caladrius?"

The librarian took the black pamphlet. She read slowly with her index finger tracing line by line. "Oh, I get it! I know. This is just the Winter Festival. We sacrifice a bird!"

"A bird gets sacrificed to a bird?"

"It's very silly, isn't it?"

"Why is it called Great White?"

The librarian smiled halfway, amused. "They can get big. There's a rumor the really big ones live down in the shelter. But it's a joke. It's funny. Kids pretend they've seen them. They sleep down there and scare themselves silly. We have a lot of fun with Hollow."

"Can you tell me exactly what happens in the tunnels at the Winter Festival?"

"All kinds of things happen. It's a party. A celebration."

"What about the black ribbons?"

The librarian put the pamphlet down, away from Linda, like Linda'd lost her pamphlet privileges. "They're just decoration."

Linda felt a panic in her chest. A feeling of something wrong. "That's it?"

"Mostly. We prefer not to spoil it for new people. It's best you experience it firsthand."

This woman looked normal and sane. Then again, everyone there looked normal and sane. So maybe appearances weren't the salient feature. "Everyone keeps telling me that I'll love it," Linda said.

The woman relented, perhaps remembering that Linda wasn't accustomed to this place. "It must be so hard. I spent my whole life here, and I still have questions. I mean, a smelly bird? They make fun of us in Palo Alto . . . But it really is just for fun."

Linda waited, hoping she'd say more.

"There's a VIP room for people with golden tickets."

"Yeah?"

"But only a handful of people have access."

"What happens in there?" Linda asked.

She raised her brows, grinned innocently, like they were talking of nothing of consequence. "How would I know? My final review isn't for three years."

• • •

Back home that night, she found Russell in his office.

"Did the EPA ever testify against Omnium?" she asked.

This second court case was coming up. He was more stressed about it than he'd been about the last one. His typically neat workspace was surrounded by empty mugs, tea bags staining random papers, and crinkled-up snack bags. This was not unusual for most people in the throes of a deadline, but for Russell, it was shocking.

"This again? We've always testified in its favor," he answered, his eyes blinking and bleary from overuse. "The data always backed it up."

She told him about *the blight*, its concurrence with the first Omnium mill. She asked him again about Ireland's settlement, for trillions. "Could you get me a file on that—the republic's stated case? Because the Omnium-processing plant there was one of the biggest in the world."

Russell rubbed his red eyes. Mumbled without looking at her. "I can't get somebody else's case. Who does she think I am?"

"Russell? Are you okay?"

He let out a breath. "Yeah."

"You don't seem okay. What's going on with this case? Can I help?"

He shook his head. "I should never have let you see the numbers last time. It's not allowed."

"Right. But they don't have to know. Come to bed and get back fresh in the morning? You could use the break."

He blinked a few times, like his eyes were too tired to focus. "Listen, I know you loved Fielding, but I checked. Chlorine isn't ever involved in Omnium waste processing. Ireland's suit was fraudulent. They were bankrupt, we were low-hanging fruit. Omnium's the only reason krill and tuna and whales are still alive—the only reason the ocean's still spitting oxygen."

"Sorry," she said.

"Don't be. I get it. But I'm so tired, Linda." She saw that he was. If she thought on it, he'd been tired for as long as she'd known him.

She came over to his desk. He shut his laptop so she wouldn't see. "What can I do?"

"Nothing. I just need to get through this."

And then the next thing, and the next, she thought. "It's late. Come upstairs. It'll all still be here in the morning."

Smiling strangely, he got up from his desk.

They started walking. "Do you want Esperanza to clean for you?"

"No."

She drifted off around midnight and woke to a gasping sound. She reached across the bed. Her hand came back empty. A light shone under the master bath's door.

She crossed the room, listened. There was an analog skeleton keyhole in the event the house powered down. She peered through it, and there he was, sitting on the lip of the toilet, bent over and breathing into a brown paper bag. In-out, in-out, the thing expanded and contracted like a crinkling, artificial lung.

He'd done this once before, hidden in a bathroom and hyperventilated. At the time, he was assisting at a lab where they sacrificed rabbits. He claimed the work didn't bother him. He could see the greater good and that was all the consolation he needed. Then she found him like this, red eyed in the middle of the night.

"Honey, you okay?" she now asked.

"Yeah!" he answered, hiding the bag fast. But still, it crinkled. "My stomach's off. I ate something bad. Go back to bed."

"No, come out," she said.

He took another few minutes to open the door, and when that happened, he came right out, climbed back into bed, turned out the light, and pretended to fall asleep.

• • •

Trish Parker, Gal's ex-wife. There was no corporation-wide directory that included Palo Alto. Through Zach Greene, Linda found the number for Palo Alto's human resources department. After a week, an admin replied with Trish Parker's contact information.

Linda called. Her message went like this: *Hi! This is Linda Farmer. I'm a pediatrician in Plymouth Valley. I hope you don't mind the intrusion, but I'm wondering if I can volunteer to act as a resource for your children's treatment. I know idiopathic leukemia is very rare and it's hard to get consensus on best practices. I also have a patient I believe might have the disease. Anyway, thank you. Please call me back.*

Trish didn't respond. In the time leading up to the holidays, Linda left three additional messages.

• • •

Christmas came fast. Linda couldn't get Hip or Josie involved, the former because he was busy with his girlfriend, the latter because she was blue. So, she went to the farm on her own and clipped a few branches from the evergreen trees, made a wreath, and set up some lights. Parson's Market had mistletoe, which she hung from the parlor ceiling.

They celebrated in their pajamas, just the family. They drank pomegranate juice and ate croissants with cured krill, cream cheese, and capers. She put on holiday music. But the presents got opened too fast, and all were from stores on Main Street—warm socks and video game apps. The Fabric Collective had finished their formal attire for the big prefestival party at the Parson family mansion. Russell and Hip both tried their suits on, and she and Josie both teasingly hooted in admiration.

Then, it was over. Everyone took naps or went to their room. Feeling lonely, Linda knocked on Josie's door. "Can I come in?"

Josie opened the door and moved back to where she'd been, lying in her bed with no books or screen.

"Tired?" Linda asked.

Josie blinked, which in its way was an answer.

Linda felt nervous. Didn't know how to do this correctly. Decided that the point was doing it at all. "I thought you could talk to someone. A doctor. There's one at the hospital who specializes in teens."

Josie's lips curled into an ugly sneer. "There's nothing wrong with me."

"No. There isn't. You're perfect. But I think something's got hold of you. I think you need help wrestling it down."

"It's not me. It's this town," Josie said.

"I believe you," Linda said. "But the town's not hurting. You're hurting."

Josie flopped over onto her stomach, her face in her pillow.

"Can you tell me why you're hurting? Didn't you like any of your Christmas presents?"

Josie didn't answer.

Linda set down the snow globe her dad had given her when she left home. It showed a bear plucking a honeycomb from a tall tree in what looked like the Catskills. "I have one more thing. I should have wrapped it."

Josie sighed out. "I don't want your junk, Mom."

"My dad gave it to me when I was about your age. It's home. Where I come from," Linda said. "Like you come from Kings. You never forget your first home."

Josie pulled the covers over her head and began to cry. "I don't want things! I'm surrounded by things!"

"I'm sick of things, too," Linda said. "Do you want to go for a walk?"

Josie stayed hidden. Her voice was low and furious. "You say all the right things but you don't do anything. Get out."

"What am I supposed to do?" Linda asked.

Josie didn't answer. Linda's instincts told her to stay. To figure this out. But Josie seemed so hurt and angry. What was the point?

• • •

"What do you think happens at the Winter Festival?" Linda asked one night, after she and Russell had gotten into bed. He was reading a screen, its light shedding a purple hue.

"They kill a bird, don't they? Or something. These people make full-time work out of some dumb hobbies." Except for his hands, which were knotted in fists, he affected poised calm.

"I'm freaked out about it," she said. "In a couple of weeks, we're spending three days and two nights trapped in a tunnel with these people."

"From what I hear, it's nothing serious. Parson'll make a speech and everyone'll get drunk. And some of 'em screw around with the wrong people. It's three days and two nights and communal sleeping. That's the secret of the PV Winter Festival. Everyone screws around."

"What if they put kids down in the Labyrinth, and leave them there? Like, the kids have to find their own way out? And maybe, sometimes, they get lost." She thought of Percy, the soccer dad who had lost his kid.

He reached over, turned out his bedside light. "I doubt that's it. But even if it is something they do, if they try that on our kids we'll tell them they're out of luck. We're not playing."

• • •

A few days later, Linda took Josie to the therapist, only Josie wouldn't go alone. So, they sat together in the office. Josie wouldn't answer any questions, and Linda didn't think talking on her behalf was a great start to open communication, so they mostly sat quietly, memorizing the painting of a ship at sea.

"Do you feel like a ship at sea?" the therapist asked.

"No. I feel like a person in a room," Josie answered. While the therapist wrote this comment down, Linda hid a grin.

On the ride home, Josie reached out, touched Linda's shoulder. "Want to talk now?" Linda asked.

"Nope." But her expression was more alert, her eyes less dead. It seemed, in the ways blood flows through the smallest capillaries, like movement.

• • •

The itch, the scratch, the waiting, the not knowing. Right before the New Year, Linda called Rachel and asked if they could meet. *Come over whenever. I'm taking a sick day*, Rachel texted back.

The town was in full lights. A collection of carved wooden mythological birds, the white caladrius at center, filled the bandstand at

Caladrius Park. Snow stuck now, packing down after weeks of storms. The temperature had turned from brisk to icy.

When Linda rang, Rachel swung the door open and walked back inside the house. There was luggage by the door—Rachel was always either just home, or just on her way out.

"Come in," she called from behind, and Linda followed her to the sitting room, which was decorated similarly to most of the other PV parlors. Upon the table was a ream of curled ribbon candy, which appeared never to have been touched. The couches were deep and soft. When she'd first come to this town, she'd thought rooms like this, and in her own home, were unique. But she'd learned that except for Daniella's flourishes, most everything was the same. The quality differed according to A, B, or C class, but she had ornamental ribbon candy in her house, too.

"Kai home?" Linda asked.

Rachel leaned her head back, closed her eyes. Her every movement seemed to cause her pain, as if her joints were grinding against glass.

"What about your housekeeper?"

"Oh, who knows," Rachel said. "She hates me. Does yours hate you?"

It seemed unfair to cast judgment on the person who cleaned your toilet. Esperanza was allowed to feel however she wanted. But she'd tried to talk to Esperanza at least twenty times and been shot down on every occasion. "Yeah. She hates me. Why does yours hate you?"

Rachel lifted her mug. Sipped. Linda got a whiff. It smelled like coconut rum. "I could be her, and she could be me. I'm supposed to know better, but I don't."

"Know better about what? I mean, I offer clothes, I offer food. I don't have money. What else can I do?"

Rachel chirped with amusement. "You *really* don't know better. They get checked at the border. They're not allowed to bring anything in or out. Black market. We could use them as mules, side hustle enough to buy a compound."

Linda let go of a long breath. "She could have told me that. I feel like a jerk."

Rachel finished the contents of her mug. Laid her head back again. *Sick day*, Linda realized, meant *bender day*. She was back to her habit. "So, why are you here?"

Linda felt the soft couch with her hands. "Is today a bad time?"

"Jack convinced Parson to push all his East Asia trips onto me as a test for my fitness. It's been a nightmare," Rachel answered. The bags under her eyes were back and worse than ever before. It was like they'd been drawn with purple-black charcoal.

Linda nodded. "I've helped people with this problem you're having. Addiction. I can help you, if you want."

Rachel's eyes burned a hole right through Linda. She was reminded, then, of her mother in a hospital bed. For just a moment, she was out of time. They looked different from the outside, but on the inside, Poughkeepsie and Plymouth Valley weren't so very different.

"Tell me why you're here."

"I've had this feeling for a long while," Linda said. "That something's wrong with this place."

Languorous, Rachel reached down beside her chair to produce a bottle of coconut rum. She locked eyes with Linda as she poured into her mug, as if daring her to say something contrary about it. It was a gross drink. The kind of thing you do because you can't stop, not because you like it. "Whatever do you mean by *wrong*?"

"What's the significance of the black ribbons?"

Rachel made her *I don't know—people here are crazy!* face, sipped more coconut rum.

"I talked to this woman who told me that every year, some sick kid or group of kids gets forced into the tunnels at the Winter Festival. There's this nuclear engineer—he spends most of his time in the mental ward. He lost his kid down the tunnels last year. It happened during the Winter Festival. From the things people have been saying, or letting slip, Sebbie and Katie Parker were chosen to go down this year. But you guys told me they're not in this town anymore. You told me they're safe with their mom, Trish Parker. But I've been calling Trish Parker and I can't get through. She won't verify it. Where are those kids? What happens at the Winter Festival?"

Rachel looked at her mug, seemed to consider having another swig, but was repulsed. Linda understood, suddenly, that either she or Kai or both had tossed out all the booze in the house. But she'd saved this bottle. Secreted it away for when she'd need it. "What do you think happens?"

"I don't know. That's why I'm asking."

"It's a party," Rachel said. "Lots of drugs. Anything goes, if you're into that."

"And no one gets hurt?"

Rachel rolled her eyes.

"It's not a crazy question," Linda said.

"It is, actually. It's a fucking stupid question because you don't know anything. You're just stirring the pot."

"So tell me, and I'll leave the pot alone."

"Do you know what Daniella used to do before she was our fearless leader?"

Rachel's eyes were sewn with red threads. It was possible she didn't know what she was saying. Was blackout. "Vegas. Think about it. What's Vegas known for? Her mom was a hostess. She worked at a BW whorehouse. The world's oldest profession. Do you know what I do on the side? All these goddamned trips?"

Linda had the feeling it wasn't good.

"I'm a fixer. I fly out, I fix things. If important people want something, I procure it. If someone needs to be shut up, I pay them so much they can't say no. That's how I got into these people's good graces. I'm good at it, because people trust me. Nobody sees me coming. Daniella was talent. She wanted in. She didn't care how. She was supposed to be his piece on the side; Lloyd likes pieces on the side. They all do. They keep them around as domestics and then they trade them in. But she's Daniella. The woman could whip a eunuch. She seduced him, got rid of the wife. Promised him she'd be better for him politically. She worked the angles. Lloyd went from low man to CEO. That's why her stepkids hate her, not because she's got the firm boundaries of a perfect parent. She replaced their mom, who has to live on the outside now. You think she's fucking around? A woman like that?

"And Anouk? Ever notice her son looks just like her dad? Ever wonder why she's so obsessed with genetic purity?"

Linda didn't understand that part. Well, she had some idea, but it was too outlandish. She picked up the candy ribbon. The bowl came with it. She pulled, forgetting that she was in someone else's house. Forgetting everything.

"Me, Daniella, your husband, Jack Lust—they have to bring outsiders like us in to do their dirty work. Third generation's incompetent. Fourth generation, like Keith? Fucking psychotic. He thinks he's the son of God.

"Jack's nanny? That's his piece. Colette is so fucking milquetoast she lets it happen. Whatever makes him happy. He goes through them like tissues. Colette is the one who sleeps in the servants' room. She says she likes it because it's closer to the baby. The nanny almost never helps with the kids. She's usually too sore. But that's better than what happens in some of these houses. Some of them—"

Rachel looked up at the ornate ceiling, her eyelids going heavy. "They like them young."

Linda was standing. She'd pulled the ribbon free. Her hands squeezed without thinking and she broke it.

"People live here for so long, they forget common decency."

Linda held the pieces in her palm, irreparable as broken teeth. So she dropped them to the floor, where they scattered.

"What's crazy is you act the part of the innocent. How do you think you got here? Hard work?" she asked. "Everyone here is—" she started, then leaned her head back and passed out.

Linda bent down. She started to pick things up.

The housekeeper came into frame. "I've got it," the woman said, polite and full of contempt.

• • •

Linda didn't go home. She didn't want to carry this knowledge back to 9 Sunset Heights, contaminate the air with it. Adrenaline pumping, she didn't let herself think as she drove across town, to the southwest quadrant, to the nightmare house.

Frozen snow had hardened, unsalted, all down the short walk. The car was still there, seemingly unmoved all this time. She knocked on the front door. Its handle was caked with ice. There wasn't that frightened, anxious feeling in her stomach she'd gotten so accustomed to. Instead, she was calm. At last, she'd returned.

She knocked again. No one came.

She walked uphill and around to the side kitchen door. Remembered that night, the sounds of children. Remembered Gal's abrupt menace. Through the kitchen window, into the living room, she could see the back of Gal's head. "Hello?" she called.

No movement. She was sleeping or watching a screenie, perhaps.

She knocked.

Nothing.

She banged. "HELLO?"

The head nodded down, reeled up. Slowly, Gal turned. She stayed there, having recognized Linda, but deciding not to move.

"It's Linda Farmer. I met you several months ago. Hello?" Linda pulled back the old screen door, turned the handle. "Gal? Hello? I want to know how you're doing."

"Bad!" Gal called. "How do you think?"

"Yes," Linda agreed as she entered the small house. "But more specifically."

Gal finally limped to the door with great stiffness. She was wearing a midthigh-length shirt. The skin along her legs sheened pink from healing burns while her ankles appeared like twisted tree knots. Her arms, which must have been bare that night, were translucent red-pink. Burnt raw to the muscle. Her face was unscathed, but she'd lost most of her hair and it was growing back only along her temples. A heart-shaped locket rested within the concavity of her neck.

"Oh, you," she said, her voice clear, all its childishness gone. "Come in."

She turned. Linda gasped. Though her front would recover, her entire hind was ruined. It was like she'd been licked by the devil.

A plausible reconstruction of how it had happened bubbled in Linda's mind: Gal had started the fire, but electrical smoke burns the eyes. It's caustic. Probably, she really had intended to burn up with her kids, but her instincts kicked in. She'd run out, saving herself.

It could have ended there. Full of nasty spite, she could have let them burn. Instead, she'd run back inside. She'd carried them out one at a time, Daniella had said. Linda pictured the scene, Gal grabbing the child nearest, shouting: *I'll be back, baby, Momma's coming back!* to the one left alone. Once outside, she'd set Katie or Sebbie down. High on adrenaline, on that promise she'd made to the unchosen child, she'd returned and done it all over again.

"How are the burns?"

Gal moved slowly, favoring her left side. "My throat's the worst," she said. "Bleeds."

"They're giving you anti-inflammatories?"

"I don't know. I'm not a doctor. Nobody tells me anything. They're too mad."

"They are. I can tell. They're also giving you epidermal growth factors but limiting it to your ventral side for now. The dorsal's too large. They don't want to risk doing too much and forcing a bad immune response. With constant treatment, you'll recover within about eighteen months."

Gal made a fart noise. "I'm not staying a year."

The house was spare, everything painted white since the fire, all the iconography gone. Linda had expected bottles of booze, but there were no such signs. Just stray breadcrumbs, some crusty cereal bowls in the sink.

"Your crosses are gone."

"Yeah. That didn't work. I was trying to pray to a god stronger than the Hollow god. Reverse the curse; cure the cancer."

"Oh," Linda said. "You think the Hollow god made your kids sick?"

"*They* do," Gal said. She sat on the couch they'd once shared. Linda took the musty armchair. It was dark in this room, despite the daylight. "I don't think anything. I don't care. I just want my kids."

"That's what you meant that night, by turning up the heat," Linda said. "You meant you were going to set a fire."

Gal took a breath. She was very different from the woman Linda'd met in September. She wasn't agitated. She was still. Heavy, even, like a wounded cat that sneaks to a hidden place to lick its wounds or perish.

"My kids are sick," Gal said. "Dr. Chernin told me they're not going to get better."

"Listen, I'm sorry. I should start by saying I'm sorry."

"For what?" Gal asked.

"I never checked on you or visited before now. I should have done that."

"That's okay. *Nobody* talks to me," Gal said.

"Oh," Linda said. She'd expected rage and hurled accusations. A few *why didn't you help me*s thrown in. But either Linda had caught her on a very bad night last time, or the experience of the fire, of her burns, of losing her children, had changed her.

"I must have swallowed a bottle of grain for courage. Or more? More. But I couldn't go through with it. Fire's awful. I didn't think it would be so awful. I couldn't let them suffer like that . . ."

Linda's eyes watered. "But why did you do it at all?"

"Because they're mine."

"My God, Gal!"

Gal's voice didn't modulate. No pleading. No hollering, either. Just flat and ragged. "I'm healed enough to walk. They said that's all I get. They're kicking me out. Can't even wait for a trial. They need me gone. I was trying to understand why they didn't kill me and then I thought: It's not part of the rules. They only follow rules. It lets them pretend they're civilized."

"Who would kill you?"

"It's a break from tradition," Gal said, ignoring the question. "Every other year, they let the parents stick around. Percy Khoury's mad as a meat axe. Guy runs all through the Labyrinth making friends out of the lost caladrius down there and he still got a golden ticket out of it, like Trish. That's how you get your ticket early—you give them something they really need. But I pissed them off. So, I'll be on the outside. I'd like to take Sebbie and Katie with me. If you can help with that, you're welcome to sit on my couch all day. And if you can't, you can get out."

Linda stood. "I don't understand any of this."

"I hurt them, yes," Gal said. "It was better coming from me. Who do you think was going to set them loose in a freezing tunnel and offer them up to Hollow?"

"That's not real," Linda said. "It can't be."

"Do you know anything about Hami, China?" Gal asked.

Linda shook her head.

"Me neither. But lots of people there are really sick. The Omnium waste gets in the river. Same thing happens when you dissolve it," Gal said. "Worse things, too. Black teeth. Messed-up eyes. The animals are mutants over there. Not even edible. I've heard they got sick like that here, until the mill closed. Now it's rare—affects just kids, mostly. Because it's still in the river. Nobody told me not to let them swim in it. Nobody tells you anything, or maybe it was on purpose. It could have been a deal Trish made before she met me. Trish could be like that—cold. I used to feel so safe with her. I thought I'd be protected by someone so mean."

She looked right at Linda. "It's not by chance, who gets black ribbons at the maypole. It's decided before. It's always whoever's sick."

The contents of Linda's stomach didn't want to stay there. "Your kids are in Palo Alto."

"They're not," Gal said. "Trish traded them for a golden ticket and she transferred to a place where they'd honor it because she couldn't stand people around here knowing what she'd done. My kids are still here. Hidden."

"It's psychotic," Linda said. "Companies don't intentionally cause cancer. Towns don't sacrifice children. It would have gotten out by now. It's not something anyone could keep a secret." But she knew from experience this wasn't true. She remembered Glamp.

"Didn't you tell me your husband, Russell, worked for the EPA?"

Linda looked at the bright spot on the wall, where the inverted cross had hung. It stung, to hear Gal mention his name, to drag him into this ugliness.

"Trish worked for the EPA, too. Don't you think that comes in handy, when you work on one side, and then you switch to the enemy?"

"He'd never do that," Linda said. "You don't know my husband."

"Maybe you don't know him," Gal said without raising her voice.

She'd been hoping Gal would be just as histrionic as the night they'd met. Hoping she'd say terrible, nonsensical things that would allow Linda to categorize her as mad. But Gal was sober: reasonable, though the things she was saying were not.

"You're crazy. Your life is a mess, so you want mine to be, too."

Gal laughed, deep from her belly. "I don't care about you. My kids with terminal cancer were gonna be taken away from me. I wanted to spare them that. I wanted the last face they saw to be the person who loved them most. I'd have done anything to keep them. I still would."

"No one gets hurt at the Winter Festival," Linda said. "It's a joke. Just for fun."

"Look around. You think a place like this is free?"

Linda was standing, somehow. She was at the door. Gal had followed her.

"They're not with Trish. They're in this town. I'll bet they never left the hospital. Chernin always keeps them at the hospital at the end. They probably think I abandoned them, too. But I would never do that. Not ever."

"You're not well," Linda said.

Gal opened her locket. Inside was a photo of two taupe-skinned children, young enough that they probably still had baby voices. This photo was familiar. Linda realized, her skin crawling, that she'd seen it before.

"Help me?" Gal asked.

"I don't know. I don't know what's happening," Linda said. And then, somehow, she was stumbling out, into the snow-blind light.

Don't You Know What This Is?

Linda called Trish Parker again when she got home. The number was disconnected. She held the device, scrolling through old messages from the ActHollow crew. The smiley-faced epigenetic links to pseudo-scientific articles from Anouk, the inside jokes and mocking asides from Daniella, the sarcasm from Rachel.

She reread Fielding's original letter and the attendant studies Russell had printed. Then she read all Fielding's letters after that. She got lost in those letters, noticing the resignation in them that she'd ignored before. *I'll miss these patients*, Fielding had written. *A bird has built a nest under the eaves of our balcony, and I wonder if I'll get to see the babies hatch. I never noticed how much I like snow. My advice to you, Linda, is to enjoy the snow.*

Before it closed, Linda returned to the library and researched PV's history again. Found the same passages and reread them. Then she went home and poured herself a glass of mead. And another glass. And a third.

That night, she left out sandwiches. Didn't bother to check if her family had eaten them, nor did she remind them to clean up after themselves and stop pushing their messes on Esperanza. She sat in the dark bedroom, too drunk to drink more.

She didn't want to get out of bed the next morning, but when she checked her schedule, she saw that Danny Morales had made an appointment that morning at the clinic.

At breakfast, her voice went raspy, her breath heavy. Even her fingernails hurt, but it wasn't hangover and it wasn't sickness. It was sadness worse than any she could remember, including as a kid back in Poughkeepsie. Including the baby blues after the twins. It was a heavy, drowning feeling.

Only Hip was at the table. Russell was already at the office. "Where's Josie?"

"She went early."

Linda sat down beside him. "Those kids gave her a ride?"

Hip nodded.

"She doesn't like them, does she?"

"I don't really talk to her," he said, his mouth full of toast.

"Why's that?"

"You know Josie. Everything's about Josie."

"I'm not sure I do know Josie," Linda said. "She doesn't like these kids, but she still hangs out with them. That doesn't sound like my Josie. Do you know what's going on with her?"

"No. I tried but I give up. People need to take care of themselves, too." He dipped his toast into his poached egg. The yellow ran all out, swirling the periphery of the white.

"Is this a PV civics lesson?"

"Just common sense." He pressed his index finger against the bridge of his nose, pushing back phantom glasses that he'd stopped wearing since the laser surgery. "Are you feeling okay?"

"Why do you ask?"

He shrugged. Between the surgery for his fixed eyesight and the growth spurt—he was taller than her now—he'd changed a great deal. He'd been a boy in June. Now he looked like a man. "Cathy's mom said she was worried."

"Yeah?" Linda asked.

"She said you took that house fire really bad. She said it haunts you. You're the kind of person who takes on a lot of responsibility for other people."

"She told you this?"

He nodded, imagining himself the recipient of a grown-up confidence. "It's true. Back home you worried about your patients a lot, too.

Sometimes you worried about them more than you worried about us. But you can't help everyone."

"When did Daniella drop this little bomb on you?"

"A while ago. She said to be nice to you because you're so sensitive."

"How thoughtful of her, Hip," she said, and if he caught her sarcasm, he didn't let on.

"Can I be home late tonight? Cathy wants to work on our golden ticket petition. We're at almost eighteen hundred."

"Sure," Linda said. "The people of PV really don't have enough privilege. It's super important we make sure they inherit it generationally."

He got the sarcasm this time. "You talk like an outsider. I hope you keep that to yourself when you're around ActHollow. So can I go?"

• • •

Friday clinic. PV Extension was quiet. The snowplow had cleared only the main road leading to the highway. On the radio, scientists were testing a nuclear remediation technique in Los Alamos, and New York's governor had evaded a second assassination attempt. Locals had rioted in a Seattle company town that had bought up all the surrounding water and air rights. Riots and protests against company towns were pretty de rigueur. What was unusual—the company had asked for help from the National Guard, but the National Guard, pillaged by budget cuts, didn't have the resources to prevent the entire town from being sacked.

She parked on the street, the driveway blocked by snow. Though she'd reported the damaged caladrius shelter outside the clinic, it still hadn't been repaired and now there was something new: someone had spray-painted *kid killers* in red across the face of the building.

She stood before the graffiti for a while, trying to imagine the person who'd done it. Then she removed her coat and sweater, so that she wore just a T-shirt, and stuck out her tongue until a flake landed and melted. She stayed there awhile, imagining what would happen if she peeled away everything else.

When she got inside, she found that her assistant, who introduced himself as Matt, had arrived early. "Did you see the graffiti?" she asked.

He nodded, smiling brightly despite the circumstances. "I called PV security. They said it's not their purview. It's not part of PV's budget. They said we should call the local police."

"Are there local police?"

"Maybe in Platte?"

She blew a raspberry. "That's too far. I'll ask around, see if we can get a camera installed."

They made small talk, which she always felt obliged to do with new volunteers. She learned that he was a shelter engineer in training but liked the idea of doing volunteer work. His cousin was Colette Lust, and he was going on vacation to Sedona after the Winter Festival.

Then she headed into her office, where her papers were out of order. Her computer was on, the database with patients' names and health information on-screen.

"Hey, Matt! Could you get in here?"

He arrived with that same pleasant smile. It made her second-guess herself. "This is patient data. Did you look at this stuff or was there a break-in?"

Not a chink in that grin. "That's company data."

"Who told you to do this?"

"ActHollow on behalf of Jack Lust," he said. He lifted his hands in a show of innocence. "It's my job. I had to!" Then he turned and was out.

Linda followed, furious enough to spit. "You can't just steal—" she started, but then she noticed that Danny Morales had arrived early. He was holding a sleeping Carlos, wet boots dripping sleet to the short blue carpet.

"You're back. I'm so glad!" she said, then indicated for him to follow her into the closest examining room while Matt scuttled off.

"How's he doing? Did you get a second opinion?"

Danny placed Carlos onto the table. He'd gained very little weight. The child's skinniness was a disturbing sight. Linda worked hard not to let it show on her face. She put one hand on the baby's belly, the other on his forehead. "Sweetie," she cooed. "You don't feel so good, do you?" Then, to Danny, she asked, "I'm glad you scheduled an appointment. But what changed your mind?"

Tears filled his eyes and his voice broke. "We took him everywhere. No one can tell us what this is. You said you wanted to help."

"I do." Linda took two very small blood samples, ran the first through the system she'd finagled from Chernin. Same results as last time. She saved the report, attached it to the second vial. Started filling out the hemostatic oncology form for the PV system, then reconsidered.

"Are you mobile? Can you travel to a different state if I find a good hospital for him?" she asked.

He examined her expression, as if somehow convinced she was pranking him. When he saw that wasn't the case, he looked away. "Yes. We can leave tonight. Now, if that's best."

"I can't promise anything. But I can try. Meantime, you're doing a good job. He's bonded to you. I can tell. He can't focus on anything. Not even the bright colors. But he tracks your voice in the room."

Danny wiped his eyes with the heels of his hands. "This is so hard," he croaked.

She was thinking the child might die. He'd remember this conversation if that happened. "The hardest thing in the world," she agreed. "Nothing in your life will ever be harder than right now."

"God, I hope not," he said.

"I'm going to make some calls and come up with a plan for both of you. I'm not as convinced as I once was that PV is the best place for his treatment."

"Why not PV?" he asked, looking up at the altar of feathers and leather. There was a knowingness in the question that he needed corroborated.

"For one, they couldn't diagnose the cancer with the last blood sample I gave them. So, I doubt they'll magically manage it with a second sample. For another, I have to apply for resources that may get stuck in bureaucratic red tape. Leukemia is tricky. Lots of hospitals will send you home with some infusion therapy and that's it. But there are other places, public places running clinical trials right now, where I think you might have better chances.

"I have a hunch what this specific cancer might be. It's got a lot of names—because there's no data sharing, the hospitals are all treating it differently. Give me a few days and I'll come up with a plan," she said.

Danny picked up his baby. Despite Carlos's listlessness, he nuzzled into his father's chest.

"You're not like the last one."

"What?" she asked.

"The lady before you who worked here. I didn't like her."

"You've been here before?"

"I took my niece when she had the flu. A lotta people came here. It's why no one likes this clinic. They weren't nice. You can live with that if you have to, but they didn't help, either. Especially that doc."

"Trish Parker," Linda said.

"She wouldn't shake hands. She thought we were dirty. She thought all the kids had syphilis. Her answer to everything was penicillin. I don't think she was a real doctor. It was a science degree but not medicine. She never helped."

Linda burned with shame. "I'm sorry. That's inexcusable." And then, somehow, she asked the most insensitive question possible. "Do you know what happened to the bird shelter out front, or who defaced the building?"

He didn't take offense. Hungry, Carlos sucked on his forearm, so Danny produced a baggy of dried Cheerios and fed them to him one at a time. "No. But I'm not surprised it happened. People around here are mad. PV residents don't learn our names. All they care about is how fast the food gets delivered and if their house is clean. Look at our town. They stole all the water. They brought the dust. They don't care so long as they have their nannies and plumbers and hookers. This," he said, indicating the room, and the clinic, "makes them feel like good people. But they're not good people."

Linda leaned against the wall, wishing she could slide down. "I'm inclined to agree."

She made a point of shaking his hand, promising to follow up, and wishing them luck.

Once Danny left, Matt knocked, asking Linda for her notes. She had the feeling that this wasn't a random information raid on Jack

Lust's part. It was about Danny's son, whose appointment had been in the system.

"Why?" she asked.

"ActHollow has to have evidence of everything they're doing here."

"If we want their personal information attached to their health information, we need them to sign a waiver. Otherwise, patient identity has to be stripped."

"I'll do it. I'll strip it," he said.

She was tired of diplomacy. "You should go away before I get mad."

Matt stood there, so she got up and shut her office door. His mouth made a last-second *O* of surprise, and he lingered outside, stunned, before his footfalls retreated.

She considered calling Russell. It was possible he'd tell her she was overreacting. It was possible he'd tell her to shut up and play along. But it was also possible he'd be on her side.

"What? You can't just take patient data," he said after she told him what had happened. But he didn't actually sound surprised. She was getting used to the distinction in his voice, when he was surprised by something, and when he was pretending.

"He said they needed to prove to Jack that ActHollow was functional. But I think it's about my patient, the baby with cancer. I think it's about idiopathic leukemia."

"Jack's involved? That explains it. I doubt it's about that patient. He probably just wants proof that Daniella's not embezzling. Or, he's hoping she is, so he can take Rachel down. Lloyd, too, if he's lucky."

"I think there's something going on, Russell. I think you think it, too."

"Honey, I told you. There's nothing."

She squeezed her device in anger.

"You there? He's a king. They're all kings. They don't ask. You know that."

Linda considered throwing the device.

"I think you're overreacting. Don't blow anything up. You're helping people. That's worth something," he said. "Who cares if they mine a little data?"

• • •

New Year's Eve. For once, the party wasn't at Sirin's. It was at Anouk's dad's mansion. More than five hundred people were invited, the Farmer-Bowens among them. They were supposed to arrive at exactly eleven p.m. in order to be let in. The invitation said not to be late.

Linda was in no mood for a party. But she thought she might learn something, and invitations from Anouk Parson were not the kind a smart person turned down.

"Where's Josie?" she asked as the family assembled in the front hall. Hip was in his bespoke tuxedo, carrying a bag with swim trunks. Kids over thirteen were welcome and there was a separate indoor pool, heated just for them.

"Josie?" Hip asked. "She *says* she's sick."

Linda was so knocked off balance by his tone that she glanced up. "What?"

His upper lip curled in contempt and he used a ten-dollar word. "Malingering."

"Oh, that's too bad. She'll be sorry to miss all her friends. Should we go?" Russell asked. He was worried that if they were late, they wouldn't be let in. Rules, rules, rules. Who issues them on New Year's Eve?

"What do you mean, malingering?" Linda asked.

"Just, the usual with her. She's always miserable," Hip said.

Linda stink-eyed him for long enough that his posture slackened.

"Fine! I'm sorry! But she's not sick. She's faking."

"What's the difference? She's either sick or upset. Either way, it's nothing to tease."

He bent lower, his spine a *C* curve of regret. "I *try*. But she won't go along with anything. She sits by herself behind that stupid pole at lunch. I even asked her to sit with me and Cathy, though Cathy didn't want her. Cathy says she's weird, and she *is* weird. She never raises her hand in class. She doesn't answer teachers when they call on her. She doesn't dress for PE. She just stands there in her regular clothes and everybody notices. I put myself out, then she makes me look like a jerk."

Linda had some retorts. For instance, who was Cathy in her lame-ass outfits to call Josie weird? What kind of person comes between twins? "You disappoint me, Hip," she said. And then, to Russell, "I'll go talk to her."

"Do we have time?" Russell asked.

Linda ignored him, was already headed for the stairs. "Josie? You in there?" she called as she knocked.

"No," Josie called back after a while.

The first thing Linda noticed was that the room was free of clutter. No makeup or perfume. Nothing tossed onto the floor, no baseball caps on the posts of her bed. "What happened here?" Linda asked.

Josie was in bed, covers pulled up. Her face looked puffy from too much sleep. Maybe too much crying. "I'm tired of *things*," she said.

"So, you got rid of it all? When?"

"Yesterday," Josie said in a put-on nasal voice. But when Josie really was sick, her pupils got glazed. Today, they were brown and sharp. Cutting, even.

"It must be at the PV Extension landfill by now," Linda said.

Josie answered with silence. Early on in motherhood, Linda had interpreted silences like these as challenges to her authority. Now, she knew better. Josie was looking out the window, where the trees wore baptismal white dresses.

"My snow globe?" Linda asked.

Josie blinked, stayed watching the softly breezing trees. Her voice sounded far away, like something angry had taken residence inside her. "I told you. I can't be bought."

Tears welled in Linda's eyes. "I don't know what you're doing. I don't understand this at all."

Josie turned her attention from the swaying, snow-ribboned branches. "I'm just so tired, Mom."

Linda sat down on the bed beside her. You get used to certain things. You take them for granted. Josie was her happy bug. Josie *bounced*. She saw now that she'd been in denial. Because clearly, Josie didn't always bounce.

"Tired of what? There's so much shit to be tired of."

Josie didn't answer. She looked older, more adult, just like Hip. This town had aged them both.

"I'll start," Linda said. "I'm tired of trying to figure out how people want me to act and falling short. I'm tired of no one saying what they mean."

Josie sighed out, looked at Linda. "You know, he's not as good at math, but he gets the tutor. I'm actually having problems with history, but you don't even ask."

"Do you want a history tutor?"

"What's the point?"

"BetterWorld University? Getting out of here and never coming back?"

"Don't you understand? I don't fit! I try. I want to. But I don't belong." Josie's eyes squeezed tight. She was tolerating a pain inside her, trying not to cry out. "You don't *see* me."

"I do," Linda said. "That's not fair. I'm up here every night, lately, trying to get you to talk."

"No. You treat me like less. You treat me like you treat yourself." The room was so empty their voices echoed.

"I'm calling bee ess," Linda said. "You're feeling sorry for yourself."

"I have to be good at everything and I can't be a problem and Hip can do whatever the hell he wants. You have to be good at everything and you can't be a problem and Dad can do whatever the hell he wants."

The words stung, peeling at a hidden truth.

A car horn honked. Linda didn't know she was mad until she stomped to the window, flung it open. The boys were in the car, eager for their big night out. "Calm yourselves! Give us a second!"

She turned to Josie. "So, are you coming, because you're obviously not sick."

Josie glared.

"Fine. It's too late for you to get dressed, anyway," she said, even as she was overcome by the urge to stay home, too. To blow off this stupid goddamned party. To sort this out with Josie, even if the sorting involved yelling.

"You don't have anything to say?" Linda asked, realizing only after she'd spoken that she'd given Josie no space to answer. Russell honked again. Face hot, body shaking with senseless fury, she raised her voice: "You've been moping around for months. All I've done is try to help, and now you want me to believe it's my fault? I'm at a loss here, Josie. And my snow globe. Everything I ever came from is dead and gone, and that was all I had left and you knew it."

Josie's expression hardened with something larger than anger. Linda was struck by it, her knees weak from the intensity of it, her heart carved out and plopped to the indigo-dyed rug on the floor.

"Fuck you," Josie said, rage tears sliding down her cheeks.

"No. Fuck you, you spoiled brat!" Linda said, only her voice came out shrill and defensive. It was wrong and she knew it even as it was happening. Then she was flying down the stairs, out the door, into the car, her whole body shaking.

She climbed into shotgun. In his rush, Russell didn't wait for her to buckle up. He was already pulling away. "We're late," he said.

"Who cares?"

"They said the doors won't open," he answered, confused and distracted as he navigated the snow on their driveway curb. "Invited people have to go or it looks bad. They bring it up at the review."

The review, the review, the review. She was so tired of worrying about this review, which would lead to another review, and another, and another, and for what? So they could survive long enough to turn into assholes, too?

Linda looked out and glimpsed Josie through her bedroom window. The girl—young woman—stood a foot or two back from the glass. With the expanse of the large room looming over her, she didn't look angry anymore. She looked alone. Forgotten, even, like a toy.

It all felt so wrong. *I should get out*, Linda thought. *Tell him right now to pull over*. "It was a scene in there. I screwed up. I made it worse."

Russell raised an eyebrow for show. She could tell he wasn't listening. Possibly hadn't even heard her words, was reacting only to their tone. His mind was on the party.

"She said something upsetting."

Russell rolled through a stop sign, gunned the gas. It felt like running in the wrong direction.

"What'd she say?"

"Something bad. And then I said something that made it worse," Linda answered. "Russell, could you talk to her?"

"What?" Another stop sign. He turned to her with agitation: They were late. They might get in trouble. So why was she talking about Josie?

"Could you talk to her about what's going on? I screwed up."

"Oh. Yeah. Sure," he said, gunning it again. Even as he said it, she knew he wouldn't. When had he ever talked to them about anything important? For years, she'd put forth the appearance he was involved in the rearing of their children. She'd given him credit for things he'd never done, wrapped gifts and put his name on them. For whom? For the kids, so they didn't feel neglected? For him, in the event he changed his ways, so there was a space for him? Or for herself, so she didn't have to admit what was happening? The whole pretense was kabuki fucking theater.

• • •

They arrived ten minutes late, which seemed within the confines of reasonable, but the valet was gone, and the party was so loud that no one heard them ring the bell. It took another five minutes before the butler, wearing an actual butler's costume, answered the door. He acted like he didn't know why they were there, despite the scores of parked cars, the revelry.

"The party started," the butler announced.

"We're new here. We didn't realize," Russell said. "Next time we'll be prompt." His voice wheedled. He smiled wide and phony, made prayer hands. Hip made prayer hands, then a peace sign.

"We got confused about where to go—that's all. It won't ever happen again," Russell added.

The butler smiled indulgent forgiveness, admitted them inside.

A man guided Hip to the back, Linda assumed to the pool house. So focused on getting everything right, on pleasing Cathy, he didn't look back or say good-bye, even after Linda called out to him. Russell followed the original butler. She stood there for a while. Considered getting back in the car. Remembered it was his car and wouldn't drive without his handprint or the keys.

The hall opened to a grand ballroom. A string quartet played. The thirty-foot arched ceiling was blighted with helium balloons, some of which were falling in lazy arcs, their strings curlicued in pigtail fronds. Russell pushed through the crowd to Heinrich and his office crew.

"Hey!" she heard him chirp as he glad-handed Heinrich, then hugged him with a back clap: "You're looking spiffy!" And then, to someone else: "Oh, I see they let the riffraff in!" Then some comment about his tie being an improvement, but it might get cut anyway, and laughs and laughs and laughs.

The faces here were older and more established. These were the people with golden tickets, or with *potential.* Because of ActHollow, she and Russell had been judged as potentials. Greeting everyone up front were the powers that be: Parson Junior, Anouk, Jack, Lloyd, and Daniella. Keith Parson drank red wine on the stairway half landing, looking down. No costume or crown tonight. He looked out of place in his bright yellow Omnium tracksuit. With everyone in black tie, he appeared like a thirty-year-old kid at a grown-up party, his face sweaty and sallow. *Sick,* she thought. His body was outsized and wrongly proportioned. *Steroids,* she finally realized. *In a town with so many competent doctors, this kid's got heart failure.*

She moved past the gauntlet before they could see her or call out. A black goat was tied with a slipknot to the banister. *What a sweetie,* someone mumbled, soft and baby-talking. *I hope they untie it, so it can hang out,* another person added.

She kept going, to another room far from the people she knew. Waiters crossed her path with platters. She ate a lentil bird's nest, a liver pâté amuse-bouche. She would go home to Josie as soon as the ball dropped, she decided. She would tell her happy New Year.

A waiter passed with a tray of glasses filled with red wine.

"Careful!" he said as she took one. "It's strong."

It tasted just the same as usual, only earthier.

By the long sofas, a cluster of beautiful women and men talked animatedly. They were the dayworker housekeepers and drivers of the most elite families, Jack's nanny among them. They gave Linda the uneasy sense that there was a hidden class structure within the system here. In other words, how often do housekeepers and drivers have surgically enhanced faces and bombshell bodies?

She headed in the direction of the kid party, where a wall of glass with a sliding door at its center led to a pool. There, she spotted Hip and Cathy, both in bathing suits, drinking real champagne from tall flutes. They were in the deep end of the pool, elbows tucked on the sides to hold them above its ten-foot depth.

Around them, kids chitchatted. They held grownup cocktails and accepted hors d'oeuvres. The invitation hadn't specified that the hosts intended to serve alcohol to young guests. It had not said, "by the way, hope you're cool holding your kid's head over a toilet when you get home." But perhaps it hadn't needed to do that, because no teen rebellion was happening here. Nobody did a cannonball, or shoved a friend into the water as means of flirtation. Nobody shouted or seemed drunk. In their designer swimsuits and cover-ups and robes, they were caricatures of callow and decadent adults.

She spotted Josie's "friends" by the tables and chairs. They were huddled and laughing, but they did so softly—not like the monkey banter of typical kids. "That girl's full of poop," one of them said.

In a way that was pretending to be kind, but was actually self-serving, another added, "She's *so* sensitive."

Then, the girl—Jeanette—who'd fake-asked Josie out said, "I still like her. But I'm worried. Have you noticed her weight gain? Like, a lot? Which is totally fine. But also, not healthy."

"If she gets a B in history, she's in trouble. You cannot have a B on your transcript and get into the honors track at BWU," someone added. "She better stay good at soccer. But if she gets any bigger, she won't be able to run the field. Not that there's anything wrong with that."

"I'm *so* worried," Jeanette said.

Linda kept walking, knowing that in her angry state, whatever she said would only make things worse. She went outside. Breathed the cold, perfectly filtered air. Partygoers strolled along the tall trees, offering treats to the thinned-out caladrius among the rows of shelters, but mostly, she was alone. In the distance, she could see Anouk's little cottage. The stars above were so clear that the bright ones could have been floodlights behind punched velvet, the dim ones scattered glitter.

How did I get here? she wondered.

But then, an oddly familiar scent. It had been years. Those crops had mostly died out. Tobacco smoke. Who around here still smoked cigarettes? Would it be the kind of person who didn't like this place? The kind of person undertaking a small act of rebellion, to signify a larger one? Around the corner, in an Adirondack glider, she found Rachel.

Linda stood there, caught.

Rachel made the sound of lazy laughter. Waved Linda closer. "Want one?"

"Too much like Glamp."

"These are just tobacco. But they'll kill you, too," Rachel said as she exhaled.

Linda sat on the glider next to Rachel. Found, despite what had happened between them, that she was more comfortable there than inside.

"Do you remember talking to me at your house?" Linda asked.

Rachel sucked on her smoke. "No. I'm told I've been telling tales. Did I tell you tall tales?"

"Yes," Linda said.

"How tall?"

"Whoppers," Linda said. "Were they true?"

Rachel exhaled a perfect ring. "Probably." She indicated her cigarette. "I know my benders are almost done when I start smoking. This is the tail end. I promised Kai I'd stop again tomorrow."

"Did he give you an ultimatum?"

"He's done that so many times we've both stopped counting. It's not for him," she said. "Though I do love him. He's been loyal. More loyal than me. He's got plenty to complain about, but I'm doing it because Daniella's pissed. It's bad when Daniella's pissed."

"Oh," Linda said. "Either way, it's good you're taking action."

Rachel nodded. Linda sat back. They were quiet. She finished her wine. Noticed a soft, organic deposit at the bottom of the glass. Used her index finger to taste its earthiness, like a porcini mushroom.

"Careful with that," Rachel said.

"Why?" Linda asked.

"Why? Why? Why?" Rachel imitated in irritating singsong. "You'll see. You'll see! You'll see!"

It was close to midnight. She wanted to leave, so they weren't stuck together when the New Year began. But she didn't want to go inside, didn't want to have to watch Russell kiss every ass he could find.

Rachel reached into the bag beside her, pulled out a small bottle of sherry, and tipped back. "It's too much bother to go stand in line at the bar," she said. "This way I can clear the house for sobriety tomorrow."

"That's one way to look at it," Linda said. She took the bottle from Rachel and swigged to make sure it hadn't gone vinegar and would make her sick. "The other way is that you need to be in a hospital."

Rachel waved her hand in lazy dismissal. "It's not the addiction. It's the habit. I don't know how else I'd get through my days."

"You could change things in your life. The quitting would follow." *You could leave here*, she wanted to add, but she didn't dare.

"Change," Rachel said, and she sounded, to Linda, like Josie. Spent and trapped. "When I first moved here, I had so many plans. CEO, it could have been a clean slate for everyone."

"You're not getting it?"

Rachel shrugged. "I fell down in front of Parson tonight. It doesn't look good."

"I heard you were sabotaged. Jack hurt you."

Rachel nodded. Closed her eyes, as if disappointed in herself.

"He shouldn't get away with that. The other night, you told me that you procure," Linda said carefully. "You fix. I assume that means you bribe whistleblowers and regulators. You arrange prostitutes. Maybe you stop," she said. *Maybe you gather all that damning evidence, and you give it to the lawyers on the outside, or that governor in New York*, she wanted to add.

Rachel blew a cloud of smoke. "Once you're in something, you're in it. I'm so bloody. I'm covered in blood."

Linda nodded, looking at the stars.

In the big house, the countdown started. She got up and walked toward the fake light.

• • •

On her way, she passed the pool party, and found Hip and Cathy kissing, Hip's hands roving the small mounds under Cathy's bikini top. No one seemed to be looking especially at them. Plenty of other kids were making out, including a few of the soccer kids. They were doing it in front of the servants, and it was as if they'd decided these servants were invisible.

Linda headed for the edge of the pool. Pressed her shoe against Hip's bare back until he startled, pulled his hands out from under Cathy's bikini. "I don't give a damn what the rest of them are doing. Don't be a creep."

They separated, Hip mortified, Cathy irritated with insult. Who was Linda to tell Hip anything? Hip belonged to *her*. Before the kids had the chance to answer her, Linda moved on to the big house ballroom, where all the balloons had been timed to drop at once. Kai was standing between parties, looking through the crowds of people, his eyes finding Rachel. But he didn't go to her and there was something so sad about that—that Rachel was in one place, and he was in the other. In her sickness she didn't know to look for him. In his exhaustion, he'd become done seeking her.

"Five!" everyone shouted.

"Four!"

"Three!"

"Two!"

"One!"

The balloons dropped.

Daniella cozied to Lloyd, kissing a trail up his neck to his mouth. He really did look love drunk. Jack pressed his groin against his nanny (who was possibly a sex slave), one hand on her bottom, the other squeezing her breast. This was far away, with the balloons falling fast and smeary.

Everyone was cheering and happy. Laughing and having a good time. She looked for Russell. He was hugging the many friends he'd made there, going from one to the next. He looked happy, like for the first time in his life, he'd found people who appreciated him.

She started toward Russell Bowen, her husband. He would kiss her and hold her and maybe not forever, maybe not for even a minute, but for a moment, she'd feel close to him. She would not have this annihilating feeling inside her—that their marriage, their family, their life together in this place, was over.

But then, Russell headed a few steps back, to say hello to Tania Janssen's husband, and between them, small and still—bored, even—stood Gal Parker's children.

FEATHERS THROUGH TIME: AND THE AVIAN SHALL PURIFY THE EARTH

All gods who receive homage are cruel. All gods dispense suffering without reason. Otherwise they would not be worshipped. Through indiscriminate suffering men know fear and fear is the most divine emotion. It is the stones for altars and the beginning of wisdom. Half gods are worshipped in wine and flowers. Real gods require blood.

—Zora Neale Hurston, *Their Eyes Were Watching God*

—Preface to Anouk Parson's third collection of poetry, self-published, 2053.

PART IV

It's Exactly What You Fear

(The Plymouth Valley Winter Festival)

"Gladiatorial games functioned to build consensus—a *we versus you* mentality. Said poet Juvenal, *they were the circus to Caesar's bread* (1). The Mayans cracked skulls on the steps of Chichén Itzá (2). We can also see community-building in Plymouth Valley's skin furniture (3) and through blood sacrifice in Holland's 8,000-year-old peat bog fossils (4). In times of greatest scarcity, bodies were hung, stabbed, and castrated by entire communities, each playing their part as executioner, in what archaeologists term *overkill* (5)."

—AI-generated library research using the keywords "Human Sacrifice," "History," and "Scarcity," Kings Public Library, Main Branch, 2079.

Blutkitt (blood cement)—the tendency for morally corrupt actions to calcify group attachments.

For example, when groups commit murder together, their individual guilt has the opposite of the expected effect. Instead of leaving the group, members feel they've passed a point of no return. They're bonded, perceiving those outside the group as less *real*.

Members tend to be groomed, given morsels of knowledge and responsibility, tasked with proving loyalty at each step. By the time they commit violence, they've typically transgressed so far past their moral codes that they can no longer conceive of the deeper line they're crossing.

It's only after gang and cult members commit murder that they're assigned the greater honors and leadership responsibilities of indoctrinating new members. This is because they're **Blutkitt**.

—CORPORATE CULTS FROM SEOUL TO PLYMOUTH VALLEY, by Trebor Meier, Verlag Press, 2074.

Mirage

The Parker children were small for their ages, possibly from prolonged sickness. Their hair was black, their eyes brown. Around them, the world moved. People laughed and hugged and balloons fell. But the children were still.

In screenies about the great deserts of South America, people often imagined water shimmering off the great sand expanse. With each step, the water shifted farther away, luring coyotes crossing borders to their deaths. She thought about that as she advanced through the parlor, and the children seemed to fade.

Everything else could be ignored. But not this.

Linda pushed through the crowd of people like wading through animated dolls. Tania Janssen hugged her. "May this be the most fruitful of all years!" she cried with drunken delight, her shirt stained with wine, her mouth red with it.

"Fruitful of years," Linda parroted.

Jack Lust stalked past the altar, a murderous dandy. His body obscured and then revealed two wraiths holding hands. Linda came closer, and as she did, she remembered the nightmare house. She thought of Gal, who'd once sewn all her children's clothing, married to Trish, a woman who'd never examined her patients with her hands. More balloons. One of them popped with a *bang!*

The path opened again, and there was Zach the unctuous tour guide, who'd made PV look so fine, ushering the children to the recesses of the closed-off parts of the mansion.

Linda weaved through hugging friends and lovers and more gunfire-popping balloons. Like canned music or hundred-year-old screenies in black-and-white, it all felt dead to her, the whole valley a tomb.

She chased Zach to a hall beneath the stairs.

"Linnie?" Russell called.

He's dead, too, a dreadful voice whispered.

She went deeper, but the door she'd seen Zach and the children pass through was gone. Did the walls move here, like in the Labyrinth?

Slow and boozy at first, Russell followed.

"Where are they?" she asked. The house steamed from so many warm, crowded bodies. Sweat rolled from Russell's matted blond hair and down his neck. His eyes widened with terror: his wife was about to make a scene. He lowered himself, a tall man extending his arms, tucking his head over hers to keep the party from seeing her. To undo her, like a thin and badly knotted chain.

She raced around him but now all the doors were walls. She searched with blind hands for a secret passage. Everything was cold and dark and smooth.

"What are you doing?" he hissed. "Don't you know we're not supposed to be here?"

"Sebbie! Katie! Do you hear me?" she shouted, loud as a horn.

No answer. She swerved back along the short hall. Some revelers stayed celebrating, but just as many stopped their blessings and hugs. In bespoke Fabric Collective ball gowns and black ties, they paid witness.

"Katie! Sebbie!" she bellowed.

Everything stopped, even the music. Eyes drilled.

This felt like a nightmare. How could this be happening? How was she a screaming woman at a party? "Katie! Sebbie!" she shouted as she raced through the pool house, and then around the corner, to passed-out Rachel. The party cleared a path.

She was panting, hands on thighs beside gawking caladrius, when Russell caught up. "There you are!" he cried, affable and stage loud. "Honey! What's the joke? Let me in on it!"

He took her hands, kissed both cheeks, then her lips. Whiskey-breathed, he held her too tight, too long. "Have you lost your mind?" he whispered.

"You didn't see them?" Linda asked, her cheek pressed against his fancy new suit. "Gal's kids?"

"I didn't see any kids. There's no kids here."

She pushed on him until he loosened his hold. Gawkers had followed them out. The soccer parents Amir and Farah, of course. And Ruth Epstein. Jack Lust, too. It felt surreal. These people were ghosts. Everyone was a ghost, shadows of the people they'd once been. They'd lived too long in fairyland, and now they could never go home.

"I saw," she said. But what, exactly, had she seen?

His face was smeared. Everything smeared. "Did you have the wine? It's laced with psilocybin," he said.

Things swam. Russell was holding her again, too tight. "Help me find them," she said, crying now. "Why do you keep lying to me? Why won't you help me?"

"Where? How? Do you even know what they look like?"

Everything spun. Linda stopped fighting. She leaned into Russell. The air was bending, becoming dense. She was swallowing too much. "Jack's asked us to leave. I need to get Hip. Stay here," he said, then thought better, and took her by the hand as they crossed back to the pool and collected their son. The party was quiet now. Between straggling balloons with curlicued pig tails, eyes watched.

They were back in the mansion. The goat wasn't tied to the banister anymore. It lay vacant and heavy, its body too large for the altar, its head and neck sloping down on the one side, its raggedy hind weighing down the other end. Everything melted, colors all around. The goat dissolved into the floor, and blood sprayed out across the party like sprinkler water, caking them all in death.

"Do you see? Do you see the goat?" she asked, meek now.

"Affirmative," Russell whispered, squeezing her too hard. "Quiet down."

"They killed the goat. They're murderers."

"No. It's a prop, like on Samhain. It's not real," he said as he reached out his finger to the red, turned it in the light where it glistened. "It's corn syrup." She snatched that finger, tasted its confusing sweetness.

"My God, what is this place?" she begged.

The BetterWorld and ActHollow boards of directors were by the altar. Jack's expression stayed flat, his eyes dead as coal, but there was something in his upturned lips that seemed like amusement. Lloyd appeared horrified, his mouth gaping in shock. Daniella and Anouk followed her with their eyes. They looked *through* her, and it felt to Linda like a thousand small knives.

She followed Russell, pushing through to the front door and out. Lights strung across the porch smeared into lines, burned holes through the dark revealing the awful beneath.

"What happened? Is Mom okay?" Hip asked from far away. She was between her son and her husband, each of them holding an upper arm as they all headed for the car. Hip's voice was scared. For the first time she understood that a war was happening inside him. The Farmer-Bowens were all fighting private, lonely wars.

"Too much wine," Russell said.

A flicker, like a light switch. Hip's compassion died. His fear won. "But everyone said to be careful with the wine. She should have been careful."

They were in the car somehow, Russell driving.

"I saw them. I know it," Linda said.

Russell's jaw locked in anger. "You did a lot of damage."

"What did she do?" Hip asked.

"Insulted our hosts," Russell said.

"You ruined everything!" Hip cried.

She turned to Hip in the back seat. Everything was bleeding and running. The car was melting and underneath it was the Great White Caladrius from the history book, from the shelter that first day she'd toured. It had been waiting all this time. They were in its belly.

In Linda's mind, everything went red. The belly became teeth. She kept her eyes on Hip, but she couldn't see him. Not clearly. He was smeared. They were all bloody smears.

• • •

In the morning, everything hurt. But that didn't stop her. She left the house before any of them were awake. She went to Gal's house, opened the back screen, then the aluminum door, both unlocked.

Change had happened. The kitchen was scrubbed clean, the appliances all new, some still Omnium wrapped. The living room furniture was gone. In its place, two overstuffed suitcases.

The sound of a flush. Gal came out from a small washroom. Dressed appropriately for the weather for the first time, she was in slacks, her crimped fingers laboring to align the zipper teeth of a puffy, coat-length parka.

She didn't startle at Linda's presence. "Oh. You again."

"You're leaving?" Linda asked.

"Yeah." Stiffly, she favored her left leg.

"Where will you go?"

"There's a halfway house in PVE, I guess. So, what do you want?"

The psilocybin in Linda's system hadn't worn off. Things *wonked* and pulsed. "You said your kids were still here. You said they're not in Palo Alto."

"I said that."

"Do they sacrifice a goat on New Year's Eve at the Parson Mansion?"

"Nope," she said, like this break-in, this random conversation, was the most normal and expected in the world. "It's stuffed. They haul it out every year and take the real goat back to the farm. I think. I mean, I've never been to one of those things sober."

"Me neither," Linda said. "Why do they do that? Make it seem like they're doing something awful when they're not? They had these skulls on Samhain. They looked real, too."

"I don't know," Gal said.

"Is it because they want us to be confused when they do the actual awful things?"

"I don't know," Gal said. Her movements were heavy, her speech slow. But her eyes were focused. This was sadness, not drugs. "I don't care."

"Why did you say they sacrifice people at the Winter Festival?"

Gal tried to bend her fingers to work the zipper but her scarred skin had lost all elasticity. She couldn't get a decent grip. "Maybe they don't. Maybe I'm crazy like everybody says. Maybe my kids are safe and healthy with their mother who hates them."

"Is there a way I could contact Trish to verify your story? You must have a way to reach her." Linda's voice echoed in this house now, because it was so empty.

"Trish got what she wanted and she's gone."

"Where are your kids?" Linda gasped.

Gal gave up on her coat, opened her locket. Linda came closer though she didn't want to. Gal didn't spit or lunge or try to kiss her. She seemed just as uncomfortable with their nearness.

On the left of the locket, Katie. On the right, Sebbie. A cold chill ran all down Linda's spine and radiated icy electric shocks.

"That's definitely the kids I saw last night."

Gal closed and touched the locket to her chest. "You saw them?"

"I think so. I was high. But I think so. They were okay. They were holding hands. Zach Greene took them inside the mansion and I looked for them but I couldn't find them."

"They were holding hands?" Gal asked. She sounded dazed.

"Yeah. I think so. It happened fast. I made a scene, looking for them. But I couldn't find them. I could be wrong. I want you to know."

A tear slid down Gal's cheek. "They fight like cats and dogs. But I always knew," she said. "I knew if things got bad, they'd be close. I did that right. I did some things wrong, but I never played favorites, never turned them on each other, so I did that right."

"Yeah," Linda said. "Where are they now, do you think?"

"I told you. Try the hospital. That's where they keep them. Maybe the tunnels. But the tunnels are scary, and they want to be humane about it. They trot them out sometimes—the black ribbon winners—so maybe at some event if you pay attention."

In the way that everything happening lately was surreal, Linda didn't react when Gal took hold of her waist and awkwardly, painfully, lowered herself to the floor on gnarled knees. "Please," she begged. "Get them out."

The door opened. In came smiling Sally Claus and Cyrus Galani, both with guns holstered. Their smiles didn't waver at the sight of Linda. It was as if no one had anything to hide, and Linda had all the reason in the world to be in this house, saying good-bye to Gal, who was begging at her feet.

"Ready to go?" Sally asked.

"No," Gal said. Linda helped her up, lifting her by the tender underarms. Then she took the fabric of Gal's coat in her hands. She aligned the slider and zipped her up. The gesture felt so intimate that Linda couldn't look at her as she did it.

Sally and Cyrus each took a suitcase.

"I'll burn this whole town down if I don't get to see my kids again. I'll murder every one of you," Gal said, flat and disconsolate.

Then they were out the door, headed for the gate.

Back in the car, Linda started the engine. "Don't panic," she whispered to herself, hands on the wheel, heart beating unevenly, like a gunshot victim who's bleeding out.

• • •

She didn't let herself think about it, or the fact that it was still early in the morning. She programmed Chernin's name into the GPS.

He lived in a tidy brick colonial on the north side of town. A nurse answered the door and led her into the kitchen, where Chernin and Louis were having morning tea, Louis through a straw. Chernin sported a two- or three-day gray stubble beard and wore a ratty bathrobe; Louis was neatly clad in crisp pajamas. Though the latter was the one in the wheelchair, Chernin looked sick. His hair was unkempt, the wrinkle crevices along the sides of his mouth stained with tea, his eyes bloodshot.

"Dr. Farmer, hello!" he said with real warmth, then introduced her to the nurse and to Louis, who nodded without looking away from his screenie. The program was puerile, a fast-paced cartoon with cats and dogs shooting guns and blowing up dynamite. Chernin acknowledged the strangeness of this to Linda with a shrug.

"To what do I owe the pleasure?"

"I have a question about Katie and Sebbie Parker."

The air popped with sudden static. Very slowly, Louis looked up.

"The Parker children, yes? Yes, yes, what's your question?" Chernin asked.

"Where are they?"

"Palo Alto," he said, scratching his dry cheek, where white flakes pulled away from his skin. "I released them to their mother. Yes, yes. Clean bills of health. I suspect they're still there."

Her unease built like bubbles in shaken carbonation. More, faster panting. "I saw them last night at the Parson Mansion."

"You did?" he asked with exaggerated surprise.

"Is there something special about idiopathic leukemia?"

"What's that?" He made direct eye contact for the first time since she'd known him. The look was a warning.

Still standing, she held the back of an empty breakfast chair and squeezed. "Their cancer. That's their diagnosis. I asked you about it. You treated them for it so you must have heard of it. You'd prescribed them a chemotherapeutic drug and I asked if that was best practice and you never answered."

"I never answered?" he asked with mock innocence. He wasn't looking at her anymore. He was looking at his slippered feet.

"No," she said. Her head was hurting. A dull throb all along her temples. The room smelled like toast and medicine.

Slowly, holding on to the table, with the sounds of popping knee joints, Chernin stood. "It's very early. Yes, an unreasonable time for a visit."

"I know."

"Those parties at the Parson Mansion go on. You've exerted yourself. Did you drink the wine?"

"I'm not confused, Dr. Chernin."

"Yes. I believe you are. Linda, I'm going to do you a favor and forget this happened. It's time you went home and slept this off."

Frail and slow, he showed her to the door. When they got there, away from Louis and the nurse, he leaned in close, the skin along his uneven beard thin as the bunched membrane inside an eggshell. He put his mouth to her ear.

"It's not your problem," he whispered, the sound tickling her skin. "Yes. Yes. I'm trying to stop it. I'm fixing it from the inside."

"Fix what?" she begged.

His eyes filled with water that didn't produce tears. They were drowning.

"Mitch?" Louis called.

"Dr. Chernin?" the nurse called. "I need help with the catheter."

Chernin pulled back. His eyes went distant with that spaciness she'd come to expect. He retreated someplace, like a floater picked clean by scavengers until all that's left is heavy bone.

Without saying good-bye, he shut the door.

• • •

Home, Linda went. Still early, she climbed into bed and stayed there. Even after the sun shone through the windows, the Farmer-Bowen house stayed quiet. It carried the musty emotional charge of an unwound clock.

"Honey. It's not your fault. I'm not blaming you. But can we do some damage repair?" Russell asked around noon. He stood in the doorway of their bedroom, his shadow long. Despite their soft delivery, his words felt like an accusation. "Heinrich told me the board wants a written apology."

"Later," she said.

He spent the day working in his increasingly chaotic office.

Hip and Josie stayed in their rooms. When they came out, she didn't hear wrestling in the kitchen or laughter at the way one or the other garnished toast. There were no funny voices, no jitterbug delights.

In the early evening, Hip brought her a glass of juice. *Are you okay, Mom?* he asked as she lay open eyed in bed, too upset to sleep. *They said you weren't supposed to drink that stuff. Why did you drink that stuff?*

Close the door, she told him.

The Dump

By morning, staying in bed required more energy than getting up. She was already dressed and trying to figure out what to possibly do next when Josie knocked.

"What is it, hon?"

Shoulders hunched, Josie padded barefoot into the room. "Can we leave Plymouth Valley? Is it allowed?"

Linda misunderstood. *I want to*, she thought. *But how do we get the rest of the family to come with us?*

Josie clarified. "Could you take me to the dump? I want to find that snow globe."

• • •

At the gate, Sally checked the car for contraband and found none. Linda couldn't tell if it was the lingering effect of the psilocybin, or just her mental state, but she and the world were out of synchronicity, like ballerinas on separate music boxes, spinning at different speeds.

"Hey, good-lookin'. You really tied one on at Parson's party, huh?"

"Yeah," Linda said.

"Got everybody worked up," Sally said without smiling. When a dumb person stops smiling, you suddenly realize they're not as harmless as you'd thought.

"Did I? I drank the wine. It was a bad idea."

Cheerless, Sally held on to Linda for an extra beat. "You're not working at the clinic today. Why are you here?"

"We threw something out by accident. We want to go to the dump. See if we can find it."

"What did you throw out?" Sally asked.

Maybe they weren't allowed out without a reason. But that didn't make sense. The Farmer-Bowens weren't essential. People would literally kill to have their spots here. "A family heirloom. Do you know where the dump is at?"

With much less cordiality than Linda was accustomed to, Sally gave directions. It was three kilometers past PVE, on an unmarked road. She also pulled two gas masks from her booth, logged them as borrowed, and handed them to Linda. "You'll want these. It's stinky as poop!"

With that, they left PV. It was easy, Linda suddenly realized. This place wasn't a prison. She could leave with her whole family any time. She could pack up and go.

• • •

The air today was cleaner than usual because of a recent snow. Linda's sinuses didn't instantaneously clog, nor did she feel the need to don a mask.

The ride was quiet. Linda's conversational openers had been misfiring for months. She had no confidence she'd say the right thing this time, either. "I had a bad day yesterday. I'm sorry if I frightened you."

Josie dead-eyed straight ahead. When kids are little, you do so much together that your thoughts are often in lockstep. You know what they're thinking. Then they get older, and they look like adults. It's right and healthy that they should separate, but the access you once had to them is gone. Sometimes, they even seem like strangers.

"I felt overwhelmed," Linda said to this pained young woman sitting shotgun.

"Oh," Josie said. A tear rolled down her cheek.

"Why are you crying?"

"I don't know."

"I didn't mean to yell at you about the snow globe. That was an accident. I was upset."

Josie sniffled, looked at her hands. Linda appreciated that they were driving in a car past so much snow, and not trying to have this conversation while sitting inside that big house at 9 Sunset Heights. It felt safer here.

"You're not spoiled. Or if you are, you don't act it."

Josie rolled the window a crack, breathed the frigid air.

"And maybe you're right. Maybe I do treat you differently. Maybe I treat myself differently. When you're living a thing sometimes you're too close to know."

Josie didn't answer for a while. Linda looked ahead at the snow, the small houses, the salt on the road that kept her tires from skidding. With the open window, their breath fogged the air. "It was a good snow globe," Josie said at last.

"I'd put it at medium to junky with high sentimental value," Linda answered.

They passed the clinic and went down the small main street, the run-down and shuttered stores. Josie wiped her eyes with the back of her hand. "Why did you leave me alone on New Year's Eve?"

They passed the last store, Diem's Auto, and were on the road going opposite the highway. Only one lane had been plowed. There wasn't any place to pull over. But it was an early weekend morning. There weren't other cars around. Linda cut the engine and stopped right there.

"I made a mistake," she said.

"Oh," Josie said.

"It's hard to know the right thing to do in the moment. I didn't know. I felt bad all night. I wanted to come back to you." She was tempted to add, *Daddy and Hip, too. We all missed you.* But Josie would smell the lie. She wouldn't see it as a kindness. She'd see it as an insult. "You have to tell me what you want, Josie. I can't always think of it. If you'd told me, I'd have stayed."

"You were mad at me," Josie said. And then, eyes scrunched tight: "I know I should tell you. But I don't *know* what I want."

The cold air felt good. PV was oppressive. Its walls were oppressive. The people were oppressive. Even the air, cycled through vents, tasted both fresh and dead, like a recording of music instead of the real thing.

"What's going on with you?" Linda asked. "Can you try to tell me?"

Josie pursed her thin lips and seemed to think. Then she did try, and Linda had the idea it wasn't because she'd said anything right. It was necessity. Things couldn't go on as they had been going. Josie had to tell someone. "It's like I'm not here. Like, I can see everything. I can see me, but it's not me. Sometimes it's like . . . like my heart."

"What about your heart?"

"It's beating too fast. I think I'm dying. But I know I'm not. I never was like this back home. I'm going crazy."

Linda's eyes watered. She'd been crying a lot lately, and on every occasion, it had happened because she'd learned something new and disquieting about this town. It had felt like carrying a heavy weight that kept getting heavier, until yesterday, when the weight had sunk her and she'd stayed in bed. This time, with her daughter, her tears didn't feel like a weight. They felt like a release.

"God, Josie. You're not crazy. It's this place. Crazy is the only sane reaction."

"No one likes me," she said.

"From what you say, they suck, so you're better off."

"No. Not them. They don't matter. Hip doesn't like me. And Dad doesn't."

"No," Linda said. "Hip's in girlfriend land. It doesn't have anything to do with you. And your dad, he shows his feelings differently. He wants to succeed for all our sakes. He doesn't have room to think about much else."

"I know all that," Josie said, tears falling down her cheeks to her lips. "But isn't that the same as not liking me?"

"They like you. They love you. They're just being mediocre relatives right now. I probably shouldn't judge. I've had my selfish phases . . . I wasn't mad at you the other night. I was scared," she said.

"Why?"

"I need you," Linda said at last. "It's not fair to tell you that. I'm supposed to tell you that I care about you and I'm trying to reach you because I want to save you or something. That's what a normal parent would say. My mom and dad used to tell me they needed me, and I hated it, because it meant I had to take care of them. I never got to be a kid, or a person, really. I was a crutch. They never considered me. So, I'm sorry. I don't want you to take care of me, but I do need you. I've always felt we understood each other. It makes everything okay, when someone understands you. Hip's busy and you had your finger on something when you said your dad gets away with things. It hit a nerve, I guess.

"It's wrong I'm telling you this. I know I shouldn't. I'm sorry already, but I don't think he's ever understood me. Feelings aren't his thing. He's good in other ways . . . People aren't perfect. We have these notions they're supposed to be perfect, but they're not. I got scared because since we moved here, I keep losing you. I can't find you. I don't know where you've gone. I come to your room every night thinking you'll be there and I won't be alone anymore. I can't stand these phonies and I'm pretending. I'm forcing myself so you can live in a better world, and I get home and all I want is to be with all of you. But Hip's someplace else. He's bought in. He's becoming one of them. And your dad's so haunted by the possibility of failure he can't see straight. He's this genius and it's never worked for him until now. No one ever saw it except the people here. And then there's you. And I go to you. It's so scary when you look at me like you can't stand me."

She'd been searching for the right words for a very long time. These felt like the opposite of that. Too adult. Too selfish.

Josie unbuckled. Scooted over. "Oh, Mom," she said. Linda held her tight, like she'd done a long time ago, when her daughter had still been small.

• • •

Linda suggested that they turn back around. She didn't care that much about the snow globe, anyway. But neither wanted to return so soon to PV. They drove on, smelling the dump before they saw it. It wasn't rotting organic material, like she'd expected. It was chemical: ammonia and burnt protein.

They'd both worn old clothes—jeans and boots with rubber soles. Helping each other, they walked across the modest and very odd garbage pile. About a half a kilometer around, its mound was only about six meters high. The whole thing was caked in green sludge.

"I feel like an astronaut," Linda said, trudging through muck that suctioned her feet.

"What *is* this?" Josie asked. She'd stuffed her hair into a ponytail, and her voice both echoed and dampened through the rubbery gas mask.

"Omnium disposal. But it's supposed to be separated from the other trash so there's no contamination. This is *not* separated."

"That snow globe's all sad. It's like: 'What did I do wrong?'" Josie said in her old, jokey way. "'Why did that mean girl throw me into a toxic waste site?'" Her mood had picked up since their talk, and as they walked, they stood close. Linda'd missed that closeness, their old banter. She felt lovesick at its return.

"It's inanimate," Linda said, game and cheerful. "It's like: 'I'm glad I'm not sentient or I'd be worried about the future of my existence.'"

"It's like: 'What is snow, anyway? And why is my representational snow just synthetic?'" Josie said.

They both looked across the landscape, green goop and garbage. It would be hard to find a small snow globe here.

"I really am sorry, Mom," Josie said. "It was a spoiled brat thing to do."

"I'm done caring about it," Linda answered.

The place was empty and surrounded by emptiness. There wasn't any organic material here—PV and PVE both composted that more locally. So, birds didn't swoop to feed. Rats didn't scavenge. Through the gaps in her mask, it smelled like burning tires and ammonia. It smelled wrong. She thought of those kids, those disease indices, wondered how much contamination was too much.

"Coming here was a mistake. Let's go," Linda said. "We can take showers at my clinic."

Josie ignored her and strode for the center of the pile, where it looked like the most recent truck had deposited its load. This was mostly Omnium material, but also junk like old chairs and bikes and Christmas-present rejects. Household items and bleach, too. So, chlorine. Right here, alongside Omnium and GREEN.

"Stop!" Linda's panicked voice was raised so Josie could hear it through her mask.

"I'm finding that snow globe," Josie called back.

"It's not worth it."

Josie kept going, traversing the muck. The generally-recognized-as-safe green slurry, chemical-scented muck.

"Screw it, Josie. There's only one thing here that I want and it's you."

• • •

They drove to the clinic, used the office bathroom, which had a shower. Linda put all their clothing, including their boots, into Omnium shrink bags like it was a biohazard. Maybe it was. They wore hospital gowns and sat at the staff kitchen table. Both were hungry, but there wasn't any food.

"We could go to the Quik-Bite, but I think they only take credit," Linda said.

"How much credit do you have?" Josie asked.

Linda mimed searching for pockets, coming back with nothing, then understood that the question was more open ended. "We're broke. This move cost everything."

"That's okay," Josie reassured. "We'll figure something out." It wasn't the typical Josie thing to say. Back home, she'd have whined and told Linda to figure it out because she was hungry. But she'd changed. Life there had shaved away her arrogance and girlish giggles.

She remembered Glamp, then. The way she'd been a kid one day, a woman the next. Or, she'd lived a woman's life inside the mind of a child. "It occurs to me I should ask: Is anything happening to you? Is anyone hurting you?"

Josie shook her head. "Not like how you mean."

"Then how?"

Josie picked up the pepper shaker, poured a sprinkling into her palm, and licked it. "I don't know. The houses, they're all the same. The people are all the same. I keep picking stuff up—the dishes and couch cushions. I look under the tables, the bed. I keep thinking they're not real. They're like, props. At school, after every test the kids are like: *What'd you get? What'd you get?* Every weekend it's like: *Where'd you go? Who'd you hang out with? How far is your daddy or mommy from a golden ticket? I'm third generation, except I sound like a dumbass because I don't cuss. I'm all scatological and can only say* poop! *I'm so special. My parents got their tickets early because they do side jobs. We're all so frigging special.* And it's like, do you realize the goddamned ocean just drowned the Maldives? Fuck you, dude. And seriously, what are these side jobs? Are these families all hookers?"

Linda gave her a look, like, *Maybe. They might be hookers.* "It's the same thing for me with ActHollow. My job isn't to be a doctor. It's to make them look good," Linda said, raising her arms to indicate the clinic. "We don't have enough patients. The patients we do have, we can't adequately treat."

"That must piss you off," Josie said.

"I've been in denial. I couldn't admit it until now. Nobody to admit it to."

"I wanted to like this place," Josie said. She'd wrapped her arms around her waist, gathering the material so that it bunched and puffed. "I tried. I'm still trying. I like the math. And I learned a lot of new ball skills when we started soccer, so I thought it could be good. I thought once everybody started inviting us places that it was going to work out. It would be like back home only with better stuff. But it's not like that. If anybody texts me I have to text right back. If I blow it off, it's a drama. They all talk about it like it's the end of the world. I have to conference with everybody from the team at night. Arnie Nassar runs it. He's this drill sergeant. He calls on us. We have to be like: *Yeah! Soccer's great! Yeah! School's great! Yeah!* They're always in my room. Even my room isn't safe. They can tell I don't like it, so they made me into a project. I'm a challenge. They have to rehabilitate and save me. But they don't actually care. It's just something to do."

"That sounds miserable."

"If I don't sit with them at lunch, there's payback. My lunch goes missing. My papers get stolen. So I have to hide behind that smelly freaking beam. They're the ones who smashed Hip's lunch. It was payback for losing the game.

"And the lunch people—they love to pick on the loners. They're so mad at us residents they can't wait. They screw with my food. Like, give me half or the wrong thing and then they pretend not to hear me when I complain. I know their lives suck and everything, but they suck, too.

"One time I sat with Hip. Just for the relief, you know? Cathy freaked! Lost her mind! He gave me his green beans because he knows I like them and she was all: *Why didn't you ask me first! I'm the girlfriend!* She was all afraid I was gonna steal him away from her. Like I'm gonna break them up . . . Hip didn't talk to me the whole time, just to keep her happy. God forbid Cathy Bennett ever feel unhappy. She might have an anxiety explosion. And the worst part is, I have to go through all this garbage, but I'm probably not even going to wind up in a company town. Even if I got the grades and the job, I can't stand these people. It's for nothing."

"You could go back to New York. You like it there."

"It's falling apart, plus I'd never be able to see you. Because outsiders aren't allowed in. And you couldn't see me except on some special occasion like if I died. Because you'd have to use real money to visit. And you don't get paid in money."

The idea that golden tickets broke up families should have occurred to Linda before now. But twenty-five years seemed so far away. Even one year had been more than she'd wanted to think past. Now she realized: Russell might get a golden ticket, but the kids might not. "We don't know how things are going to shake out."

"We do. It's how everything bad happens. You'll get used to the idea and it won't seem so horrible. You'll get so used to it that it seems inevitable. I'll leave and Hip and Dad'll stay, so you'll stay, and you won't even be that sad about it, because you'll have worried about it for so long that when it happens it'll be a relief. And Dad and Hip'll think I'm a rebel. They'll be like: *Oh, Josie, she marches to the beat of her own drum. What a character.* But you'll know, because I'm telling you right now. You'll know, but I bet by the time it happens, you'll forget this conversation. I will, too. We'll both be so used to the idea that it doesn't seem that bad at all."

"Josie . . . That's not true."

Josie's eyes were wet. She'd been fiddling with the blue gown on her lap so much that she'd torn it. "When you dropped me off at the police station, you said nothing was as important as me."

"And I meant it."

"But this place is bad for me."

"Yes," Linda said.

Josie's jaw hardened, and Linda saw that underneath all the tears and sadness, she really was angry. "Then why are we still here?"

Linda's eyes welled. This was it: the reason for the divide between them. "I'm trying to figure it all out, Josie. There's a lot to figure. We have limited options. You're not the sacrificial lamb. If we leave without a plan, we're fucked."

"You're on my side. And you're on ActHollow's side. And you're on Dad's side. And you're on Hip's side . . ." Josie bunched her hands, the whole gown coming undone, splitting in two at her waist. "You don't do anything. Nothing changes. It never has. Even back home. Dad said something, you got mad. Dad got what he wanted and worked late or didn't come home for dinner or watched screenies while you did the dishes. You yell and no one changes and then you don't follow up. It's like giving permission."

"Stop it," Linda said. "You're going too far."

"I want to go home," Josie said.

"Home's gone. We have nothing, Josie. This is it. Where will we go? What will we do?"

"I don't know!" Josie cried. "That's your problem!"

"Josie, I'm trying!" Frustrated, her words slipped out. "Your dad's got an excuse for everything happening here. I need to present hard evidence. He understands numbers. I swear to God, I'm trying. I've been trying. Give me some credit."

Josie's wet eyes got big. "You're looking for dirt?"

"Yeah," Linda said. "I hadn't thought of it that way, but yeah. I'm looking for dirt."

Josie smiled very faintly. "What dirt?"

"This Omnium sludge—I think it's carcinogenic. The missing

kids—their mom Gal Parker thinks they're still here, stolen someplace. There's a lot that doesn't add up."

"You think those kids got stolen?"

Linda let out a long breath. Looked to Josie. Felt sorry to weigh her down with this information but knew holding back would be worse. "Yeah. I do. Gal thinks they're going to be used in the Winter Festival. She thinks they'll be hurt. I don't know about that. I just know those kids are still in this town."

"Beware the sacrifice," Josie answered, and Linda's skin crawled.

"What?"

"All the signs say that. Everybody at school says it, too, as a joke. It's written inside practically every bathroom stall. But maybe when someone warns you like that, you should believe them."

Linda pressed her fingers to her temples and rubbed. "I can't tell if they're serious or it's twisted humor, like those sugar skulls or the dead goat. The race sucked but nobody died. The haunted maze scared the crap out of me, but we all got out okay. You didn't get in serious trouble for the stop sign. So far the threats are huge, but the consequences are light. Even Gal was exonerated, and she almost murdered her own children! It feels to me like expulsion is their greatest punishment. But I don't know. They keep saying the Winter Festival's indescribable. We have to be there to understand. Have you heard anything about what happens?"

"Not really," Josie said. "But we'd better figure it out because it's happening in less than a week."

"So soon? It snuck up on me. Do you think the festival will put us in danger, physically?" Linda asked. This should have concerned her long before now, but she'd been preoccupied.

"I don't know," Josie said. She seemed relieved to be talking about this, too. To finally be in Linda's confidence. She was taking every question seriously, feeling its weight. "They're polite so it's hard to picture."

"I keep thinking something bad might happen," Linda said. "But I don't really believe they'd do anything openly violent. They'd never get their hands dirty."

"Yeah," Josie said. "I feel like it'll be crazy. It might even be bad, like they'll dissect a horse while it's still alive and then feed it to the birds, and they'll all be like: *The sacrifice! The sacrifice!* But no, I'm not scared of getting hurt. Everybody at school's always talking about how they're wild rebels but they crap themselves over Bs."

Linda nodded. "It's hard to tell, honestly. Maybe they're dangerous to us, maybe not. I can't figure it out."

"I wish we'd never left home," Josie said.

"I know. But you need to be patient with me. I need evidence. It's the only way we'll get your dad and Hip to come."

"I can respect that," Josie said, her voice softer.

Linda realized that she could respect it, too. She had a plan.

"I'm not a milksop, Josie," Linda said. "I've made compromises and I don't regret them. I don't regret you or your brother and I certainly don't regret marrying your father. I'm proud of everything I have and none of it was easy."

"I'm sorry," Josie said.

"I don't need you to be sorry. I just need you to understand."

"I do." Her daughter had given up her blue gown and had stripped off the bottom half. She held it now, a crinkled wad of blue paper. "But Mom, can I help you?"

Countdown

Sunday

The hospital in Cleveland sent her an email. They'd looked at Carlos's bloodwork, agreed that his illness fell under the idiopathic leukemia umbrella, and were glad to accept him into the trial, as they needed more participants. Long before first light, Linda tried to call Danny Morales, but her device didn't have outside reception. Before anyone was awake, she drove just outside PV's walls, passing a night guard who wasn't Sally, and called from the clinic.

Danny said he could borrow a truck for the journey to Cleveland. He'd leave that Friday, drive through the weekend. She had no solutions to the practicalities of his situation—would he have a place to stay? Battery-charging money? When she said as much, he was surprised. "I'll be fine."

When she returned to PV, the sun was rising, but still not visible behind the eastern wall. The town was awash in a red glow. She stopped at the river and collected a sample of the water, then returned home and went through the day like it were any other.

That night, she waited until Russell was asleep, and slowly climbed out of the bed. She was surprised to find the door to his study locked. In the darkness, she walked the perimeter of the house. Sunny was out wandering and followed her, looking for food, even though she'd caught a struggling mouse between her teeth. It wriggled as she toyed with it, sucking it into her mouth, letting it climb out again.

Russell's office window wasn't locked, but the ink-wash screen inside it was. She banged it out, breaking it away from the frame and setting it aside, then gently lifting the window.

The ledge was about shoulder height. She hoisted herself, swinging first her right leg, then her left, and pulling herself through. She closed the window behind her, made sure the screen was hidden by the hedge. Sunny watched, her doll eyes shining, the mouse now still.

The room was a mess—piles of paper, crumby plates, and cups everywhere. She opened Russell's laptop, tried her birthday as his passcode. It stayed locked. She tried his birthday. Didn't want to risk trying a third and making the system lock.

She picked it up, left the study, crept up the stairs, and held it over sleeping Russell's face. The screen pinged with recognition, then unlocked. Russell stirred and sat up.

She wished she'd thought this out better.

"What are you doing?" he asked. His voice was colder than she was used to, but then again, she'd broken into his work computer in the middle of the night.

She set the screen on his lap. "I'm trying to figure out what the hell's going on."

Russell shut the screen. "So am I. What the hell's going on, Linda?"

"Idiopathic leukemia and Omnium. I think there's a connection. Gal's kids, who have it—I saw them at the Parson Mansion."

"Honey, you were high," he said, his voice still groggy.

"Okay, fine. They weren't there and I'm crazy. I never used to be crazy. But suddenly, I'm crazy?"

Russell threw back the covers. "I didn't say that. I'm saying you can't break into my system. Just ask me if you want to know something."

She felt a little ridiculous. "I know you. You're hiding something."

"If I saw two little kidnapped kids at a party, I'd notice it. If I thought Omnium was killing people right now and there was a way to stop it, I'd stand up." He said this with shining eyes, with conviction.

"I want to believe you. I really do," she said.

"Then believe me."

"I guess right now I'm feeling trust but verify, Russell. I'll be satisfied if you do two things for me. I want you to run a tox screen of the river water, and I need you to correlate the Omnium waste-processing centers with idiopathic leukemia incidence on a map. And in the absence of that data, all cancers and autoimmune diseases."

His face reddened. She couldn't tell if it was impatience or something more. "I will if you keep this between us."

"Why?"

"Because they're touchy. Haven't you noticed? You screamed at a party the other night. You accused these people of kidnapping. Now you're going after their miracle product. Let's keep a lower profile."

"You'll run the test? You'll do the mapping?"

He sat up, covers over his knees, screen pushed aside. "We won't find anything. I promise you we won't. But I'll look."

"Can you get the results to me before the Winter Festival?"

He smiled at her, a peculiar smile that twisted his lips but didn't change his face. "Yeah. Okay," he said, in a way that made her feel humored. "But even if you are right and they're doing something criminal, what does screaming about it help?"

"You're conceding I might be right?"

The smile was gritty, somehow. Like sand or dirt had been rubbed into it. "I don't see any evidence. But like you said, you never used to be crazy."

Tears burned her eyes. She couldn't tell whether they were the good kind she'd felt with Josie, or the bad kind that had plagued her lately. "You swear to God you're not keeping secrets?"

"I swear on our kids," he said.

On their kids? She was horrified. That started her waterworks, the bad waterworks. "If you say that, I believe you. I have to."

"Thank you," he said, and then the ugly smile was gone. He was Russell again. It was over. She could convince herself it was over and okay and he wasn't, very obviously, lying.

"Thank you. I'm sorry I did that to your screen. I know that was out of line."

She realized that his eyes were wet, too. When had he started crying? "It's fine. Just don't do it again."

"I know you're working your ass off and it feels like I'm undermining you. But I have to understand what's happening. I have to know. For my sanity. Your help means a lot. Thank you."

"You're my wife," he said, his voice gruff. "I'm always on your side."

They were sitting closer now. She leaned into him.

"We've been in different places lately," she said, though, now that she thought about it, they'd more often been out of synchronicity during their marriage than in it.

"I'm really tired, Linda. I'm tired all the time." Her sympathy returned. This was Russell, her earnest, dependable husband with whom she hadn't always agreed, but whom she'd always respected.

"Can I do anything?"

"Make nice with ActHollow?"

"Okay," she said. "I can do that. Russell? Can you do something?"

He let out a sigh that seemed to indicate *not one more thing*.

"Can you talk to the kids?"

"About this?" he asked.

"No. Not this. I just think you should talk to them. Josie's feeling lonely. And Hip . . . this thing with Cathy's getting serious."

"Sex?" His demeanor changed, and he seemed quietly proud.

"If it hasn't happened yet, it's coming. I don't mean to be the typical bitch-in-law type, but the more I know her, the more it feels to me like Cathy's selfish. She likes him because she thinks he's got no other options. She can push him around."

"I hope that's not true," Russell said, finally putting the laptop on the night table.

"Yeah. And if he's intimate with her, it's very important he do it right. He's a good kid. I believe in him. But he needs to be told explicitly how it all works. How to make sure everything's consensual, to the letter of the law, for his own sake."

"He'd never do anything untoward. That's not him, Linnie. Not ever."

"Yeah. But it needs to be said. Everything needs to be said. Would you talk to him? Not just say you'll talk to him, but actually talk to him?"

"Okay. Yeah," he said, sounding tired. It was, after all, three in the morning. An ungodly hour for a surprise confrontation with your spouse.

"Don't you want to?"

"Yeah. I just feel like you'll do it better."

"Why?"

"You all talk the same. You make the same jokes. They're like mini-Lindas. I don't know what I have to add to that."

"You're their dad," she said. "They only have one in the world. Honestly, just for your scarcity, I think they like you better."

Russell didn't answer for a bit. Blinked up at the ceiling. A tear fell. "They'll really listen to me?" In the time she'd known Russell, they'd had many missed connections. It's easy, when that happens, to assume the worst—she was a cog in his life, interchangeable. The kids were accessories. He resented her, had been afraid she'd leave him, and so had sat on her career, forcing her dependency. Though these interpretations were, on some level, true, they were the cruelest iterations of the truth. It was just as possible that he wanted to help but had no idea how to do it, or even how to ask for instructions and admit the deficiency.

On a few lucky occasions, like now, they talked enough to pierce through all the nonsense and arrive at the truth: he loved her. He wanted good things for her and for their family. She loved him. She wanted good things for him. That didn't mean they agreed with one another on the means to acquire those things.

"Yeah," she said. "They'll especially listen to you."

"I don't know what I can teach that kid about sex. At fifteen I wasn't close."

"You knew some tricks by the time we met," she said.

"All acquired from porn, none from experience," he said, and they both chuckled. "Okay, I'll talk to him. I'll talk to them both."

They rolled together in the bed. He pushed his groin into her and he was hard. It might be a good idea to make love tonight. It might make them feel closer. They were both considering, hands probing lazily, but they considered for too long and he fell back asleep.

She awoke a little while later to the sound of the shower. For reasons she couldn't explain, she didn't knock. She looked through the keyhole. He wasn't breathing into a paper bag. It was more disturbing than that. He was staring at the floor, naked and utterly still.

"Russell?" she asked. "Are you okay?"

Slowly, he walked into the water.

Monday

Josie opted out of riding with Arnie Nassar and the soccer crew to school. Instead, Linda dropped her off, along with Hip. On the ride, Hip rambled about universal golden tickets. He and Cathy were working on getting everyone to sign the petition, but since New Year's Eve, residents had been reluctant to add their names. Some were even asking for their names to be removed. They were afraid that Lloyd might not become chairman and that if a new regime came along after Parson retired, there'd be retaliation.

Josie interrupted from the back seat. Her voice was jaunty. Perky, even. "Could you forge 'em?"

"What? No! Why would we do that?"

"I dunno. Why would you pick universal golden tickets as a cause? Why not the society for rescuing dead cats? Or the conscientious citizens for increased child labor?"

"People have a right to care about their own lives. Everything doesn't have to be about rescuing the poor or cleaning the air," he answered from shotgun. "And in a way, universal tickets *are* about life and death. Outside is bad."

"Yeah. But also, you and Cathy are lame-bot express. Trust me. Her next cause she's gonna drag you into is harvesting spinal fluid from Pakistani babies so she can live longer, because this whole death from old age thing is really scary. Existentialism is giving her a panic attack."

What Josie'd said was not nice. Linda knew that. When you love someone, you support the people they choose to love. But maybe that's what siblings were for, breaking those rules, because damn, it was a bull's-eye.

Hip lost his mind. "How can you say that? You're so selfish! You think you're a good person but you only ever care about yourself. You're all sad lately and we're supposed to feel sorry for you, but why? You don't ask how anybody else is doing. You don't care. You don't clean up. You don't ever say *thank you* to Mom. You're a freak. Nobody likes you. At least I *have* a girlfriend. At least people want me around."

"Whoa," Linda said. "Stop talking. Too far, Hip."

The rest of the car ride was tense. Hip fumed. Josie tried to hide her tears by staring straight ahead and not wiping them. Linda didn't wade in. She knew from fifteen years of peace-brokering that they were both too raw.

When Linda pulled up to the designated drop-off area, Hip busted out and didn't look back. Left his door wide open, which was how Linda knew he wasn't just angry, but distressed. Josie got out, shut her door, then leaned into shotgun.

"He didn't mean it, Josie," Linda said.

"No?" Josie asked.

"Okay. Maybe he did mean it. But that doesn't make it true."

• • •

After her shift at the hospital, Linda checked the kiosk for Katie and Sebbie Parker's files. True to Chernin's word, they'd been marked as discharged back in September. After that, she checked every pediatric patient registered at the hospital. None resembled the Parker kids.

In the absence of any leads, she decided on a physical search. She took the stairs to the fourth floor, which was divided into maternity and mental health. She found two sleeping babies in the nursery, their milk-fed mouths open in satisfied little *O*s. A sole attendant read her device at the front desk. Linda passed from the east wing to psychiatric in the west wing. She hesitated only briefly—wasn't sure she was allowed there—then palm-accessed her way inside.

It was shocking.

The sound-tight door opened to bedlam: ambient beeps and

whines, screeching wheels on rushing gurneys, yelps and shouts from patients and professionals alike. Everything whizzed, a fast-paced contrast to the rest of the hospital—the rest of Plymouth Valley. There were two whiteboards, both full. On the floor, a maintenance person was cleaning a quart-sized pool of blood, his mop's yarn strings saturated with red. She skirted around that, kept her eyes wide for two small children.

The air had a fissure to it—a crackle. She passed one open door after the next, all occupied. Some were young people in their teens and twenties. More were middle-aged. Through the open door on her left, she saw a drooling, heavily sedated brick of a man. Spittle gathered along his lower lip and ribboned down to the shining floor. She froze. It was Keith Parson. The Beltane King.

He smiled slowly, a wide, ugly grin that showed too much gums and too many teeth. "Hello to you," he said, patrician and arrogant, like that first day she'd met him, in Anouk's cottage.

Linda walked faster, away from him. "It's okay, honey. Don't you know everything's okay?" she heard a nurse ask a woman in the next room, who was weeping. Linda recognized her, too.

"It came to me on New Year's Eve through the eyes of a goat," goalie soccer mom Ruth Epstein answered. "It said I'm the new prophet. I'm God now."

Afraid she'd be recognized—caught—Linda kept walking. She passed more rooms, didn't see any kids. Someone at the end of the hall was howling to be let alone. It was a scarecrow-skinny man in his late thirties, his arms and legs strapped down. Percy Khoury. Red Rorschached through the white gauze of his freshly bandaged wrists. Like fairy-tale breadcrumbs, it streaked a smeared, hastily mopped trail leading out and down the hall.

"Mr. Khoury, this is too much. You know very well that you're not allowed to do any maintenance on the reactor until you're medically cleared to go back to work. You have to stop going there. Do you want expulsion? Because that's where you're headed."

"I have friends. They're bigger than you think. They're coming for you."

"Do I have to adjust your olanzapine, too?"

He noticed Linda. Locked eyes with her as the nurse depressed the plunger on a hypodermic into his blood-smeared arm.

"You're liars," he said, his voice fading as he nodded off.

The nurse noticed Linda and launched: "Where's your access pass?"

Linda shrugged, like: *Oh, was I supposed to have a pass?*

"Get out," the nurse said.

• • •

She didn't leave the hospital. She found the stairs and walked the length of the third floor, through surgical and recovery. Then the second floor, mostly offices. Halfway down the east wing, she was at Chernin's office. Her hands shaking from all she'd seen, she forgot to knock. She needed to see him. To talk to him. He'd wanted to confide in her the other morning. Maybe he would do it, now.

She opened. There was Chernin, lying on his office couch, his eyes closed. His chest rose and fell in deep sleep. It wasn't unusual for doctors to nap during work breaks. It was a habit she'd developed back as an intern, when she'd been working long hours. She was about to back up and let him rest when she noticed the tank on the floor beside him. Rubber tubing ran out of it, ending in a mask that Chernin clutched in his left fist.

NITROUS OXIDE, the label read.

He wasn't sleeping; he was high.

How had she not guessed this? It was so obvious. Every sign: the big pupils, the spaciness, the general wishy-washy lack of accountability that characterized every junkie she'd ever known—she'd seen all of it before, back in Poughkeepsie.

She shook him by the frail, thin shoulders. Maybe he'd be so high he'd think he was dreaming, and she'd get a straight answer. He grunted. It was a pain sound, though she wasn't shaking him hard. "Where are the Parker children?"

His dilated pupils didn't adjust. Squinting through the bleariness, he sat up, still holding the mask, as if believing that if he did not let it go, she wouldn't notice it. She saw that his wrists were bruised with pinprick centers. He'd been injecting something, too.

Like my dad, she thought, who'd given up snorting Glamp and by the end had been shooting it.

"Where are they?"

"It's not time for them yet, you maniacs," he muttered.

"Time for what?"

His eyes regulated, the black shrinking. He reached for his glasses and pushed them over the bridge of his nose with a shaking hand. "No, no. You're not permitted here." His voice was slow, confused.

"You're not permitted to practice medicine while high," she said.

With great effort, he stood. His voice was clearer than the rest of him. "This is none of your business, Dr. Farmer."

"What are you doing?" she asked. "What's going on?"

He eased toward the device on his desk, like he thought she was going to jump him. He picked it up, clumsily dialed. "I'm being attacked. Help," he said, his voice flat.

She made no move to stop him. They stood there, waiting. Chernin's eyes stayed lowered. Linda's stayed pointed.

"She's threatening me," he told security when they arrived. "She's not well."

Linda indicated the nitrous.

They were both taken to the police station, Linda in cuffs, Chernin freely. He gave his statement first. Linda watched him leave. He glanced at her, the skin around his mouth dry and red for reasons she now understood, his expression so calm as to seem dead.

Linda was ushered into a back office to meet with the police chief, a guy named Pratt. "I did not attack that man," she said.

Pratt gave her a side-eye, which she took to mean, *Obviously.*

"He won't press charges if the hospital agrees to put you on leave, which they've done," Pratt said.

"I'm fired? That guy's a junkie!" she said, louder than she'd intended.

"He's a diabetic. He was treating himself," Pratt said.

"You don't treat blood sugar with nitrous oxide."

Pratt stood. "I've spoken to the higher-ups and this is their decision. Their patience is thin on you and your family. The public drunkenness, the stop sign your daughter broke, sneaking into the mental ward . . . We'd typically push for expulsion today. Right now. But your husband spoke in your favor. He agreed that if you cause any more problems, he'll commit you to a minimum of three months at our psychiatric facility—the fourth floor."

Pratt walked out, leaving her there on the comfy couch, where she picked up the letter Russell had e-signed, agreeing to the recommendations of the board, which had convened in the time she'd spent in the waiting room. Then she heard his wheedling voice: "Linnie?"

"I had no choice," Russell explained on the ride home. "You put me in the worst position, Linda. You promised a low profile and you did the opposite."

She listened to his logical arguments, heard out his indignant frustration. In the midst of it, she interrupted. "Are you saying that if I fuck up one more time, you're going to commit me to the PV mental ward? Do I have this right, Russell?"

"Of course not! But I had to promise them something or we'd be out on our asses—no deposit, no car, no nothing. We'd literally be on the street."

When they got into the house, he seemed to think that she'd follow him to his office, where they'd talk more and in private, figure out how Linda would make her many apologies, keep this shit show going one more day.

He stood in the doorway, waiting.

She saw that grin again, scratched with sand or dirt. Imagined it bleeding through lace in the land of nightmares. "Naw," she said. Then she was up the stairs, locking the door to her bedroom.

Russell didn't come to bed that night. Perhaps he used the guest room or the fold-out in his study. Would his back hurt? She hoped so.

Tuesday

The next morning, she didn't get up to take the kids to school. What the hell did school matter? But at seven fifteen a.m., Josie knocked.

"Come on in," Linda said.

"Are you okay?" Josie asked.

"I'm still thinking on the things we talked about," Linda said. "I'm working on them."

Josie seemed relieved.

"I'll figure it out," Linda promised.

Just then, Russell poked his head in. Linda had the feeling he'd been listening. "I'll take them."

• • •

That afternoon, Linda drove through falling snow to the PV Hospital's back lot. Foggy laundry steam poured from a vent in the basement.

She tried to palm her way inside the employee entrance, but her access was denied. So she went around front to the emergency room entrance, where she flashed her badge at the dayworker attending at the front desk. "I'm having an ocular migraine—I can't see the palm access in back, so I thought I'd come through here?" she lied.

He let her through.

She went fast, passing regular staff like Greg Hamstead. If he saw her, he didn't say anything. She found the stairs. Went to the last place she hadn't searched: the basement. The door was locked. No access. She tiptoed to the rectangle of glass just above eye height, saw two PV-uniformed cops in their country club green uniforms. Cyrus Galani was one of them.

She retreated, sitting on the stairs as she tried to figure out how to get in. She could lift Chernin's palm print from his car handle or head back to his house and peel it from his front door. Make a mold and use that to gain entrance. But this seemed complicated, and likely to go wrong, and she had no idea how she'd competently execute any of those things. She could also just wait and see what happened.

After about a half hour, a nurse emerged from the basement elevator. She wheeled a cart with two trays into the guarded room, then came back out empty handed.

Hours passed before anything else happened. No one came down the stairwell. Her worries of getting caught subsided into boredom and, after that, doubt. This endeavor was, incontrovertibly, absurd.

But then, the elevator opened again and there came Dr. Chernin and Pratt, the chief of police. Pratt was holding two teddy bears and a brunette baby doll. Cyrus opened the door for them and suddenly the hall was empty. They were all inside.

A jolt ran through her, bursting and zinging with electricity.

Fifteen minutes later, Chernin and Pratt left the way they'd come, without the doll and teddys. It was the end of the day. Cyrus and his partner had to be leaving soon. They'd take this back exit where the staff cars were all parked. She placed a pen with a wide cap on the ground, within the arc the open door would make. Then she hid in the nook under the stairs.

No movement.

Around dinnertime, she texted Russell and the kids to figure out dinner on their own. Ninety minutes later, her door opened. Cyrus and his partner headed straight for the exit. She rushed around the corner. But the pen glided out of the way. No time to grab the handle.

It shut with a hard *click!*

She waited another hour. The relief guards in the hall now were older and seemed like good friends. "Dumb thing bit Jessie so he kicked it," the one said. "Now it limps. Don't tell any of these Hollow fanatics."

"Pooping hate these pooping birds," the other answered, and then, scandalized, both laughed.

It was time to go home.

She was distracted enough that she almost missed the turn for her house. As she headed inside, lumbering Sunny crossed her path and hissed.

Inspired by the old security guard's confession, she came closer, felt extra weight in her right foot. It was itching to swing in a low arc. Send Sunny flying like a football, make her limp, or die mysteriously from internal bleeding.

Most animals can feel violence before it happens. But Sunny wasn't scared. She was bold. She hissed louder: *SSSSSSSSS!*

Linda swung, knowing even before her foot landed that she wouldn't be able to carry through and hurt a living creature. She kicked air near the bird and the bird hissed harder. She kicked closer, grazing her fat, feathered side. Sunny got scared and backed up. Linda followed, kicking and stomping, until Sunny retreated into her shelter. Her temerity gone, she hid in the very back.

"You're a lying piece of shit. You lie to me, you lie to the kids, you lie to yourself. All you ever do is lie," Linda told the bird.

• • •

Inside, Russell was waiting. He wore an Omnium robe, cinched, and it didn't seem like he had pajamas on underneath. There was something urgent and wild in his eyes. "Late night?"

"Yeah. Where are the kids?"

He pointed above, meaning upstairs, in bed.

"I thought we were going out tonight," he said. "Daniella and Lloyd had that prefestival get-together. Everyone missed you."

"You didn't get my text?"

"It didn't explain where you were."

She caught something in his expression. "But you turned on the locator. You know where I was."

After so many years, she knew that his lack of response was an admission. He started for his office, where their voices were less likely to carry. She followed. Inside, he sat behind the desk with his hands in fists against the classic chestnut wood. The mugs were all still there. The papers and tea bags and mayhem, too.

"Those kids aren't with the ex-wife in Palo Alto," she said. "They've been keeping them locked up in the basement of that hospital. If they were in a clinical trial on the outside, they'd be getting marrow transplants. I doubt that's happening here, where they're trapped behind a locked door. It's like the residents want to keep them alive, but not cure them. They're keeping them for the festival."

"How can you know this?" he asked. On his desk, he seemed to notice the mess for the first time. He stacked and realigned in a kind of panic, but the mess was overwhelming. "Did you see them?"

"No. But security's guarding the door. Chernin brought toys. Who else could it be?"

"But you didn't see them."

"I've never seen gravity, either."

Russell's neck and jaw—his whole body—went tight, as if he were pulling a tug-of-war rope. "So you don't know."

"I do know. What I want to understand is why they're hiding them. What goes on at this Winter Fest?"

Russell's fingers ticked the scattered items on his desk, as if they might provide an answer. "Linda, these people you're talking about, this *they*—they're your friends. Gal gave you alcohol poisoning. She set her house on fire. Would you rather those kids went home to her? Isn't it better they're kept away and safe? I'm not saying it's true, but if it is, there's a reason no one told you. It's not your business. Maybe they don't like the ex-wife, either. Maybe you're right, and they plan to involve the kids in the festival. But for all we know, it's a healing ritual. The myth of the caladrius is that it eats sickness. These people don't have cold-blooded murder in them. Why would anyone trust you with the truth when you act like this?"

"Russell, they lied!"

Russell opened his device and turned the screen to face her. Their bank app was opened, and the balance was laughably low. "What drives me wild is that you don't know anything. But you're taking it upon yourself to blow up our lives."

His words hit, but they made her angry, too. "What's the deal with Omnium?"

He paled.

"Josie and I went to the PV Dump. The sludge—this Omnium sludge—has an awful smell. Does it cause make people sick? If I accessed the cancer or aplastic anemia or birth defect incidence in Hami, China, would the numbers be through the roof? Is that why they moved production out of PV? Is that why they hired you, because you can cover it up?"

He reddened. "I told you. I don't have any data that supports what you're saying. And honestly, that's insulting. I worked for this. I *earned* this."

"Have you seen the sludge?"

His face went to stone. Muscles tense, chin locked. "It's safe. Every study says so."

Linda ran out of gas. There was no point in this. She needed data. But she had the awful feeling that he had the data. It was on that laptop. Maybe he'd gone so far down the rabbit hole of justifications that he didn't know it, himself. But he was lying.

"Everything I've ever done has been for you. Even this town, I did it for you."

"This wasn't for me," she said. "It wasn't for Josie, who's falling apart. It wasn't for Hip, who's turning into a jerk."

"It's always for you," he said. He was looking her right in the eyes and he seemed sad. Disconsolate, even. Like it was tragic that she wouldn't believe him. Like they'd be fine right now, if she'd just trust him. The problem here was her lack of faith.

The whole thing was so confounding, so confusing. "Why are you being like this?" she asked, high pitched and trying not to cry.

"We could work here. We could live and be happy. All you have to do is shut up."

"But Russell," she said, standing now. She hated the squeaking sound of the defeat in her voice. "They're lying."

Russell came over and stood beside Linda. He took her hands in his, full of concern. "You're pushing yourself too hard on this. You don't eat. You don't sleep. I'm worried you're having a nervous breakdown."

She didn't know what came over her. She'd never done anything like it in her life. She swung her hand back, slapped him. Then she stomped out, furious and on fire.

• • •

He stayed downstairs, and slept down there, too. She went up. Pacing like an animal, she started packing her clothes. But the winter items were bulky, and she didn't have enough bags for all the mementos—the photo albums and her wedding dress. And how would she transport all these bags?

She stopped packing. Even if she figured out a rental car service, who'd take her account on a handshake? She needed to lease a home, still, and figure out where that home ought to be. It was too late to wake the kids. They'd need an explanation, and even after she provided it, Hip wouldn't go along. Probably, it would be best to just lie—stick both kids in the car and tell them she was taking them on a vacation.

But lying's not okay.

. . . Was she ready to leave Russell?

She stopped packing. She sat up half the night, wheels spinning.

Wednesday

The next morning, she came down early to the kitchen, intending to keep the kids home from school and have a talk with them. But Russell was waiting. "I think you should keep all this to yourself," he said.

"Why's that?"

"You'll upset them. They'll worry about you. Like I'm worried about you." She noticed that his shirt buttons were mismatched, the left tail longer than the right. He hadn't shaved, either. "Say I believe you, what's to be gained?"

Linda held her head. Which was hurting. She'd lied about migraine aura before, and now she was having a real one.

"Russell, how bad is Omnium?"

"Just stop it," he said.

• • •

He took the kids to school. She heard the car door shut, the purring solar engine of Russell's sedan. Then the house was empty. Even Esperanza wouldn't arrive for another couple of hours.

She went to Russell's office. He still hadn't cleaned. On the floor, several pairs of cast-off shoes. What was new since last night: statistics texts opened to random pages, which meant he'd been ignoring the software's algorithms and doing the work by hand. After sixteen years, she couldn't help it. She carried the dishes to the kitchen, tidied the floor, collected the shoes by their heels and set them outside the door. Then she opened his screen.

She tried the kid's names and birthdates but nothing. She tried their old address on Bedford Avenue, and their new one here in PV. These didn't work, either. The system locked her out for an hour. During that time, she read the scattered papers, all statistically significant indices of "positivity" in large and small studies.

She tried the password again, and, in a moment of frustrated nihilism, typed *idiopathic leukemia.*

It unlocked.

He'd stashed a lot of files on his hard drive. Over the following five hours that he was at work and the kids were at school, she read them all. It turned out he had done that research for her. She found a recent tox report on the PV river water, and a map analysis colocating disease with Omnium waste-processing facilities. PV water contained trace amounts of PERC and benzene, known carcinogens. Cancer and autoimmune diseases in populations near Omnium waste were higher than average and statistically significant. It was all very damning.

At one point, Esperanza knocked. Feeling overcome, Linda told her to come in.

Esperanza brought her bucket and mop—the old-fashioned kind with yarn-like loops.

"I'm reading about Omnium," Linda said. "Apparently, in the presence of chlorine and GREEN it creates a toxic sludge. Outside the walls, everyone near a waste station gets contaminated. But here in PV, it's mostly children who swim in the river. It's got a thousand different names, because we're like the Tower of Babel. Nobody assimilates data anymore, except the big companies.

"Gal Parker's kids got it. The toxins haven't been entirely remediated from the river, so they had that exposure. It's hard to get a handle on the outside numbers, but they're much bigger. Has it hit PVE very hard? If so, I can see why people might avoid the clinic."

Esperanza looked at Linda like she was out of her mind, took the bucket and mop, and walked back out, shutting the door behind her. Linda didn't blame her. On the contrary, she showed good sense.

"I want out," Linda continued, like there was still someone listening.

• • •

It was the deepest heart of winter, and the town was dark for a long time before anyone came home. In the interim, Daniella called. "Hi, sweet thing. You haven't been answering my texts. Are you sick?"

Linda held her device at a distance. Daniella's voice felt malignant in her hands. "A little. Low grade. Sorry."

"Oh! That explains it! The assistant at the clinic said you were refusing to give him your notes?"

"He exceeded his authority. He went through my desk."

"Oh. I see," Daniella said. "But it's not your desk. It's ActHollow's desk."

"They do it differently back home," Linda said.

"Don't worry. Just cooperate next time," Daniella said. "But did you get the file Anouk sent? She found a list of specialists willing to teleconference."

"I saw that," Linda said. The list was composed of random specialties totally unrelated to pediatrics and would be useless.

"We can start next month. With the Winter Festival, we obviously can't meet this weekend, and we'll want some time to decompress after that. I'm looking at the scheduler right now. We haven't increased traffic in weeks. Publicity needs to be the big agenda item for our next meeting."

"Is the MRI coming?" Linda asked. "Or the drug printer?"

"Oh, soon. Very soon," Daniella said. "Also! I found another doctor willing to volunteer. This one's a PhD, not an MD, but she's game."

"I didn't know you'd found another . . . practitioner."

"Can't have too many! With your suspension, we need to show the board we're serious. We can't have our main doctor be a person who's barred from the hospital! Or is it banned?"

"Oh," Linda said. "So, you've decided."

"For now. But the door's open for you once you get yourself unfucked with the powers that be. You're still on the board, too. For now. I need you or I won't have any board at all. Oh! Right, I should tell you about Rachel. She had to make a choice."

Linda's stomach hollowed. "What kind of choice?"

"Kai tried to leave with the children. He claimed it was just a visit to relatives. After twenty-four hours they tracked the vehicle. Stopped them at the Mexican border."

"Oh, no!" Linda said.

"He's such a dummy. Who the hell wants to live in Mexico? They recycle sewer water."

"Right," Linda said, though she had no idea whether Mexico was bad. She'd never been there.

"Anyway, we had to kick it up to New York. The judge made an emergency decision because of the kidnapping. Rachel got sole custody. But then Kai said he was sorry, and Rachel took him back. They recommitted. It was adorable."

"Wow," Linda said, imagining the scene with horror. Man wants to leave with his kids; man gets stopped; man goes back to same life, pretending he's happy. Wife apparently doesn't give a shit, so long as she gets decent childcare.

"But Kai had a condition: Rachel had to check herself into the hospital and dry out. It's a good thing, too. She was getting out of hand."

"She was," Linda agreed.

"Apparently, I'm a whore," Daniella said. "Can you imagine?"

"No," Linda lied.

"I'm all for gossip but she went a little far. Anyway, she'll be out of commission for a while. You'll see her at the Winter Festival—she has to go to that—but otherwise, she's taking a break. I told her she's out of ActHollow. She can come back once she apologizes. I'm a little miffed, to be honest. It's okay to talk about *other* people, but it's not okay to stab your best friend in the back."

"Right," Linda said. "It must have hurt your feelings."

"Feelings? No. Nothing hurts my feelings. I'm a grown-up. But I helped her. I had her in good position. She was going to be in leadership, and now that's gone."

"Jack's definitely getting CEO?" Linda asked.

Daniella blew a frustrated raspberry. "It's going to make Lloyd's job much harder, having Jack around. Mine, too, without Rachel. She's been my person for a long time and now I'm alone," Daniella said, flat and angry, like the sorrow in there was an underwater volcano. She had no access to it.

"Is she going cold turkey or are they administering something to ease her symptoms?" Linda asked. "I don't mean to sound alarmist, but alcohol is the only drug where the withdrawal can literally kill you."

"Oh, who knows. She's done it enough you'd think she'd have written a manual," Daniella said.

Linda pulled the device away from her ear and stared at it. "I'm so sorry you had to deal with all this," she said.

"Thank you," Daniella said. "Honestly, between your little revolt and Rachel falling apart, things with Lloyd have been shaky. It's every man for himself."

Thursday

Russell was avoiding Linda, and Linda was too angry to seek him out. He'd been sleeping in his office. They walked circles around one another. As if she could no longer be trusted, he'd taken it upon himself to drive the kids to school. That Thursday morning, she went to the border.

"Today's not your day!" Sally said, waving big and seemingly over her anger.

"I know! But I wanted to have a look at the halfway house I've been hearing about."

Sally's eyes widened. "Oooh! Hot gossip. Are you visiting someone?"

"No. I just want to let them know that the clinic's open to them if they need it."

"Sure. Just be careful. Too many trips outside starts to look bad."

It was snowing and had been snowing. Drifts settled across lawns and sidewalks and sides of streets. PVE looked clean for once. The car wasn't great on the ice—and neither was Linda. She skidded, rolling across the median. But there wasn't any oncoming traffic.

She passed the clinic, and after a short kilometer made a left at a ten-foot-high snowbank. Then down that street. She was surprised to see that the houses here were tended, their shutters freshly painted. Great air purifiers were mounted to side yards. PVE's middle class—engineers, plumbers, and architects.

On the radio, a story about the fall of Berlin. Another story about nuclear capture. Working in tandem, United Colonial scientists and Chinese scientists had made another breakthrough that they were now testing in Nevada, Tehran, Chernobyl, and Yangjiang. Except for Tehran, which had been badly hit, the new technology had scrubbed all ambient radiation within forty-eight hours. People in Chernobyl were wandering through overgrown fields that had once been roads. The scientists involved in the breakthrough had been arrested for espionage and sedition to overthrow their respective governments. Instead of seeking asylum, they'd surrendered and were facing death penalties. In a Chinese-American joint statement, they announced whatever was done to them was worth it. They believed it was important to stand trial in the hopes of proving their innocence and paving the way for more open communication.

Despite all that was happening in her own life, a feeling of wonder rippled through her. You get used to people doing terrible things. You get used to being told that only suckers take risks. You hear this so much you believe it. You believe that if you try, you'll try alone, and because of that, you'll fail. But here were people who'd done something, who were willing to die for that thing. They existed. Always had.

She made a right at the next block, which followed the Omnium River. The snow at its banks was an unnatural, oil-slick grayish black. She went another kilometer, the car skidding the whole time. She stopped in front of a run-down Victorian house with smoke pluming from its chimney. It reminded her of Poughkeepsie.

Upon knocking, the door opened to Gal's familiar face. She was wearing a wool cap that covered the scars along her scalp, along with a long-sleeved shirt and plain trousers. Her hands glistened with some kind of ointment she'd probably applied for the pain.

"Hi," Linda said. It oddly felt like she was talking to an old friend.

Gal's eyes welled with tears. "You found them."

"Maybe."

Gal leaned against the door for support. She looked older. She'd somehow gone from twenty-five to forty years old in less than half a year. "Can you get them?"

"I don't know."

Gal backed up. Linda came inside. The house was pleasantly messy. To the left, three couches made a wide circle around a large screen where cartoons played. A pair of bored tweens watched a wolf blow down a house of straw. To the right was a dining room where an odd lot of about ten people ate and talked softly. Gal waved to the one who looked like a supervisor.

"It's okay. We can do my hands later. My best friend's visiting," Gal said. Then she led Linda straight ahead. They sat on the hall steps.

"How many people live here?"

"I can't tell. Everybody comes and goes," Gal said. "It's people from PV who got kicked out, but it's also for people in general. Townies volunteer to do night watches and check bags and make sure we're not loaded. But you can't call them townies. They don't like it."

"Yeah. Don't do that," Linda said. "Are those Kim Jackson's kids watching the screen?"

"I think so? The principal, right? She got kicked out last week. They said she couldn't write good recommendations."

Linda told Gal what she'd seen. After that, they talked practicalities. To retrieve Sebbie and Katie, she would have to access a locked basement at a hospital from which she'd been barred. She'd have to retrieve the kids and drive them across the border. This wouldn't be easy.

Gal made a claw, scratched her forehead. "My Katie and Sebbie won't cause any fuss. Just tell them their mommy sent you. Say 'heaven's gate.' That's our special saying. They'll walk right out. They'll know it's me. Sally won't stop you. She won't know what to do. Nobody expects you to risk your golden ticket. They couldn't even imagine it. And once it's done, they'll never confront you. Katie and Sebbie aren't supposed to be there. They'd have to admit that."

Linda wondered at that, figured very possibly they *would* get angry. They *would* confront. But Gal was desperate, saying anything. Linda didn't blame her. "Do you really believe they're going to hurt your children at this festival?" Linda asked.

Gal took Linda's hand in hers. The skin was tough as shark fins. "Ask Percy Khoury."

"I'm asking you. Are you sure these people mean harm?"

"I'm sure," Gal said, but she hesitated.

"You've never seen it, though, the festival. You don't know."

"No. But you can know a thing is true without having to see it."

"You're asking me to take a huge leap of faith," Linda said.

"Not really."

Linda looked ahead at the arched entrance, the old lead windows leaking air. She liked this house. "I don't know if I have this in me. Even if I wanted to help you. People are good at different things," Linda said. "I'm not good at whatever this is."

"They'll die if you don't," Gal said.

"Russ said they're being treated in secret. They know Trish isn't fit, and they think you're unfit, too."

"Do you believe that?" Gal asked.

No. She did not. "You nearly killed them once. Why should I deliver them to you?"

"So don't give them to me. Give them to strangers. Give them to anybody but Hollow."

Linda thought on all that, said the thing she'd known she'd say as soon as she'd gotten in her car. "I'll help you."

They worked out the logistics. "I'd like something back," Linda said before leaving.

"Anything," Gal said.

"I'd like your room here, once you're gone."

• • •

"I need you to be honest with me," Linda said. Russell had just walked into his office. She was sitting behind his desk.

"Linda—" he started, making a show of exasperation.

"—Don't," she said. "Tell me the truth. If you don't, I'm taking Josie and Hip and we're leaving right now."

Russell sat hard in the opposite chair. He was still wearing his coat. Snow melted and pooled in wet drips at his feet. His face reddened and he smiled at her, an awful, empty smile. "It's just a little bad," he said.

"Omnium sludge?"

"It's double the average pediatric cancers and aplastic anemias. Idiopathic leukemia's a made-up name they use to hide the disease. They use other names, too. Adults can get just as sick, but they need a high, chronic exposure. Kids need less. It gets into their growth factors. I didn't know any of this until you had me looking. The numbers were all input wrong so I did a lot of the work by hand. Even then, I wasn't sure. I just knew something was off, that they were hiding something. The relationship I found isn't causal. There isn't enough data. It's not even enough to take it off the market. There'd have to be more trials."

"That's what Rachel fixes," she said. "She pays people off, so no one runs more trials."

"That's not my lane. I just run the numbers."

She winced at that. After a while, he looked away.

"And they hired you to lie," she said.

"No," he said with great certainty. "I've been telling you—I use the data I get. They liked that I come from the regulatory agencies. I know how things work."

"How far have they gone to keep this secret?"

"I don't think there's any violence," he said. "It's money and NDAs. Everyone takes the money."

"Gal's kids are sick because of Omnium," Linda said. "Because they swam in the river, and no one ever remediated there, because no one will admit the problem. They blame it on epigenetics. That could have been Josie or Hip. We swam in the river before I knew better. I was at that dump out there. It was supposed to be house trash, but they'd combined it with Omnium waste processing. The liner's at least sixty years old. Don't tell me it's not seeping into the aquifer. So even if you're not doctoring the data, the silence is killing people. Hell, Russell, that aquifer's our drinking water. It's probably poisoning us, too."

Russell shrugged. "I can't say."

"We have to report this. We're obliged."

He shook his head. "It won't make any difference. The Parson family's been divesting, getting all their money out. They're spinning another company called Caladrius. Lloyd'll run it. Caladrius'll be all their non-Omnium holdings—their tech and banks. They'll be clean. As soon as the Omnium patent's over, BetterWorld plans to release all its data and the remediation starts. It's less than a year, now, actually. Maybe just six months."

"I don't get it. They kept the secret for eighty years and now they're going to open their books? Why?" Linda asked.

"They won't be able to make any more money off of it, and the generics'll be running their own studies. So it'll come out either way. Essentially, they're going to stop making Omnium very soon. What we do about it now doesn't matter. If we say something, it will literally have zero effect. The EPA's useless on this. There isn't a whistleblower in the world that has the teeth. We wouldn't save a single life. And to be honest, I'm not even sure Omnium is actually bad. Plastic caused a lot of sickness, too."

"You're saying you think Omnium's an improvement?"

"Yeah. Maybe."

"How would you know? How would anyone know, when you don't have the data? I've been here over six months and met three kids that Omnium is killing. That's already a very high incidence. This thing could be huge, Russ."

He nodded. She was surprised to see she'd scored a point, and he'd heard her. "Yeah. It might be very, very bad, just like Fielding told you. Worse than anyone imagines. But I want you to know I didn't figure it out right away. It's been a process. And the thing is, we're trapped in this. We might as well get something out of it."

"You didn't trust me to tell me," she said.

"I told you, I haven't been sure."

Growing up, she'd learned obliviousness. When people are puking all the time, or high, or lost and wandering the house they've known their whole lives, it's upsetting. You learn not to see. Not to get upset.

That was how she'd managed to grow up and still love her family. Still appreciate the occasions when meals were cooked, and fresh clothing appeared. When her dad had given her a snow globe, instead of spending that money on Glamp. Probably, this was why she hadn't noticed Chernin's obvious drug addiction. Possibly, it was how she'd overlooked Russell's struggle. The man had hyperventilated into a paper bag, and she'd still gone to sleep that night, woken the next morning, and let it roll off her like water off a duck. She'd seen this mess of an office, so out of character that he may as well have scraped the word *help* into his chest, and she'd let it go.

The emotion inside her was something much deeper than sorrow. It was a shift of everything deep down: an inversion and a break and a decimation. "You're lying to me, Russell Bowen," she said. "You've been lying to me our whole life together."

• • •

An hour later, he appeared in their bedroom, where she was packing. "Leaving won't change anything."

Linda felt a pull inside her, a pain not so different from when Fielding had announced her terminal cancer. An incredible loss.

"What is this, between us?" she asked.

His eyes got wide. Panicked. "What are you asking?"

"I don't know what's between us. I don't know how we work. I'm a sham doctor and you're a cancer shill. We're not heroes."

"I love you. I love our kids," he said. "That's real."

"But what does that even mean?"

He sat hard on the bed, his hand on her suitcase, holding it closed. "Wait."

"Why?"

"I'm sorry. I should have told you as soon as I found out."

"Why didn't you?"

"I kept thinking I had it wrong. I was never sure."

"No. That's not why. I want to hear you say it, Russell."

He played with the latch on the case. "I knew you'd want to leave or blow a whistle."

"Thank you," she said.

"I didn't do it for me. I did it for you and the kids."

"That's a lie," she said. "You might believe what you're saying, but it's still a lie."

He shook his head. "It's bad out there, Linnie. It's only getting worse."

"I know that."

"Survival isn't worth anything if you're not with me. It's more than love, the thing I feel. I don't have words for it," he said, his voice cracking. "There's never been anyone in my life except you. I don't care what happens to me. I want this for you."

Words like *love* become meaningless when you've been with someone for long enough. Love is beside the point. You've built something. You're not going to tear it down. Possibly, you could love someone else just as much. Possibly, your union was based on timing, and this person you're with is not your soul mate. This is irrelevant. There are no soul mates. You think this. And you go on thinking it. And then you hear a speech like this, and realize that in fact, you are loved not because of the things you do, but for who you are, the specificity of you.

Russell loved her. More than anything, he did. And it occurred to her then, as it had not since their early, messy barroom years, that she loved him in the same way.

But this love, she was beginning to think, had become a cage. "I can't stay in this, Russell." She didn't know whether she meant their marriage, or this town, or both.

"Okay," he said.

"Okay?"

"Yeah. I understand. Can you do one thing for me?" he asked, as if it were the only thing of her that he'd ever asked, and perhaps that was close to true, because historically, he hadn't asked. He'd just done. "Can you wait until after the Winter Festival? Because I think nothing's going to happen. I think even if they have those kids, everything you're scared about isn't coming to pass. We're safe here. They need me. I'm doing good work. The company's about to go clean. I'll be doing research on totally different products. There's still time to repair. We haven't even been here the full year. It's too soon to decide."

"What if I want to leave right now?"

He made no expression, no move, and she understood he'd already thought this out. "I'll stay here so you have something to come back to if you change your mind, or a bomb drops, or one of you gets sick."

"And the kids? Are you going to fight me?"

"No," he said, that awful, gritty smile returning to his face, and then tears welled in his eyes and his voice got very soft. She'd expected a fight. That he'd use them as bargaining chips. But in her anger, she'd underestimated him. "Please don't take my kids away from me."

They stood there, at an impasse, in the mansion that for a little while had felt like home.

Friday

With the Winter Festival starting Saturday, Linda tried to sneak out of the house early that Friday morning, but Josie caught her.

"I can't go to school today," she said. "Dad keeps making me. Don't make me."

Linda drew an index finger to her lips, and they walked together to the front hall. "I'm doing something. I need to do it alone."

Josie's expression showed this wasn't going to happen quietly unless Linda confided. So, she did.

"Can I come?"

"I'd rather they're just mad at me, not you."

"I thought you said you'd let me help. I thought you said we were in this together. I'm not going to school. I won't," she said, her voice rising in a way that threatened to wake the house.

"Okay," Linda said. "You got me."

• • •

They left for the PV Hospital. Linda parked in back. "Do you want to stay in the car?"

Josie was already getting out.

They went around front. "My daughter's sick. I need to take her to triage," Linda said.

Josie stood there, not acting sick. Then realizing she ought to, she held her stomach like it hurt.

They went through. Instead of heading for triage, they took the stairs down. Linda placed a pen cap like she'd done last time. But no one came. Cyrus Galani leaned against the door inside, where she assumed those kids were in beds.

"This could be bad and very embarrassing," she whispered. Then she knocked. Cyrus came to the door, smiling.

"You two! To what do I owe the pleasure?"

Linda waved happily like she was delighted to see him. "I'm supposed to take their vitals for ActHollow. It's for their data collection on pediatric cancer."

Holding the door, he backed up. "You're still with Daniella Bennett?"

"I am!" Linda said, with excessive enthusiasm.

His expression showed doubt. He opened his device, typed something. A reply arrived in a quick *ping!* And Linda felt all the blood drain from her body.

Cyrus glanced back at Linda. "You really are still on the board."

"I am," Linda answered, breathless.

"Go right on in!"

A small part of Linda didn't believe she'd find Gal Parker's kids in this room. Then Cyrus opened the door.

They sat at a round table. Two beds were pushed along the wall. The girl was drawing a tree under rainbows, the boy handknitting with purple yarn.

She bent down to their height while Josie shut the door behind them. Fine featured and small for their ages, possibly because of the cancer, the children were the same as in the photos. The same she'd seen at Parson's party, the same cutouts that she'd seen shoved inside a pomegranate her first night at Sirin's.

It should not have been such a shock. She'd expected this. It was why she was there, risking PV's wrath. It was, nonetheless, a shock.

"Sebbie? Katie?" she asked.

They responded to their names, but did so slowly and without great interest.

"What's that drawing?" Linda asked.

Josie kept a distance, listening.

"A drawing," Katie said, her voice flat. Then she turned the drawing over to its blank side. The behavior reminded Linda of Gal and it made her smile.

"And what are you knitting?" Linda asked the boy.

Sebbie was the younger one, his voice still babyish and small. "It's a scarf for Mommy."

"Oh, it's pretty," she said. "Which mommy?"

"I only have one mommy. There's also Mother," he said. "But she went away."

"And then Mommy went away," Katie said. She was angry-scribbling on the reverse side, not looking up, her voice still matter-of-fact.

"I guess you miss them," Linda said.

Katie pushed harder on her crayon so the yellow came out extra deep.

"Did she teach you to knit?" Linda asked.

"With fingers," Sebbie said, wiggling his fingers through the yarn like a puppet spider.

Often, in abusive upbringings, the children are developmentally delayed. Though they were small, their energy unusually low, Sebbie and Katie had met their milestones. Their fingers were dexterous, their postures straight, their apprehension apparent.

"Is Mommy Gal Parker?"

Katie put down her crayon and squinted. Then she tore up her paper. "You don't get to know. Nobody gets to know anything."

"Mommy's in the tunnels," Sebbie said. "That's why we have to live here. We have to wait for the festival, and then they said they'd let us out, so we could find Mommy."

Linda felt an incredible unease, as if all the atoms in the room had entered gelatinous excited states.

"But is she Gal Parker?"

"—Don't tell her, Sebbie," Katie said. "They break all their promises."

"I'm still a kid. I don't break promises," Josie said.

"How old?" Katie asked.

"Fifteen," Josie answered. "Almost sixteen."

Katie looked her up and down. Apparently liked what she saw. "My mommy's Gal Parker," she said.

"Would you like to get out of this hospital? Are you tired of being here?" Linda asked.

Katie glared; Sebbie nodded.

"Your mother's outside Plymouth Valley. We can take you there. Would you like that? Your mom said to say 'heaven's gate,'" Linda said.

The kids looked up, and for a moment, before the suspicion of this strange adult returned, their expressions were like flowers to sun.

• • •

Linda told Cyrus Galani that she needed to take the children upstairs in order to examine them better. He took this news without obvious suspicion. It seemed likely that they'd been escorted by Chernin plenty before and this was nothing new.

Katie preferred Josie and took her hand—little girls love big girls—so Linda took Sebbie's very small hand. They took the steps one at a time to accommodate Sebbie's little legs. Her heart staccatoed. They opened the door to the winter dark, and then arrived at the B-class sedan. Josie sparked, alert as a high beam, during that short walk. At last, after all these months of indecision, she was doing something.

At the car, Josie took control. She pulled the blankets Linda was transporting to the clinic from the trunk, instructed the kids to get into the footwells of the back seat, and covered them. "We're really taking you to your mom, but we have to get out of here first," she said, her voice, beside these small children, sounding very grown-up.

"Is it a good idea to hide them?" Linda asked once they were on the road, passing sleeping houses with sleeping birds inside shelters.

"Yes," Josie said. "What's the downside?"

"Where's my mommy again?" Katie asked on the drive.

"She's outside Plymouth Valley," Josie answered.

"Are you lying?" Katie asked.

"No. You'll see," Linda said. "We're telling you the truth. Since the fire, you're all she's talked about. She loves you both very much. She'd do anything for you," Linda said, her voice cracking with emotion, because she believed what she was saying to be true.

"I know she loves me. I don't need to be told," Katie answered from under the blanket, her cadence the same as Gal's.

"My mommy's a princess," Sebbie said.

"Be very quiet," Josie told them as they approached the border. "Can I get an okay?"

"Okay," little voices chimed.

They got to the border. Sally left her steaming tea in her booth. Early-morning dead of winter. It was still so dark that she had to shine her flashlight into the back and the front. Linda popped the trunk and she looked there, too. After all that, she returned to Linda's rolled-down window.

"Why so early?" she asked, sounding annoyed. "You're creeping all over lately."

Linda drew a complete blank.

Josie leaned over: "I left something important at my mom's office."

Sally gave an eye roll. "You're not a careful kid, are you?" And then, to Linda: "I told you this doesn't look good. I warned you to stop doing this."

"Yeah," Linda said. She thought about it, gave gratitude hands for the first time. "I heard you. I appreciate you. This will be the last time."

Sally seemed pleasantly surprised.

Josie followed Linda's lead, gave prayer hands, too. "I hate outside," she said. "It's so dirty and ugly and the food's the worst."

Sally grinned. "So bad," she mock-whispered. "The people are dirty. It's not their fault. But they're infected inside and out. Syphilis. Epigenetic viruses. I don't know how you do it, Linda. Touching them."

"Me neither," Linda said. "But it's my side hustle!"

Sally let out a laugh. She'd been shining her light on the back seat, looking at the blankets on the buckets below. "What's that?"

"Oh, patients' blankets," Linda answered. "I took them back to clean them here but forgot."

Sally made a sour face. "Are they used?"

"Yeah. Pretty dirty. We had some very sick patients. Do you want to have a look at them?"

Sally pulled the back door handle but didn't open it.

"Sorry about the smell," Josie said. "I think somebody puked on one of them. Was it norovirus, Mom?"

"Worse. Giardia. It's a parasite," she said to Sally. "We good to go? Sorry again about being so much trouble."

Appalled by the thought of opening the door to so much sickness, Sally waved them on.

• • •

The roads were icy and black, the streetlights nonexistent. They crept impossibly slowly, like scenery-gawking Sunday drivers. The kids climbed out from under the blankets and buckled in. "You're okay," Linda reassured them, and then Josie, too. "We're all okay."

Twenty minutes later, they parked behind Danny's truck at the halfway house, where they'd agreed to meet. Gal came racing out. The kids threw themselves at her and didn't let go. All wept with happiness and emotion.

As Linda and Josie watched, their hands joined. *My daughter*, Linda thought. And then: *But where are my husband and son?*

Danny's mother-in-law stayed shotgun while he opened the back door of his truck and Gal helped her kids climb onto either side of sleeping Carlos. "My babies. You're cold. We'll turn up the heat and get you all cozy." Then, to Linda, "I didn't think you'd do it. I was so scared you'd back out."

"Me too," Linda said. "I didn't think I'd do it, either."

"I lied. They'll be mad at you." Her voice had lost all childishness. She was a different Gal. At peace. "Crazy, scary, Jack Lust mad. Don't go to the Winter Fest tomorrow.

"We're leaving tonight," Linda said. "Keep your room warm."

"Be careful," Gal told her.

"You too. I spoke to the people in Cleveland. They think the medicine's been wrong and that you'll see an improvement. Not every child responds, but a lot of them do. There's a solid chance. They know your history, about the house fire, so I don't know what'll happen there. My guess is you'll be in some trouble with whatever police have jurisdiction. I'm sorry. I know it may be overcautious, but I also instructed Danny and his mother-in-law not to leave you alone with Katie or Sebbie."

"I don't care if I get tarred and feathered so long as I can smooch on them this whole drive," Gal said.

Despite her frailty, Gal hugged Linda hard. Then she hugged Josie. "Your mom's fucking crazy," she said, which Linda understood to be the highest of compliments. And then, suddenly, Linda was shaking Danny's hand, touching her hand to Carlos's forehead, and wishing them all the best. Then, the truck was gone.

• • •

They were back at 9 Sunset Heights by midmorning. Russell and Hip had left for work and school. "I think we should pack up," Linda said. So, they did. Josie packed Hip's things, too, and Linda figured what the hell, and packed a bag for Russell.

At first, she felt good. So did Josie. They'd done the right thing. Hopefully, Hip and Russell would believe them and come along. They'd get out before the Winter Festival and call this whole experience finished. But the hours passed. Neither Hip nor Russell answered their devices, and the bags stayed packed with no one to claim them.

• • •

Long past dark, Russell walked through the back door. He wore the disturbing rictus smile she'd come to associate with his PV persona. The longer they stayed there, the more it chafed, this persona, but he insisted on wearing it.

"What happened?" she asked.

"That's my question," he said.

The two of them passed the packed suitcases and took opposite seats at the formal dining room table. Josie followed.

"I need to talk to your mother alone," Russell said.

Josie shot Linda a nervous glance, retreated. Linda didn't imagine she'd retreated far.

Succinctly as she was able, Linda described escaping with the children and delivering them to Gal. They'd forgotten to turn on the overhead lights, so the room was dark.

"They told me. The whole board called me in once they found out. I thought they were joking, Linnie," Russell said.

"I had to."

"You gave those kids to a psychotic."

"It's not like that."

Tears of indignation filled Russell's eyes. "Jack explained everything. They were trying to save those kids. They were working on their own clinical trial. They were going to recommend best practices as soon as the patent expires. By pulling them out, you signed their death warrants."

Emotions flooded Linda. None were confusion. "You believe them and not me. But all they do is lie."

Russell surveyed the room, its nice furniture, its hand-painted wallpaper, its ribbon candy. He wasn't hearing her. He was running dialogue from some imaginary conversation with an imaginary Linda that had already happened. "It's a mess, but I fixed it. I had to beg," he said, his voice going distant and soft. "I got down on my knees in front of Jack Lust. I was literally on my knees. For you."

"I'm sorry," she said, but she wasn't. It's just something you say, when you're accused of something bad. An automatic response, as thoughtless as a heartbeat.

"We cut a deal. I'll finish the next case and win it for them, but I won't pass the first-year review. We'll leave then. So long as it's the full year, Jack and Lloyd promised to give our deposit back. We need that money. That means you play nice. We go to every festival, we follow every rule, we stop asking questions and sneaking around and breaking into places we don't belong. Even your boss, Chernin, was there. He likes you. But he voted to kick you out. He wants you gone tonight."

"I want that, too," she said.

"If we leave now, with nothing, we won't make it. People are dying out there."

Dying. The word was a kind of warble in her chest, expanding and collapsing. "There's a halfway house in PVE. I have a room for us. I'm your wife and I'm telling you we should go. Forget the deposit. Let's cut our losses."

Russell looked over. He was talking to her, but not really. He wasn't seeing her. "We can still win. Unpack those bags. No one's leaving."

• • •

The thing about epiphanies, they don't always lead to change. Sometimes you have them, and know they're true, then forget about them because you're not ready. In her darkest moments, she'd wondered whether she ought to have done everything in secret. Lied to the kids and fled with them, leaving Russell on his own. But epiphanies are easy to ignore. You think: *Nothing's an emergency. It can't possibly be that bad. I'll deal with that later when I have a cooler head. For now, I'll pretend everything's fine.*

She knocked on Josie's door. "We're going."

They packed all the suitcases into the car. From the locator on his device, Linda knew where to find her son. She drove to the Bennett house. Instead of a servant, Daniella came to the door, smiling carnivorous and shit-eating.

"Is Hip here?"

Daniella sighed, deep and theatrical. She was wearing those same tight blue coveralls as when they'd gone out to Sirin's for the first time. "So much emotion. So much weeping."

"Why's that?"

Daniella looked at her sidelong. "You screwed the pooch. Your whole family's in serious trouble. But these two idiots had their fifteen-year-old fantasies of getting married."

Linda could tell that Daniella expected an apology. At the very least, an explanation. "Can you get my son?"

Daniella leaned into the doorway an extra beat, deciding. Then, catlike, she turned.

A minute later, Hip was at the door, his eyes deep red.

"I need you to come with me," she said.

He lowered his voice. "Is it true, Mom? Did you kidnap kids from a clinical trial and give them to a crazy lady?"

"Yeah. Come on."

He took a step deeper into the house. Linda noticed Cathy on the stairwell, eyes red and swollen. She stood under an altar of feathers and meat, the Geiger counter's watch hand at a steady low level.

"Why would you do that?"

"For their own good," Linda said.

"But they were getting better," Hip said.

"I doubt that."

He looked back, seemed ashamed that Cathy had to see this, that Cathy had to have a bad thing happen tangentially to her. Delicate little Cathy. "It reflects on me, Mom! It reflects on Cathy! We'll never get universal golden tickets passed now. She's been crying for hours."

Linda didn't mean to be so cold, but the discrepancy between fantasy and reality here was obscene. "I'm sorry, Hip. But that kid doesn't know her ass from her elbow and neither do you. Now get in the car."

He didn't move.

"Now!" she yelled.

"Mom!" he said, his eyes ragged, his voice ragged, everything about him holding the stance of the betrayed.

By now, Josie had come to the door. "Come on, Hip," she said.

He sneered an ugly sneer. "I knew you wouldn't let me have this."

"Have what?" Josie said.

"You liked it when I followed you around. When I had nobody else," he answered. "Both of you. But I'm happy. I'm the one who belongs. And you couldn't let me have it. You had to mess it up. I never ruined anything for you, Josie."

"You mess your own shit up. You never needed my help," Josie answered.

"I'm staying over here tonight. They said I could," Hip said. Then he shut the door on them.

• • •

They drove to the border. Linda planned to set the luggage in the halfway house and leave Josie there, then head back and try to salvage what she could. But the gate was blocked. Sally, Cyrus, and Pratt all got out of the security booth.

"No passage!" Pratt said, genial and sympathetic, like he was sorry for the inconvenience.

"I just need to get something at my clinic," Linda said.

"No, you don't," Sally answered, her thick brows knitted in fury.

"You're right," Linda agreed. "I want to leave. Let me out."

Pratt leaned down into Linda's window, made gratitude hands at her. "Hi! Sorry, but this is the site of an ongoing investigation. Until we clear things up, no one comes or goes."

The Plymouth Valley Winter Festival

Fleeing through the mountains would never work. It was at least a three-day hike through winter cold to the next town and they had no supplies. The wall was impossible to climb. They drove back to 9 Sunset Heights. For Josie's sake, Linda pretended none of this was serious. "We'll be fine," she reassured. "We'll try again in the morning."

"But the Winter Festival's in the morning," Josie answered.

"We'll be fine," Linda repeated.

They went to their separate bedrooms. Linda sat upright in her day clothing, heart beating hard as the hours ticked by. Russell came just before dawn. "My back hurts," he said.

"So come here," she told him.

He lay down, his side touching her thigh as she stayed upright.

"You didn't leave," he said.

"They barricaded the exit," she told him. "And Hip wouldn't come. It's a clusterfuck."

"You really think they were going to hurt those kids?"

"I don't know," she said. "I only know they were lying."

"Where are they now?"

"On their way to somewhere safe."

"You're not going to tell me?"

"No. You'll tell Lloyd to cut us a deal and you'll tell yourself it was the right thing."

Lovingly and without denial, he squeezed her leg. What he said next frightened her deeply. "I talked to that guy, Percy Khoury, tonight while you were out. The nuclear engineer you told me about from the first soccer game."

"Yeah? Why?"

"He lives across the street. Who knew? These houses are so big it's hard to see the neighbors. Anyway, I saw him, so I came out. He had this huge tool belt . . . or I don't know. He's weird. I get the feeling the guy could go berserk any second."

"He vibes that way, doesn't he? Like a shooter? What happened? Did you talk?"

"He's obviously crazy. I didn't want to poke a tiger and ask him about his son. I just asked if something bad happens at this festival."

Her body went stiff. She'd been asking that very question for a long time now, but was still afraid of the answer. "And?"

"He heard me. But he looked right through me. 'Get out,' he said, and then he shoved me and got into his car, which by the way, was loaded with power tools."

"Huh. Did he mean 'get out of the way,' or 'get out of town'?"

"It's a coin flip. The guy's a maniac. What's the difference? The thing is, once I asked the question out loud, I had this bad feeling. I've heard you and the things you've been saying, Linda. But I haven't been thinking them through. I haven't compared the logic of the two arguments—yours and PV's—because their foundations are rooted in such different premises.

"On the one hand, we have civic pride and a lot of unnecessary secrecy. The residents want to believe that they're better than outsiders, otherwise they'd have to admit that they have an unfair allotment of wealth. It's classic snobbery. On the other hand, we have a group of people so corrupted by their own complicity in polluting the earth while simultaneously hoarding its resources that they've invented a religion to exonerate themselves from guilt, from the literal thousands, maybe millions of people they've murdered indirectly. We have festivals that you might consider masses led by the founder and his board of directors, who are essentially henchmen with dimples. We even have gestures of prayer to clandestine gods. Who are these gods? We don't know. But they're represented by the very birds the town has engineered. It's incredibly self-centered. They're the creators, worshipping what they've created while also gorging themselves on it.

"Every historical precedent informs us that religious fanatics can be violent, particularly in the presence of a demagogue. Is Parson Junior that demagogue? Maybe. Frankly, I've spoken to him personally and he's not very bright. I think, if anyone, his father was the demagogue and he's just carrying on tradition. Lloyd and Rachel are reasonable people. They're likely to shift this thing in a better direction. But Jack . . . he's bad. I've heard things, Linda, that I'd rather not tell you about. He's got notorious appetites."

Goose pimples rolled all down Linda's body from scalp to legs.

"Religious fanatics tend to believe that their violence is self-protective—they're fighting an existential threat. In this case, the threat is nuclear disaster, or the end of Plymouth Valley, or possibly even the end of their own hegemony, once BetterWorld is finally indicted for its environmental crimes. They commit human sacrifice as a ritual, a superstitious admission of their own guilt, in the hopes that a higher being will cleanse and protect them from their own demise, only they *are* this higher being. It's a screwed-up circle jerk that eats its own future.

"So, we have here, two arguments. One is mundane, if ugly. The other is malignant. I've been playing devil's advocate with you for a long time, despite my private misgivings. I don't know why. It just seemed like the right approach. We couldn't both be standing out, asking questions, making scenes. But it occurred to me that these two arguments may coexist.

"What's interesting is how it started. This town was just a corporate headquarters in the 1980s. They didn't build the shelter until twenty years after that. Did Parson Senior begin these festivals as part of a corporate retreat? Did they evolve over time, along with the corporation, into something violent? There isn't any real government here. No laws. For a very long time, they've been able to do whatever they've wanted."

Russell liked big concepts and big words, especially when he was nervous. He liked talking big when he was avoiding feeling something, too. "What are you saying?" she asked.

"Maybe it's nothing. Maybe it's real. Having never been to a Winter Festival, we can't possibly know. Viewed under the lens of a particular kaleidoscope, the Parker children may have been in the path of harm. I would not have done what you did. You risked our family for the sake of another family and to me, that's wrong. Your loyalty ought to be to us. But the act, itself, was rational. Brave, even. But that's not surprising."

"Yeah?" she asked, though she sensed by now where he was going.

"As you know, I draw conclusions with greater deliberation than you. This has been a benefit on occasion. My doggedness is what kept me employed for as long as I was on the outside. It's also what got the attention of BetterWorld. I don't think you'd ever have managed that kind of slow drudgery I performed at the EPA. That's the work that fueled our livelihood."

"True," she said. She might have added that she could have gone back into medicine full time, and he could have helped more. Combined, they'd have made a little less money, but their lifestyle back home would have been about the same. But that regret was a buried conch washed away into the ocean. It was gone.

"Admitting fault is hard for me. People can be unkind. Sometimes, and I don't want to start a fight, Linda, but you've been unkind."

She felt a tightness in her throat. "I know. I remember some of the things I said to you and I feel sick about it. We had a bad dynamic."

"Yes," he said. "It might still be bad. I don't know. I keep telling you I love you and I understand that it's not enough. But I don't know the answer to these problems we have."

"What are you really saying, Russell?"

He let out a long breath. "I think about all the times you disagreed with me, not just in Plymouth Valley. I think about how I ignored you. For years, if I didn't like what you were saying, I ignored you."

This admission cut deep. It felt like a cold scalpel through the center of her, opening her wide. She should have felt relieved. She wasn't crazy or oversensitive. He really had been blowing her off. But the emotion inside her wasn't relief: it was shame.

"It's because I thought I was right," he said.

"I know."

"But a lot of times, I wasn't right. I can be very blind. You're a head-strong person. Sometimes I was surprised you stayed with me. Why did you?"

She thought about crazy Gal, who'd set her own house on fire to get out of something unthinkable. To either save or end her family. She thought about the many ways she might have made big, terrifying decisions without him, which could have gotten them all out of this a long time ago. "Maybe I'm not that strong a person. It's just a story we told about who we were as the Farmer-Bowens."

"It's a different kind of strong," he said. "I think you really just love us that much. You haven't wanted to risk losing us. I haven't always been happy, either. This has been hard. But I've been doing what I've been doing for the same reasons."

It occurred to her that this was a postmortem. They were talking about something dead and gone. Since moving here and rescuing those kids, she'd changed. She'd proven to herself that she was the kind of person who could make big, terrifying decisions. She'd become a woman who could leave.

"Why are you telling me this now?" she asked.

"I don't know. I've just been thinking," he said. But she knew. The Winter Festival was tomorrow. These things needed to be said, in the event they never again had the chance.

Unable to sleep after that, they made love. She had the most terrible intuition that it was for the last time.

DAY 1

In the morning, Russell drove. Linda sat shotgun and Josie took the back. The bags remained in the trunk. According to his device's GPS, Hip was at the Bennett house. They went there, but no one was home. He must have already headed to the festival and left his device behind.

"What now?" she asked.

"We get you and Josie out, and I find Hip," he answered.

As they drove to the wall, they passed crowds of people headed in the opposite direction, for the festival. Most walked toward any of the six entrances all over town. Like this really was the Ark, members of the Beautification Society gathered caladrius into livestock trucks.

When they arrived, they met new faces at security. Armed, these guards turned the Farmer-Bowens away.

At a loss, the three of them drove the periphery of the town, looking for chinks in the wall. They found none. Slowly, the populace dwindled. The town emptied. When they got to 9 Sunset Heights, Pratt and Sally were waiting.

Everything inside Linda jangled like dissonant piano chords. A scream would let some of the tension out, but she kept it inside her, instead looked back at Josie, who'd gone pale.

Russell rolled down the driver's side window, smiled pleasantly. He had a good poker face. "To what do we owe the pleasure?"

Pratt issued prayer hands and smiled affably on this cold, bright day. "House check," he answered while Sally stood beside him, glaring.

"Hmm?" Russell asked.

"Every PV resident must attend the Winter Festival. We check from house to house to make sure no one's left behind."

"We're not feeling well," Russell answered. "Linda thinks it's something she caught on the outside. We don't want to pass it on to anyone, especially in such closed quarters. We're going to have to skip it."

Pratt touched his hand to his gun. "Everyone goes to the Winter Festival."

• • •

The police car escorted them to Caladrius Park just as the livestock trucks had finished unloading their cargo. She spotted the last of the caladrius waddling down the Labyrinth entrance. Like homing pigeons returning to their point of origin, they required no direction.

"Are we in trouble? I was assured there'd be no retaliation for my wife's actions," Russell said to Pratt once they were all out.

Sally sneered, fists clenched. Linda'd made her look stupid and would not be forgiven.

"No trouble at all," Pratt answered, stepping ahead of Sally and talking before she had the chance. "This isn't a serious event. It's a party and it's just for fun. We escort people all morning. As a matter of fact, we have to be off. Some of the older residents need reminders. Enjoy your time!"

The Farmer-Bowens stayed close. The line of residents descending into the entrance moved briskly. All variety of scenarios played out in Linda's mind. They could run. But there were guards here, too. What if one of them got shot?

And Hip. Where was Hip?

They arrived at the mouth—the same entrance she'd taken on that first day they'd toured with Zach. Cyrus Galani checked their names off a master list.

"Did Hip Farmer-Bowen go through?" Linda asked.

Cyrus checked the list. "Yeah," he said with a frown. "Looks like he was one of the first . . . You played a real prank on us yesterday."

He was inside. Linda's heart sank.

"My wife's very sorry," Russell said in his wheedling, pleasing voice. His gritty smile was pasted on, a kind of parody of happiness that in fact looked like misery.

Cyrus looked behind them, at Percy Khoury. His wrist wounds were freshly bandaged and he wore a bulky knapsack on his shoulders. "Look at you! Finally ready to go back to work at another festival. Thanks for keeping the shelter online. We owe you our gratitude and we appreciate you. Go on down!"

Slowly, his pack cumbersome, looking disregulated as ever, Percy descended. Cyrus signaled for the Farmer-Bowens to do the same. Linda scanned the area, trying to decide whether to flee. But what would running do when they had no place to go?

Down they went.

The Labyrinth was decorated with feathers glued into tapestries hanging from every wall. Warm heat lamps glowed every few feet. They reached a coat and bag check at the bottom. By then, the crowd was so teeming that there wasn't any turning back.

They went through the hidden door and into the belly of the place—the shelter. To the left, the caladrius hissed and warbled from an indoor stockyard, furious at being penned in, and probably more furious at being stuck with so many of its own kind.

The Farmer-Bowens followed the crowd to the right, into a wide room where Beautification Society and Civic Club volunteers distributed uniformly sized hooded white robes. "May you always shine," Heaven Gelman said to each person as she handed out each folded gown. "For longer than the stars."

• • •

They dressed in communal chambers divided by age group, storing their street clothing in cubbies. The older people and the more self-conscious kids changed behind screens erected specifically for that reason. Time passed slowly, Linda's heart beating hard. The festival lasted three days and two nights. How would she and her family possibly get through it?

After everyone was dressed and ready, Heaven Gelman spoke into a megaphone to deliver her announcement. "Greetings, Plymouth Valley! Welcome to the sixty-first Plymouth Valley Winter Festival! All residents are accounted for and all exits have been sealed. Please proceed to lunch."

The exits were sealed?

They followed the crowd to the main reception chamber, where they found a sumptuous buffet. They'd killed most of their livestock for this. There was goat meat and cow meat and deer meat, all sliced and cooked and garnished with all the fruits she'd thought were extinct: raspberries, strawberries, pineapples, mangoes. There was so much of it that no one rushed or took double helpings.

The three of them did as expected, serving themselves and then searching for Hip. The crowd was larger than she'd realized. She'd thought by then that she'd have met everyone in this town, but she was wrong. Forty-five hundred people are a lot of people.

She roamed outside the banquet hall, was intercepted. "Party's in there," Sally said, her lips pulled back into a sneer.

Thinking of exits and fleeing, Linda asked: "Can I look around the rest of the shelter?"

"No."

"And what happens if I ignore you?"

Sally touched her hand to her revolver. "I hope you try."

Linda pegged this as a bluff, but didn't see the point testing the theory, given she didn't have her family with her and she'd be running away without them.

She returned to the hall and found the Bennett family, who greeted her with surprising warmth, as if nothing had happened. Lloyd gave his usual sunny smile and firm shake. His three kids hung back. Daniella hugged Linda long and tight, just like that first time, when Linda remembered having felt protected. Accepted.

Hip and Cathy looked sad and tired. He was holding her, his lips pressed to her blond hair.

"So much drama!" Daniella whispered with the same effusiveness as ever. "I had to play mediator all night. Or meditator? Pooping both! Hip talks a lot. Too much. I had no idea. No offense, but poor Cathy. Has she been listening to that jibber-jabber all these months? It's like a drill. Not that she's easy. The kid's as spoiled as they come. You're welcome for letting him sleep over, by the way. Five kids in one house is too many kids."

"Thanks," Linda said. "Did they resolve anything? I heard Cathy's upset that what I did will reflect badly on her agenda."

"We all are!" Daniella said brightly.

"Sorry," Linda said.

"Cathy's the one I'm worried about. I've spent fifteen years protecting that girl from certain realities about this place. She's so tender. I told them both, no point getting attached when it's only going to end badly. I told her to break up with him and she agreed. Besides, he's been dominating her time. She's like me; she's into making the world better, and she can't let some boy distract her from that. Forget the Fabric Collective. She's got a future here as a politician."

There was much insanity and some stupidity in what Daniella had said, but Linda tried to stay focused. "They're broken up? But they're standing together?"

"These two. It's been one long good-bye."

"Poor kids," Linda said.

"Poor me. They kept me up half the night."

"Sorry about that."

Daniella's smile went flat. "You should say it like you mean it. I've got a lot of damage to repair. Because of my association with you, Lloyd's on the outs with Parson. Not even Anouk can smooth it over. I told you when we met, everything reflects."

"That's unfortunate," Linda said. "It was something I felt I had to do. It wasn't an easy choice."

Daniella squeezed Linda's shoulder, digging her nails. "It must be so hard, being better than everyone else. You fucked me, you cunt." Still smiling, she broke off to make small talk with Tania Janssen and her family.

Her cheeks flushed and her breath coming fast, Linda headed next for Hip and Cathy. "I'm sorry," she said, and this time she was sincere.

In her too-loose robe, the sleeves long past her wrists, delicate Cathy averted her eyes from Linda like she couldn't stand the sight of her.

Hip's whole body was hunched, as if carrying a great burden. Linda had the feeling they really had been up all night, talking. Only Cathy, with her mother backing her, had been accusing and ranting, and Hip had been consoling and apologizing.

Linda reached out and took his shoulder. It was narrow, like the rest of him. But solid. In their time in this town, he'd grown half a foot. "You both need rest," she said. "This is too much emotion. You can't be thinking clearly."

"Mom, we're fine," Hip said. But she could see that he was in over his head. He needed extraction. "Give me some space."

"Sure," Linda said. "But I want you back with the rest of us by dinner."

Cathy began bawling, loud and with great theatrics. "Your mother's awful!" she bleated. The hall's cacophony drowned her voice. She looked around as she cried, to see if anyone had noticed. When she saw they hadn't, she bawled louder.

"Okay," Hip agreed, seeming grateful, holding Cathy now in his arms. "See you at dinner."

• • •

Scanning the room, Linda saw all the other residents of Plymouth Valley. Jack and Colette were together with their little ones, no nanny in sight. Looking angry but nonetheless smiling, the Bennett stepsiblings stood by the grilled goat, peeling strips from its carcass, hyena-like. Far up at the grand table was John Parson Junior, Anouk, and Keith in his crown. Even Ruth Epstein, whom she'd seen ranting in the psychiatric ward, was sitting with her husband and kids like nothing in the world was wrong.

After lunch, they all scraped their own plates and filed into the kitchen, where, in an assembly line, they washed, dried, and put them away. Then came the greetings, where everyone said hello. Linda expected people to snub her. With the way news traveled in PV, they had to know what she'd done. But they didn't snub her. "May your star always shine bright," they said to one another as she hugged her neighbors, and the soccer parents, and Russell's friends, and Better-World's board.

Rachel, helped by Kai, was the last to greet them. She'd paled and lost weight she couldn't afford to lose. "Dry for two days," she said. "Like a rotting boat."

"Good for you!" Linda said. "But that's early to be out. Are they giving you something for the withdrawal? White-knuckling this kind of thing can cause some damage."

"They've got me on Glamp," she answered, and Linda felt, for a moment, like she might vomit. "Smooth ride, baby. Best shit I've ever had." She took Linda's upper arm.

"You can't take Glamp. It'll make everything worse," Linda said, urgent and low.

Rachel smiled at her with needle-width pupils. She raised her voice so Daniella and everyone else nearby could hear. It radiated desperation. "I said some things that scared you. We can talk about it all later. But you should know I was sick."

Linda nodded, going along with the performance. Rachel looked so weak she might collapse. Kai appeared equally wretched. Had Daniella forced her to check out of the hospital to make her rounds of public apologies?

Yes, Linda realized. She had.

"I was out of my mind," Rachel said. "I'm just hoping everyone forgives me."

Linda's voice got loud and wrong with fake enthusiasm. It broke a little, too, because she wanted to cry. "I'm sure they will!"

Then Anouk burst between them. "We're all here! Even naughty Linda! Guess what? Daniella and I did so much begging! And now Daddy's happy about the clinic and he says he won't close it after all!" she whispered. "Isn't that amazing? I did it! I did it all myself because I help people! Even though it's not my fault people get sick, it's bad parenting and bad genes, I help them. That's my calling!"

Rachel took a breath, looking to Kai, who Linda just then realized reeked of booze. So, now he was the one drinking, and she was on an even worse and faster journey to oblivion. Poor Rachel. Poor him. This was awful. "Ready?" Kai whispered.

"Yeah," Rachel said. Then he was helping her through the crowd, where she said the same thing over and over. "I've been hospitalized! I'm two days dry! I said some things that were wrong. I'm so sorry!"

• • •

Before dinner, they were ushered into a giant hall with perfect acoustics, where BetterWorld's board issued their annual report on the state of the company and of Plymouth Valley. They'd had their eleventh year of contraction, but remained solvent. This tracked, given global population and resources had declined accordingly. "As you all know," Jack Lust said, "we'll be spinning off our most profitable industries into Caladrius Corp beginning the next financial quarter. BetterWorld will manage only Omnium."

Everyone clapped in synchronicity. Parson then announced that some positions in the governing body would shift. Rachel Johnson would be stepping down from leadership, replaced as compliance director by Farah Nassar. Lloyd would remain on the board, but would not be promoted to chairman of Caladrius. The position of his successor, chairman of the board, was going to Jack Lust.

The cheering ceased. The room went still, the rock ceiling seeming to lower. "Oh God, no," someone nearby whispered. The formerly neat rows everyone had been standing in, naturally equidistant, fell into disarray. "He's a monster," Ruth Epstein whispered.

Onstage, Lloyd's gorgeous, dimpled smile turned rictus. Linda had the feeling he was in shock. Jack had been in competition with Rachel for the CEO spot, hadn't he? Since when had he wormed his way into the chairman job Lloyd had been fighting for all these years?

Jack's wife, Colette, a shell of a woman with a toothy, cadaver grin, clapped her hands once, twice. No one in the crowd followed until Parson clapped from his chair. The Jack Lust sympathizers on the board of directors clapped, too. These claps were out of synchronicity, confused squawks from an injured organism. Slowly, the crowd joined and momentum built.

Skinny, black-suited Jack Lust bowed playfully like a funereal wraith. Maybe from hysteria, emotions pent without egress, people began hooting with fake, desperate joy. And then the whole hall was clapping and hollering and even screaming. Weakly, Linda, Russell, and Josie joined in.

Jack Lust, a quiet monster, would now run Plymouth Valley.

• • •

Evening came, and they all filed through the kitchens and got their meals on their own from what had been left out. Hip joined the Farmer-Bowens at a four-top in the large dining room. "Are you okay?" Linda asked.

Hip's eyes got wet and he quickly wiped them. "Yeah."

"She's not—" Linda started.

"Don't say anything bad about her," Hip interrupted. "I know she's overreacting. It's because she loves me so much."

"I won't say anything bad. I wasn't going to," Linda said.

"But why did you and Josie do something like that?" he asked. Linda noticed that the people at the tables surrounding them were listening.

"I'm sorry. I know it means I ruined things for you. But I'm also not sorry. It was the right thing to do."

She'd known this kid intimately for nearly sixteen years. Away from Cathy, exhausted and raw, his defenses were down. He heard her.

After dinner, the children's choir, all in angelic white, sang songs about John Parson, followed by actual labyrinth dancing. The ceiling was high, and someone had put up lights there, to look like stars.

"It's pretty," Russell said as he held her.

She pressed into him as they tried to match the steps. "Do you think we can sneak out?"

"No. I looked around. Even if we got past the guards, everything's locked."

Bunks were assigned. Linda found the barracks guard. "We sleep a lot better at home. Do you think we could leave?" she asked.

"I'm sorry," Pratt answered. "This is fun, but it's also mandatory preparation in the event we have to live down here for real."

After lights-out, Hip tried to talk to Cathy, whose room was just in the next chamber. "I can't," Linda heard her whisper. "This is too painful for me. I need a clean break." Then he was back in his bunk, sniffling, his face pressed tight to the wall.

A little later, Josie climbed in with him. "Go away," Linda heard him whisper.

"No, you doofus. I won't."

"I mean it. Get out."

Josie got out, crawled into bed with Linda, who held her. "What's going to happen?" Josie asked.

Linda wanted to reassure, but doing so felt irresponsible. "I don't know," she said.

As if reading her mind, Russell leaned down into the lower bunk where she and Josie were lying. "I'll keep watch. You two get some sleep."

Josie knocked out, her breath deep in minutes.

Linda expected to stay up all night with a pounding, terrified heart.

But she'd played all her cards. There were no more moves. All that was left was to wait for the reveal, the flop, the thing behind door number two. She held her daughter, her eyelids going heavy, and slept like the dead.

DAY 2

Can mundanity be excruciating?

She searched for signs of horror and human sacrifice and instead encountered lectures. A scientist from Russell's department got on a podium and explained the sustainable garden and the manner in which the caladrius would be sacrificed for their meals, should they live down here long-term. Then BetterWorld's general secretary, Mary Coburn, explained how the new Caladrius Corporation planned to prevent global disaster by contributing more to charity. "ActHollow will receive a ten percent increase in funding," she announced, and everyone clapped and hooted, like she'd just announced she'd brokered world peace. "Can the board please come up and take a few bows?"

Daniella and Anouk were onstage. They waved for Linda to join them and she complied.

"A little boy and his father came to our clinic recently," Daniella said with such poise that she must have rehearsed it. "The child has asthma. Now, because of ActHollow, he's going to get the treatment he so badly needs. Another child came with anemia. Because of our clinic's state-of-the-art technology, we were able to analyze his blood on the same visit. All he needed to change his life were iron pills!" She then talked about the tele-meet component for specialists and the decision to add a new staff member. "Under our new clinic director's purview, of course. Tania Janssen, please step forward!" Daniella declared with a beatific grin.

Teeth stained with red wine, Tania Janssen stood and gave prayer hands. Daniella and Anouk returned those prayer hands. Linda just stood there. Then Anouk handed out her dumb pamphlets and read them word for word.

The rest of the day went by in a blur. More games, more dancing. "This is excruciating," Josie said.

"Yeah," Linda agreed. It was dinner. They were seated all four together.

"I went to the Caladrius Park exit. Palm access is disabled," Russell said.

"I tried the one on the south side," Hip said. "Same thing."

"You did?" Linda asked with surprise.

Hip nodded, as if he'd somehow been on the same page with the rest of them, all along. "If something bad happens, we'll have to hide. There's no out that I can find."

• • •

All the same people were assigned their same bunks that night. "I don't think there's a point to one of us staying awake on watch," Russell said, and Linda agreed. There were 4,500 people down there, including dozens of armed guards. What would possibly be the point of watching out for a sneak attack?

This time, it was Hip who went to Josie's bunk. They whispered softly. "I said some ugly things," Hip said. "I didn't mean them."

"You did so mean them," Josie answered.

"I really didn't."

"You were right, though. I liked being cooler than you back home. It's this thing that just occurred to me. I always thought I was helping you when I talked for you. I really did. It made me feel good about myself to help you. I thought it was my job. But I don't think I *was* helping. I think it was making you feel bad about yourself. I got, like, high off it," she answered. "This is bad, but I always just assumed people liked me better. So I was doing you a favor, just being near you."

"You suck," he said. "You're like, a self-esteem vampire."

"Yeah. You suck too, though."

"It's not all your fault, though. Mom treats me the same way. Like I'm incompetent. You just did like she does."

"Does she? I'm the one she's hard on."

"That's because she thinks men can't do anything. She goes easy on them. That's why Dad gets away with so much. She thinks he's a house with holes in its roof."

Linda heard this, knew it was true. Hadn't expected Hip to have guessed as much, which proved his point.

"Shit," Josie said. "You might be right."

"I am right," Hip said. "I'm always right. It's just nobody listens. It's like when I talk in our family, all anybody hears is singing cats."

"I listen."

"You don't," he said. Then, softer, quivering, "It's hard being in this family. It's hard knowing what everyone thinks of you and those thoughts aren't good. Dad hates himself. Like, *hate*. And he's convinced we're the same people. Mom pities him. She pities me. I've never understood why she's stayed with someone she pities. Dad and I aren't the same."

"Oh, Hip," Josie said. "Fuck them."

"Easy for you. You're the favorite."

"I've never felt like the favorite."

Linda heard a rustling. Saw in the shadows that Hip was draping his arm around her for a hug. The whispers got even softer. She strained but couldn't hear. A few minutes later, a little louder, Josie said: "But why?"

"I don't," Hip said. "I mean, it's fine. I can make myself like anything. I'm not like you. I can, you know, adapt."

"I can adapt."

"No. You can't. But that's okay. I like this place because Mom's not sick here. That's why Dad likes it, too. He told me."

"What?"

"Don't you remember? She was always coughing back home. She doesn't cough anymore."

"She coughed?"

"Do you notice anything except yourself?"

"Well, don't get mean."

"She coughed. She was always taking medicine. As soon as we got here, she was better. Remember she used to spend, like, a day out of every week in bed?"

"Right!" Josie said. "I forgot!"

"Yeah. That's why I like PV."

"I thought it was just Cathy."

"I like Cathy, too. But I'm not stupid. I wasn't doing universal tickets just because she told me. I was doing it for Mom."

"That's fucked up," Josie said.

"Why? No it's not."

"No. I mean, it's fucked up I never noticed she stopped coughing. I think it just became white noise for me, and then the white noise was gone."

"You're white noise," he said.

There was more whispering that she couldn't hear, and then Josie said, "I wouldn't call it kidnapping. I'd call it a caper."

"But what if you were wrong?" Hip asked.

"Mom's not dumb."

"You'd think if she really wanted to take this place down because she thought it was corrupt, she'd have been more subtle," Hip said.

Josie let out a soft laugh, had a hard time talking without laughing: "She's, like, the noisy spy."

"The awkward avenger."

They were both laughing.

"Mom and Dad are both so crazy," Josie said.

"I know," Hip said. "I'd hate them, but I like them better than everybody else's parents."

"Yeah."

They got quiet after that; everyone seemed ready to doze. All kinds of bombs had just been detonated, but Linda didn't feel bad. She took pride that she'd done a good-enough job raising them that her children could openly talk about such things at fifteen, instead of trying to unknot them at thirty or forty, if ever.

If she got the chance, if they got out of here, she'd tell them she had no favorites. Tell Hip she was sorry and not to worry so much about her. Tell him that if she'd been pitying him, she hadn't intended it. She'd stop. A lot of changes would happen, if they got out of this.

They were all close to sleep when Russell's voice spoke clear in the dark. "I don't hate any of you. I love you."

The kids, probably shocked, pretended to be sleeping. Linda considered answering. Decided instead to let him have the last word.

Throughout the shelter, there was shifting in the night while the Farmer-Bowens slept. Soft whispers all through the barracks. Briefly, doors opened, then shut again.

DAY 3

When they woke the third morning, most of the bunks surrounding them, in the rooms surrounding them, were empty. Her heart, which had taken a respite, thumped hard again.

She, Russell, and the kids donned their robes and met the remainders for breakfast. She counted about five hundred.

"Where'd they go?" she asked Daniella and Lloyd, who were in front of them at the buffet.

"Last day's only for people with golden tickets and their kids," Daniella said.

"Oh! We should leave!" Linda said. "How do we get out?"

"Oh, no! With ActHollow, you're part of this. It's expected."

• • •

Together and apart, all four tried again to find working exits. There were none.

The group of remainders gathered in the lecture hall. Since the big announcement on his successor, Parson had been sidelined, his chair wedged into a corner with Jack Lust at center stage. Now, Jack talked about scarcity. Global predictions indicated that there would not be enough food to feed 50 percent of the world population in another decade. The nuclear meltdown in New Mexico was no fluke, and while news reports had touted a remedy for radiation, they didn't trust it to work.

"We're not happy about the side effects of Omnium," he said. "But we've done what we can to mitigate. With the patent's expiration, BetterWorld's likely to collapse under lawsuits. Caladrius should carry us through the next fifty years.

"These tunnels are equipped to support exactly 4,500 people. With new births and the necessity for fresh, bright minds, our resident numbers must be regularly culled. This year we expunged twenty-eight long-term residents, keeping us on track."

Around them, the audience clapped in syncopation. Smiling for the first time she could remember, his grin utterly predatory, Jack waved his hands in false modesty for them to stop.

• • •

With fewer people, the party moved to the kitchen, where they served themselves dinner and ate all together. Keith Parson appeared, wearing his crown and eating with Anouk and her father. Grandson and grandfather looked alike. "They could be twins in a relativity experiment," Linda said with a sick feeling in her stomach.

Russell squinted, and then his eyes widened in fresh alarm. "They could."

Anouk, Daniella, and Rachel, with Kai's help, were getting seconds at the salad bar when Linda bumped into them.

"Linda!" Anouk cried. "Did you hear? Daddy says I can go to the eugenics conference in Palo Alto this spring! He's never let me before because he's afraid I'll get hurt. But he's promised because Tania says she'll join me. They're having their annual convention on genetic purity versus its variability. Me and Keith are just diverse enough. We don't have any trauma. We have hardly any trauma. Or if we have trauma, we're protected. There's a protective effect because of our strong genes. That's why people like us never get sick. It's also important not to swim in the river."

Drunk, she close-talked, her robe cinched tight. Linda noticed that her front teeth were false, her eyes sunken. The scions of this town were wasting away.

"Congratulations," Linda said.

"It'll be inspirational," Rachel said.

"Or do you mean sensational?" Daniella asked.

"I mean neither," Rachel said. "You're a monster. You're all monsters."

They all laughed, except for Linda.

It occurred to Linda that this was what happened to people who actively upheld a system they knew was wrong. It either turned them into monsters or killed them. Sometimes, it did both.

• • •

More playacting. After the meal, families mingled. The kids all clustered in one area, the adults in the other, Keith Parson standing alone. He wore a robe like the rest of them, though the shirt under it was black and shiny.

Her crying done, Cathy joined the older soccer kids. She was more confident now, sporting the experience of a love affair in her easy walk, her tinkling Daniella laugh. They accepted her like a wayward family member who had finally come home.

"I just think we need more access to the Scottsdale residence. What's the point of having vacation-request sheets if no one reads them?" Daniella said.

"What a good idea. Let's take notes," Anouk said.

They were never getting an MRI or a drug printer. Once Tania Janssen took over, they wouldn't even have a doctor.

Early evening, the crowd thinned again. The youngest children disappeared. Drinks were served. These had the earthy taste she remembered from New Year's Eve. Linda received hers last. "Don't drink it," she told the rest of them. But in Russell's case, she was too late. Thirsty, he'd downed his glass.

More circulating, more talking. Linda's heart stayed thumping. A sheen of sweat spread across her skin. She found herself touching her children, grabbing hands and shoulders, wanting them near. "Be careful," she whispered to Russell, though the drink had made him bleary.

The air was electric. It crackled. Something bad was going to happen. She could feel it.

Another meeting was called. Passing her, Chernin pushed Louis in his chair. He looked through her. The spaciness, she realized, didn't necessarily mean he was high. It meant he'd been disconnecting from himself for so long that he was only ever half there.

The four Farmer-Bowens sat together, united at last in their fear.

"There's only about two hundred people left," she whispered. "Where are they going? Can't we sneak out, too?"

"I just checked again," Russell answered, his pupils dilated from the hallucinogen. "The exits I tried are still locked."

"Did you really tell Hip we should stay here for my health?"

He nodded, his eyes wet with fear. "Those granulocyte blockers you used to take have a lot of downsides."

"I didn't know you worried like that."

"Honey, the person I love most has been sick the last decade. What is it you imagine I worry about?" he asked.

The thing about epiphanies, if you have enough of them, they begin to stick.

Many times over the years, she'd imagined they'd been out of synchronicity. Between the people called Linda and Russell, this was true. But as it pertained to the Farmer-Bowens, it was false. All along, the family had been working toward something. He'd taken one role, she'd taken the other, and together they'd driven it forward.

Their methods were different—he was infuriatingly secretive; she was open. He made the money; she raised the kids. But this was how they'd always worked, each with their eye on the larger prize: survival for their family—the Farmer-Bowen Corporation. Again and again, she'd upheld a system while complaining about it, without ever taking responsibility for being a part of it. It occurred to her right then that Rachel was right. She was and always had been complicit.

• • •

They were called into a new chamber, deeper into the belly. Above the arch, engraved in neat script across the stone:

Beware the Sacrifice!

The chairs there were larger and made of soft bird leather. By then, fully tripping off their mushroom drinks, the guests stared at ceiling lights, watched their hands make trails.

Linda looked around, noticed that Cathy was gone, and Daniella's stepkids, too. Hip and Josie were the only kids left, of a crowd that had once again shrunk by half.

John Parson took the stage. His voice was small and didn't carry. He didn't speak up; people quieted to hear. "It is not by luck alone that we persist. Every year, the gods demand a price."

Linda felt something very cold inside her. A sleeping thing awoke.

"Around this ritual, we built Hollow. But I should say we discovered Hollow, because it has always been here, just as God has been, made incarnate through our caladrius. He is old, but soon he will be new."

He sat down in a chair with wide arms and a tall back—a throne.

Jack, the new king, ascended the podium. He pressed his hand against the heavy stone door behind him, and nanoparticles coalesced into a handle. He opened it, and there was the Labyrinth.

"Every year, one of our children, and sometimes more than one, become sick from the very product that gives this community life. We ask our God to heal that sickness or accept its hosts as offering. Every year, we participate in a town-wide race, from which the slowest is culled. That slowest is offered up, to be renewed, or accepted as sacrifice. Every year, we participate in a challenge of strength. That champion acts as the executor of these tasks. And so it is, this year."

Linda looked over to her family, and she could see their tight expressions.

"Our sick have been stolen. And so they must be replaced," Jack said. "Our last was not last. There was one person who never completed the race."

The faces in the crowd all turned.

PART V

Run

(The Labyrinth)

The Labyrinth

The leaders of Plymouth Valley made a fifty-foot aisle that ended at the Farmer-Bowen family, a gauntlet of white robes.

"All things in Plymouth Valley are fair, and so the exits are unsealed. If the chosen make it out before the Beltane King catches them, they win," Jack said. His eyes were narrowed in anger but his tiny-mouthed grin went wide. This was what happy Jack looked like. He hooked the arm of the small-hipped young woman beside him, who couldn't have been older than fourteen. She was beautiful in a muted, childlike way.

Linda thought of the first time she'd met him, and the way he'd daintily stepped over so much trash.

Sally Claus pushed through the crowd and shoved Linda, hard. Lloyd Bennett, charming Lloyd Bennett with dimples that could melt any heart, spit on Linda's cheek. It was hot and thick and stuck before sliding inside the neck of her robe.

The chatter grew. There were catcalls, and shouts, and laughter. Daniella threw a rock at Hip. "Creepy fucker!" she cried. "You didn't deserve to pop her cherry."

Heinrich charged, fist flying with a weak sucker punch that grazed Russell's jaw.

Ruth Epstein, who'd recently declared herself God, slapped Josie in the back of the head, her ring catching Josie's hair and snagging a lock from her scalp. Strong and distracted, Josie didn't look back, just cupped her cranium from behind.

Hip watched this, and Linda could tell he was trying to figure out how to stop it, though he'd been told his whole life not to lay hands on other people.

Nanny Jones, who'd wanted Russell's job back in September, smashed their glass against Russell's cheek and sliced a sideways letter *C* along the fullness of his nose. He fell on his ass, hands bracing from behind, blood dripping. He got up slowly and caught the blood on his sleeve with dulled, drugged surprise.

They were driven like cattle. Josie tripped while climbing the steps to the podium. Hip, alert now, yanked her back up before someone could stomp her hand. Russell trailed them, pinching his nose and opening the wound even worse. Probably, he thought the blood was coming from inside. He didn't know he'd been cut.

The robed mass converged. She saw white and she saw skin and she saw faces of rage as angry as Gal's had been in the nightmare house. They were all like this, on the inside. From his corner chair, the forgotten titan John Parson hissed—

"SSSSSSSSSSSSSSSS!"

Then they were all hissing. The sound reverberated in Linda's chest, and she had the sensation that these weren't people anymore. They were something bigger and less human than that, with a soulless kind of intelligence.

The members of ActHollow met them at the Labyrinth entrance. Daniella stayed a little back and it occurred to Linda that on the day Mr. Scaley took that bullet for her, a part of Daniella had died along with him, trapped under the burden of so much mess. What persisted was the stunning shell, and the drive to survive.

Beside Daniella, as she had always been and would always be until it killed her, was Rachel. Throughout her time in PV, Linda had always felt that Rachel was different. She was honest with herself. Now, high on Glamp, her face was contorted in misdirected rage. As if her person had been erased, this expression made her look, at last, like everyone else. "You did this to yourself!" she screamed, her eyes wet with maniacal tears.

Finally, Anouk. She handed Linda, Josie, and Hip each a cluster of fresh sage wrapped in black ribbon. She didn't appear insane, but she was insane. The myriad contradictory thoughts, the cognitive dissonance, had reversed inside her like fish scales, cutting and slicing until what remained was a broken, bleeding, hollowed-out thing that spoke words without meaning, that parroted ideas, that walked and saw and heard but nonetheless was deaf and dumb and blind. She smiled at Linda like this was a regrettable, but nonetheless fitting and necessary, end to their friendship.

"Upon such sacrifices, my Linda, the gods themselves anoint. You're so lucky!"

The Farmer-Bowens were at the door, just under the sign that read: BEWARE THE SACRIFICE. Russell trailed them, moving slowly up the steps, bewildered as he'd been that night she'd spied him through the keyhole, naked and vacant.

"SSSSSSSSSSSSSSS!"

They kept on with their hissing and their spite.

Linda felt a presence. She turned, and down the aisle at the other end of the room, like a groom, was a man in all-reflective black, wearing a crown of bones.

"And the three must go, with five minutes' head start," Jack bellowed.

Linda faced Keith Parson. This was not a joke. This was really happening. Her whole family was about to be slaughtered by the Beltane King. Even as she knew this, even as her body felt the truth of it all through to her marrow, she thought: *impossible.*

"We have to go through there?" she asked, looking at the stone door, her voice loud to be heard over the hissing.

"Into the Labyrinth to meet your fate, for the glory of us all," Anouk said.

"But we don't want to."

"Too late for that," someone muttered.

"He'll kill them right here, at this rate," someone else said.

Linda's knees wobbled, her joints gone soft. Everything shook with adrenaline, but she had no place to funnel it.

"Mom. We go!" Josie cried. And then, Hip, too. They pulled either side of her. "Mom!"

The three of them were through the door, and into the Labyrinth. From behind, Russell chimed in at last. "It's a joke, right? You're kidding? Even so, it's unacceptable. We surrender our deposit. This is over. We're leaving now."

In his shining black, Keith seemed to float down the aisle, his chest puffed as if this were his promenade.

"Absolutely not," Russell said, once he noticed Keith.

"Get out of the way," Heinrich said. "There's room for you here. Enjoy the party."

"But it's not serious. It's a game," Russell said, as a kind of question, even as the crowd continued their *SSSSSSSSSSSSSSSSSSSSSS!*

"It's a game," Lloyd answered, only all his charm was gone, his expression slack, his eyes drugged and glossy.

"Can I go instead? Let me be the one. Take me instead," Russell said. And then, to Keith in his shining skin suit, who had closed in, "Back up, okay? Can you back up?"

"Too late to switch," Jack bellowed. The sound was unlike his soft speaking voice. It was that of a megachurch preacher. The girl nuzzled his wrinkled neck. "This is the law! This is the way of Hollow. Too late to switch!"

"Back up!" Russell barked as Keith approached. He blocked Keith's entrance to the Labyrinth with his body.

Linda and the twins watched through the aperture. Everything in the Labyrinth was dark, everything in the belly of the shelter bright. It was like watching a screenie in a theater, all their attention focused on Russell and the crowned, bulky man in fluid black.

In stories, this part was where the reluctant hero comes to Jesus. He figures out that he was blocked by something outside the story, a Byzantine force, and something within, too. In a story, Russell would have connected his childhood to this moment. He'd have recognized some haunting, buried trauma that had made him the type of person who buried unpleasant things. The type of person who froze at a raised voice or a paradox. He'd have seen how this past had rippled through to his present, compromising his ability to connect to his children, because when they most wanted to talk, to tell him about their bad day or a feeling inside them, he least wanted to listen. He'd allowed only his wife through this complex network of defenses. In his quest for peace, he'd sometimes lied to keep her there. Often, he hadn't even known he was lying.

The hero would have had a great, life-changing epiphany, not a glimpse that unwound itself into nothing after every second guess. His love for his family would have been the fulcrum of change. It would have given him near-superhuman strength. He'd have killed Keith Parson, made a speech, and left town with Linda, Josie, and Hip. Gathered evidence and taken it to the courts, offering himself as a whistleblower. The Farmer-Bowens would have driven off into the sunset of the unknown.

Real life is very different from screenies. He came to Jesus. He had all these epiphanies, and it was too late.

They watched this scene, framed by the door, and it didn't seem *less* real. With the hissing and the thrumming, it seemed like something that was happening not just outside, but inside their bodies, too.

Keith bumped his chest against slender Russell, who staggered back. "What is this?" he asked, his voice muddy from the drink.

"Just stand back," said Heinrich.

SSSSSSSSSS!

For a moment, it appeared as if Russell would retreat by necessity, to save his own life. But then, he glimpsed his family through the door, in the dark. His eyes washed over them like a flashlight, settling on Linda. Much was exchanged in that look: fear, regret, pain, disbelief.

There was too much between them, too much to possibly ever say, and then again, there was just one thing: love.

"You can't interfere!" someone shouted.

"The choice is made!" said another.

Keith advanced, his hooded face so shining black that it seemed like empty space. Russell shoved him, hard. But he was a rock. "This isn't happening today," Russell said. "You can pick other people. We're leaving. We're done."

SSSSSSSSSSSSSSSS!

Keith unsheathed a machete from a deep pocket along the side of his costume. First handle, then steel pulled out from the black, as if by magic. Russell didn't back down. "You don't get to do this!" he growled, like a dog giving one last warning before it bites. Linda'd never seen him so angry, had never guessed he had it in him.

Then, Keith Parson lifted the knife. He slashed Russell Farmer-Bowen, age forty-two, of Plymouth Valley via Meredith, New Hampshire, and then Kings, New York, from throat to groin.

• • •

When terrible things happen, time goes excruciatingly still. You try to rewind it, even in the moment it has happened. You keep doing that, stretching seconds. A minute is a year, because in that time, you've lived so many alternate lives. Russell lay flopping on the ground like a fish, holding his insides to keep organs from falling out. Soon, he was still. The blood was enormous. It could have coated the entire auditorium.

She wanted to go to him. Keith blocked the way. He stood in the door, knife raised. She had no speeches to give. She had no cutting comments or insightful and dreadful parting gifts for the women of ActHollow. She had nothing.

"Is the murder of a nonparticipant allowed?" came a voice.

"The Beltane King acts as a conduit. It is not ours to question his discretion," answered Jack with great glee. He was into this. In subsequent Winter Festivals, there would be more ornate sacrifices, she understood. This party would only get bigger.

Behind Keith, the crowd removed their robes. Naked, they took turns caking their feet in Russell's blood, then embracing one another, indifferent to whom it was they held. They were bodies, twisted and kissing, coiled and indistinct. On the floor, Russell's green eyes weren't looking at her anymore. They never would again.

"May the sacrifice cleanse us," voices murmured.

"One minute left," Jack called. "Better run."

• • •

The Labyrinth. They stumble-ran down the hall. Motion-sensor lights followed them, illuminating narrow rectangular pieces of their path and then going dark again once they'd passed. They came to a crossroad. Panting, she hesitated. Josie and Hip stopped short.

From the direction they'd come, there was sudden cheering, and she imagined Keith Parson entering the Labyrinth. All three went left, passing Winter Festival adornments tacked to the walls—feathers and fur arranged in runic swirls.

Another crossroad. They ran straight this time, igniting more motion-sensor lights, giving Keith the jump on their route. Josie, the fastest, led the way, though none of them knew where they were going. The halls curved, led to a dead end. Scrambling, they doubled back, picked a different direction.

The walls moved. They were in one hallway, and as they ran, the crossroad it fed into changed. It was impossible to keep track of where they were coming from or going. Behind, footsteps. He was coming. He knew this place very well. Had been its murderous king for fifteen years.

They reached the center of the new crossroad, one they hadn't seen before. "Here!" Hip whispered, placing his palm on a shallow cavity. A handle emerged, only it didn't lead to an exit. It led back inside the belly of the shelter.

More panic. All alarms sounded inside her body. *Deeper inside? Wasn't that much worse?*

"If we can find a way to the kitchen I know the exit," Hip said.

That was all Josie needed. The two of them ran through, leaving her no choice but to follow. They found themselves in a candlelit room with a dirt floor. It was the same room as the candy skull and corn syrup cemetery from Samhain, only the furniture, obscured by decoration, was now revealed. A pew was pushed against the far wall, overlooking at least a hundred skulls. These were not fake. They were polished, with straight gleaming teeth. There were adult skulls, but, just as often, child-sized ones with soft and sometimes translucent sagittal sutures. They were human.

Along the back wall was that same massive altar, only the blood dripping down wasn't candy. It was fresh, from a recently slaughtered goat. The air there smelled mineral rich, of calcium and salt.

"It's this way!" Josie pointed to the tunnel on the left.

But Hip stopped. He nodded, and they saw. In rows between the pew and altar were wooden chairs, their seats and backs made of pink, brown, and black leather. These were soft and supple looking, some shaded with hints of down, some thick with short hair. Humans. This leather was human.

It takes a second after something like that. You need everyone to see it, to acknowledge it, so that you know you're not going mad. And even then, what you've seen may be too hard to accept.

"The sacrificed who were killed running the Labyrinth. They skinned them," Hip said.

Linda felt the blood withdraw along her scalp and groin, felt her skin go tight. This could be anyone. It could be them.

Hip ran his hand along the short strands of black seat-back hair from what had originally been a chest or arm. Along it was a stretched-out peace sign tattoo, which drove home to Linda that this really had once been a person, living and breathing, who'd shelled out a few bucks to the dude with the ink shop on the corner. The design hadn't been so original, but maybe they'd just wanted to do it, for the sake of doing it.

There were scores of these skin-chairs . . . Was this the Fabric Collective's secret back-room project?

"Oh God," Josie said.

Just then came the sound of the Labyrinth door opening. Keith's footsteps slapped the hard floors as he followed their trail of overhead lights.

"We have to keep moving," Linda said.

But there wasn't time. Like an elegant shadow, Keith Parson was upon them.

• • •

It happened so fast Linda couldn't parse it. All she knew was that she and the kids were running. She could sense Keith behind them, gaining. When she felt him get close enough, adrenaline kicked in. She pivoted hard. Kicked out her leg. He tripped, landing on his knees.

Before he had the time to recover, she was on him, her thumbs over his eyes, pushing hard. He reacted fast and strong, punching her head, a real sparks-flying closed-fist punch, her soft temple taking the brunt. She went blind in pain and rolled down beside him but didn't let go. His eyes were wet and so were her thumbs. He rolled on top of her, screaming in fury, and she thought, *If I can loosen his eyes from their sockets, he won't be able to find the kids.*

He bore his entire weight on her, knees grinding into her chest. Her spine made a *crunch!* against the floor. At least three ribs broke with distinct pops. His hands squeezed around her neck.

Thwock! Something slammed the side of Keith's head. His crown skittered into the wall. The bones broke apart.

After all that, she thought. *A dime-store crown.*

Josie was holding a rock. It took Linda a second, her brain fuzzy with pain, to understand that she must have hit him with it. Josie seemed bewildered, too, by her own violence. She stayed still and close. Keith reached up and grabbed her wrist. She dropped the rock. He squeezed until they all heard the soft, sandpaper *crunches* of small bones as they broke.

In her shock, Josie didn't cry out or fight.

But then came Hip. He slammed Keith with another rock from directly overhead—a better angle. Blood sprayed down on Linda in aerosol and also in drips. She launched again at his eyes, stabbing with her thumbs. One *pop!* Then the other: *Pop!* Both eyes broke free from their sockets and hung loosely from their jellied optic nerves.

Screaming a wild, terror scream, eyes dangling against his cheeks, he flailed to his back. He didn't seem to understand what had happened—that his eyes were no longer inside his skull. He could still see, she knew. But with one eye pointing down and left, the other down and right, his mind wasn't creating a useful picture.

No longer screaming, but whimpering, he reached his hands along his face until he found and cupped his eyes. Now was the time, she knew. She ought to tear them from their nerves, smash him with a rock. Finish it.

She didn't do these things. She scrambled up, got back near the kids.

He tried in vain to wedge his eyes under their lids and back inside their orbital nests. As he worked, he didn't weep or keen. He uttered soft, disconsolate whimpers. His breath caught in gulps and gurgles. "Is anyone there?" he begged. "Are you there?"

Linda and the kids stayed still and close.

"Please?"

It was strange. She was tempted to help him. Josie even took a step toward him before Hip caught and held her.

Keith heard the sound and went very still.

Unmoving, they waited. It was a kind of purgatory.

Keith let go of his eyes. His hands moved to the left side of his chest, where his palms stiffened and turned to claws.

A heart attack.

They stayed that way in the silence. She guessed only a few seconds, though it felt longer. Hip broke their paralysis. Having lost all trepidation, all decorum for now and maybe forever, he took his rock and bashed that same bleeding side of Keith's head with it. *Crack!* Keith went utterly still.

It's awful to see your child do something like that. In many ways, they're no longer your child or anyone's child, once they've committed murder. She felt great compassion for him, and only wished she'd spared him this act, and had done it herself.

More than all of that, she felt relief.

• • •

Panting, the three didn't take the time to huddle or check injuries. They ran through the nearest hall, marked PARSON PRIVATE QUARTERS, into a suite of rooms. The first room was a library with those same human-skinned chairs. The second was a small bedroom, a low cot, and shining Beltane King costumes on the white tile floor like ragged black holes. Along the faux window shelf, through which an artist had depicted mosaic caladrius, were two rows of Beltane Crowns, the back row stacked halfway over the front one. On the nightstand, a scatter of used hypodermics.

Keith's private room.

She didn't pity him. He didn't deserve that. Still, she felt a pang, imagining him on this cot, alone.

They kept going into the connected room, which was five times bigger and much brighter, its mosaic windows taking up nearly every wall. The bed was sultan-sized and the furniture was all Daniella's trademark velvet. Each side room led to large dressing rooms and studies. Linda recognized Anouk's ugly caftan shawl hanging off the side of the bed. She recognized her father Parson's cane on the other side.

She didn't think about what all that meant. Now was not the time to care about what had driven Anouk Parson and her son insane.

They kept going through to a solarium with a ceiling made of mirrors. The next room let out to an unexpected place: the stairwell leading down, down, down, to the reactor. The showstopper.

• • •

"Now where?" she croaked, wringing her sticky, wet hands. Then came a wild and hurtling sound that echoed. She could hear a man's keening, his large body slamming against walls as it tracked them, following light.

Keith Parson came crashing through the doorway. He'd shoved his eyes back into their sockets, but they moved out of synchronicity. He panted, his fingers and lips cyanotic blue, his face bloody and red. She'd seen this before in people right before they died, though she hadn't expected it now, when Keith had been so badly hurt. Though his pursuit was unwelcome, it at least meant that Hip would not have to carry the burden of having dealt a death blow.

Semiblind and coursing with adrenaline, Keith swung at the air with the indignant fury of a young man whose time has prematurely run out. They were cornered. Josie raced down the clanging metal stairs, so Linda and Hip followed. Flinging blood, shrieking animal sounds of fury, Keith held to the railing.

They had a lead but lost it. Keith jumped from stairwell to stairwell; even as he landed wrong, crunching his ankle, slamming his knees, he seemed to feel no pain.

Down, down, down. This was all so awful that her mind wandered.

She thought of the disrobed people in that room, their feet wet with Russell's blood. She thought of all the plans and jokes and routines. The sides of the bed they slept on, the way she liked to doze while he drove. She thought of all the ways that life gets complicated when lives are intertwined, in ways that are impossible to explain except for the people living inside the tangle.

They got to the bottom—the reactor.

The machine was composed of networks of giant metal barrels connected by more metal tubing. These groaned and ticked in a way that seemed wrong and that she had not witnessed on the last visit. Heat came off the center of the thing in blurry waves.

Keith threw his machete to the landing, then jumped the last set of stairs. She was out of breath and in too much shock to come up with a better plan. She grabbed the knife by the dull end, threw it aside. In her peripheral vision, Hip and Josie hustled for it.

Keith's costume was torn, revealing the pink-skinned man beneath. There was something tender in that pink—a human trapped under monster skin. Panting, wheezing, he stayed squatting, even as he struggled to stand. Closer now, she saw that his head was hemorrhaging blood in pulsing, heartbeat waves. He wobbled, landing on his bottom.

Linda came forward. How much he saw, she couldn't guess. "Please," he whispered. "Help." Then, slowly, like something unwinding, he lay down on his back.

Linda felt his carotid artery. No flow. His blue fingers curled again and finally into stiff claws. His mouth opened and locked.

She pulled away his hood, a sleek Omnium material. She could see his sickly, once pleasant face. Full lips and small eyes. The end of the Parson line.

There were hands by her side. The kids. No one was ready yet to hug. You can't hug when you're that full of adrenaline. They stood over the body, not seeing that body, but thinking of Russell's body.

How much time passed? Seconds? Minutes?

"Hello?" a voice asked.

They all three jumped. Between a coil composed of hundreds of rods and its attached metal barrels came Percy Khoury.

"This is the Beltane King?" he asked. His expression bore that same stunted fury as the first time she'd met him, way back on the soccer field in early September. Careless of the blood, he twisted the neck of Keith's limp body to see his face. "You got him?"

Had they gotten him? It was hard to remember that far. Hard to think about anything except Russell on the floor.

Percy didn't wipe his hands clean after touching the body, but stuck three fingers into his mouth and blew, loud and whistling. The sound was primal. It resonated, its meaning clear: *Come here, pet. I have something for you.* Linda and the kids backed away. She knew, even though, if asked, she wouldn't have had the words to explain. You know some things on a deeper, wilder level, in a place without logic.

They heard rumbling. She remembered the thing in the dark with its knowing eyes. The sound was a kind of scuffling, feathery lumber, and she knew: *it* was coming.

Muscles shaking, bodies heaving, the family formerly known as the Farmer-Bowens did not have it in them to run.

Out from a crevice of the reactor lumbered the thing she'd imagined, and dreamed about, and feared: the great white caladrius. It was real, after all.

The size of a large and awkward man, it picked its way toward the stairs and crouched over Keith's body. It nosed against his belly, the gesture almost loving, nudging him to wake up. Then, with sharp teeth, it tore open his trunk from groin to chest and began to eat.

The twins turned away. She watched. She needed to see. It left the skin and ate only from the insides. This included the bones. Then came two more giant caladrius and they, too, began to eat. She saw now that whatever personality she'd imagined for this species from tending Sunny was a projection. They were a mindless tide of dirty white predators drawn to the fresh smell of blood.

They hunkered, obscuring Keith's carcass. She saw only cellar-filthy feathers that would never fly.

"He had that coming," said Percy Khoury, the mad soccer dad without a child. "But don't worry. They're sneaky poopers. They won't go after big game like humans. Just carrion."

"What are you doing down here?" Linda asked, soft to avoid the attention of the creatures.

He wore that same outfit he'd been wearing when she'd first met him, his belly revealed under a loose, unbuttoned trench coat. She noticed, too, that his tool belt was now open and spread across the floor: big, specialized drills and coils and saws.

Percy's eyes lit up. "God came to me. He told me to rain down the fire. I'm vengeance." Then he put his finger vertical to his lips: "Shhh."

• • •

Too numb to properly fear or understand what was happening, they took care, stepping softly as they passed the feeding scourge of caladrius. Then they climbed up, up, up. They found the kitchen. Things got familiar. They went into the Labyrinth, straight past the crossroads and then left to the stairs, just like Zach had taught them on their tour.

Blood covered, they summited at Caladrius Park.

In the bright midday sun that Monday following the great and final Plymouth Valley Winter Festival, the family once known as the Farmer-Bowens could be seen trudging through snowbanks, underdressed in slippers and bloody white robes. The few cars on the road slowed as they passed. Faces looked out. No one rolled down their windows or stopped, though a few pointed their devices.

Linda, Hip, and Josie climbed into their B-class sedan stationed just a few blocks from the park. Shivering though they didn't know it, they drenched the car leather with melted snow and blood.

They didn't stop at their house or bother to wash the gore from their hands. The suitcases were already packed and in the car. On the ride, no one said his name. They couldn't bear to say his name.

They arrived at the wall.

Sally was there, along with her dad, Heinrich. Both were still high, their pupils narrow as hay needles. "Congratulations! You got out!" she said. Josie and Hip had gone still. Linda thought it was probably shock. They didn't own the car, so they emptied it—one rolling suitcase for each of them, two for herself. They started walking.

"You don't have to leave!" Heinrich said. "People get golden tickets for less. You won fair and square!"

The cold biting their skin, they kept going. The halfway house was only three kilometers away and though the day was cold, the sun was bright. Hip looped back to Linda, took the extra suitcase—Russell's suitcase—from her. Then he forged ahead, and walked beside Josie.

Linda stayed a little behind. Never the sentimental type, she told herself not to look back. But this was impossible. She took one last glimpse of the place as its walls closed. The slanted winter sun washed everything behind them in red.

She could see, most likely, their future.

The three of them would consider the Great Lakes. They would plan and talk and behave as if this were their destination. The start of a new life. But in the end, they would return home to New York. She would take over Fielding's position, and at first they would live in the storage basement at the Kings' Pediatric Clinic, where she worked. The children would go back to their school, though they would be so changed that nothing would quite fit as it had.

They would talk of Russell and remember him. They would at first venerate him, as if he'd been a saint. Eventually, his feet would become clay. They'd talk about the flaws in him, and the way he'd never answered direct questions, the way he'd tucked secrets closer to him than his family. She had never been a romantic person. No ounce of sentiment. This would not inoculate her against the loss of Russell. She would never get over him.

BetterWorld would probably come after them. But she'd smuggled no damning evidence to take the company down. They'd likely leave her alone so long as she stayed quiet. Maybe this Caladrius spin-off corporation would work out. Maybe it would crash and burn under the corrupt agenda of a demagogue. The world would keep unwinding. But then again, maybe this low point was the bedrock from which people would rebuild. You can't ever know such things when you're living inside them. You can only hope and do your part.

They say you never get over the loss of a loved one and that's true, but the human condition is resilient. There would be nightmares and skittishness. There would be unhealed wounds and distrust of new people. But because they had one another, this would mostly pass. They would move on, and learn new things and forge new attachments. There would be sickness. Unless by some miracle the air in New York got clean again, her health would probably not survive outside. If her sickness returned, she knew already that she would keep it a secret from her children, a burden she didn't want them to carry. There would be struggle. There would be joy. There would be life.

"Bye," she said.

Then they headed back into the world, the fucked-up, falling-apart, beautiful world.

CHAPTER 5 SUMMARY: Plymouth Valley Case Study: The Fall of the Anthropocene, the Rise of the Modern Global Ecosystem

But as we now know, the Maginot Lines that these corporate cities erected protected against the wrong things. For instance, on the last day of their annual Winter Festival in Plymouth Valley, a disgruntled employee initiated a nuclear meltdown in the very survivor tunnels built to protect against radiation.

It's an Oedipal tragedy (metaphorically, but also literally, if accounts of John Parson Junior are to be believed). The Great Lakes Disaster Relief Consortium evacuated Plymouth Valley Extension's residents. But the people of Plymouth Valley proper refused to believe their own Geiger counters. Like passengers on the *Titanic*, they could not conceive of what was happening. Rather than leaving the valley, or even seeking higher ground, they gathered in the very survivor tunnels that were poisoning them, dying within hours. The caladrius (a now common North American pest) were less sensitive to ionizing radiation. They shifted their diet from insects to meat, gorging themselves on thousands of human remains.

The Chinese-American Scientific Consortium rushed their nuclear-absorption device to the disaster site, testing it live for the first time while the world watched: Could the genie be forced back into its bottle? The successful remediation of Plymouth Valley became a watershed of human wonder as momentous as Neil Armstrong's 1969 moon landing. Despite the executions of the scientists who'd invented the device, the technological feat ushered a wave of optimism and faith in science. Plymouth Valley was habitable within the year, its vegetation edible within the decade.

Crises precipitated change. The Great Unwinding halted. The age of the Anthropocene ended and the era of the Global Ecosystem began. Solar energy and soil advancements delivered exponential agricultural yields. Air pollution and algae blooms brought a respiratory crisis, and global leadership responded, copying BetterWorld's dome policy for the majority of its cities. The pilot program for the first public Bell Jar was started in New York.

Unable to expunge corporate and political corruption from within, popular uprisings forced change from without. In London, São Paulo, Mexico City, Seattle, Omaha, Beijing, and St. Petersburg, the dayworkers joined together, and tore the walls down.

It's rumored that some Plymouth Valley residents still live in the tunnels. Fearing the outside world, and unable to care for themselves without dayworkers, they remain there, like Morlocks. For those trivia buffs out there, Plymouth Valley's disaster is the reason Halloween is now celebrated on Day of the Dead—Samhain. Revelers dress like PV Morlocks rising up from underground to steal children for meals down below. But of course, this is a myth.

—From THE FALL OF THE ANTHROPOCENE, by Jin Hyun, Seoul National University Press, 2093.

Acknowledgments

This book took too long to write! Hopefully it's the better for it. It evolved in my imagination from a simple story about the breakdown of an American marriage to something bigger and, to me, more interesting, about the convenient stories we tell ourselves to get through our days and the goblins those stories tend to hide.

Since my last novel, I lost my mother, Carole Joan Langan (1942–2020), and my father, Peter Robert Langan (1944–2023). This was bad and sad, relieved only by the time I spent with my brother, Christopher (and Kara!); my uncles John, Michael, and Rick; and family friends Marilou Astudillo and Connie Vecchio during the week of June 19, 2023.

Lots of people helped with this novel. To start, my stalwart agent (I know I've described you this way before, Stacia, but I can think of no better word), Stacia Decker; my brainy and brilliant editor, Loan Le, who seems to have faith in me when I don't (thank you!); Jimmy Iacobelli (How did you do it? This cover is spectacular!); David Brown (I want to win the Roomba Thunderdome so much!); Maudee Genao (thank you!); and the whole excellent Atria team (Libby McGuire, Lindsay Sagnette, Dana Trocker, Dana Sloan, Elizabeth Hitti, Paige Lytle, Liz Byer, and Nicole Bond)—I love working with you. Thank you.

Early readers Meg Howrey, Sarah Tomlinson, Chris Terry, and J. Ryan Stradal proved invaluable. I've appreciated the general support of Erin Jontow; Alison Benson; close friends Kirsten Roeters and Dave Eilenberg, who have us over for holidays and let us pretend we're family; and Maura Maloney, who noticed how badly I was flailing some years ago, and with great tact made an appointment for me with an entertainment lawyer. Thanks to Dr. Adella Johnson, who talked to me about clinical pediatrics in Nassau County. Your help was much appreciated, and everything I got wrong is entirely my fault.

Thanks also to my former Brooklyn-based writing group Who Wants Cake, Antonio D'Intino, Lawrence Mattis, Hilary Zaitz Michael, Sarah Self, and Darren Trattner. For being people I can text in a pinch, thanks to Paul Tremblay, Grady Hendrix, and Victor LaValle. For being cool neighbors I can text any time because I want a laugh, a cry, or a driveway beer (and once, a schoolyard martini), who are nothing at all like the clowns in PV, thanks to Chelsea Scade, Valerie Gordon, Ellie Speare, and Malaya Rivera Drew.

Writing about a marriage when you happen to be married is a little crazy, and also a little stupid. As it happens, I'm married to someone who gets it. Thanks, JT, for the rush read and for making the suggestions I needed, not the ones I wanted. Thanks also for watching the kids and letting me hole up in the garage for weeks on end and not saying anything when I wandered into the kitchen, drank some milk from the carton, and wandered off again, mid-thought on this behemoth of a novel. Finally, when I said, "This husband in my book doesn't come off so good. I'm worried people will think it's you. Should I write a disclaimer?" you said, "Do your worst."

Thanks finally, and especially, to Clementine and Frances. You are the best.

About the Author

Sarah Langan, a Columbia MFA graduate and three-time recipient of the Bram Stoker Award, is the author of several novels, including *Good Neighbors*. She grew up on Long Island, and she currently lives in Los Angeles with her husband and daughters. Find out more at SarahLangan.com.